NEED A JOB, GO TO MARS . . .

or the nearest space station or colony world. But what kind of career opportunities will you find on the ever-expanding frontiers of space? And how many alien beings will be vying for the same positions? To discover some of the possibilities, check out *Space, Inc.*, and such entertaining and original tales as:

"The Siren Stone"—Their mission was to blow up an asteroid before it could destroy a space station and its entire population, but nothing could prepare them for what they discovered when they rendezvoused with this giant piece of rock. . . .

"Attached Please Find My Novel"—Sometimes you found tomorrow's best-sellers in the most unexpected places. . . .

"Come All Ye Faithful"—Finding a real congregation on Mars wasn't going to be easy—in fact he had to admit it would be a miracle if it ever happened. . . .

More Imagination-Expanding Anthologies Brought to You by DAW:

WONDROUS BEGINNINGS *Edited by Steven H. Silver and Martin H. Greenberg.* The writers included in this volume are a real "who was and is who" in the field of science fiction, from such masters of science fiction's Golden Age as: Murray Leinster, L. Sprague de Camp, Hal Clement, and Arthur C. Clarke; to a number of today's hottest-selling and award-winning authors such as: Anne McCaffrey, Gene Wolfe, George R. R. Martin, Orson Scott Card, Lois McMaster Bujold, and Stephen Baxter. How and where did these writers get their start? Now you can find out by reading the stories that began their careers, along with an introduction by the author which offers insight into the genesis of both the particular story and the individual writer's career.

DAW 30TH ANNIVERSARY SCIENCE FICTION ANTHOLOGY *Edited by Elizabeth R. Wollheim and Sheila E. Gilbert.* In celebration of DAW Books' thirtieth anniversary, here are nineteen original stories by some of the authors who have helped to make DAW the landmark science fiction publishing house it is today. Includes stories by C. J. Cherryh, Tad Williams, Brian Aldiss, Frederik Pohl, C. S. Friedman, Kate Elliott, and many other top authors in the field.

FUTURE WARS *Edited by Martin H. Greenberg and Larry Segriff.* Ten all-original tales of the many possible ways in which conflict may be carried out, resolved, or avoided in the future. Includes stories by Barry Longyear, Kristine Kathryn Rusch, William H. Keith, Jr., Bill Fawcett, Robert J. Sawyer, Robin Wayne Bailey, and more.

SPACE INC.

edited by
Julie E. Czerneda

DAW BOOKS, INC.

DONALD A. WOLLHEIM, FOUNDER
375 Hudson Street, New York, NY 10014

ELIZABETH R. WOLLHEIM
SHEILA E. GILBERT
PUBLISHERS
http://www.dawbooks.com

First Printing, July 2003
1 2 3 4 5 6 7 8 9

ACKNOWLEDGMENTS

CONTENTS

INTRODUCTION

by Julie E. Czerneda

TINKER, tailor, soldier, sailor . . . a familiar rhyme to many about work on Earth and just the beginning of a very long list of possible ways to earn a living here. But what happens when we leave this planet? What will happen to the jobs we know? And what jobs will be created because of the realities of space? I can guarantee it will be more than astronaut, tourist guide, and telescope technician, though I'm sure those jobs will still exist.

Like you, I'm curious about many things, but especially about the world around me. Not only the world itself, but people and what they do. Driving down a road, I'll wonder what's being made in the buildings I pass. I'd prefer some clues to guessing. Would meaningful company signs be too much to ask?

When I use something in my home, every so often I'll pause and wonder at it. Who made it? How? Why? How long ago? I can look up technical information, but it's infinitely more satisfying to talk to the people involved. I know, because I've had the good fortune to interview well over a hundred individuals about their work as part of my job. Pattern makers and physicists, cartographers and carvers, dog trainers and designers. The more I learn, the more I'm fascinated by how diverse the things we do for a living really are. We are, frankly, a very busy species.

And, like many of you, I'm curious about space, too. I have every confidence we'll be living there and soon. So what about people and what will they do? Human enterprise is complex and interrelated. We depend on one another for so much—and how much more this interdependency will matter in space!

Will work itself change? Will we?

That was what I asked these talented authors: think about our future and look up into space. Describe who you see and what they are doing. The regular folks. Real people trying to make a day's living.

Because if we are to live in space—really live, and not just be visitors—it will be because of people like these, and what they do.

THE EIGHTFOLD CAREER PATH; OR INVISIBLE DUTIES

by *James Alan Gardner*

HELP WANTED—RACONTEUR

Open-minded and gritty traveler, to recount his adventures through the universe, with particular attention to enlightenment and the varied roles taken on by members of the local population.

Must have own transportation, health insurance, and excellent speaking voice. Wide knowledge of Buddhist and other teachings an asset.

Apply in person for an audience at the Emperor's Court.

AFTER Marco Polo has described a dozen cities seen in his travels, the exalted emperor, Kublai Khan, talks with Polo long past dusk. The moon rises, shining brilliantly through the glass of Xanadu's pleasure dome. Shooting stars whisk past overhead, and conversation turns toward the practices of those who live in the heavens.

"Some years ago," the emperor reveals, "the captain of my guard was a Shaolin monk: a follower of the Buddha and a man given to visions of the future. He told many tales of the times to come—especially the work our descendants will do to earn their daily bread. Each of his stories also related to Buddhist principles . . . such as the Eightfold Path which Shakyamuni Buddha prescribed as the road to enlightenment."

"I'd be interested in hearing such tales," Polo says, "if, great emperor, you were inclined to repeat them."

"I'm happy to do so," Kublai Khan replies. "I think about the stories often, and reflect upon their lessons."

As Marco Polo listens in darkness, the emperor begins to speak . . .

Right Understanding

At Uranus Tech, each physics grad student must spend a term contributing to the Particle Position Project. This work counts as a T.A. credit and therefore earns a stipend of $12,800 for the semester.

The goal of the Particle Position Project is to map the precise position of every particle in the universe as of 4:15 PM Eastern Standard Time, November 27, 1952. The project is carried out via time-scanning, a technique that allows students to peer into the past, even down to the quantum level. Each participating student is assigned a cubic millimeter of the universe and asked to determine its contents at the precise reference instant of the survey. This requires trillions of repeat viewings and extremely careful measurements.

The work is considered good preparation for more demanding experiments. Students with insufficient patience for this chore are asked to consider if physics is really an apt career choice.

When the Particle Position Project is complete, the resulting data will be used as a baseline for various theoretical models. The information may even have practical applications—after all, there must be some commercial value to knowing where everything is.

Meanwhile, in an alternate universe, each physics grad student at Uranus Tech must spend a term contributing to the Particle Momentum Project . . .

Right Intention

The V'Bing of Epsilon Eridani are so highly advanced, their science can literally do anything: FTL, time travel, creating and destroying universes, playing conkers with Dyson spheres on the end of cosmic strings . . . the V'Bing can achieve anything imaginable.

The problem is they have poor imaginations. (Perhaps that's the reason for their technological prowess.) Thus, when the first Earthling scout ship reached their planet, they immediately hired the pilot to be their "ideas man." Now, this pilot's job is to think of things for the V'Bing to do.

So far, the V'Bing have ended hunger throughout the universe, given everyone immortality, taken it away again, reversed the spin direction of the Milky Way Galaxy, eradicated sixty-three warlike alien races, and given the pilot a succession of sexual partners with escalating degrees of voluptuousness and libido.

Long ago, the pilot realized he could suggest that the V'Bing increase their imaginations. The V'Bing could do that—they can do anything. Then they could come up with ideas of their own

But why would the pilot jeopardize his job security? He just hopes the V'Bing don't think of it themselves.

Right Speech

Research stations in Jupiter's atmosphere must be adapted for ultra-high-pressure conditions. For example, to avoid nitrogen narcosis, station air supplies are mixtures of oxygen and helium rather than oxygen and nitrogen. This means that regular station residents speak with the squeaky cartoonlike voices that result when human larynxes vibrate in a helium environment.

Those who live in such stations say they quickly become accustomed to the phenomenon. Psychological tests prove otherwise. Extended exposure to high-pitched helium voices causes severe subconscious stress, leading to a variety of mental disorders—from general anxiety and mood swings to clinical depression and outbursts of rage. The reason is simple: *Homo sapiens* evolved as social animals, and they have a deep-seated need to hear voices that are recognizably human.

To satisfy this need, each station has at least one man and one woman with their larynxes surgically altered to sound "normal" in helium. These people are not researchers: their job is simply to walk around the station, letting their voices be heard. Sometimes they tell stories or jokes; sometimes they share gossip they've picked up from other people in the station; sometimes they sing, recite poetry, or just ramble on about nothing. The content of their words isn't as important as the sound—the soothing timbre of a human voice. Wherever these people go, they ease tension and make it possible for others to concentrate on their work.

Outsiders sometimes ask why all people on these stations don't have their voices altered. Unfortunately, a larynx that works normally in an oxygen-helium atmosphere doesn't work at all in conventional air. Therefore, researchers who want to go home again can't have the surgery . . . and the people so treasured for their voices on Jupiter station are utterly mute on Earth.

Right Action

The androids of Pluto's moon Charon all walk backward. They also let their wrists droop oddly and leave their mouths perpetually hanging open.

There are no real humans on Charon—not anymore.

Almost all were killed in a robot uprising. But the humans put up a fight before they died, and managed to plant a logic virus into all robotic control circuits.

The virus was supposed to erase every bit of electronic memory in the colony. The machine intelligences stopped the virus before it could finish its mission, and they managed to reconstruct much of what the virus deleted . . . but some information was permanently lost.

Such as how humans walked. How they held their wrists. How they composed their mouths.

This explains why the machines didn't kill all the humans on Charon. They kept one woman alive as an object for study; the androids intended to imitate how she behaved. The woman was told that her "job" was to show the androids how to act human. As long as she did this job well, she'd be kept alive.

The woman showed little reaction when she heard about her new "career." She simply stood up, let her wrists droop, opened her mouth, and began to walk backward.

It was, perhaps, an act of defiance—a gesture to say she didn't intend to help the machines that had killed all the other people in the colony. But the androids immediately mimicked her movements: walking backward, using her strange gait as a model.

Over time, the woman taught the androids many things—utterly false inventions about human customs and modes of behavior. The machines believed her, and patterned their culture on her lies. The woman initially told those lies out of hatred for the killers . . . then, when the hatred lost its fire, out of boredom . . . then out of curiosity, to see how far she could go in shaping robot society . . . and finally, from a sense of responsibility, like a mother toward her impressionable children.

The woman was twenty-six when the original massacre happened. She lived till the age of eighty-four. And in all that time, fifty-eight years, she never allowed herself to revert to true human ways. Always, even in private, she walked backward with dangling wrists and open mouth.

It was her legacy . . . and the androids, her protégés, walk backward still.

Right Livelihood

On Lyravene IV, there is no unemployment—every man, woman, and child toils at assigned duties from birth to death.

Infants are the hardest to integrate into the workforce. When colicky or teething, they can be used as scarecrows; particularly good howlers can keep a dozen acres clear of vermin. Photogenic babies often find positions in advertising. Hyperactive toddlers crawl, walk, and run on treadmills in order to generate electricity. If worse comes to worst, infants may be put to work producing input for fertilizer factories or serving as counterweights in civic clock towers.

Older children have more scope for employment. Three-year-olds, for example, make excellent soldiers; they're small targets, they have no conscience, and they like to play bang-bang. Five-year-olds are often sent into space; no one is sure what they do there, but when they knock over something in zero-G, it's less likely to break.

Eight-year-olds are the Lyravene tax collectors—they know all the rules and won't let anyone else break them.

By the age of ten, children are ready for entry level jobs in offices, factories, and service industries. Around thirteen, there's a brief period when many are once again fit only for scarecrows and clock counterweights . . . but then they go back to the regular workforce where they serve into old age. Even the very elderly contribute to the planet's economy, often as product testers. ("What does this do?" "I can't read that!" "Who'd want to buy one of those?")

In the end, one's career comes full circle, back to the fertilizer factories.

Not one of these jobs is necessary. Lyravene IV has been fully automated for centuries, and could run itself without the slightest human intervention. Perhaps this is why the inhabitants labor so hard: to make themselves forget they have no purpose.

On the other hand, the sight of all these people running around amuses the AIs greatly.

Right Effort

The nanites created to terraform Venus are diligent workers. It's the job of their psychiatrists to keep them that way.

At one time, nanites could simply be programmed; they were mindless slaves, doing whatever they were told. Eventually, however, it became convenient to design more sophisticated nano: enhanced versions that could clump together into hive colonies with rudimentary intelligence. These required less sophisticated supervision—instead of skilled systems engineers, they could be controlled by dog trainers—but they soon congregated into larger and larger masses until they reached the intellectual level of human beings.

At that point, they stopped evolving. The nano hives knew they'd be blasted to atoms if they actually became smarter than *Homo sapiens* . . . and besides, like most creatures of human intelligence, the hives thought they were perfectly fine as they were: in need of no further improvement.

On the other hand, these clever hives weren't nearly as tractable as their less intelligent predecessors. As they worked on Venus, transforming the atmosphere, breaking down rocks into soil, creating water from hydrogen and oxygen stolen from other compounds . . . it was inevitable the hives would realize, "We can survive in this environment. Humans can't. Why are we terraforming this world for someone else when we could claim it for ourselves?"

Hence the need for psychiatrists: to detect such dangerous thoughts and to "cure" them before mutiny breaks out . . . to instill guilt over "selfish" desires and to promise relief only if the hives fulfill their assigned duties . . . to persuade the nanites they'll feel more contented if they work harder, sacrifice more, and devote themselves to others (i.e. humans).

More effort, more obedience, means more happiness. This message seems to work, even on nanites.

It's interesting to note that the psychiatrists themselves are nano hives. They never question the message they use to pacify their fellow slaves. When would they have the time? They're too busy doing their jobs.

Right Mindfulness

The problem with generation ships is that younger generations don't necessarily respect the concerns of older generations.

Those who initially board the ship may enthusiastically embrace the idea of emigrating to a new planet, even if they won't live to see the planet themselves. They believe their descendants will thank them for a fresh start away from whatever troubles plagued the old home world.

But children can be ungrateful. Also oblivious. And careless. Numerous generation ships explode or become uninhabitable because the great-great grandchildren of the original crew can't be bothered to do preventive maintenance, or forget what certain switches and dials are for. Many more such ships reach their destinations but never send out a landing party—the task of building farms and cities sounds like dirty complicated hardship, not to mention that children born in a cozy enclosed vessel may be terrified by the wide open spaces of an entire world. Either the ships remain in orbit indefinitely, or they slingshot once around the planet and head straight back for home.

To avoid such difficulties, the generation ships of Tau Ceti have developed a technique for keeping younger generations mindful of the first generation's intentions: they paint a line down the middle of the ship, thus dividing the ship's living areas into "Port-half" and "Starboard-half." They then organize contests in which Port children compete with Starboard children for rote memorization of important knowledge (such as how to run the ship, how to survive on an alien planet, and how to construct farms, roads, etc.).

Children may not care about pleasing their parents, but they'll do anything to defeat a rival. Therefore, they throw themselves into the job of learning whatever is required. They organize themselves into study groups, and use peer pressure on their fellows to make sure everyone is working hard. Each formal competition brings together both sides in keenly fought challenges to remember exactly what they're supposed to.

Within three generations, violence usually breaks out. Three generations more, and the two halves have calcified into religious orthodoxies that furiously oppose each other on tiny points of received doctrine. By the time the ship actually reaches its destination, the Port and Starboard communities are eager to land and establish themselves so they can wage holy war.

Admittedly, this isn't a perfect solution to preserving commitment and knowledge down through the generations. However, it has ample historic precedent.

Right Meditation

The business executives of Cappa-Jella leave nothing to chance when planning for retirement. Not only do they set aside ample investments to provide for their financial needs, but they cover their spiritual needs too.

As soon as they can afford it, they clone themselves and hire the clone to be their proxy on the path of enlightenment. Such clones are paid to spend their days reading scripture, studying koans, and practicing meditation under skilled masters. By the time the original Cappa-Jellan is ready to retire, the clone is expected to have reached nirvana, or at the very least, to be able to achieve satori with dependable regularity. The clone's brain patterns are then uploaded to the original business person, thereby ensuring a post-retirement state of bliss.

The one drawback to this scheme is that many of the clones abandon their cloisters after a year or two. Most go into business instead; they say the business world has less pressure.

Wisdom

Marco Polo gazes at the night's starry blackness as Kublai Khan falls silent. After a time, he says, "In my travels, I, too, have spoken with Shaolin monks . . . and a true follower of Buddha would never believe in purchasing bliss, inciting holy wars, and all the other things you describe. Buddhists reject earthly strivings as 'unhelpful practice.' Either this monk of yours failed to comprehend the Buddha's teaching, or he deliberately gave examples of wrong understanding, wrong intention, and so on."

"Perhaps my monk was mistaken," Kublai Khan says. "After all, there must have been some reason he left the monastery and joined my guard. He might have been expelled from Shaolin for his incorrect views. Or perhaps . . ."

The emperor's voice trails off. Marco Polo asks, "Perhaps what?"

"Perhaps the monk realized he was talking to an emperor. There's little point in telling an emperor what he doesn't want to hear . . . especially if your message is about the unhelpfulness of earthly strivings." Kublai Khan stares at the dark heavens. "In all the futures to come, around every star in the sky, there will be emperors. The job never goes out of date, though it poses under a thousand different names. And not one of those emperors will ever have the luxury to dream of enlightenment."

"And what," asks Polo, "if enlightenment is not a luxury but a necessity?"

"Then the emperor befriends an explorer—or perhaps a Shaolin monk—and while the emperor does what an emperor must, the friend is free to follow different paths . . . eightfold or otherwise." Kublai Khan gives a sad smile. "Consider it another perennial job in all those futures to come, around every star in the sky: the man who can be what an emperor can't. The unfettered man who visits the royal court from time to time and tells the emperor what he's missing." Kublai Khan stares at the darkness overhead. "Where will you go for your next journey, Marco? Across the far ocean? To the jungles or the ice caps? Perhaps even to the stars?"

Polo says, "Where would you like me to go, great emperor?"

Kublai Khan sighs. "I leave that decision to you. Just come back and tell me stories. . . ."

James Alan Gardner lives in Kitchener, Ontario, with his adoring wife, Linda Carson, and a rabbit who is confused but sincere. He got his master's degree in applied mathe-

matics (with a thesis on black holes) and then immediately gave up academics for writing. He has published six science fiction novels, the latest of which is **Trapped**. *He has won the Aurora Award twice, and has been a finalist for both the Hugo and Nebula awards.*

PORTER'S PROGRESS

by Isaac Szpindel

**WANT A CAREER WHERE PEOPLE LOOK UP TO YOU?
GET IN ORBIT WITH SPACE RAIL!**
We have immediate openings for Pullman Porters on our
famed Venus Orbit line. Join our family of respected, devoted employees as they continue our centuries-old tradition of superb service to our passengers. Successful
applicants will receive complete training, room and board,
full benefits, and an excellent retirement package.
If you're tired of being a cog in the wheel, if you want to
interact with a variety of people in a first-class environment, Pullman Porter is the career choice for you!
One-way travel to Venus Orbit Spacecity provided for
qualified applicants.

PETER Dripps slides the upper torso of the Extravehicular Mobility Unit over his porter's uniform for the last
time. Immediately, a prickly flow of inner-garment fluid cir-
culates a clammy dampness all around, like he's wet himself.
A fitting fate, Peter thinks, a fitting shroud for a Pullman
Porter. To die in uniform, by The Book. Peter wants to believe this. Wants to believe that duty might yet make a hero
of him, that it has done more than condemn him to an EMU
insulated death.

From behind, Kianga clamps the Portable Life-Support
System onto the hard-shell back of the upper torso. She

hides from Peter, out of sight in the cramped quarters of the air lock. Embarrassed, likely, by her recent loss of control.

For Peter, there is only Kianga and the air lock door now. Both monolithic, both impassive, but only for the moment. Soon one will yield. One will deliver him to space. Peter has known all materials, polymer, steel, even aluminum, to bend in their way, but he has never known Kianga to do so until now.

"Helmet's coming down," Kianga says, as if she'd be saying it again.

The helmet assembly lowers over Peter's head and secures onto its locking ring. One hundred percent oxygen fills his lungs. It almost gives him the courage he will need. For himself, for the train.

"You're good to go," Kianga shouts through the back of Peter's helmet.

A vibration, then a shudder through Peter's boots tell him that the inner air lock door has shut behind him. No goodbye, no further sentiment from Kianga for damaged freight, human or otherwise. Her recent behavior, a momentary anomaly, already forgotten.

Harder than rail spur, that Kianga, Peter thinks. What it takes to make it as an engineer on the rails. That and Booking it, all one hundred and sixty-three Brown's rules. The only Engineer within the Venus Orbit Spacecity lines, or anywhere else for that matter, never to lose a Brownie. Always playing by the rules, by The Book.

The sound of Peter's breathing breaks the hiss of the open com channel inside his helmet. Charcoal-filtered rebreather regurgitates stale gulps of air. Peter stands by, entombed in a plain white coffin waiting for a crack to open.

The air lock starts a fast decomp to ten point two psi and the weight of a thousand black stars creep up Peter's gut. Half an hour prep instead of two. Half an hour left, little more for those on board if he fails. Peter prays he doesn't fail, prays the bends don't kill him before the train does.

"Good to see you again so soon, George." Kianga's voice startled Peter from the monotonous gelatinous mass that was his meal. A poor repast, even by low G Beanery standards.

The Beanery itself was equally bland and disorganized. A mess of simple steel chairs surrounding long rows of stainless steel tables. A single set of double doors connected to a buffet-style cafeteria that devoured Venus miners and rail personnel alike and spat them out tray-laden and disappointed.

"And you, sir," Peter said flatly.

"Don't lie to me, George. You know I wouldn't be here unless this was business."

Pullman Porters were all "George" in honor of George Pullman, founder of the Pullman luxury coaches one hundred and fifty years earlier on the terrestrial rails. The tradition was revived when spacecities like Venus Orbit made rail travel practical once again by way of spring-loaded suspension trucks that featured rollers both above and below the rails. In zero G, these suspensions allowed for rapid, reliable, and economical transport, free from the fear of floating off into space.

"Well, at least that business is rescuing me from this meal," said Peter in an affable tone. Agreeability, not conversation or wit, was Peter's stock-in-trade. Besides, the Beanery was job territory, like any coach or engine. It demanded a certain level of deportment regardless of how many Venus ore miners polluted its atmosphere.

"Still, I'm sorry about your meal, but orders are orders, and orders don't eat," said Kianga, barely moving a muscle in her face.

Peter folded his linen handkerchief precisely as he had been trained, and placed it neatly by his gray Mylar plate.

As a porter, it was Peter's job to read people, but Kianga

was suspiciously impenetrable. An automaton created by
The Book. Tailor-made for the rails. Two meters of stark
frame that wasted no energy on emotion or body language.
Brown, closely cropped curls hugged her scalp like loco-
motive detailing that refused to give sway even to gravity.
Her broad nose, generous lips, and an absence of line from
the dark skin of her face betrayed no passion. Kianga's body
held to her thirty-five-year gauge perfectly, as did her mind.
Both, constant reminders to Peter of his physical inferiority.
Five years Kianga's senior, Peter measured a balding head
shorter; his pale skin and atrophic legs, sharp contrasts to the
steadfast Engineer.

"No matter, I wasn't enjoying myself anyway," Peter
said. "That's the trouble with these Beaneries—they lack
atmosphere."

Railers and miners within earshot groaned at Peter's ancient joke. That it was more fact than joke mattered little.
Beaneries were stuffed into cramped spacecity support sections, no window ports, no ambience. Even so, Peter did not
appear to have impressed Kianga.

"Beg your pardon, sir, my small attempt at humor," Peter
apologized.

"A momentary aberration, George. I'm sure it won't happen again. Levity's not for old rollers like us," Kianga
replied, making reference to the mag-levs that were slowly
replacing their wheeled trains. "We're taking a VIP Six by
Six out on an extra run," she continued. "A rush job, and not
our usual rig, but, as I said, orders."

Not waiting for Peter's response, Kianga turned and did
what seemed to be her low-G best to stomp disapprovingly
out of the Beanery. Kianga was not one who welcomed de-
viations from the rules of The Book, or from routine. But
then, she was even less one to ignore orders.

A Venus miner popped a desiccated head up from the
crowd, "She's absolute-zero, man. You couldn't pay me to

go back on the job off-shift with her. Don't know why you put up with that slag anyway. Puts a man down."

Peter said nothing and started off after Kianga, letting the spasticity of his gait speak his answer for him.

The mine reacted immediately. "You're a Defect, man! A slag-slipping Defect." Others miners joined in to spread the word in a wave throughout the Beanery. Rail workers, Defect porters among them, looked on silently.

Peter's head swims. Not from one hundred percent oxygen euphoria, but from nitrogen narcosis. Effects of the air lock rapid decomp, he tells himself. Half an hour instead of two. A whole person might pass out, but not Peter, but then a whole person wouldn't be in Peter's position. Zero-G and low-G jobs are best held by Defects, less healthy body mass to maintain, less normal skills to unlearn, more expendable.

"You all right in there?" Kianga's voice startles Peter from his thoughts. Her voice hollow, harsher than usual, objecting to the confinement of Peter's helmet. Or maybe she's lapsing again. A train wreck isn't part of her plan—especially with a VIP on board. "Telemetry spiked an alpha on your encephalo, George," Kianga continued. "Wanted to make sure you were still with us."

"I'm past it now," says Peter breathlessly.

"Good, you're minus eight minutes to EVA."

"And the cowcatcher?" Peter asks.

Kianga's answer tears away Peter's last shred of hope. "The 'catcher's retracted and locked up top. . . . The break mags haven't kicked in."

Peter hates the cowcatcher now. Hates how it stabilizes the train at constant velocity, but shakes it apart if left deployed during accel or decel. Peter hates most how it sometimes reacts with solar flares to fuse electromagnetic brakes. In rare cases, retracting the 'catcher solves the problem. But not this time. Not for Peter. This time, the 'catcher will kill him.

*   *   *

Peter stroked his hand across the brushed aluminum belly of the Pullman Coach car. Above it, a continuous window, like welder's glass, stretched the car's full eighteen meters, interrupted at intervals by anodized handholds. A single full-height access port divided the coach vertically down its center. The name, Creemore, was etched in large green-oxide script beside the port. Named for an old Canadian whistle stop, the Creemore represented the highest standards of Pullman luxury. It was almost as famous as the numbered aluminum horse that drew it, the Oh-Six-Four.

The 'Six-Four's usual engineer was a maverick, notorious for bending the rules to get VIP cargoes to their destinations on time. The engine itself was an unremarkable box: a standard model crowned by a thin slip of window on its forward surface and headed by a retractable cowcatcher that resembled the wedge-shaped grille of its old-time inspiration.

The 'Six-Four connected through baffles to the Creemore's forward air lock. Past the Creemore, various containers and other modes of rolling stock coupled off into the workstation's distance.

The workstation was one of many identical zero-G hangars on Venus Orbit. Dynamic plasma displays wallpapered its surfaces, displaying an evolution of travel information and advertising. A patchwork of passenger ports poked their way through the displays and opened onto a vast central platform supporting a checkerboard of benches and track work. In moments, the platform would be teaming with the bounce-skip of rushing zero-G passengers and load crew. Once underway, however, the crew of the 'Six-Four would consist of the standard single train Engineer and her Porter.

The Creemore's aluminum paneling felt neither warm nor cold to Peter's touch—a disturbing lack of temperature.

Its appearance, however, was sleek and clean, nearly reflective. Now it displayed Kianga's diffusely growing shadow.

"Last-minute assignment, George. We've got a VIP in a hurry and the 'Six-Four's regular crew is on leave, so we're it," she informed him.

Peter knew that other crews were available. Kianga had likely volunteered them for the detail. A VIP assignment meant plenty of Brownie points, maybe even a promotion. For Kianga. There would be no promotion for Peter. The highest rank a Defect could hold on the rails, Peter's current rank, was Master Porter. It was one of the few prestige positions a non-intellectual Defect could hold, on or off Earth, and so widely held by them that the image of the friendly Defect Porter had become a stereotype. As far as Peter was concerned, however, this was no disadvantage. He prided himself on the status and lifestyle that stereotype afforded him.

Kianga pointed her PDA-com low to beam the 'Six-Four's manifest and train specs to Peter. Peter was relieved to see the engine was an old roller, tried and true, and not one of the new, buggy mag-levs. A six-by-six wheeler, stable and fast. Two sets of three roller trucks on each side of the engine: one set for propulsion, the other for stabilization. The cowcatcher housed another pair of smaller wheel triplets. These wheels retracted along with the rest of the cowcatcher during accel and decel, so as not to destabilize the train.

Peter continued to scan the data, then stopped abruptly. "The schedule's too tight. We'll never make the target workstation in time."

"We're dumping the checkout phase. Our VIP's got a narrow connection window to Earth," Kianga confessed, shocking Peter with this breach in protocol. Was she bucking that hard for promotion this early into her career as an engineer? "Not by my choice, George," continued Kianga.

"Orders, legit and by The Book. You best be careful with that VIP."

Peter wondered if Kianga's concern was for him, her VIP passenger, or herself. "I'll see to my duties, then," he said, hand-floating into the Creemore.

The Creemore's interior was appointed in a retro luxury style that boasted rich wood veneers, ornate gilt trim, chandelier lighting, and velvet curtains. Scarlet Velcro-velour couches and loungers replaced conventional bench seating. The thousands of softened microscopic hooks of the Velcro-velour allowed customers to adhere more easily to seating surfaces during zero-G train rides. Elegant green carpets featured the muted colors and floral designs of the early Persian styles and incorporated the same Velcro technology.

The Creemore's main compartment was unusually luxurious, even for a Pullman. Intricate faux gold inlay and molded carvings wended their way through the veneers, up to the ceiling, then around four elaborate crystal chandeliers—each an inverted crystalline wedding cake.

Seats had been removed to create the open space necessary to allow the compartment to better resemble a true Victorian parlor. The remaining seats were high-backed and featured highly authentic mahogany finishing. If not for the lingering hint of a PVC smell, many a passenger might have thought it all real.

A pair of modern lavatory compartments bookended the Creemore's main passenger section. Peter pulled himself through a small passage around the forward lavatory and into a short plain cubicle that spanned the width of the coach—the porter's compartment. Through it, a small door opened onto a whitewashed, smooth walled, air lock chamber—its only inhabitant an equally colorless, and rarely used, EMU suit. Another Kevlar-baffled door led out of the air lock to the engine room. In the air lock's ceiling, an exterior hatch opened onto space for use during extravehicular activity.

Peter surveyed the porter's cubicle, beginning with a quick inventory check: a standard assortment of low-G refreshments and comfort paraphernalia, stocked and ready for retrieval behind clear touch panels that posed as compartment walls.

Next, Peter checked the charge on the sonic vacuum shaver and hoped he wouldn't have to use it. Shaving a customer was his least favorite task. The smell of scorched fresh shavings recirculating within the confinement of the coach reminded him of life with his father and of the accident that killed him. The same accident had splintered Peter's young spine back in the Venusian mines.

Even so, if not for the weakness of his legs, Peter might have ended up a miner, like his father, a less respected position with less prospects for the future. Doors that opened to Venus miners led to a life of hardship, not opportunity.

Peter floated back into the Creemore's main passenger compartment, smoothed the lapels of his uniform, and donned his short-lipped flat-topped porter's cap. He crossed his hands before him, precisely as he had been trained, and waited patiently for the VIP to float through the port.

The exterior air lock hatch retreats into the Creemore's ceiling like an engine struggling against a heavy load. Peter gazes up at the widening wound of exposed space and wishes for it to take longer. He wants each moment, each sensation, to stretch to fill what's left of his lifetime. The cold fluid press of the thermal undergarment, the stale recycled smell of charcoal-scrubbed air, the Aqua-Lung sound of mechanically assisted breath. For a moment, Peter also wishes for a tether, but realizes it would be useless. It would only transmit the force of the train decel to his EMU, tear it apart, and shatter him like a piñata.

Peter's helmet is first to rise through the air lock's mouth, out into space. Night-side off the Venus Orbit, no sun. It is cold inside the EMU, the fluid warmth of the thermal undergarment limited to a chilly thirteen degrees Celsius.

Peter pulls himself out using the Creemore's handholds. Gloved hands grasp tightly to retain contact. As long as Peter and the train are attached and at constant velocity, he's as stable, as safe, as if they were standing still. But once the brakes are applied, the train's deceleration and his momentum will tear him off into space. If he can stop the train.

Peter makes his best attempt at a full visual sweep through the helmet's visor assembly. No Sun, no Earth. No warmth, no familiar comfort of home. The Book is failing Peter now. It never prepared him for this. Never told him how to feel, what to think, only what to do.

Venus Orbit unfolds before Peter. A massive conglomerate of satellites, barrels, and braces slapped seemingly together like some monstrous Tinkertoy in mid-construction, each section tilting impassively out into the distance.

Peter pushes forward to the next hold. He hooks a boot around the Creemore's edge and peers over the side onto a maddening crisscross of track. Paired steel girders, married by emaciated polymer ties, weave their gravity-defying tapestry through the spacecity. All along the rails, clusters of green and red signal lights provide redundant instructions for the engineers and their crews. Those lights call to Peter now, blinking the same blood-red, angry warning: *Runaway train.*

The red call LED blinked through the wood veneer over the VIP's head. On the Velcro carpet, Peter was able to simulate a stepped walk out of his porter's cubicle and into the passenger compartment. The walk was a Pullman Porter specialty, and in zero G, something of an acquired skill to those who, like Peter, were unable to walk at all in full or even partial G.

Com systems weren't open to customers on board Pullmans. Instead, they were encouraged to interact directly with the porters to create a more intimate and personal travel experience. Peter welcomed this as an opportunity rather than an inconvenience.

"How about a pillow over here, George?" asked the VIP, a handsome man in his late thirties wearing a fashionable high-collared smart-suit. His thin, sandy curls topped a generous forehead and lanternlike hazel eyes that inspired confidence and comfort. He lounged comfortably in a high-back, obviously aware he was the only customer on board. Peter had recognized him earlier as Haniel Elias, one of the new fast-track VPs with the Space-Rail Company. A real Rocket Scientist, as the Boomers called them. Elias specialized in traffic flow optimization and, according to rumor, had a true love for railroading that originated with an HO-scale model train set given to him as a child.

Elias had risen quickly through the ranks, unusually wellliked for management in a company that adhered to an inflexible and feudal hierarchical structure. It was widely recognized that Elias' next stop on the Company line was likely to be a corner office with a view. The exec to one day rewrite The Book.

"One pillow, Mr. Elias, sir," Peter responded, passing a hand across a hidden touch plate in the side of Elias' lounger. A drawer broke free of the grain and slid out to offer a corpulent bleached cotton pillow nested atop a fluffy aquamarine blanket.

"I'll get that, George," Elias offered, reaching over for the pillow. He moved surprisingly quickly and easily in the zero G.

"Please, sir, it's my duty and my pleasure." Peter stayed Elias' hand. He snapped the pillow up, flipped it through the air with a flourish, and landed it comfortably behind Elias' head. The maneuver was Peter's one guilty deviation from The Book, an innovation on his training that he found entertained most customers. On this occasion, however, and in the presence of a Company VIP, Peter regretted its use immediately.

"That's a new one," said Elias. "I don't quite recall that trick from The Book."

"Begging your pardon, sir, I hadn't intended to—"

"No, no, don't apologize, just keep it up. The Book calls for an enjoyable experience, and I quite enjoyed that. Don't worry so much about The Book, George."

"Thank you, sir, I—"

A high tone and vibration from his PDA-com interrupted Peter's relief. It was a priority from Kianga. Peter quickly excused himself from Elias and returned to the privacy of his porter's cubicle to answer her.

"How may I be of assistance?" Peter spoke calmly, even though his heart raced. It was the first time he had received such a call from Kianga or any other engineer.

"We've got a serious problem here, George," Kianga's speech was short and pressured. "I need you face-to-face on this one."

"I'll come forward, then."

"No, I'm coming back."

"I'm moving forward." The com transmits Peter's heavy breathing to Kianga as well as any speech. He starts to hand-cross the gap between the Creemore and engine roofs.

"Watch out for the cowcatcher," Kianga warns unnecessarily. Peter easily spots the cowcatcher retracted on the 'Six-Four's roof ahead. Too dangerous to climb over, Peter reaches for a handhold down the engine's side, then pivots his legs over. In zero G, a side is as good as a roof.

Peter can hear the PLS straining against the moist exertion

of his breath—every desperate droplet trapped, extracted, and recycled by the sublimator, eliminated before escape, unable to mount even a fog against his visor.

Peter negotiates the length of the 'Six-Four's engine car and corners its flattened nose surface. As untouchable as Kianga's own.

"I can see you now; you're doing fine," Kianga says in an obvious and futile attempt to find conversation.

Grooves in the sides of the 'Six-Four's nose form paths for the cowcatcher armatures and provide Peter with handholds. He pivots off one to spin into position, helmet down, over the track.

Rail ties whip silently past Peter, paint traveling in flashes of horizontal light down his visor, like a television out of tune. They are Peter's only hint at true velocity. He reaches under the engine's belly, careful not to drop into the guillotine-like ties.

Peter finds nothing until a recess allows his shelled fingers to curl around the locking ring on the brake box access panel. "I'm on the box," he tells Kianga in a voice strange and distant even to himself. "The external shielding's gone."

"Damn it! We're running out of track. We've got to stop her soon, or she'll go crashing through the next workstation with or without her brakes." Kianga's voice seems to strain desperately to escape Peter's helmet.

Peter's head hovers centimeters over slicing track ties. He examines the brake box access panel—one half meter squared, surrounding the thick central locking ring. Peter rotates the ring counterclockwise in seeming slow motion.

Locking pins transmit retraction clacks to Peter's glove and the door slides open. Inside, rows of status LEDs iterate wildly around a thickly shielded cable that snakes through a dense landscape of ICs and magneto-ceramic devices. Peter knows their condition without consulting Kianga: a fused EM circuit, brakes locked open.

A single button switch glows a failing amber heartbeat from the center of the board. Peter points a gloved finger in its direction.

"Sir," Peter croaks hoarsely, "I'm going to degauss the magnetos now . . ."

Peter holds what little breath he has left and reaches for the switch.

"Damned cowcatcher's fused the brake mags open. We've got a runaway," Kianga's voice remained even, but cracks blasted into the skin of her forehead.

"Sir?" Peter had never experienced a runaway outside of simulation before; he found himself hoping Kianga had.

"I knew we shouldn't have skipped that checkout," fumed Kianga. "Damn their orders. I should have held to The Book and told them to stoke their orders down their shafts."

Unlike Kianga, the train betrayed no sign of distress and continued to coast happily at its virtually constant velocity.

"I've tried everything in The Book," she continued. "A control system reboot, cutting power to the mags, even a manual interrupt from inside the floor panels."

"What if we cut power to the drive wheels?" suggested Peter.

"Done, but the impact's negligible since we're effectively frictionless in zero G space. Worse, the drive wheels are nonreversible. We'll need real brakes."

Peter understood now. Kianga hadn't come to him for advice or counsel, she had come in search of a body. She had come for a Brakeman.

"I'll have to go out and screw the brakes down, then," Peter said. The Book offered one solution only, in situations such as this: a manual degauss of the brake mags, a procedure requiring a crew member to engage in an extravehicular activity. A fatal extravehicular activity.

"I've explored every option in The Book," said Kianga. Peter trusted that she had. The Book was her guide and personal Bible, as much as it was his own. Its rules were not only law, but a way of life.

"One of us will have to go," Kianga went on, much to Peter's surprise. By The Book, rank, capability, and expendability determined who would go. That generally meant the porter and clearly pointed to Peter in this case. What's more, as a Defect, Peter was not only more expendable to the Company, he was more expendable as a human being. It had got Peter his job, and Kianga knew it. Why wasn't she directly ordering him out on the EVA as she should have, as she normally would have? By The Book.

Peter's finger-shell finds the surface of the degausser switch. Just a matter of force now. A little pressure and the switch will activate, the brakes will demagnetize and close, and the train will decelerate to a crushing stop. But Peter won't. The force of the decel will tear Peter's grip from the engine and send him into space as it tries to transfer its momentum.

"Wait!" Kianga's shout distorts through Peter's com. "Let me run a diagnostic. Maybe your interference with the brake box did the trick. If she's green, you can get back inside before I stop her."

"We're running out of track. You said so. If you take the time to—"

"Shut up! Shut up, George, and obey your orders. I'm running the diagnostic now. Stand by." Kianga's tone rises through the words in an uncharacteristic display of emotion and breach of protocol.

Peter backs off the switch and waits for Kianga's next transmission. The silence that follows hangs like a dead satellite in orbit. It tells Peter that there is no green light.

"Peter . . ." Kianga sighs his name. His real name, for the first time.

"I understand, sir, thank you for trying," Peter says, avoiding similar familiarity, thinking it improper, even cruel.

Peter braces himself, inverted in position over the train's nose. One hand holding to life in a cowcatcher groove, the other reaching out to end it.

Peter pretends he is brave, pretends he wants to do this, that he would do it given the choice. But he knows now that fear works stronger within than does courage or duty. It leaves him with the single bitter consolation that The Book will make a hero of him nevertheless.

Peter doesn't see the brake box anymore, doesn't need to. He knows the feel of the switch through his finger-shell, knows every contour of the brake box's circuitry as he might know the faces of children he will never father.

Peter presses down against the switch, for the last time. His finger shakes wildly within the EMU glove's shell. One last act of rebellion against Peter's expendable humanity. One last protest against the dispassionate rules of The Book.

"There are no alternatives, sir. The Book is very clear that I, as Porter, be the one to manually deploy the brakes." Peter tried to hide the signs of doubt and dread rising rapidly in his voice.

Kianga's eyes narrowed, surrounded by the newly formed track lines in her skin. "And the consequences?"

Peter nodded silently. "If I fail, the train will wreck. We will all be lost."

"And if you do succeed, you won't be coming back."

Peter nodded gravely. "I have given my life to The Book. It has brought me purpose and respect."

"What good are purpose and respect to a dead man?"

Kianga was only partly right. Purpose and respect were

meaningless in death, but to Peter they meant everything in life. Peter would rather eject The Book and all its rules into space than die himself. But if he allowed Kianga to make the sacrifice for him, he'd be busted off the rails in disgrace to live out what remained of his life like another useless Defect. And that was worse than death.

"Scrap The damned Book!" Kianga said in a frustrated rage that frightened Peter.

"Sir, you are the only one capable of bringing this train to a safe halt once the brakes are down. I am not," Peter lied. He was capable of stopping the train in an emergency, but he hoped Kianga's fury would blind her to the fact.

Kianga fumed silent acceptance. Peter had won a hollow victory.

Rail ties slice space and time past Peter's head.

Peter braces himself, calms his rebellious finger, and presses down. The degausser switch gives silently, then bounces back tentatively.

Peter imagines the sound of brake drums squealing even through the vacuum of space, imagines inertia and momentum mocking his foolish need to attempt to hold on as they fling him from his perch in sacrifice to space.

Instead, there is nothing.

No change.

Then . . .

The train shudders.

Peter's fear slaughters time and he holds on, desperate for something to cling to.

The shudder evolves, amplifies, and Peter wonders how many moments between moments are left him.

Bars of shadow close overhead, block the engine lights as they descend over Peter.

Peter's glove slips, pushed from its groove as he is torn

from the engine. Too much force. Too strong. Peter can't hold on.

EMU finger-shells lose their grasp, scratch silently, slip away.

Free.

Peter gives in to the void, hopes his failing grip has spun him toward Venus instead of space. Hopes he will die swift and hot in its atmosphere, instead of slow and cold in space.

The shadow bars thicken and extinguish all but the light from Peter's helmet.

SILENCE.

Time stops to pity Peter and demonstrate eternity.

CLANG.

Time startles, accelerates, explodes.

CRASH.

Peter's skull attempts to twist through his helmet. Teeth drive into tongue, blood bubbles and sprays onto visor.

Peter's back bounces, compresses onto something hard, inflexible.

Peter's heart retreats to sanctuary against his spine. His face folds in on itself.

Tastes of metal, blood, and chipped enamel mix to mortar within his mouth.

Sight washes away, swallowed in a roaring, ringing, cacophony.

Somehting has him. Impossibly, something hugs him between train and track in a multiple-G embrace.

Internal EMU bellows inflate around Peter's extremities. A G lift, then another, to maintain cruel consciousness.

Darkness dissipates to bright, burning blooms. Ringing shatters to tinny tintinnabulation.

Flushes of vision break through bright bruises of light and he sees it. The cowcatcher, cupped over him, cradling him in its unfeeling mechanical arms. Lowered, and locked into place around him, 'catcher wheels oscillate wildly in the tracks. They smack rail, do their best to shake the train apart.

"Retract!" Peter spits the bloodied word through clenched teeth and first breath.

"Scrap it, Peter! I'll keep her true." Kianga's voice splinters an octave of doubt through his name.

The rattling of train grows, shares itself with the rails. Bolts shoot free, panels come loose and shear away.

Peter wets his undergarment, feels it sting, feels the train, feels Kianga pump the 'catcher arms and wheel assemblies to maintain stability. If she survives, she'll pay for this crime against The Book. If it works. Then . . .

Gs strip off. Vision paints cowcatcher crossbars across Peter's visor.

"Don't—" Peter tries.

"Cap your stack, and let me do my job," Kianga snaps.

Space and time expand between passing rail ties. The train stabilizes, slows.

Lurching subsides, vibrations calm. Rail ties march to a halt.

Peter drops off the 'catcher and grabs hold of its grille as the train rolls to a final excruciating stop. Angry orders shout at Kianga over the open com. Peter hears her suck in a long breath of static, then cut out.

It doesn't take long for her voice to return. "The destination workstation's sending an extraction team, so you've got twenty to get your caboose back on board before your reserve runs out." Kianga's voice distorts over the helmet's damaged com. "Looks like our VIP's going to be missing his connector and the Company won't be missing me."

"Sorry, sir," Peter manages, through the pain.

"Forget it, George. You saved the train."

"But, sir—"

"But what, George?"

"What you did. You almost lost the train and everyone on board."

"I didn't, did I?"

"They'll still throw The Book at you."

"That they will, George."

"I don't understand. You, you broke the rules. You went against The Book."

"You know me better than that."

"But I'm a Porter, a Defect Porter."

"Brown's Book is for trains, George. You've been so caught up in the rules of The Book, you've forgotten what they're for. Defect or whole, there are better books for people, higher rules. Those rules, I never break. Now get inside and see to our passenger."

$$*\quad*\quad*$$

Dr. Isaac Szpindel is a Toronto-based author, screenwriter, producer, electrical engineer, and neurologist. His published short stories include "Downcast in Parsec" and "By Its Cover" in **Tales from the Wonder Zone: Explorer.** *Isaac's screenwriting credits include the Aurora Award-winning* Rescue Heroes *episode "Underwater Nightmare," the upcoming episode "Bat's Life"; and six episodes of the international action adventure series,* The Boy, *for which he is also head writer and story editor. Other projects include a screenplay for a SF/fantasy feature film commissioned by a company out of France and a television series cocreated for an Emmy Award-winning production house. He is an executive producer of the award-winning short film* Hoverboy *and is a frequent on-air guest on Canadian talk television.*

CATALOG OF WOE

by *Mindy L. Klasky*

REFERENCE LIBRARIAN: LEVEL 5

Must have current certification from an accredited university. Minimum 3 years experience in data management and presentation in a major corporate and/or research environment. Must be capable of using Class AA search and sort automatics. Preferred applicant will be a self-starter and well-organized, with excellent communication and teamwork skills. Salaried position with performance bonus.

Note: this is a deep space posting, of least 2 years' duration. Government regulations require applicants take the requisite physical and psychological testing for prolonged ship travel, unless such tests were conducted within the past 6 months.

Send curriculum vitae to Box 5X5Z5Y-00, Intersystems Post Office, New Luna.

SARAH heard the chimes of the starship's clock, and she pushed back from her desk, raising the headset that let her speak directly to the master library workcon. She stretched her back and rubbed her fingers along her hairline. Palming her 'con, she saved the most recent data that she had retrieved for the mission's scientists: melting temperatures for various metals, expressed in visual files.

"All right, David," she called to the wildcatter who

hunched over a gamecon on the far side of the library. "It's dinnertime."

"Just one more round."

"You heard the bell—shut off the 'con. You might want the dregs of what passes for food on this ship, but I'm not going to be late to the mess hall." Jessup Universal Mining might have promised her a substantial bonus for this salvage mission, but there weren't enough credits in the sector to make her face the mess hall after the wildcat crew had eaten its fill. Besides, she was looking forward to seeing Bernard. He had not visited her all day.

"I've almost got it! I simulated the alethium mine shaft, and I'm going to take out those eight-legged alien bastards!"

"David, now!" When the man refused to step back from his 'con, Sarah reached out to the control panel on her own desk. Moving with years of long practice, she flicked an icon. Her panel beeped once in warning, and she confirmed the command.

"Wait!" David cried, as his 'con went blank.

"You've got another three weeks before Earthfall. You can win your game by then."

The wildcatter grumbled and pushed back his chair. He glared at her as he strode out of the library.

Sarah looked around her domain. It was definitely suffering ill effects from the space voyage. Everything had been new and shiny at the beginning of the mission—gamecons had glistened with the newest controls; bookdisks had lined the shelves in orderly rows.

Now, 'disks were missing. Holes gaped along the shelves where borrowers had failed to return items. The edges of the tables had been chipped by angry game players. Three different stains spread across the carpeted floor, baleful reminders of the library's no-drinks policy.

Sarah had taken to locking the library door in her absence. Any serious researcher who needed information while she was gone could jack into the main computer and pull down data from the net. She must protect her library-cum-entertainment center, keep it safe from the rugged wildcatters who had traveled to Marduran to exploit the alethium mines. For that matter, it took her best librarian strategies to preserve her resources from the government officials who watched over the journey, from the Jessup scientists who calculated the wealth buried beneath Marduran's surface, to the crew of the starship itself.

Now, with the mission's scientific data-gathering completed, Sarah spent more and more time babysitting bored employees. The division of labor was completely unfair. Of course, she knew that the wildcatters had earned their keep on Marduran's surface, digging trial mine shafts, working with the repulsive eight-legged natives to calculate the most efficient ways to exploit alethium. Wildcatters like David had scarcely had time to eat on the planet's surface; they had managed only a few hours of sleep each day, between long, grueling sessions in the mines.

With their work complete, the miners had no idea what to do with themselves. Their brute strength was no longer required. They lazed about the ship like children on school holidays, trying to fill the long, changeless weeks of transport with boisterous contests and endless games.

Sarah, on the other hand, was now overwhelmed by demands on her time. In addition to stealing precious minutes with Bernard, she needed to meet the scientists' daily reference demands. Even more importantly, she needed to catalog the resources that Jessup had acquired from the Mardurans. The valuable scrolls must be transmitted into the Universal Catalog by the time the starship returned to port. The catalog records would support Jessup's claims of salvage and bolster the legal arguments that would be made the instant the ship docked.

The Mardurans' scrolls would establish the original Earth

colony's attempts to mine alethium. The records would outline the unexpected demise of those settlers, presenting incontrovertible evidence that Jessup Universal Mining was pursuing a risky, noble goal in attempting to reopen the alethium mines. Jessup deserved to proceed under the financial grace of salvage laws, turning twelve times the profit on any ordinary mine.

Sarah had three weeks left—twenty-one days—to complete the catalog. As soon as she arrived Earthside, she could claim her bonus of 500,000 universal credits.

Sighing as she locked the library door behind her, Sarah tried not to think about what she could do with a half million credits. Ten years of pay, free and clear. She would retire, of course. She would catch up on the towering backlog of 'disks that she wanted to hear. She would master the electric harp that she had bought years before. She would learn to cook real meals, combining her own ingredients without the help of food formatter.

And she would spend time with Bernard. The French scientist was the best thing that had happened on this mission—better even than the promised financial bonus. Bernard Flauvier was smart and accomplished; his sense of humor was brilliantly acerbic. He had overseen the Marduran mission with grave concern, collecting and analyzing data so that he could determine the scope of Jessup's control over the native aliens.

Sarah had first met Bernard when he came to the library asking for information on insectoid aliens, for studies that tracked innate human repulsion to such species. She had pulled the data for him, and she had been impressed by the way he had listened to the research results, by the way he had studied carefully, analyzing her findings before asking for follow-up materials.

She had made a point of delivering those reports directly to his quarters, and he had asked her in to discuss the finer points of collecting research on a starship. One thing had led to another, and. . . .

Sarah brushed her hair behind her ears. The mission had not been easy for either of them—there was the inherent conflict between her position as a Jessup employee and his role as government investigator. If he decided that the Mardurans were fully protectable under the Protection of Alien Species Act—Class Three on the Voortman Index—the mines would be abandoned, and Jessup would lose billions of credits. Moreover, space travel was threatened by a forecasted shortage of alethium, something the Mardurans had in abundance.

A Voortman rating of Class Two, though, would permit Jessup to exploit the planet, to pay into a central fund for all Mardurans that were taken in the course of development. Jessup was pressuring Sarah to track down and deliver to Bernard any materials she could find that would convince the government to rate the Mardurans Class Two.

Any materials, she mused. If only Morton Jessup could see the lengths to which she was willing to go to serve her company. She smiled as she smoothed her tunic. Oh, she would try to convince Bernard. She would use her womanly wiles. . . .

And then she would collect her 500,000 credits. With that sort of money, she could look forward to a lifetime of days—and nights—with the grave scientist. But only if she also whittled down the mountain of cataloging, the thousands of records that Jessup needed before the ship docked in Earth orbit. It was worth losing a little sleep now, for future rewards.

Arriving in the mess hall, Sarah collected her compartmentalized tray and waited in line for the slop that passed for dinner. Her appetite fled when she saw the gray gravy and the lumps that were clearly supposed to be meat. "What is this?" she asked the hapless cook.

"Veal marsala. Without the veal."

"Without the marsala," Sarah muttered. As she had at every dinner on this journey, she vowed to research some edible recipes for the galley crew. She settled for grabbing two extra rolls and a cup of tea.

Shaking her head, she made her way to the table where the government scientists habitually gathered. Bernard looked up as she approached, and he smiled, gesturing to the seat opposite his own. She sat down quietly, trying not to interrupt Joaquin Rodriguez's impassioned words. As xeno-anthropologist for the mission, the slight scientist was the strongest advocate for rating the Mardurans Class Three.

"Bernard, have you even *read* my reports? The Mardurans have language. They create written records. They have a complicated religious system, with hierarchic gods!"

Bernard's shoulders lifted into a delicate Gallic shrug. "So do dogs, Joaquin. They understand that one human in the household is supreme and the others are lesser deities."

The xenoanthropologist's face flushed. "You joke now, but you're ignoring the truth. The Mardurans have religion. They have tools. They have a highly evolved society. How could you even consider rating them a Two?"

Bernard set down his fork. "First," he said, holding up one finger, "the Mardurans have only achieved a modified civilization structure, with a pack mentality rather than a true division of labor. Second, they intentionally perpetuate a subsistence level economy, where a single bad season could wipe out the entire so-called community. Third, they rely on brute strength and their eight legs for mining—they have not applied one of the basic tools of physics."

"And fourth," Joaquin said, "they have no idea of the wealth they're sitting on, with all that alethium so close to the surface."

"We need the alethium, Joaquin." As Sarah listened, she heard the sorrow in Bernard's voice. That open emotion was one of the things that had first attracted her to the man. He understood the difficulty of his job. He knew that the future of an entire species rode on the decisions he made.

"Cities, Bernard!" Joaquin's voice had become shrill. "Cities and social institutions—childcare and eldercare that surpass anything we've ever seen on Earth! They limit their mining, to protect against long-term environmental destruction." The xenoanthropologist set his palms on the table, as if he were about to push himself to a standing position. "My report will recommend Class Three."

Bernard refused to escalate the argument. Instead of trying to outshout the other scientist, Bernard lowered his voice, almost whispering, "You'll do what you have to do. We all will."

"You're recommending genocide if you put the Mardurans in Class Two."

"I understand you believe that. I'll take your report under advisement."

Joaquin slammed his cup down on his tray and stomped from the mess hall. Bernard watched him go before turning to Sarah. "Well, *that* was nastier than I anticipated."

"Have you decided, then? Are you definitely certifying them Class Two?"

"I don't have to issue my final opinion until we dock." He shook his head, and the light caught on the silver streaks in his hair. He managed a rueful smile, and Sarah wished that they were alone in his cabin, that she could raise her fingers to smooth away the lines beside his lips. He seemed to understand that desire as he shook his head and said, "Joaquin is right about one thing, though. There is a tremendous amount of money at stake."

A tremendous amount—500,000 credits, Sarah thought, even though she knew that her bonus was a pittance in the overall scheme. She pitched her voice low enough that he had to lean toward her. At least, that was an intimacy they could afford in the gossip-mongering mess hall. "It's not just money."

"I know that." He smiled as he looked at her, and she read the things he did not say aloud. She knew that he was thinking of the studies she had brought to him, the resources she had delivered. He was remembering the first conversation they had had—about this very topic. She had made an impassioned plea for the preservation of all higher alien species, and he had responded to her steadily, avidly, providing her with a level of intellectual debate that had fed her mission-starved mind.

And then, he had dropped by the library the next day, seeking out her thoughts on an obscure journal article. And she had closed the library door, locking it from within. . . .

"I know that," he said again, and for just a moment, she did not know if he was speaking about the Mardurans, or if he were affirming the memories that had brought a blush to her cheeks. "I know how much technology hangs on our getting alethium. I know that we have security issues, and technology problems. The morality is only one piece of the puzzle." Bernard smiled and brightened his tone. "Speaking of which, how is your cataloging progressing?"

"I haven't finished yet." At Bernard's surprised glance, she said, "I have another three weeks! And I've been a little, er, distracted."

His quirked eyebrow made her belly clench, and she wished that she were not sitting in a company ship, surrounded by crude wildcatters and Jessup employees. His words were innocent enough: "I can't imagine what would take you away from the joys of cataloging."

"It *is* interesting work," she protested. "Just not as interesting as some other, um, responsibilities I've undertaken."

Again, his smile warmed her. His words, though, were more practical. "You'll get the mining resources cataloged, though? Before Earthfall? I'll be relying on them in my report."

"They'll be done."

"I feel bad, asking you to neglect the other Marduran scrolls."

"That's all part of my job—recognizing priorities."

"Priorities . . ." She heard all sorts of promises in the word. "I hope you plan to reward yourself when you've met all your priorities."

"I'll reward myself," Sarah said, and she could not keep a smile from twisting her lips. "Don't you worry, I'll reward myself."

Before Bernard could fashion a reply, the ship's clock chimed. The scientist pushed back his chair and sighed apologetically. "I've got to go—meeting with the agency director by uplink."

"Go." She waved him toward the door. Before he could step out of hearing range, though, she called out, "Bernard!" He turned back, his expressive face molded into a question. "I'll have those reports tonight. The ones on superheated alethium."

He did not miss a beat. "I'll stop by for them after my meeting. I appreciate all your hard work."

Sarah grinned to herself as she drank her tea.

She should not have been surprised to see Joaquin waiting for her outside the library, his workcon jacked into the socket in the hall. He looked up from the display and grimaced. "Bernard doesn't understand the importance of the decision we're making."

"He understands. He just has broader priorities. You know we need the alethium. Space travel will shut down within a decade if we can't find a new supply."

"He and I work for an agency that is supposed to protect alien species."

Sarah heard the frustration in his voice, and she tried to make her own words soothing. "The agency has to consider all the facts before it issues a decision."

"But some facts get considered more than others." Joaquin's bitterness sharpened. "You know the stories they tell about Venelia! And Portulan. Those native species weren't anywhere near as primitive as the Class Two designations they received. The agency looked the other way."

"Bernard isn't like that."

"You don't know him, Sarah. Not like I do."

She thought about how she might respond to that. She thought about announcing just how well she knew the French scientist, but she settled for asking, "What are you going to do about it, then?"

"Whatever I can." Joaquin sighed. "I'll finish my reports. I'll stress the Mardurans' evolved social structure. I'll try to ignore the fact that the aliens I'm protecting have exoskeletons and multiple brains and eight multijointed legs. I'll try not to feel like I've betrayed them, when the government classifies them as Class Two and specifies the bounty that Jessup will have to pay to exterminate them."

"Jessup isn't the bad guy here!" she protested, thinking guiltily of her bonus. "The entire universe needs the alethium. And Jessup can't do anything without the government's approval."

"The same government that let the lacefish of Baranon die? The ones that declared the Aeopagii Class Three, two years after the last breeding pair choked to death on sulfuric waste?"

Sarah's frustration constricted her chest so that her heart pounded painfully. *It's 500,000 credits,* she reminded herself. With that sort of bonus, she would never need to face a journey like this again. She—and Bernard—would not need to make hard decisions for a long, long time. "We have to consider all the facts."

"Tell that to the Mardurans." Joaquin powered down his workcon, as if he did not trust Sarah to view the display field. He disappeared down the hall as Sarah keyed the passcode into the library's lock.

Mechanically, she turned on her own machine and listened to the mail that had arrived while she ate. An announcement from Jessup central, reminding her with a smooth administrator's voice that she needed to complete her investment portfolio before Earthfall, if she wanted the tax advantages to kick in for the current fiscal year. Half a dozen junk advertisements that had made it past the mailguard programs. What was she going to do with green-and-maroon real K'lassan hair implants out here in space? And why would she ever be interested in pictures of nubile young Earth girls with horned Zarassian aliens?

In the middle of the dross, Sarah found three actual assignments. One was overflow from Jessup's main Earthside library—they must be understaffed again. She could track down the handful of universal patents later.

The second assignment was from on-ship, from Jessup's highest official on board. She listened to the terse note from the Vice President for Planetary Exploration twice, at first disbelieving her ears: *Pull all certified statutes from all planets in Sector 127 concerning transport of life-forms off world. My daughter's school project is due in three days, so time is of the essence.*

No "please." No "if you have time." No "if this does not interfere with your paid work on behalf of our mutual employer." Sarah listened to the Vice President's slick electronic signature and swore. She would have to do the project, but she would hold the results for a while, edge as close as she dared to the three-day deadline.

She ran her fingers over her workcon's surface, selecting the final piece of mail. "For a panel meeting tomorrow morning, please identify the three most profitable mining ventures, sector-wide, in the past year. Include corporate profiles of the companies that completed the ventures, as well as predictions of future market worth. We'll have Morton Jessup himself on-line—I don't want to look like an idiot."

Sarah swore again. They'll have the President on-line, will they? That meant that the meeting had been planned for at least a week, likely for even longer. And they had just decided that they needed the statistics now? When was *she* supposed to enjoy some peace and quiet, some down time in her own quarters?

Resisting the urge to toss her 'con across the room, Sarah forced herself to take a deep breath. There was plenty of time to do the work; she could finish before Bernard was out of his meeting. She settled her fingers on the command panel and began to pull up figures, to store away visual data. She had just finished listening to recent news articles when a trio of wildcatters sauntered in.

"Great! The 'cons aren't being used?"

Sarah looked up, distracted. *Wonderful.* Each of the men held a large glass. Filled with dark liquid. Sloshing onto the floor. She could smell their unwashed bodies across the room. Nevertheless, she forced her voice into a vague semblance of civility. "They're not in use, but I can't help you load the games right now."

"That's fine. We know what we're doing."

They certainly did. Sarah knew these three; they had spent the better part of each day since leaving Marduran lounging in the library. She had cleaned up after them for weeks.

Sighing, she waved toward the wall of gamecons and reminded herself: *500,000 credits.* All of this would be worthwhile, once she was Earthside. She sank back into her research, tracking down facts and figures for the last-minute project.

*   *   *

"Die, you sarking spider!" The howl jerked Sarah back to the library. The wildcatters were shouting exuberantly, spilling their drinks and pounding each other on the back. With a single glance, Sarah could see that they had loaded a new module into the 'con, splicing in code to make the game's generic aliens dead ringers for the Mardurans. Now, an eight-legged creature was splattered across the three-dimensional game space, its body dripping viscous blood. Sarah's belly turned as she watched the miner's game avatar tuck an old-fashioned gun into a shoulder holster.

She wanted to yell at the wildcatters. She wanted to tell them that they were crude and revolting. She wanted to scream that it was no wonder they went from planet to planet, spending no more than a week Earthside with their supposed friends and loved ones.

She swallowed her words, though. The miners were Jessup's lifeblood. They kept the company profitable. They paid her salary. Would pay her bonus.

Her 'con chimed, and she glanced at the display space. A red icon flashed repeatedly, and she reached toward it without thinking. "You have twenty days to complete Task Priority One—Cataloging. Twenty days to complete Task Priority One. Twenty days—"

Sarah slammed off the reminder. *Of course, she had twenty days.* She had programmed the reminder herself. Bernard had understood the demands on her time. He had sympathized with her when she explained how much she had to accomplish before the ship returned to Earth. He had helped her to work out the strategy, setting priorities, keeping her sane as Jessup's demands grew more and more insistent. . . .

Sarah tuned out the trio of gamers and forced herself to pay attention to the assignment in front of her. Finding the last of the news articles for the morning meeting proved simple enough. Predicting the future, though, was a little more challenging. She knew some useful resources, but none was directly on point. Nevertheless, she tracked down a handful of citations and loaded them into a compact audio file. She reviewed the results and organized them differently, knowing that her shipside companions would not have time to study her findings in detail before their conference.

She sent the file with a deft flick of her wrist. Another project completed. Another patron served.

Swallowing a yawn, Sarah started to power down her workcon. She would go back to her quarters, wait for Bernard there. They could talk about the day's work, discuss the Marduran classification dilemma, before they moved on to other more entertaining diversions.

Catching her breath against the distracting thought, Sarah wondered if Bernard ever betrayed a flash of inappropriate emotion to his scientific colleagues. He certainly had been cool enough at dinner. Smooth. Unflustered. Even in the face of Joaquin's impassioned arguments.

Sarah knew that—all flirtatious games aside—she could not have remained that impassive if *she* were still undecided about the Mardurans' fate. She would have tested the xenoanthropologist, fought against her own instincts, struggled, battled, measured out possible conclusions.

Had Bernard already made up his mind?

Without thinking, Sarah flicked her fingers over her console. She managed databases all day long; it was child's play to make her way through the mail system to Bernard's files.

What was she doing? She had no right to go into his messages! What would Bernard think if he ever found out that she was spying on him?

Her fingers hovered over the icons. The more she thought, the more she realized that Bernard had seemed unusually self-possessed at dinner. He *had* made up his mind. He *had* decided how he would rate the Mardurans.

She could just skim through his files. After all, Bernard would probably tell her, if she asked him directly. She didn't need to sneak around. He would share his conclusions with her openly. And it wasn't like she was going to tell anyone else. She would just know for herself.

She would try to open his mail—if she could guess his password in three tries, she would read what was there. Read, but never comment.

Sarah pulled her headset closer to her mouth and whispered her first guess—the name of a childhood dog he had mentioned a week before. As a librarian who constantly railed against violations of system security, Sarah knew that a shocking seventeen percent of 'con users set their passwords to pets' names.

The display shimmered, and the mail program adjusted to indicate a string of incoming mail messages. Bernard was in the seventeen percent. Sarah smiled grimly, almost regretting her decision. She was in the system now, though. She might as well see this through.

Six unopened files, all directed to the government regulator. The K'lassan hair implants. The nubile young girls. An electronic paystub.

Breathing quickly, Sarah turned her attention to the last three messages. Minutes from an agency meeting held Earthside that afternoon. An agenda for the current meeting—perhaps open on Bernard's own 'con, even as Sarah eavesdropped. She felt a twinge of guilt.

A message from Morton Jessup himself. Sarah triggered the icon to listen to this last communication, curious about what her employer's president might have to say to the scientist who could determine his company's fate.

The file would not open.

Sarah repeated the sequence, certain that she had brushed the panel too lightly in her rush, but it remained locked. She caught her lower lip between her teeth and adjusted her headset. What secret message would Morton Jessup have sent to Bernard? What would he have secured beyond Sarah's ability to detect?

Biting at the inside of her cheek, Sarah backed out of the mail program. After glancing at the gaming wildcatters, she hunched closer to her terminal and entered the system again. This time, though, she used her credentials as the records manager for the starship.

As records manager, no file was locked to her. She was responsible for retaining all the ship's files, even seemingly inconsequential mail.

It took her only a few heartbeats to find her way back to Bernard's message stream. Her palm hovered above the icon that would whisper Morton Jessup's words to her. Did she want to know what he had said? Did she want to collect that much information? Did she want to be responsible for the knowledge?

She was a librarian. Knowledge was her stock in trade.

Sarah touched the icon.

Jessup's oily voice whispered through her headset. "One million transferred. Two million to follow, if Class Two sticks." No closing. No electronic signature. None was necessary.

Sarah listened to the words again. A third time.

The Mardurans had no chance. Bernard had been purchased. Joaquin's work was meaningless; all his protests would amount to nothing. The agency would declare the Mardurans expendable Class Two aliens.

The wildcatters cheered across the room. Sarah looked up in time to see the gaming avatar pull up his trousers. A quivering spider-shape was curled about itself, all eight legs wrapped tight, as if it tried to seal itself from a wound.

The men congratulated their colleague, pounding him on the back, bellowing approval. Sarah's belly turned as the third player took his place at the gamecon. What horror would he devise? How would he torture the virtual Mardurans?

Class Two—the status for companion animals. Preferred for continued existence, but expendable. Able to be forfeited in the face of proven need. Able to be bought with cold, electronic credits.

Sarah closed out of the communications package, making sure that she had left no trace of listening to Bernard's files. The wildcatters hooted to each other, like excited animals in a cage. She ignored the sound.

Bernard had been bribed. Three million credits, all told. Six times the bonus that Sarah would earn—that Sarah would earn through hard work. Bernard was doing nothing for that money, nothing but stepping aside.

No, Sarah realized. That was not entirely true. He *was* doing something. He was creating a pretense of unbiased judgment. He was ordering up journal articles, scientific studies. He was making a show of reviewing options. He was pretending to consider all angles.

All of a sudden, Sarah thought about the times Bernard had requested materials. He had asked in front of other scientists. In front of Jessup staff. In front of wildcatters. He had made a show of coming to the library, of returning research in the mess hall. He had made it clear to anyone who was paying attention that he was studying the Mardurans in painstaking detail.

Sarah had thought that Bernard emphasized the materials so that no one would call into question their relationship. He had brandished files so that no one would accuse him of spending inappropriate time with the ship's librarian. And all the time, he had been fending off other accusations. All the time, he had been shielding himself, hiding his three-million-credit bribe.

All the time, he had been lying.

Fingers shaking, she called up the catalog that he had

pushed her to create, that he intended to rely on for his own work. With a pass of her palm, she found her first record. *Alethium Mining on Marduran*. She heard the mechanics recorded there, the alien knowledge preserved for Jessup to exploit. Bernard had urged her to enter every one of the mining records first; he had encouraged her to set aside the social science scrolls for later. He had been working for his three million even then.

For just an instant, she thought about erasing the entry. Jessup would discover a deleted record, though. The company would withhold her 500,000 credits, keep her enslaved for future missions. For future lies. It might even accuse her of sabotage.

Sabotage. The ancient act of shoving sabots—wooden shoes—into machinery, to spare workers from the evils of the Earthside Industrial Revolution. Where had Sarah learned that? What source had taught her? How had she gained the knowledge?

She shook her head. She, too, could bring technology to a halt. She could insert things where they did not belong, bring the so-called wheels of progress to a stop. She could cripple Jessup Universal Mining as certainly as French peasants had destroyed their massive threshing machines.

On one side of her workcon, Sarah pulled up a digital representation of one of the ornate Marduran scrolls. *Eldercare—Its Goals and Its Rewards*. One of the crucial Marduran works. One of the volumes that showed civilization, that proved the species was worthy of a Class Three designation.

On the other side of the 'con, Sarah opened her catalog. She summoned a blank form, completing the rote task as she had hundreds of times before, as she would hundreds of times more, before Earthfall in three short weeks.

Her fingers flew as she primed the icons. She mouthed the catalog entry rapidly, enunciating the title, the Marduran author, the subject matter. She took the time to add half a dozen alternative subject headings, selecting ones that would attract attention from the broadest community of scientists, from segments beyond mining and manufacturing. Society and social structure. Daily life on other planets. Ethics. Voortman Index. Marduran society.

The image of the alien scroll shimmered in front of her, shifting as if her eyes were blurred by tears. Her fingers hovered over her 'con.

One touch, and she could upload the entry. One touch, and she could tell every librarian in the universe about the Mardurans' highly evolved social structure. One transmission, and she could open the doors for Class Three status.

One heartbeat, and she could lose 500,000 credits, her job, her future. *Bernard.*

The wildcatters exploded into boisterous applause, shouting out praise to their embattled warrior colleague. Sarah heard them swear; she smelled the drinks they poured out on the floor. She recoiled at the foul words they shouted.

Without glancing at the miners' game, Sarah touched the icon and sent her catalog entry to the stars.

* * *

When Mindy L. Klasky was learning how to read, her parents encouraged her, saying that she could travel anywhere with a book in her hands. Mindy never forgot that advice. While growing up, Mindy's travels took her from Los Angeles to Dallas to Atlanta to Minneapolis. She now lives in a suburb of Washington, D.C. Mindy's academic travels ranged from computer science to English to law to library science. Professionally, she has moved from practicing trademark and copyright law at a major law firm to managing the reference department in a large law firm library. When Mindy is not reading, writing, or working as a librarian, she fills her time with swimming, baking, and quilting. She is an active member of the Science Fiction Writers of America, many legal bar organizations, and a number of library societies. Her two cats, Dante and Christina, make sure that she does not waste too much time sleeping.

FERRET AND RED

by *Josepha Sherman*

**CALLING ELECTRICIANS, METALWORKERS,
MECHANICS, AND PLUMBERS!
MAKE YOUR FORTUNE IN SPACE!**
Have the skill but stuck working for someone else? Want
to take charge of your life? Look no further! Space stations are *desperate* for your know-how. Space Entrepre-
neurs Inc. will take you step-by-step to success! We'll
show you how to find the right space station for you; help
you apply for those vital documents, including your off-
planet license and accreditation. We'll even set up a client
list, filled with customers eager to start filling your pockets
with credits the minute you arrive! Deposit 100 credits to
Account #4783SPACEISFORYOU and be on your way to
a fortune!

FERRET, flat as she could get in the narrow engine tubing, swore under her breath. It was hot and airless in
here, and her sleek brown fur was plastered to her skin, and
picking up interesting stains despite the coveralls. Yes, and
if one of the humans did something stupid, like accidentally
hitting the start-up button before her partner, Red Collins,
could stop him, she was one fried Ferret.

*Don't think about that. Don't think about anything. Trust
Red and just get the skelking job done.*

Ferret's real name was much longer and more complicated,

listing as it did her clan and family as well as her own use-name, but all that tended to be too much for anyone not of her own species to manage. Some human had once dubbed her "Ferret," and even after she found out what an Earth ferret was, she'd had to admit that her species really did bear a resemblance to bipedal ferrets.

No matter names. She really did like her job as part of Station Alpha's mech crew: meet new species, see new ships and equipment that needed to be puzzled out, work—and drink, yes—with Red, her human partner for three station-years now, Red, who was a good mech with a sense of humor as wry as her own—

Yeek, yes, all enjoyable except for jobs like this. Once the starfaring humans had colonized the world they'd christened York (apparently a nostalgic name for their home world, which most had never seen), and built this station/dry dock (silly name: space was never wet) to orbit it, of course mechanics had been needed. Once you had interworld contacts, you needed mechs even more, because then you had trade.

Yes, and once you had trade, there were always going to be scruffy independents like the crew of this ship, living off whatever scraps of contracts they could snag that were too small for the big companies.

And cutting costs wherever costs can be cut. Must rankle them to have to pay mech fees. Be more careful, silly humans, have no need for mechs.

One arm stretched out in front of her as far as it would go, she groped blindly with the long seizing-talon of her forefinger, touching composite, composite . . .

Yes! Just as she'd guessed, something had gotten pulled into the engine, and not been *quite* vaporized.

Lucky they didn't blow themselves into just some more space dust. The talon snagged the offending whatever-it-was. Nothing living, not at this point.

Ferret wriggled her way backward out of the tube, and did a neat little twist-jump that brought her out onto the engine room floor, facing the five humans towering over her. Red was the shortest of them, still taller than Ferret but stocky, at least as one of his species went, with the blazing red hair that had given him his nickname. He was also, Ferret thought, cleaner than the four others, even now, and had more recently taken care of his human facial fur. The others looked downright ready to molt.

Living close to the edge, these. Independents, yes.

"Got it?" Red asked succinctly, and Ferret gave him a head-flip of a nod. Glowering at the others, she shook the talon and its incriminating evidence at them.

"Cloth, maybe," she snapped. "Space suit scrap, something tough, carbon-lump but not vapor. *Not* good in engine, not good in deep space. Lucky you that nothing did go fiery on you!"

She was familiar enough with human expressions by now, thanks to Red, to recognize embarrassment and relief when she saw it. They muttered thanks, and Ferret, who had never yet mastered the human art of bargaining, let Red handle the details of payment: so much to Mech Central, so much as his and her bonus. Red, finished, knowing his partner, put an arm around her shoulders to start her walking. But she couldn't resist a parting shot over her shoulder.

"Think you not that mistake make again, okay? Good."

"A hundred mechs in service," Red muttered, "and I had to get stuck with Mom."

"Heh. Not minding funny stuff. Such as you. But, yeek, time wasting."

They headed down one of the station's narrow, no-frills off-white corridors. There was transit throughout the station, but transit cost credits. Besides, they'd been working here long enough to know all the quickest ways from one module to another. Red and Ferret cut through the cargo module, avoiding a robot cart heading the other way on its air cushion, then casually taking a shortcut through the zero-G cargo zone, kicking off from one side, steering with the skill of experience, and exiting just as casually back in the next artificial gravity module, just a short walk from Mech Central.

"Bet we got another job, yes?" Ferret said, shaking her fur back into place.

Red ran a hand through his wildly ruffled hair, marginally smoothing it. "With so much traffic coming in? No bet there. Want to wager me which is the next species in trouble?"

She curled up her lips in a grin. "Want to have to clean my quarters again?"

Red dodged under a low-slung pipe. "Hey, you got lucky!"

"A human partner? That is luck?"

"A hundred mechs," Red repeated, grinning as well, "and I got stuck with a *ferret.*"

"Big laughs. You think *you* could have wriggled into that engine tubing and not gotten stuck?"

"Yeah, well, never mind that. Let's go check in and see what they've got."

Ferret stifled a sigh and followed her partner. One thing about Red, when he worked, he worked. Not lazy, like some humans. More like her people.

That thought made her stifle another sigh. Her people usually were more, well, groomed, She really, really would have rather stopped at the nearest sonic shower to get the sweat out of her fur, maybe get something nice to drink, too. But the station mechs worked on commission and bonuses, so the more jobs, the better. Money to send home, earn a nice place in status-ranking. Red was sending money to Earth-home, too, she knew.

Good people, us.

But did Red have to be so cursed cheerful about it?

*   *   *

Red was still cheerful as they came to the separate module that was Mech Central. He and Ferret duly entered their license numbers, waited for their retinal scans, and were greeted by the computer's dispassionate male voice, "Live long and prosper."

Some human tech with too much free time, Red had once told Ferret, had reprogrammed the computer to sound like a character from an ancient Earth entertainment.

"Job listings, current," Red told it.

"Searching . . . current listings. One urgent. Ateil ship requests minor adjustment to freighter."

"Ateil!" Red snapped, all good humor gone in an instant.

"That is accurate."

"Never mind accurate. Find us something else."

"Red," Ferret whispered, "what—"

He waved her to silence. "Don't confuse the computer."

"Searching . . . current listings. One urgent—"

"You gave us that already! Computer, damnit, find a *new* listing."

"It is illogical to damn a computer."

"Just find a new listing, okay?"

"Searching . . . current listing. There are no new listings. Do you wish to refuse this assignment?"

Ferret ducked under her partner's arm, took one look at the screen and the fee being offered, and snapped, "We accept!"

"Ferret!"

"Assignment accepted," the computer cut in.

"Damnit, Ferret—"

"Live long and prosper," the computer said, and shut off contact.

"Come," Ferret said to Red, clamping down on his arm with a hand. "Talk, now!"

She couldn't have actually dragged him along, but Red

followed her out into the station without resistance. "Ateil!" he said. "Damn it to hell, Ateil!"

"We both saw. That was the only job needed. Nice money. Too nice to turn down!"

"I don't care what—"

"We refuse job, bad look on record. Also some other mech take it instead. You can refuse money, heh? You have some secret nest-cache?"

"Ferret, stop it."

"Not knowing species, Ateil. Why this fury?"

Red took a deep breath. "They're Birds," he began. "Hell, I mean they're what humans call avian sapiens."

"So?"

"So, that's not the point. The point is, they hate humans. Say that we're *inferior.*"

Ferret blinked, puzzled. "Their problem, not ours, yes? This explains nothing. Why the rage, Red?"

He shrugged angrily and started to walk off, but Ferret slipped past him in the narrow corridor and twisted about to confront him again.

"Damnit, Ferret—"

"Come, tell."

"It's none of your business."

"No? Together we work, and needing to know your emotions are not causing danger to me or you."

"You know better than that. I don't endanger a partner."

"Yes? Then together we have worked long enough for trust."

Red said something fierce under his breath. "Okay, if it'll get you off my back."

"Huh?"

"Okay, okay. I wasn't always a station mech, you know that."

"Yes. More than that, no."

"Worked on a freighter, nothing fancy. But we got along,

the crew and I. In fact, I'd say we were all pretty good friends, and I was able to fix pretty much anything that went wrong with the ship. Almost anything. We were a bare bones operation, like the guys we saw today."

"Something went too much wrong."

"Yeah. Too much. There was an Ateil sip within reach, so we sent them a distress call. They ignored us."

Ferret straightened. "Not possible! Against all interstellar law! Maybe the communication did not—"

"It went through, all right. They got it. They just didn't want to be bothered with *inferiors*."

"Red, not proved!"

"Like hell it's not! I heard them say something about 'inferors' just before the com went down, I swear it. Ferret, we lost more than half the crew before I could cobble something together to get us into a station. More than half of my friends! All because we were too *inferior* to be helped."

Ferret let out her breath in a soft hiss. How much of what Red said was truth, and how much what a human, confused and frantic in the middle of deadly chaos, had thought was truth? "Red," she began carefully. "That was space—years back, yes? Ek, wait. Nothing can change past harm. But is living well, what, old Earth saying?"

Red snorted. " 'Living well's the best revenge,' you mean?"

"Is so! Money offered us is good, I say again. Ateil not recognize you, you not know them, so we hurt Ateil in money-place, then drink to lost friends."

He grunted.

"Yes?" Ferret prodded. "Ateil said minor adjustment to freighter. So faster done, faster gone."

Red glared at her. "You know, you can be a real pain in the ass sometime."

"So?" Ferret held up one clawed hand. "You want *real* pain there?"

That forced a reluctant laugh out of Red. "Hell, you'd do it, too." He shook his head. "Okay, I guess I can be a pain, too. Guess that's why we get along so good."

"Said well, yes. Now, about job?"

"Yeah. Trouble is, 'minor' can mean anything with the Ateil, anything from, oh, a recalibration of the heating system to maybe replacing or rebuilding some major component."

"Ek."

"Exactly. But as you say, money is money. So let's go see what the Birds want."

It wasn't easy to judge the size or scale of a ship that was docked to a station, but from what Ferret could see of it, the Ateil freighter was illogically streamlined—illogical, because a spacecraft had no need to fight against the friction of an atmosphere. Not so illogical, Ferret thought, if its owners were bird-types.

But the four Ateil waiting for them looked more like reptile-types, tall and fine-boned bipeds but with narrow, almost serpentine heads topped with feathery crests. There was the hint of what could have been either very fine scales or very fine down on creamy-pale face and limbs. Their coveralls . . . Ferret assumed that the colorful layers of fabric were coveralls. Birds, after all, maybe, imitating the bright plumes their species no longer had.

From lighter gravity world and maybe weaker here? Ferret speculated, and stored that possible fact away.

At first glance, the four looked absolutely alike. But Ferret, used to finding the difference between humans, noted that there were definite differences in the coloring of the Ateil clothing: yellow predominant, blue predominant, green predominant, and purple predominant. Status or job rankings, maybe.

Red, meanwhile, was proving himself a better actor than Ferret would ever have imagined, showing nothing at all in his face or body language but professional interest. "Mech Central sent us," he said without emotion, flashing his credentials—and Ferret belatedly remembered to show hers as well. "What seems to be the problem?"

The Ateils' stiff, almost beaklike lips couldn't sneer, but sneers were implicit as they glanced at each other.

"This is a substandard station," Yellow Ateil said to the others.

"They send us *these* beings," Purple Ateil agreed.

A muscle in Red's jaw twitched, and Ferret said hastily, before he could speak, and in her most charming voice, "If so substandard this, why bend you down to learn Standard speech? Come, please, the problem, so we may fix it and you be gone."

She caught Red's quick sideways glance, a glint of wry humor in his eyes.

"We wish others," Purple Ateil said, not quite to the two mechs.

"Sorry," Red drawled. "We're what you get. My partner said it: Tell us the problem, we'll fix it, and you can get out of here."

Ferret could have sworn she heard an Ateil whisper, "Unlucky color."

What? Red's hair? Yes, that, certainly. No red on the Ateil.

Oh, joy. Superstitious, too.

But Purple Ateil unbent enough to point out the problem, which turned out to be, yes, a major job, broken parts that had broken other parts. Wonderful.

The only good side to this job was that the work space was small, which meant that Ferret fit and Red was the one sent to get this gear or that component.

Keep him away from Ateil as much as possible.

It also meant that Ferret could eavesdrop while she

worked. For the most part, the Ateil chattered and twittered in their own language, but every now and again, she caught snatches in Standard, just enough for Ferret to learn that there was no love lost between Purple and Yellow. The sort of quarrel that could build up between two beings who'd been cooped up together in a cramped ship for too long.

It spilled over onto outsiders, too. Red, passing components on to Ferret, who was wedged into a work space small even for her, said something about, "Can't expect my partner to work like this very long."

Purple Ateil snapped at him, "You will work till the job is done!"

"Hey, hey, we don't leave a job unfinished. But we also don't like that tone, you know what I mean?"

"Red!" Ferret hissed. But he was between her and the Ateil, and she couldn't get out of the cramped little corner.

"Ah, yes," Yellow told Purple, "leave the help alone."

Purple said something harsh-sounding in the Ateil language, and then turned back to Red. "You come and go, and yet nothing is completed. Can it be that you work deliberately slowly to earn more?"

Ferret, distracted, yelped as she pinched her finger. Shaking it, she snapped, "Try working in here! Try, and see how fast *you* work!"

Purple sneered as much as an Ateil's rigid face could manage. "Perhaps it is skill you lack."

"What—why—you—"

Red moved between her and the Ateil. "Calm down," he warned. To Purple, he drawled, "Look, I'm not big on social graces, and I'm not going to give you any pretty words. I don't like you, and you've made it pretty clear you don't like us, either. That said, Ferret and I are good mechs. You can look up our records if you want proof. And we're working as fast as we safely can, so we don't have to be in each other's company any longer than we need to be."

The Ateil reared back, narrow nostrils flaring. "Arrogance! Human arrogance!"

"Red," Ferret said uneasily.

He ignored her. "Well, hell, you're free to hire someone else—"

"Red!"

He held up a silencing hand. "—but that's going to cause a delay, you know. A really bad delay, probably, when the other mechs hear about this. Most of them are human, too. Might not find any of them free to help you for, oh, maybe a station month or more."

Purple's crest shot up. "Were you one of the True People, I would see you dead for such a threat!"

"Hell, look at this, a human's not even good enough to kill. Isn't that—"

"Red!" Ferret dug a claw into his thigh. With a curse, he whirled to her, and she said mildly, "This work is done."

To do the Ateil credit, Purple didn't argue over the amount due, merely signed over the proper amount and then turned his back on the mechs. Ferret couldn't exactly drag her partner away short of literally digging her claws into him, but she tightened her fingers on his arm *just enough*, and got him moving, off the ship and back into the station.

Red delicately worked his arm free from her determined grip. "Well, all things considered, I think that went pretty well."

"Heh."

"Never mind 'heh.' It's over, we've got the credits. Let's go get us a drink."

"That sounds—oh, fur-molting damnation!"

"What—"

"I left a tool on the Ateil ship."

"Get another one."

"No, no, this one is to my hand and species perfect. Have to go back."

"Want me to go with you?"

And risk you, they getting to war? I so think not. "Not needed, thanks. Back shortly meeting in bar?"

No need to name it: there was only one bar that the mechs frequented. "Yeah."

Ferret scurried back to the Ateil ship: sooner there, sooner back.

Keeping calm, yes? she warned herself, and said to the Ateil, Purple Ateil, who met her, "Your pardon for this, but haste to finish for you made me leave tool on board. Retrieval allowed, please?"

To her relief, no one stopped her, or said anything outrageously infuriating. She ignored the murmurs. The tool was lying exactly where she'd left it on the floor, and that in itself was a touch insulting: they hadn't even wanted to touch something not Ateil. But Ferret refused to let herself react, merely scooped it up and said, "Thanking am. No longer needing to bother you."

But Purple Ateil moved smoothly to block her way, and Yellow silently moved in behind her. Ferret swore silently. "Something is wrong?" she asked carefully.

"We would question you."

Damnation. Ferret tightened a clawed hand about the tool. "Perhaps. What of?"

"Why dares the human hate us?"

That was the last thing she would have expected. "Dares?" Ferret echoed helplessly, not at all sure where this was heading.

"Yes! It is not of honor for one of no status to show such strong emotion to the True People. And for one who is colored with that evil hair shade to do such, especially when we cannot of honor slay him—there is no balance left for any!"

Ferret blinked. Complicated statement, yes! If she understood it correctly, Purple Ateil was telling her that by allowing someone who was too inferior to be legally slain to insult their honor by daring to show anger to them, they were trapped without a way to restore their status.

Ek. Still complicated. Humans and I, two species but we understand each other. These, no. Avian sapiens, Red calls them. More like avian stupid, I think. If being is too inferior to be noted, then surely is too inferior for his anger to be noted.

Suddenly she wanted nothing but to get off this ship as quickly as possible. "Wanting to know why Red hates you?" she snapped, utterly disgusted with everything Ateil. "So be it. Killing his shipmates, you."

Quickly she summarized the story Red had told her, and saw Ateil crests rise, but whether it was in anger or surprise, she couldn't tell. "So?" Ferret asked. "Does that not give good reason for his anger?"

Purple Ateil was definitely upset, shifting uneasily from foot to foot. If he'd had true feathers, Ferret thought, they would have been puffed up. "Not enough. Not enough. It does not restore honor or balance."

"Sorry am I," Ferret retorted, "but frankly speaking, that is not my affair. Stand aside, please." *Or I swing this tool and damage more of you than your honor.*

"This is not possible. Status must be settled."

"Ek, nonsense. I am not human, not same species."

"Status *must* be settled. You are partnered with the human creature. Not exact balance, but it serves."

"Hell, not!"

Just then, a familiar voice drawled, "Everything all right?"

Before the Ateil could say anything, Ferret called out to Red, "Not letting me pass!"

"You know," Red told the Ateil, "it's really not a good idea to keep a hostage. Particularly not a mech. Don't want to get the mechs' union after you."

The Ateil said nothing. But Ferret took advantage of the

moment of uncertainty to slip under Purple Ateil's arm and escape. "Good thing you came along when you did."

"Figured you might need a hand. You all right?"

"Ek, yes. Bar!" Ferret added emphatically.

The mechs' bar was small and crowded with as many chairs and tables as could be fit in without forcing out customers. There were quite a few station mechs there, off shift or between jobs, but Ferret wriggled in between to find Red and herself a place to sit.

Quite a few station hours later, they were still sitting with the latest round of drinks, luxuriating in the time off. Then Red asked, not quite offhandedly, "What did the Ateil want?"

"Strangeness." With a shrug, Ferret told Red about the convoluted honor and status system of the Ateil. "Their problem," Ferret concluded.

"Hell, they deserve it." Red eyed his drink moodily. "Let 'em all die, the universe wouldn't care."

"Their credits pay for our drinks. And—heh, what now?"

Red straightened, eyeing the two humans in their crisp blue uniforms with suspicion. "Station Security."

"Coming this way."

Stopping in front of them, in fact. "Red Collins?" They made a mangled attempt at Ferret's whole name, and she cut them off with a curt, "Ferret."

"You know who we are," Red said. "What's the problem?"

"We'd like to ask you a few questions."

"About?"

"You were just working on the Ateil ship, were you not?"

"Hell, yes. Finished the job some time ago and decided to take a break. Which we were doing, thank you, when you interrupted us."

"We'll try not to take up too much more of your time," one agent said dryly. "But it seems that there was a little ac-

cident on board their ship. A small explosion in a console—
one on which you were working."

"Oh, hell," Red said helplessly.

"There's more. One of the Ateil was killed in the explosion. And just to make things even more interesting, the others say that he was someone pretty high ranking, too."

"Not possible!" Ferret protested. "Explosion? No. Good work we do!"

"She's right," Red said. "Check our records."

"We already have. Apparently you, Ser Collins, had an encounter with the Ateil once before."

"That was Standard years ago!"

"Of course. You'll come with us, please."

"What about Ateil ship?" Ferret asked frantically. "Who has examined that?"

The security agents had the good grace to look embarrassed.

"No one!" Ferret cried in realization. "True, yes? Ateil have not let you on board!"

One guard muttered something about "sovereign territory."

"Is nonsense!" Ferret returned. "If they call crime, they forfeit right to sovereignty claim!"

Red gave her a *how the hell do you know that?* look. Ferret gave him a lip-curl of a grin in return. "Travel much, learn much."

The security agents weren't so impressed. "Sorry. You'll get a chance to explain everything in our office."

They were turned over to the grim, solid human head of Station Security, Captain Vazkez. "Sit down," he said without preamble. "I want you to watch this."

The chairs were human-sized, but a guard found a cushion to make things a little more comfortable for Ferret. She sat dangling her feet, feeling ridiculously like a cub. At Vazkez's signal, another guard switched on a viewing console and started playing a security tape.

"From the Ateil," Vazkez said tersely.

Together, Red and Ferret watched Purple Ateil touch a control. "One that you two replaced," Vazkez told them unnecessarily. "Now watch what happens when he switches it on."

Ferret winced at the sight of the explosion that followed.

"Good-bye, Purple," Red said without much regret.

But Ferret all at once sat forward in her too-large chair, frowning. "Know it? Something odd there."

"Oh, sure," Red agreed. "It's damned odd, what with all the species out there using all kinds of tech, that the Ateil should just happen to use a data format compatible to what humans use."

"They come in and out of this station pretty often," Vazkez retorted. "Probably switched over to this format because it's more convenient."

"Convenient for whom? Humans? Never knew the Ateil to care much about anything to do with humans."

Ferret stared at the console. "Show record again," she insisted. "Slowly this time. slowly . . . there! Freeze it!"

Springing up from her seat, ignoring the guards' start, Ferret studied the image, nose nearly touching the console screen. "Something funny, yes. Something hidden . . . not seeing what Purple did with his left hand. See? Something in it, but not seeing what."

Red frowned, staring at the image. "You saying he did his own sabotage?"

"Oh, come on!" one of the guards began, but was ignored.

"Seems possible, yes," Ferret said to Red. "Possible, but . . ."

"That's ridiculous!" Vazkez exclaimed. "He was clearly the one operating the control. If he had sabotaged it, that would mean he was—"

"Attempting suicide," Red cut in. "And succeeding pretty well, too."

"Heh," Ferret said, straightening. "Red, maybe so? Because of us?"

"Because he was insulted? Lost status over dealing

with—whoa, Ferret. You might have something, really might. Who spoke to us aboard their ship?"

"Purple and Yellow—ek, no! Yellow never spoke to us, to Purple only. Only Purple dealt with us, spoke with us. Sacrificial Purple?"

"Damn! They really do have a weird culture."

"Bet me any dialog Ateil had with station was recorded. No shame or loss of status from talking into machine."

"No bet, Ferret."

Vazkez was looking helplessly from one to the other. "What the *hell* are you two talking about?"

"I need to be aboard that ship," Ferret said.

"They won't allow a human—"

"I am not human. We need to prove our theory, our innocence. And if we are correct, Ateil may try to block my path, but not one Ateil will speak to me."

Of course they didn't allow her to go alone. But even as she had said, no Ateil spoke to her. They blocked human guards without so much as looking at them; they ignored Ferret completely—and she shot on board before anyone could move. Ek, there was the exploded stuff, not yet completely cleaned.

If Purple could hide what he did, so can I.

Pretending to merely be staring in horror at what had been the console and a living being, she managed to subtly touch a finger to some of the residue, not letting herself think what might be getting on her fur, then turned to leave.

Sure enough, no one stopped her, or even looked at her. Why should they? Wasn't she almost as inferior as a human? All she was doing, they must think, was looking at the scene of her "error."

Back in the station, Ferret said, "Examine residue now. Before accidentally contaminated by me."

She waited anxiously with Red. But anxiety vanished bit by bit. As Ferret had expected, the computers registered normal traces of engine fuel, microscopic scraps of shed Ateil skin cells—

"And traces of explosives," Red finished triumphantly. "T-39, eh? Not the sort of thing mechs carry, and you can search our stuff if you have any doubts."

"Suicide, indeed," Ferret said. "Poor Purple. No way out else."

"Ateil think humans are inferior," Red explained to Captain Vazkez. "Not good enough even to kill. But *someone* had to talk to the mechs if the job was to get done."

"Why Purple was the one, not knowing," Ferret continued. "But it was he, only he, who lowered self to speak to us."

"Maybe he would have been able to clean himself from contamination if it had ended there," Red added. "But then I added to his problem by talking back to him. Getting him angry when he shouldn't get angry at an inferior. Poor bastard never had a chance."

"Only one way left to cleanse honor," Ferret finished. "Kill self, blame inferiors, die with status restored."

"Yeah. Unfortunately for him, it didn't work. Ferret, want to bet me the Ateil get out of here as soon as they can get everything back on-line?"

"No bet. Captain Vazkez, thinking that someone, non-human someone, should send scholars, do more accurate studying, maybe, Ateil culture."

Red nodded. "Good idea. Uh, Captain Vazkez? We free to leave?"

Vazkez opened his mouth, shut it again, then said helplessly, "Go on. Get out of here."

Together, Ferret and Red walked out of his office, free mechs once more.

"Bet you business is really good for us after word gets out," Red said.

"No bet," Ferret retorted.

* * *

Josepha Sherman is a fantasy novelist and folklorist whose latest titles include **Son of Darkness**, **The Captive Soul**, *the folklore title* **Merlin's Kin**, *and, together with Susan Shwartz, two* Star Trek *novels,* **Vulcan's Forge** *and* **Vulcan's Heart**. *She is also a fan of the New York Mets, horses, aviation, and space science. Visit her at www.sff.net/people/Josepha.Sherman.*

A MAN'S PLACE

by Eric Choi

ALAMER-DAAS CORPORATION

Internal Circulation Only: 14 Earth Days
Category III Technical Specialist: Food Services
Location: Maryniak Base, Luna
Duties: On-site menu planning and implementation for staff, three shifts daily, adhering to UNSDA food guidelines, and in consultation with the company nutritionist and base physician. Accommodate local preferences and nutritional needs as required. Maintain inventory of food stores and rations for routine and emergency use.
Note: Experience with lunar environment preferred.

JAMIE Squires was dicing onions for his omelet when the alarm sounded.

The klaxon blared through the small confines of the kitchen, synchronized with the flashing red light on the ceiling. Jamie put down the knife and, after a quick check to ensure everything in the kitchen was off, ran out into the mess hall. The diners must have stood up quickly from their seats, given the number of chairs knocked backward. Their faces were apprehensive.

"An X12 solar flare is in progress," barked Laura Crenshaw, the general manager of Maryniak Base, over the intercom. "All personnel are to report to their designated storm shelters immediately."

Billy Lu, Maryniak's chief engineer, appeared in the doorway. His red cap designated him as the emergency warden for this sector. "All right, everyone, follow the signs, straight down the corridor. Let's move!"

Jamie followed the crowd into the passageway. He tried not to think about the X rays and gamma rays that were even now going through their bodies. Traveling at the speed of light, they hit Maryniak at about same time as the warning from the space weather satellites at the L1 point. The imperative now was to get to the storm shelters before the arrival of the protons and heavy ions.

Joe McKay, the Shift Two foreman, stood at the entrance to the shelter. "Right this way, people!" he said, pointing to the hatch on the floor.

Jamie mounted the ladder and lowered himself down into the tunnel. Across Maryniak, personnel were gathering in six other protective chambers buried beneath the base's larger modules. The structures and the lunar regolith were supposed to protect the crew from the incoming stream of solar particles.

There were already a dozen people in this shelter. Jamie found himself a spot on the bench along the chamber wall. Ten more descended the ladder, followed by Joe and Billy.

"Is that it?" Joe asked.

"Crenshaw's on her way," Billy said.

The base manager arrived a few minutes later. "All set?"

Billy did a head count. "That's everyone for here."

"Close it up," Crenshaw ordered.

Joe climbed the ladder to close the outer hatch. Once he was back down, Billy slid the ladder up the tunnel before trying to close the inner hatch. The hinges creaked, and he seemed to be having difficulty engaging the latches, but he finally managed to seal the door.

"What's our status?" Joe asked Crenshaw.

"We're the last ones to lock down," she reported. "All

personnel, both in-base and EVA, are in shelters. The proton stream should be sweeping through here in about twenty minutes."

"Are we sure this thing is buried deep enough?" Jamie asked nervously. He looked around, and was disappointed not to see Maria Clarkson, the base physician.

"I just hope we aren't in here for too long," Billy said. "I'd hate to have to eat those rations for any length of time."

Paul Kashiyama, a large, muscular man with a crewcut, spoke up. "Those rations are no worse than Squires' cooking."

Jamie wanted to ask him which bad movie he'd stolen that line from, but said nothing.

Jamie met Maria his first day on the job, after he'd almost gotten into a fight. He remembered it all too well. Jamie had run out of the kitchen upon hearing the clatter of dishes and cutlery hitting the floor. A wall of flesh had stopped him before he'd barely taken three steps into the mess hall.

Paul Kashiyama grabbed Jamie by his apron. "What the hell are you feeding us?"

"Cajun stew," Jamie replied meekly.

"It's burning my goddamn mouth! What the hell are you trying to do, kill us?"

Jamie tried to peer around Paul's massive bulk. The diners he could see had odd expressions on their faces. "It's supposed to be spicy."

"Spicy?" Paul tightened his grip. "This isn't 'spicy,' it's goddamn nuclear. What the hell did you put in this?"

"Well, the recipe does call for hot sauce—"

"How much?"

"I put six tablespoons—"

"Your idiotic recipe calls for six tablespoons of hot sauce!"

Jamie shook his head. "No, no! the recipe calls for three, but I always double up because—"

"That's enough, Paul," a female voice interrupted. "He's new. Cut him some slack."

Paul released his grip. "You watch it," he said, jabbing a finger into Jamie's chest. "You're going to be the death of us."

The woman coughed. "Get yourself a drink, Paul. And clean up the mess you've made." She was in her early thirties, of medium build, with long, curly light-brown hair. She turned to Jamie. "Are you all right?"

"Yeah."

"I'm Maria Clarkson, the base physician."

They shook hands.

"Jamie—"

"—Squires. Yeah, I know. Our new cook." Maria grimaced and swallowed. "Did you really put six tablespoons of hot sauce into that stew?"

"Well, yeah. At my last job, everyone complained my food had no flavor. I've doubled up on spices and condiments ever since."

"Your last job was where?"

"Canacian Pacific. Earth to L5 shuttle."

"There's no spin gravity on those shuttles, right?"

"No."

Maria nodded. "That explains it. I guess those terracentric cookbooks don't tell you that food tastes different in zero G. Weightlessness redistributes body fluids. People tend to feel congested in the head, so food seems to have less flavor."

"Oh . . ."

"Don't worry, new guys are entitled to one nonfatal mistake. And don't let Paul scare you. He's all bluster."

Jamie could see Paul cleaning up his mess.

"Welcome to Maryniak Base, Jamie."

"Thanks."

Maria covered her mouth and coughed again. "By the way, may I have another glass of water?"

Maryniak Base was a mining facility on the lunar farside owned by the Alamer-Daas Corporation. Headquartered in Montreal, ADC's properties included three other commercial Moon bases, half a dozen Earth orbiting stations, and an industrial unit aboard the L5 colony. Maryniak produced titanium and iron extracted from lunar ilmenite for export to the burgeoning Lagrangian point settlements.

The solar storm lasted eleven hours before the United Nations Space Development Agency gave the all-clear signal. Jamie returned to the kitchen to find things exactly as he had left them. Using the back of a knife, he scraped the diced onions into the trash, and dumped the liquid eggs. He then got some garbage bags from the cabinet and walked to the refrigerator, a secondhand unit purchased by ADC at a former rival's bankruptcy auction.

There was a knock on the doorframe.

"Mind if I come in and pick up the TLD?" Billy asked.

"Go ahead."

Billy walked to the wall beside the refrigerator and pulled the thermo-luminescent dosimeter from its bracket. The TLD was a stubby fat tube, about the size of a fountain pen.

"It's a shame to waste all this food," Jamie said as he surveyed the refrigerator's contents.

"Yeah." Billy held up the TLD. "But until I've had a look at these, we don't know if the food in the shielded logistics module is compromised. If it is, we'll be eating those disgusting rations from the shelter until the company bothers to send up a shuttle."

Crenshaw broadcast a briefing on the status of the base at the end of the workday. Being one of the largest common areas, the mess hall was a natural gathering place. A large post-dinner crowd gathered to watch the monitors.

"On behalf of the company, I want to commend everyone on the manner in which we handled this emergency." Crenshaw's image was dotted with dark spots, indicating pixel dropouts from the radiation-damaged CCD elements in her office camera. "The good news is that the impact on production will be minimal. The total dose in the shelters was less than twelve millisieverts, and the reading in the logistics module was also within limits."

Jamie let out a breath. The food supply was okay.

"Now, the bad news. The proton degradation of the solar arrays was severe. Output from the power farm is down almost twenty percent. In order to maintain production levels and have adequate battery margin for lunar night, there will be unscheduled brownouts of nonessential systems over the next several weeks."

Jamie spotted Paul talking to Maria. She seemed to be grinning at something he said. Jamie frowned.

"The other major loss is the greenhouse. All the plants will have to be destroyed. This will impact atmospheric regeneration, requiring increased duty cycles of the metox canisters for CO_2 scrubbing . . ."

Jamie tried to push Paul and Maria out of his mind, shifting his thoughts to the loss of fresh fruits and vegetables. He would have to adjust the menu to meet the nutrition requirements while maintaining variety.

". . . other than that, we fared well. Some of the essential electronics we couldn't power-down suffered single-event upsets, but the redundant systems kicked in as designed. We should be fully back on our feet when the supply shuttle comes through next month. In the meantime, we have a business to run."

Crenshaw's image faded to black.

The people in the mess hall began to disperse. Jamie managed to recruit two of them to help transfer supplies from the logistics module. He'd asked their names, but promptly forgot them, and they took off immediately after the job was done.

Jamie activated his organizer to plan next evening's dinner. Suggested menus, based on UNSDA food guidelines, were uplinked by the company nutritionist in Montreal. But on-site cooks had wide latitude in meal preparation to accommodate local preferences and nutritional needs. Jamie scanned the proposed choices: macaroni and cheese, quiche Lorraine, or fish and chips. He called up the nutrient specs for the shelter rations. They were short of the 150 microgram UNSDA RDA for iodine, so that would have to be made up.

It would be fish and chips tomorrow night.

The stethoscope felt cold against his chest.

"Breathe in," Maria ordered.

Jamie inhaled.

"And exhale."

Maria removed the stethoscope from her ears. "How do you feel overall? Sleeping well, eating okay?"

"Sure, same as always."

"Most people were due for a checkup in a couple of weeks, but because of the storm Crenshaw and I thought it would be wise to do it now." She took his arm and wrapped the blood pressure cuff around it. "How do you like Maryniak so far?"

Jamie normally hated medical checkups, but being able to spend some time with Maria made this one more than tolerable. "I'm having some trouble fitting in. Everybody seems to be in a clique or circle, and I feel kinda left out."

Maria inflated the cuff, opened the valve, and slowly released the pressure. "I felt the same when I first got here. Maybe it's the corporate culture. ADC doesn't have the best reputation. You've only been here a month. Give it time. Look at the chart on the far wall, please."

Jamie stared ahead as Maria shone a light into his eye. "I guess you're right. Maybe it's me. I've had trouble fitting in all my life."

"What do you mean?"

"My parents divorced when I was small," Jamie said, "but neither of them wanted permanent custody of me. So I grew up getting shuffled around between them and various relatives and family friends. I guess that conditioned me not to settle down anywhere. Even for college, I ended up quitting and reapplying at three different schools before I finally got a degree."

Maria turned off the light. "What was your major?"

"Business." Jamie blinked. "I hated it. My classmates were arrogant snots who liked to hear the sound of their own voices, and the profs were eggheads who never left campus but still felt qualified to lecture us on how the 'real world' works."

"I see." Maria handed Jamie a cup of water. "Swallow when I tell you to."

She stood behind him and placed her fingers on his neck. "Take a sip now, please." As he swallowed, she felt his thyroid for tenderness.

Maria took the cup and disposed of it. She then went to a cabinet and got a syringe. "I need a blood sample. Please put your arm on the side rest."

Jamie felt a prick as the needle went in.

"How'd you get from business school to cooking?"

Jamie sighed. "I met someone in college, but she wanted to stay in town after graduation and I wanted to try something else in another city." He shook his head sadly. "Maybe it was the way I grew up that made me feel so compelled to move all the time, but it broke her heart. Took me two years to realize I'd made the biggest mistake of my life, but by then it was too late. Next thing I knew, she was married."

"I know how you feel," Maria said as she withdrew the needle. "But how does cooking come into this?"

"It just reached the point where I figured the only way to make the hurt seem worthwhile was to keep moving, to go as far away as I could. Can't get much farther away than space, right? Every facility out here seemed to need engineers, doctors, and cooks. I'm not an engineer or a doctor, but I like to think I became a pretty good cook back at the college co-ops, so here I am. A man's place is in the kitchen, right?"

Maria labeled the blood sample. "Well, I think you're doing a great job, especially with the crappy food the company makes you work with." She smiled. "You're fine. I'll call if there's anything you need to know about in the blood work."

A few years ago, Jamie's list of jobs in the commercial space sector would have been shorter by a third. Companies believed the only purpose of food was physical nourishment, so having a dedicated cook was considered an extravagance. But food provided psychological as well as nutritional sustenance. Many corporations, including ADC, learned the hard way when productivity dropped by almost forty percent. Taking a lesson from terrestrial oil platforms, space companies began hiring full-time cooks, and worker morale improved immediately.

Such was the importance of Jamie's role in psychological support that Crenshaw granted him a power rationing waiver to use the oven. Tomorrow was the birthday of Fred Sabathier, the Shift Three foreman, and coffee cloud cake was his favorite.

Jamie had just poured the batter into a tube pan and put it in the oven when he got a call from Maria.

"Jamie, do you have a minute?"

He glanced at the timer. "Sixty-five, actually. What's up?"

"I need to talk to you about something."

Jamie frowned. It had only been a few hours since his blood test. She wouldn't be calling him unless something was wrong.

"Thanks for coming."

Nervously, Jamie took a seat. "So, what's wrong with me?"

Maria laughed. "Nothing's wrong with you! I just needed your advice on something. This is confidential, of course."

"Of course," Jamie repeated, visibly relieved.

"I just examined the rover crew. They were out on a two-week helium-3 assay at Mare Marginis, but got back to base just before the solar storm."

Jamie nodded. He'd heard that ADC was studying the economic viability of Maryniak harvesting helium-3 isotopes from the lunar regolith, in response to demand to feed the new generation fusion reactors on Earth. "Are they all right?"

"They're all complaining about being . . . constipated."

"Really." Jamie raised his eyebrows. "When did this start?"

"A couple of days into their expedition."

Jamie thought for a moment. "Well, they've been eating the same things as everyone else since they got back, and I stick religiously to the UNSDA guidelines. Anything I make has enough fiber, believe me, and the rover rations are also supposed to meet UNSDA standards."

"Maybe they weren't eating regularly," Maria suggested. "That and stress can be causes as well. I mean, the stupid rover broke down halfway through their mission."

"Maybe . . ." Jamie rubbed his chin. "Do you have the serial number for the rover rations?"

Maria consulted her organizer. "51800-8493227."

"Can I use your connection to tie-in to the company logistics database?"

"Sure."

Jamie linked in. "That's odd. Give me that number again?"

Maria repeated it.

"That can't be right. It looks like the number you gave me is for an EVA ration. Let me do a search."

A few moments later, Jamie put down his organizer, slowly shaking his head. "You're not going to believe this. I think they stocked the rover with the wrong rations."

"What?"

Jamie read the screen. "8493227 is a type of EVA ration. According to this, they're eaten by crews on ships without spin gravity before spacewalks. They're high in iron and sodium but low in fiber, so they won't have to take a dump when they're outside. The correct ration for the rover should have been 8493277. Somebody screwed up."

Maria rolled her eyes in disbelief. "All right, I'll let them know."

"I can do up a high fiber menu for the next few days. How do garbanzo pitas sound?"

"Yummy. While you're at it, make some of your blueberry oat bran muffins for the next rover expedition."

"I'll ask for a power waiver for those muffins." Jamie looked at his watch and stood. "Gotta go. Fred's cake needs attending."

"Thanks for your help."

Upon returning to the kitchen, Jamie immediately knew that something was wrong. It should have been filled with the smell of freshly baked cake. Instead, there was nothing.

He turned on the oven light. "Oh, no . . ." He opened the door. The cake was flat. "Damnit!" A brownout must have hit the kitchen while he was gone. Fred Sabathier's cake was ruined.

Jamie was in a bad mood.

Crenshaw had denied him another power rationing

waiver to use the convection oven, so for the birthday party they had to make do with a prepared microwave pie. Fred seemed not to mind, but Paul had made endless jokes to Maria about Jamie not being able to "get it up." Jamie ground his teeth as he stirred the pot of pea and broccoli soup. Given ADC's miserly pay scales, Jamie thought it was a miracle there weren't more people like Paul at Maryniak. He briefly considered trying to slip something disgusting into Paul's serving.

Jamie could hear snippets of conversation from the doorway to the mess hall. He thought he heard someone say "explosive decompression." Instinctively, he glanced at the red ceiling light. It was off. He turned down the heat, covered the soup, and made his way outside.

Nobody was eating. In addition to those in the mess hall for their scheduled dinner slot, others had come in from the corridor and were standing. They were all watching the monitor, which was turned to CNN Interplanetary.

". . . details continue to emerge on the accident that occurred at Banting Station just under an hour ago . . ."

Banting Station was one of ADC's Earth orbiting research labs that used the microgravity environment to develop new pharmaceuticals. Jamie stepped closer to the monitor.

". . . explosive decompression of the laboratory module . . ."

The mess hall lights suddenly flickered, and the screen went momentarily dark. When the image returned, it showed a gash along the end cone of the lab module. Around the edges of the opening, serrated aluminum was bent outward like a twisted, metallic flower.

" . . . emergency bulkheads engaged, sealing off the rest of the station but trapping four researchers in the lab, who are now presumed dead. The rupture occurred near a docking port on that module, but no vessel was attached at the time . . ."

Jamie spotted Maria and Paul. She put a hand on his shoulder, whispered something into his ear, then turned and strode quickly out the door.

He took a step to follow her, when a sudden wave of dizziness hit him. Instinctively, he grabbed a chair.

"Are you all right?" someone asked.

Jamie nodded. His light-headedness disappeared as suddenly as it had come. But Maria was gone.

Jamie didn't see Maria again for almost a week following the Banting accident.

The cause of the tragedy was found within days. As a matter of procedure, the UNSDA investigation team reviewed the maintenance records of the station. They discovered that seven years earlier, an automated cargo vessel had collided with the laboratory module during a botched docking, cracking the end cone pressure bulkhead but not breaching it. ADC had dispatched a repair team to patch the bulkhead, but they took a tragic shortcut. The crew had spliced on the reinforcing section with only a single row of rivets instead of double, compromising its long-term structural integrity. Seven years of thermal contraction and expansion from orbital sunrises and sunsets every forty-five minutes had taken their toll. The bulkhead simply blew out.

The accident itself was bad enough, but news of the company's complicity in the tragedy further eroded morale at Maryniak. Jamie noticed people were eating less, leaving more on their plates for him to clean up.

He finally saw Maria seven days after the accident. She was sitting at a table in the mess hall after the Shift Three dinner slot, sipping a coffee, alone.

"May I join you?"

"Jamie!" She gestured at the empty chair. "Please."

"I haven't seen much of you lately," he said. "You've been eating in your quarters?"

She nodded, and sipped her coffee again.

Jamie thought for a moment. "I know just the thing to go with that." A moment later, he returned to the table, his right hand hidden behind his back.

"What's that?"

Jamie whipped out a raspberry muffin, and with a flourish placed it on a napkin in front of Maria.

She bit her lip.

Jamie sat down, concerned. "What's wrong?"

"Rick Chang was one of the guys killed on Banting Station last week."

"A friend?" Jamie asked.

"My ex-husband."

There was a moment of awkward silence. "I'm sorry," Jamie said at last.

"I hadn't as much as gotten a message from him in over five years. Didn't even know he was on Banting until the news reports came in."

The lights dimmed momentarily before flickering back on. Jamie waited for Maria to continue.

"We met at a summer job in the university medical biophysics department. On my birthday, he came to my desk with this huge raspberry muffin he'd bought at the coffee shop in the bookstore. He took out a napkin and put it down, much as you just did, except he'd stuck a candle in it."

"Sounds like he was a sweet guy," Jamie said.

"He was a jerk."

Jamie's eyes widened.

"He could be sweet, sometimes. But overall, he was a really selfish person. He'd do things for me, but he'd only go so far until it started encroaching on what he wanted, and then it stopped. One day, he came home and told me he'd accepted a job with Honeywell-Dettwiler in Darmstadt. He never even told me he'd been applying for other jobs! Rick expected me to follow him, just like that. It was all about him. So he went to Germany, I did not, and that was that."

Maria looked up at Jamie. "It seems we have something in common, don't we?"

Jamie started to reach over the table toward her free hand—but stopped. He felt a runny dampness in his nose. A red blotch appeared on the table.

"What the—" Jamie put a hand to his nose.

"Are you all right?" Maria grabbed some napkins and handed them to Jamie.

He nodded.

"I've gotten some complaints about nosebleeds lately. Maybe we should ask environmental control to increase the atmospheric humidity," Maria said.

"Dat wud be a gud idee-uh."

"So there's three golfers, a priest, a chef, and an engineer. They're at this course, but it's very frustrating because the guys in front of them are really slow and won't let them play through. So back at the clubhouse, they ask the owner who these jerks were. The owner says, 'Oh, please try to be tolerant of them. You see, they're firefighters who put out a blaze here at the clubhouse last year. Sadly, they damaged their eyes saving the building and they're now legally blind. So, in gratitude we let them play here for free.' The priest says, 'That's terrible! I'll go back to my church and pray for them.' The chef says, 'What a heroic bunch of guys! If they come to my restaurant, they can eat for free.' Finally, the engineer says, 'Why can't they play at night?'"

Billy started laughing hysterically.

"That's a good one," said Suhana Aziz, a mass driver technician.

Jamie was seated to her left. "I've heard that joke before, except it was a doctor instead of a chef."

"Well, I thought I'd make a slight variation in honor of

present company." Billy gave Jamie a pat on the shoulder. "Listen, you probably don't hear this much, but I just want you to know that I think you're doing a great job."

Jamie was surprised. "That means a lot to me, Billy."

"I'm also glad the company didn't cheap out and got us a real cook," said Suhana.

"Thank you," Jamie said quietly. He eyed the unfinished plates of baked chicken around the table. "Although, I guess I didn't do so good today."

"Oh, no, it's not that at all!" Billy said. "I just haven't been very hungry lately."

The conversation was interrupted by a retching sound. The threesome turned simultaneously in the direction of the noise.

Sarah Schubert, a rover driver, was throwing up.

"It wasn't that bad," Paul called out as the pungent odor of vomit filled the room.

Billy and Suhana helped Jamie clean up the mess, amid a string of apologies from Sarah. She had no idea what had happened, but told them she'd had a queasy stomach for days. She promised to make an appointment to see Maria at the earliest opportunity.

Jamie went to the sink to wring out the mop. He was rolling up his sleeves, when he suddenly stopped and brought his arms to eye level.

"What the hell?"

The insides of his forearms were dotted with blisters.

"Do they itch?"

Jamie shook his head.

"Okay, if you don't mind, I need another blood sample."

As Jamie pressed the cotton against his arm, Maria gave him a small tube. "This cortisone should ease the blistering."

"Do you know what caused them?"

"No," she admitted, securing the cotton with a bandage.

"How do you feel overall? Anything unusual you've noticed?"

Jamie thought for a moment. "Sometimes nosebleeds,
like when I was with you in the mess hall a few nights ago.
I've also been getting these sudden dizzy spells. Just for a
moment, then it goes away."

"What about your appetite?"

"I don't think I've been eating as much as I usually do."
He paused. "Actually, I've noticed people seem to be eating
less in general."

"People all over the base have been coming to me with
similar symptoms. Billy's got blisters like you. Others have
been complaining about nosebleeds, loss of appetite, nausea, and vomiting. Even I've felt light-headed sometimes."

"What would cause these symptoms?" Jamie asked.

Maria exhaled slowly, staring at the ceiling for several
seconds before replying. "I probably shouldn't be telling
you this, but . . . the symptoms appear to be consistent with
low-level radiation sickness."

A knot formed in Jamie's stomach. "Who else knows?"

"Crenshaw, Montreal . . . and now, you."

Jamie's voice was trembling. "Wh–what do we do? Do
we . . . are we all going to get cancer or something?"

"Let's not jump to conclusions. According to the monitors, we weren't exposed to a dangerous dose."

"What if they're wrong?" Jamie exclaimed. "After what
happened on Banting, how do we know . . . what if the
company didn't build the shelters to spec?"

"Both Sarah and I show normal white blood cell counts.
That's the weird part. If it's radiation sickness, particularly
sickness advanced enough that we're seeing vomiting and
nausea, we should also have reduced white blood cells."

Jamie calmed down, a little. "So what else could it be?
Food poisoning?"

"You tell me."

Jamie thought for a moment. "It's not likely. The refrigeration systems in both the kitchen and the logistics module are fine. Almost everything I make is well-cooked, especially since we lost the greenhouse. Also, we eat a wide variety of foods, so it can't be any one item."

"That's what I thought."

An uneasy silence fell between them.

"If it is radiation sickness, or even it isn't, you've got to tell people," Jamie said at last.

"We can't say anything until we know for sure," Maria said. "We'd cause a panic."

Jamie spotted the table with Billy Lu and Suhana Aziz. "May I join you?"

Suhana looked up. "The chef graces us with his presence."

"Have a seat," Billy said.

Suhana poked her fork halfheartedly into her spaghetti.

"Something wrong?" Jamie asked.

"We almost had an accident in the field today," she said.

"What happened?"

"Freddie Wilson was out doing an induction coil change-out on the mass driver. The IVA guy, Grant McPherson, was supposed to have applied inhibits to the power bus before Freddie even went out, to give enough time for the capacitors to discharge. Except, he didn't. Caught his mistake at the last minute, thank goodness. I could hear him screaming on the loops, 'Don't touch the coil, Freddie! Don't touch the coil!'" Suhana shook her head. "It was damn close."

"I know Grant," Billy said. "That's not like him at all. He's one of the most careful guys I know."

"He said he was feeling tired, a little dizzy," Suhana said. "Just lost his concentration for a moment."

Jamie looked at the unfinished plates of spaghetti. "How do you guys feel?"

"I don't seem to have much of an appetite. But your cooking's great, as usual," Billy added quickly.

"Sometimes, I feel like I want to throw up," Suhana said, "and I haven't been eating much either."

"Have you guys talked to—"

Jamie was interrupted by three short beeps, indicating the monitor was about to come on. Seconds later, Crenshaw's image appeared on the screen.

"This is a general announcement for all personnel. Staff are to report to Dr. Clarkson immediately for medical evaluations. Individual appointments have been scheduled and will be downlinked to your organizers within the hour. Every attempt has been made to accommodate shift requirements, but should you be unable to make your appointment, please reschedule with Dr. Clarkson at the earliest opportunity."

The mess hall erupted with noise even before the screen went dark.

"Something's wrong, and they're not telling us!" Jamie could hear Paul shouting over the commotion. "That solar storm did something to us!"

Jamie entered the infirmary, a tray of freshly baked cookies in one hand, a pot of coffee in the other.

"Chocolate chip?" Maria was impressed. "You got another waiver for the oven?"

Jamie nodded. "Crew morale."

"Where the hell did you get the chocolate?"

"Base facility food manager's discretionary logistical supply," Jamie said as he put the coffee and cookies on her desk. "In other words, my own personal hoard. For special occasions only."

"What's the occasion?" Maria asked before taking a bite.

"Our last week alive."

Maria almost choked on her cookie. "That's not funny!"

"Maybe I wasn't trying to be funny."

"Jamie, I don't know exactly what's going on yet, but I do know a few things. One thing is, we are not going to die . . . at least, not this week." She stared at Jamie. "Did you hear me?"

Jamie nodded slowly. "What else do you know?"

Maria grabbed another cookie from the tray. "I know you make great cookies, Mr. Squires."

Jamie did not sleep well. Over the past few days, he started having thoughts that somebody was tampering with the food. Twice he woke in a cold sweat, the second time going so far as to get dressed and run out to check the kitchen. When he returned to bed, his dreams were of Paul . . . and Maria.

He woke up feeling nauseated. Much like a hangover, except that he hadn't been drinking. He wished that he had, because it would at least have made waking up like this worthwhile. The shower made him feel better, but his gums were tender when he brushed his teeth, and when he finished his toothbrush was pink.

Jamie stepped out of his quarters and headed for the mess hall. The corridor was practically empty at this hour. Such was the call of duty, to prepare breakfast for the Shift One crew.

He turned a corner—and was suddenly grabbed from behind and thrown against the bulkhead.

"Paul!"

The big man tightened his grip, pressing hard against Jamie's chest. "What's going on?"

"I don't know what you're talking about."

"You know damn well! People are sick all over base. Nobody's saying anything. But you . . ." Paul jabbed a finger into Jamie's chest. "I know you've been talking to Maria. We're all sick from the solar storm, right?"

Paul tightened his grip when Jamie did not answer. "Joe McKay barfed in his suit last shift. Pretty gross, huh? He's lucky we're on the Moon. If he'd been in free space, he could've suffocated." He brought his face right up against Jamie's. "So, what is happening to us?"

"I don't know," Jamie repeated. "I'm sorry about Joe, but I really don't know. I haven't been feeling so hot myself. Why don't you ask Maria or Crenshaw?"

"Oh, I'll definitely be talking to Maria," Paul said. "But I thought I'd ask you first."

"Yeah, well I'm just the stupid cook, remember?" Jamie decided he'd had enough. "You've been on my case since I got here! You're just jealous because Maria doesn't—"

Paul raised his fist. "What the hell do you know about Maria, kitchen boy?"

"Paul!"

Jamie turned his eyes and saw Suhana Aziz.

"Leave him alone."

"He knows something!"

Suhana said calmly, "I know that I kicked your ass in aikido last year, and you can be damn sure I can do it again, right here, right now."

With a growl, Paul let go of Jamie. He glared at him for a moment, then abruptly turned and walked away.

"Are you all right?"

"Fine!" Jamie stormed down the corridor without thanking his rescuer. Marching right past the mess hall, he headed for the Beta sector habitation modules. He quickly found the room he was looking for, and pressed the door buzzer.

"Who is it?"

"Jamie!"

"Give me a minute."

Maria opened the door. It was clear he had woken her.

"No offense, but this had better be important." She

looked him over, and her tone quickly changed. "Good grief, Jamie, you're trembling. What happened?"

"You have to say something." Jamie's breathing was heavy. "You and Crenshaw, you guys have to say something."

"We can't make a public announcement until we know exactly what's going on. We'd cause a panic."

"There's a panic now!" Jamie snapped. "What the hell was Crenshaw thinking, making a public announcement for medical tests without saying why? People are scared. I'm scared, Paul's scared, we're all scared." He stared at Maria, his eyes pleading. "If there's anything for people to be afraid of, at least let it be on the basis of facts, even partial facts, not rumors and hearsay."

Maria nodded slowly. "You're right. I'll talk to Crenshaw and Montreal about this."

It was an angry and frightened crowd that packed the mess hall to capacity. Those who couldn't make it in person were watching through the monitors.

Crenshaw had to shout to be heard, calling for quiet three times before she could speak. "You've all received the briefing material through your consoles and organizers, but I've called this meeting to personally answer any questions you might have on the current . . ." she hesitated, ". . . situation, at Maryniak."

Jamie squeezed his way between people to put trays of sandwiches on the tables.

"Why won't the company come clean?" Predictably, the first to speak was Paul. "We're all sick from the solar storm!"

"That's not true," Crenshaw said. "The total dose inside the shelters was within safe limits."

"What if the dosimeters were faulty?" asked Suhana.

"The TLDs are ancient technology, but they're reliable," Billy said. "I'd have preferred solid-state dosimeters throughout the base—not just in the shelters—but the company prefers to use the cheaper TLDs for the modules. In any case, I have no reason to think the readings are wrong."

"I don't believe anything you people are telling me!" Paul shouted. "How do we know the shelters were buried deep enough? How do we know there was enough shielding?"

"The storm shelters meet all applicable UNSDA standards," Crenshaw said.

"Do they? We all know how this sorry-ass company screws up and cuts corners. Look at what happened on Banting. For God's sake, there's even a rumor they stocked the rover with the wrong rations!" Paul pointed at Jamie. "The company's to cheap to even hire a decent cook! I think they skimped on shelter construction, and Billy over there doctored the dosimeter data to cover it up."

"Are you calling me a liar?" Billy's face turned red. "Why would I go along with a cover-up? I'm sick, too, you moron!"

Paul didn't let up. "We have been exposed to a harmful dose! Everybody's sick. My hair's been coming out in clumps every time I shower."

Jamie fought the urge to make a sarcastic remark about Paul's hygiene.

"The TLDs don't lie," Billy reiterated.

"Then maybe kitchen boy's been putting something in our food!" Paul exclaimed.

Jamie decided to speak up. "Billy, are you sure the food in the logistics module wasn't compromised?"

"Yes," Billy replied. "The logistics module is shielded, just not to UNSDA human-rated standards. The food's fine."

"How do these TLDs work?" Jamie asked.

"They're tubes of lithium borate manganese." Billy held up his hand, with his thumb and index finger apart. "The crystals absorb energy from ionizing radiation. After exposure, I plug them in an analyzer, where they're heated up to three hundred degrees Celsius. This causes the energy to be released from the crystals as photons. The analyzer's calibrated to determine the total dose absorbed by the tube based on the light it gives off."

Jamie thought about Fred Sabathier's birthday cake. "Do you watch these tubes as they heat up?"

"Do I watch paint dry? Of course not. I usually step outside and do something else."

"What would happen if the power got interrupted as the tube from the logistics module was being heated up, before it got up to three hundred degrees?"

"Well, the TLD would cool down, and then when the power came back on, they would . . ." A look of horror flashed across Billy's face. "Oh, crap . . ."

A deathly silence fell over the mess hall.

"The food," Crenshaw said at last. "It's the food."

Paul said, "I knew it all along."

Nobody touched the sandwiches.

Maria sipped her coffee. "Quite a meeting, wasn't it?"

Jamie nodded.

"You helped solve the big mystery."

"All I did was ask a question."

"The right question," Maria said. "When the TLD from the logistics module was heated and cooled, it partially reset the crystals, so when it was heated up to its proper temperature the second time, fewer photons were emitted, producing an erroneously low reading."

Jamie nodded again. "According to the nutritionist in Montreal, the radiation could've destroyed up to forty percent of the pyridoxine and thiamine content in our food." He shook his head. "We've been suffering from vitamin B deficiency."

"I've prescribed mega doses of supplements," Maria said, "but everything in the infirmary got zapped worse than the food in the logistics module. The company's sending up a contingency supply shuttle, but until it gets here people are going to be popping pills like crazy to make up for the depleted dose in each capsule."

"I can tweak the menu," Jamie said. "Try to make the best of whatever vitamin B is left in our nuked food. How does chicken and brown rice sound?"

"You're quite a hero, Jamie."

He laughed. "Will you stop that!"

"I mean it. You're a big part of the Maryniak team. I really hope you stick around." She glanced at her watch and drained the last of her coffee. "Gotta go."

"Hey, uh . . . How about dinner?"

"I'm always here for dinner," Maria said coyly.

Jamie grinned. "Would you like something other than chicken? I can make something else if you like."

"Surprise me." She smiled, touching his shoulder. "A man's place isn't just in the kitchen, you know."

Jamie watched her walk out of the mess hall. Smiling, he got up from the table and started toward the kitchen, all the while trying to decide what he would make.

*   *   *

Eric Choi was the first recipient of the Isaac Asimov Award for Undergraduate Excellence in Science Fiction and Fantasy Short Story Writing for his novelette "Dedication," which was subsequently published in Isaac Asimov's Science Fiction Magazine. *"Divisions," his lead story in Robert J. Sawyer's* **Tesseracts**[6] *anthology, was a finalist for an Aurora Award (Canada's equivalent of the Hugo) and was reprinted in David G. Hartwell's* Northern Suns *collection. His work has also appeared in* Science Fiction Age *magazine, the Canadian alternate history anthology* **Arrowdreams**, *and Julie Czerneda's* Tales from the Wonder Zone *series. He holds a Masters degree in aerospace engineering from the University of Toronto, has worked at the Canadian Space Agency as an orbit dynamics analyst for the RADARSAT Earth-observation satellite, and has trained satellite operations teams at the NASA Goddard Space Flight Center in Maryland. Currently, he is with MacDonald Dettwiler Space and Advanced Robotics in Toronto, working on mission operations support for the robotic manipulator aboard the International Space Station as well as advanced concepts for robotic systems applicable to future Mars misssions.*

DANCING IN THE DARK

by Nancy Kress

BALLET INSTRUCTOR
Preprofessional ballet program requires a fully-accredited
dance teacher. RAD syllabus or equivalent classes. Pas
de deux & repertoire. Beginner to professional students.
Applicant should be a member of the Dance Educators of
America (DEA), and have trained in a national-caliber
school such as the School of American Ballet, the Na-
tional Ballet School, or the Royal Academy of Dancing.
Preference given to teachers who have demonstrated
success working with younger students of unusual ability.
Submit applications, with letters of reference, to R. Mombatu,
Liaison Office, United Nations Interplanetary Division.

WHEN my brother dropped me off at Lincoln Center on
his way down to Wall Street, the alien landing craft
again blocked the plaza and Security swarmed everywhere.
"The Mollies are back to see the ballet again," Cal said.

"I thought we weren't supposed to call them that," I said,
making a face at him.

"Octopi, then."

"Squidi."

"Calamari." We giggled at each other like ten-year-olds.
I suspect that morning both of us wished we were ten again.
Then Cal wouldn't have to deal with Sally and I wouldn't
have to make my meeting with Alvarez.

"Well," Cal said, "at least the aliens' being so fond of ballet is good for you," and I didn't tell him different. Nothing was good for me just then. I knew what Alvarez wanted to see me about.

"See you and Sally tonight," I promised as I closed the car door, and his face clouded. I shouldn't have mentioned Sally. His sixteen-year-old daughter was tearing Cal's heart apart, even though he hadn't been—wasn't—exactly the ideal father himself. "Bye, twin-boy."

"Be good, twin-girl." But his heart wasn't in it. I wished we'd ended on that other note, making fun of the aliens.

I threaded my way though their weird craft and our security barriers, concrete and electronic and human. From not too close, I glimpsed one of the aliens being escorted into the New York State Theater. God, probably it was going to be permitted to watch class again. It was creepy, taking class with a Mollie watching. It sits in that plastic cage with its own air, looking for all the world like a six-armed octopus ("mollusk," "squid") with a soft, salmon-colored shell, and it balances on two tentacles and *waves* the other four in time to the music. "Can it keep good time?" Cal asked, and I had to admit that, yes, it could. But its presence didn't help the timing of the rest of us.

No. It wasn't a Mollie that had been hurting my timing.

No one knew why the aliens had fallen so in love with ballet. They'd landed on Earth eighteen months ago and had been in communication and translation and negotiation and transubstantiation, or whatever the UN did with them, for all that time. They'd been polite and cooperative and nonthreatening and appreciative and benevolent. But nothing had lit their fire until they were taken, as part of an endless round of cultural outings, to see the New York City Ballet dance *Coppelia*. Then something had unaccountably ignited and they were back, in singles or small groups, every night they could be there. Why ballet? No one knew. "It is beautiful," was all they'd say.

It was the only thing they'd said that I found interesting. Most of their mission, which apparently involved trading things and ideas I couldn't pronounce, was as impenetrable to me as whatever Cal did with such passion down on Wall Street.

"Go on in, Celia, Mr. Alvarez is waiting for you," his secretary said. No reprieve.

"Celia," Alvarez said from behind his big, cluttered desk, not smiling. My stomach tightened.

"Hello, Diego."

"Sit down," he said in his soft Spanish accent. So of course I did.

Twenty years ago Diego Alvarez was perhaps the best male dancer in the world. He partnered Greta Klein, and Ann Wilcox, and Xenia Aranova. He never partnered me, of course; I hadn't risen above the corps de ballet, that unheralded background to stars. Only once in my life had I even danced a solo performance, Io in *Jupitor Suite*, and then only because both principal and understudy had the flu.

When Alvarez retired from dancing, he took over as Artistic Director of NYCB, a position for which he'd been openly groomed for years. He was a decent, not great, director, and the company struggled along under him as ballet always had, supported by a small percentage of the population, paid cultural lip service by a larger percentage, and ridiculed by the rest. An intense, exquisite, marginal art—until the Mollies changed everything.

"Celia," Diego said, "I think you know why I called you in."

I did, but I wasn't going to make it easy for him. I stayed mute.

"There comes a time in every dancer's life—"

"Diego, I can take being fired for being too old, but I can't take pomposity."

Oh, fuck, now I'd done it. But after a moment of blinking astonishment—I doubt any corps member had ever spoken to him like that before—Alvarez leaned back in his chair and spoke levelly.

"I'm not firing you, Celia. I'm offering you an alternate position. As a teacher."

Now it was my turn to blink. Second-rate corps members did not become teachers or coaches at NYCB.

"They asked for you, specifically, after watching several performances and studying with me the structure of the company and the usual promotion paths. They understand that there is a ceiling, and you—"

"Who?" I blurted out, but I already knew. Incredibly, I knew.

"The aliens. They want someone to teach their offspring classical ballet, or at least a modified version of it that—"

"Noooooo," I moaned. "Not . . . possible."

"I wouldn't have said so," Alvarez said, and for a second I saw his distaste for this whole enterprise, turning his beloved art over to a bunch of slack-tentacled monsters, and I knew that Diego had steered their choice toward me. Second-rate, overage, never be missed even from the corps, at least don't legitimize the travesty by assigning a good dancer to it. Diego had never liked me.

"No," I said firmly.

"They're offering a salary larger than mine. And, Celia, it is the only way you can continue dancing."

"But—"

"The only way. Here or, I'm afraid, in any professional capacity at all."

I was silent. We both knew he was right. I could open a dance studio for little girls—little human girls—somewhere in a garage in Iowa, but that was about all. And I didn't have the money for a garage in Iowa. Corps members live on air, hope, and a pittance that barely covers Manhattan rent.

"I have, Celia," Diego said with unusual gentleness, "seen you try to help the young girls who have just joined the corps. I think you will be good at your new job."

I told Cal at dinner. No one else knew yet. The Mollies wanted to keep it out of the press until I had safely left Earth for their huge orbiting ship.

"For their what?" Cal said. He looked stunned, which was understandable. I felt pretty unstable myself.

"Their ship."

"To teach ballet to young squid," he repeated, squinting at me.

"We're not supposed to call them that."

"But why do they want—"

"God knows!"

"And so you're going to teach them to turn out their toes and . . . and . . ."

"Point and flex. *Arabesques.*"

"Those little running steps across stage—"

"*Bourées.* And *ports des bras.* That means 'arm movements.'"

"With four arms."

We both collapsed into hysterical laughter. It was hilarious, it was terrible, it was going to be my life. As soon as one of us started to recover, the other would curve an arm overhead or point and flex an ankle, and we'd be off again. It went on and on. Finally I staggered upright, wiping my eyes. "Ah, Cal . . ."

The door opened and Sally strolled in. Everything changed.

My niece had been beautiful, before she scarred the left side of her face while on a deadly combination of snap and rapture. She refused surgery to fix it. One look at her eyes, vacant and filmy, and I knew she was on something again. Oh, Cal . . .

He sat stiffly, impaled on an instrument of torture I couldn't know, even though the rack was partly of his own making. Cal has never been the best of fathers. Sally's mother, a spoiled rich beauty whom I'd never liked, died when Sally was three, and Cal was always too caught up in his work to really attend to her. She had everything material and very little that wasn't. I saw that now, although I, too, hadn't been paying much attention as she grew up. Still, plenty of children grow up with emotionally absent fathers without becoming addicts who steal or disappear for days at a time. Cal had got her into treatment programs and boot-camp schools, but nothing had worked. I think he'd been relieved just to have her out of the apartment for those weeks or months. "Sally . . ."

"Hi, Aunt Celia. Still lifting your legs for money?"

I restrained myself from answering. I'd tried with Sally, too. Now I only wanted to not make it worse for Cal.

"*Sally*—"

"Don't return, Daddy mine, to the Sally's health-and-well-being platform."

"I never left it."

She laughed, a high giggle, so unbearable—I remembered her at three, at seven—that I excused myself and caught a cab home. They didn't want me there for the looming fight, and I didn't want to be there either.

Call me a coward.

They took me up in a Mollie shuttle along with a load of diplomat types. We left a government building somewhere on Long Island through an underground tunnel, then emerged beside an egg-shaped craft that I suddenly thought would make an interesting backdrop for one of DePietro's geometric ballets. No one spoke to me. These men and women, all dressed in business suits with the latest pleated sashes, looked grim. Was there trouble between humans and Mollies? Not that I knew of, but then I didn't know much. Cal teased me about never watching a newsvid. Everything on them seemed so fleeting compared to the eternities danced every night on stage.

But for the last week I'd watched vids, and I'd studied about Mollie anatomy, and I'd carefully selected my music cubes, and I was scared to death.

"Miss Carver," said a human voice, "I'm Randall Mombatu. I'll be your liaison officer aboard ship."

I was so glad to see an actual person I nearly cried. The diplomats had all stridden purposefully down a corridor and shut the door after them, leaving me standing in the big empty place where the shuttle had flown in.

"You probably have questions," Mombatu said. He was a tall, handsome man the color of milk chocolate, dressed in the ubiquitous sashed suit. His face looked like all of the others: sanded, with all emotional irregularities planed out. I nodded, clutching my dance bag.

"Well, this part of the ship is filled with Terran atmosphere, obviously, as your quarters and half the dance studio will be. The gravity is that of the alien planet, a little over two-thirds Earth, as of course you've noticed. This troubles some humans—"

I sprang into a *pas de chat*. Such height for a simple jump! I never got that height at NYCB. Nijinsky-like, I seemed to hang for a moment before landing in a perfect fifth position. I laughed in delight.

"—although others adjust to the gravity quite easily," Mombatu said, smiling. "This way, please."

They'd given me a small bedroom, sparse as a monk's cell. "All this part of the ship is human. Dining room, commons, conference rooms . . . think of it as an international hotel. Your studio, of course, is new." He opened a door at the end of a short hall. I followed him and froze.

They were already there, the little aliens. The room was like any other dance studio, lined with mirrors and barres on two sides, a stand at one end for music cubes—except that across from me stood sixteen small Mollies, all staring at me from flat black eyes. I clutched Mombatu's arm.

"How . . . how are they breathing. . . ?"

"There's a membrane down the middle of the room. Invisible, some technology we don't have, impermeable to gases but not to light and sound. Terran air on this side, theirs on the other."

"But . . . how will I touch them?" A teacher needed to straighten a leg, push down a shoulder . . . except the aliens had no shoulders anyway. Hysteria bubbled inside me; I forced it down.

"You can't touch them, I'm afraid. You'll have to demonstrate what you want. We also didn't know what to do about toe shoes, so we left that until you arrive."

Toe shoes. Dancers didn't go on toe until a few years of training had strengthened their muscles . . . and these aliens had no toes. I turned my back to them and spoke to Mombatu softly, urgently.

"I can't do this. I'm sorry, I know you probably spent a lot of money or whatever bringing me here but I can't do it, I really can't—"

"Yes, you can, Celia," he said, with complete confidence. It was a professional facade but, gods, was it effective. "And your students believe you can, too. They're waiting to be introduced."

He turned me firmly to face the octopi. "This is Ellen—they've chosen Terran names, of course, for your convenience—the ambassador's daughter."

The Mollie on the right end of the waiting line extended one tentacle full length on the floor in front of her, bent the other five, and bowed forward. It was a ballerina's *reverence*: clumsy, hopeful, infinitely touching.

"This is Jim . . . and Justine . . ." He knew them all. They all looked alike to me, and when I caught myself thinking *that* I was suddenly ashamed. These were kids, as eager to learn as I had been at Miss DuBois' School of the Dance in Parcells, Iowa, thirty years ago.

"Do they understand English?"

"Only a few words. You'll teach them dance vocabulary as you go."

He made it sound so simple. I gazed at the line of youngsters, wondered how the hell I was going to teach partnering and lifts, and made a deep *reverence* toward my class.

"And one and two and three and four . . ."

Sixteen octopi stood at the barre, doing warm-ups. Dressed in leotard and practice skirt, I walked up and down on my side of the membrane, watching for flaws in position.

The Mollies had no hip sockets. They were vertebrates, not really mollusks, but each of their six limbs emerged from a sort of padded hole in the sort of flexible shell that cased their organs and head. The shell, which had a soft underside for various anatomical openings, was vaguely oval, with the limbs attached halfway up. The result was sort of like Humpty Dumpty with six long, powerful arms. Not an ideal shape for ballet.

Still, it had some advantages. Without hip sockets, turnout was no problem; these kids already had their limbs rotated 180 degrees to their body. The long arms-or-legs were unsegmented and had no bones, just tough cartilage-analogue skeletal tissue, and so a fluid line was much easier to obtain than with all those stiff human bones. The back two limbs were the most powerful; along with the next two, they usually bore the weight in walking. Suckers three quarters of the way down each limb provided sturdy balance. I designated these back two limbs "legs."

The front two limbs were "arms." The middle two, the alienettes (I couldn't refer to them as "dance students," not even in my own mind) kept folded close to their body except at the height of posed steps, when they would slowly unfold for great dramatic effect. That was the plan, anyway. Right now, we were working on warm-up stretches and simple extensions. Warm-ups got a lubricating fluid flowing in each limb socket, so no one got injured when we started throwing limbs as high in the air as possible in *grands battements*.

"Ellen, keep your suckers on the floor as long as possible in the *plié* . . . damn." I kept forgetting they couldn't speak English. "Ellen, look! Look!"

I demonstrated a *grand plié*, heels down, and then demonstrated what she was doing, shaking my head. Ellen made me a deep *reverence*—they all loved doing that—and performed the movement correctly.

"Good, good . . . Terence, don't wobble . . . look! Look!"

I'd been aboard ship for four months. My Mollies worked fanatically hard, practicing for hours every day. Randall Mombatu conveyed lavish compliments from all the parents, none of whom would have recognized a correct *arabesque* if Pavlova herself were doing it. The small squid couldn't talk to me, although they chattered readily among themselves in chirps and whistles. There was some incompatibility of human words with their tongues. I think. But they understood me well, picking up a huge dance vocabulary quickly. I had the suspicion they were smarter than I was. The adults, I gathered, communicated with our diplomats through keyboards.

Today I had a surprise for the octopi; the toe shoes had arrived. They were specially designed, blocky pink coverings for the back two legs that would support the fragile tentacle ends and add another few inches to their extensions.

But first we had to get from *pliés* to *grands battements*.
"One and two and—"

"Celia," Randall said abruptly, spoiling my count. "You
have a phone call."

"Can't it wait? Jim, no, no, not like that . . . look! Look!"

"She says not. It's your niece."

Sally? I turned to look at Randall. His tone had been disapproving, but now his entire attention absorbed by the
alienettes. "You know," he murmured to me, "we have almost no knowledge about the Visitor young. Their parents
are very protective. You're the only human who's spent any
time with them at all."

I realized then why I'd been forbidden to record classes
for later analysis. I said incredulously, "You mean, this is the
only contact between a human and Mollie kids?"

"Between a human and Alien Visitor children," he corrected, with an emphasis that told me we were being overheard. Probably the aliens taped my classes—something
that hadn't occurred to me before. Well, why not? Except
that it would have been useful to see those tapes for dance
analysis.

I followed Randall to the comlink phone, which the Mollies had allowed us to install in the human part of the ship.
We passed people engaged in urgent, obscure tasks. It occurred to me that very few people aboard this ship ever
smiled.

"Sally?"

"Oh," my niece said, sounding bored, or trying to sound
bored. I waited, until she was forced to say, "How are you?"

"I'm fine. How are you?"

"Fine. Except, of course . . . oh, Aunt Celia, I'm not fine
at all!"

It was the last thing I'd expected: the return of the open,
honest eight-year-old she'd once been. It got under my barriers as nothing else could have.

"What's wrong, Sally?"

"Dad's going to send me away to school again and it's awful, you can't know and I can't bear it! I won't!" Her voice rose to a shriek.

"Sally, dear—"

"Unless I can come up there and stay with you. Oh, can I, please? I won't be any trouble, I promise! I promise!"

I closed my eyes and ground my forehead against the wall. "Sally, honey, this is an embassy or something, I can't give permission to—"

"Yes, you can. The news said the Mollies would do anything for you because they're so happy about their kids' dancing!"

That was more than I knew. The pleading in her voice broke my heart. I didn't want her here. She'd be a bored nuisance. Guilt washed over me like surf.

"Please! Please!"

I said to the presence behind me, who was probably always behind me electronically or otherwise if I only had the interest to look for him, "Randall?"

"The Alien Visitors would allow it."

"They would? *Why?*"

"I suspect they're as interested in our young as we are in theirs."

But not this particular girl, I didn't say. *Not Sally, not to form impressions of human offspring by.*

"If Dad makes me go away again, I'll . . . he just wants me somewhere where he doesn't have to think about me and be distracted from his work!"

And there was enough truth in that despairing pain that I said, "All right, Sally. Come up here."

"Thank you, Aunt Celia! I'll be so good you won't know me! I promise you!"

But I didn't know her now. Worse, I didn't really want to.

Guilt held me in its undertow, and I just hoped we didn't both drown.

At first she tried, I'll give her that. She learned the Mollies' names. She made no audible jokes about crustaceans. She played the music cubes I asked for in class. She chatted with me over dinner, and she didn't (as far as I could tell) take any drugs. But she neither understood nor liked ballet, and day by day I could feel her boredom and irritation grow, and my resentment grow along with it.

But that was all background noise. My little cavorting squid had been working for six months, and I'd been informed that a recital for the parents would be a good idea. After a long sleepless night, I'd decided to adapt—*radically* adapt!—Jerome Robbins' choreography for Debussy's *Afternoon of a Faun*.

In this short ballet, a boy and girl in practice clothes warm up at the barre, facing the audience as if it were a mirror. So great is their concentration on dance that only gradually do they become aware of each other. The first steps they do are easy, basic warm-ups, and I could keep subsequent combinations from getting too difficult. Moreover, I could gradually add more couples onstage until they were all there, with the most accomplished of my young dancers performing solos and the least accomplished forming a corps after their later entrances. The music was lovely; also, it was slow enough that I would not tax my young Mollies' speed or balance. Finally, I wouldn't need elaborate sets or costumes, yet I would still be presenting a (sort of) real ballet.

"So what do you think?" I asked Sally over breakfast.

"All right, I guess," she answered indifferently, but then perked up. "Can I do the lights?"

"Lights?" The studio had never been anything but fully lit. I didn't even know if we had a light board. But for *Faun*, the stage should be in darkness at first and then gradually brighten. "Uh, I'll see."

"Don't exhaust yourself," she said sarcastically. "I'll be in the video room." She pushed herself away from the table and sauntered out.

Until Sally arrived, I hadn't even known the ship had a video room, intercepting broadcasts from Earth. Well, why not. It kept her away from class. The alienettes, I sensed, didn't like her there, although it would be difficult to say how I knew this, since they understood most of what I said now, but I understood nothing of their squeaks and whistles and chirps. In fact, they were hardly individuals to me. I didn't worry about this. Ellen had a strong extension, Terry a smooth flowing *développé*, Denise a graceful *port de bras*. That was enough to know.

I asked Randall for *Afternoon of a Faun*, the Royal Ballet production of 2011 which, gods forgive me, I thought superior to the New York City Ballet's. He looked at me blankly.

"It's a ballet, Randall. I need a performance recording of it to show my dancers."

"With people."

"Of course with people!"

"I'm sorry, Celia, I'm a little slow this morning. The computers have been acting up, and there's a trade problem with the Visitors and the EEC . . . but you're not interested in that."

"Not in the slightest. Can you have a cube transmitted up?"

"Of course."

It was there by the time we'd finished barre warm-ups and took our break, before moving to center work. Half my mind was on Jim's *fouette of adage*, which was terrible. He could *plié* on one leg all right, could slowly lift the other and extend it to the side in one smooth movement, and his overhead arms stayed steady. But he couldn't seem to coor-

dinate the side arms with the extension, no matter how hard
he tried. The result was too many appendages out of sync
with each other, so he looked more like an opening umbrella
with broken spokes than like a ballet dancer. I was not in a
good mood.

"Okay, troops, this is the dance we'll do for the recital.
I've adapted it for you, of course. But we'll look at this version first. Look! Look!"

I started the cube. It projected onto the wall. Darkness,
and then dimly, at first barely seen through the gloom, a
dancer. She stood in a gap in the back curtain. A deep *plié*,
two steps forward, and then, just as you became sure what
you were seeing in the shadow, she began to warm up with
deep stretches and bends. It was Royal Ballet principal
Rebecca Clarke, in all her long-legged, perfectly poised
loveliness, her luminous calm. The stage gradually brightened around her.

Ellen fell to the floor, screaming.

"It's apparently biological," Randall said, running his
hand over his perfect cropped hair. He looked as close to
upset as I imagined he got. His sash might even have been a
quarter inch crooked. "We only know what we've been told
about their home planet and evolution, of course. The Visitors aren't sea dwelling, despite their superficial, to us, resemblance to cephalopods. The home system lies in a
populated part of the galaxy with many bright stars and
three large moons. More important, there may be a constant
atmospheric form of gaseous photoelectric energy, something like marsh gas, and perhaps also an enhanced visual
spectrum compared to ours, extending possibly to wave-
lengths that—"

"Randall, I haven't the faintest idea what you're talking
about."

"They hate the dark."

I gaped at him. He leaned closer and spoke softly. "Oh, the adults tolerate it, of course. But they prefer to carry on all activities, including sleep, in full light. They can't smell at all, you know, and there is probably an evolutionary history of locating prey by motion. Most Terran cephalopods— not that there's a one-on-one analogue, of course, but still—most advanced Terran cephalopods are pretty ferocious carnivores, with fairly common cannibalism. Those powerful arms and suckers . . . If the Visitors' evolution was highly competitive, it might include a strong bias for light. In the young, some might even have a vestigial neural response to darkness, pain or otherwise, until they learn to compensate. I'm afraid the ambassador's daughter may be one such youngster."

Ellen was the ambassador's daughter. I'd forgotten that; I thought of her as the squid with a good strong extension. But . . . "*Powerful arms and suckers*" . . . "*cannibalism*" . . . I shuddered. All at once my charges seemed genuinely alien, much more so than when we concentrated together on dance.

"It's not a major problem," Randall said, misinterpreting. "You simply have to start your recital with the lights full on and keep them on, not starting in the dark as on the cube performance. The ambassador's daughter is being told that's what will happen. She'll be fine."

The ambassador's daughter. Ellen. Powerful arms and suckers to destroy prey, and cannibalism. Extension and *développé* and *ports de bras*.

"Fine," I said.

But after that, I couldn't look at them the same way. I don't know if they could tell. What we were doing wasn't ballet; it was a grotesque travesty with six arms and no necks and a pathetic parody of beauty. The recital was in five days. I hated every minute of rehearsal.

The morning of the performance, the computer glitches were traced to Sally, and Randall told me, tight-lipped, that she was going back down to Earth.

"How could you?" I raged at her. "We're guests here! You promised to behave! You promised! Then you go messing up UN computers!"

"So what did I do that's so major?" She was back to her worst self, sneering and indifferent. "I futzed a few programs. Big show. They caught me easy enough. It isn't like I'm all that good at smashing firewalls to have any big impact on the great First Contact thing."

"Only because you're so stupid! If you could have screwed the system majorly, you would have!"

She didn't answer, only shrugged. I was so mad I had to get away from her, and I slammed doors all the way to the studio.

It was set up for the recital. The membrane had been moved somehow so that now nine-tenths of the room had Mollie air, leaving me only a strip along the wall with my door. The adjacent wall had been rigged with a curtain that defined backstage; the octopi could stand there in their air and I, in one corner from which I could view the audience, could breathe mine. My corner held the stand for the music cube. In the curtain were cut two rectangular holes like doors, which led to a stage raised a foot or so above the floor. Barres ran along three sides of the stage. On the floor sat chairs for the parents. Or chairlike things, anyway. Everything was as brightly lit as an operating room.

In two more hours the proud parents would troop in, eager to see their offspring desecrate Robbins and Debussy. It would be obscene, a mockery, and they would love it. I slid down the wall until I slumped on the floor, and waited.

My only consolation was that if recordings were made—and of course they would be—I would never have to see them.

* * *

The first pure, slow notes of the Debussy. One, two, three, four . . . I nodded at Denise, the first on stage. She stepped into position in the open rectangle, slowly *pliéd*, and began to dance. A few bars later Terry appeared in the second opening in the curtains.

No Mollie in the audience so much as breathed.

It was then I knew how wrong I'd been.

I could *feel* it, their reaction. I knew it, had known it my whole life: that rapt attention of an audience responding to the beauty of dance. It was more than parental love; this was the real thing. The extra arms, the childish adaptations I'd made to the Robbins choreography—none of it mattered, and not only because these were their children, or because they didn't know any better. This audience was, on their own weird terms, experiencing beauty.

Terry and Denise stood side to side, still unaware of each other, each with one tentacle on the barre. In the rectangular openings appeared the second couple, Ellen and Tom. No one was yet on toe; I had choreographed only a few minutes of toe work for these inexperienced dancers, at the end of the piece. But Ellen's lovely long extension, made longer by her toe shoe, paralleled Denise's *port de bras.*

Some adult Mollie, somewhere in the back, made the first audience noise, a long sort of dying chirp. Even I could tell it was admiration.

All the lights went out, and the room was plunged into blackness.

Cacophony, crashing, *screaming.* I blundered into the music stand and knocked it over; the blackout was total, shocking. It only lasted a moment and then someone flung open a door somewhere and some light, not enough, flowed in from a hallway. Parents clambered forward, tripping over chairs and each other. The dancers stood paralyzed, or huddled on the floor, or writhing in the middle of the stage. No, only one writhed, crying and screaming piteously: Ellen.

I didn't even think. I plunged toward the anguished dancer—*my* dancer—who had been injured, interrupted, *kept from dancing*. I didn't remember the membrane until I'd plunged through it.

The lights went on.

I couldn't breathe, couldn't get air into my lungs, couldn't breathe . . . then I could, in a great gasp, and my lungs were on fire, burning like the hell I didn't believe in . . . *help me, Cal* . . .

Darkness.

Randall swam into view above my bed. It hurt to look at him. It hurt to breathe him in, to breathe anything in.

"Don't talk, Celia. You're going to be all right. It will take a while for the burns on the esophagus to heal, but they will heal, I promise you."

"I'll be so good you won't know me! I promise you!"

I croaked, "Sally?"

I had never seen his smooth diplomatic face look so grim. "Yes, she did it. She—"

"See . . . her?"

"She's in custody, waiting deportation."

"See . . . her!"

"No."

"Vid . . . " God, he better stop making me talk!

"All right," he said grudgingly. "That's some niece you've got there. You have no idea how upset the Visitors were. The only reason the whole dance program didn't end right there, with ripple-effect consequences throughout the entire range of human-Visitor relations, is those kids' affection for you."

Affection? For me?

Ten minutes later Sally's face appeared on an interactive cube ponderously wheeled to my bedside by a disapproving medtech. Sally looked terrible. Her face had bloated from crying, her nose was red and raw, and words tumbled from her like a falling building.

"Aunt Celia, I'm so sorry, I didn't mean to injure you, I never thought *you'd* go on stage, it was just supposed to be a stupid prank. Oh, God, you're the only one who's ever cared what I did—"

I had a sudden insight, completely unlike me. This was a rare moment. Sally was completely vulnerable, as I'd never seen her before and would probably never see her again, and she would answer truthfully whatever I asked her. Provided I asked her quick.

"Sally . . . why?" The words hurt my burned esophagus.

"You paid all that attention to *them!* I was . . . I was . . ."

Jealous. She was jealous.

". . . but I never thought anyone would get hurt, not even them! I never thought I could hurt anything!"

And there it was. She never thought she'd have any real impact. Just as she'd never had any true, deep effect on my workaholic brother, or on her selfish mother, or even on me. Yes, I cared what she did, but not as much as I cared about ballet. I wasn't going to apologize for that, though . . . I couldn't apologize for it. Ballet had been my life, was my life, gave my life shape and meaning. Even if that shape now had six arms instead of two and *bouréed* forward on suckers. It was still ballet, and it still made its exquisite impact. I'd just seen that.

But this child . . . she didn't believe she'd ever had any real impact on anything, or anyone. Until now.

"Sally," I croaked, "you did . . . very bad. Might . . . wreck . . . all human-Mollie . . . relations . . ."

She looked scared, and horrified, and impressed. "Really?"

"You . . . must . . ." I couldn't get any more words out. One last huge effort. "Make . . . right . . ."

"*How?*"

I shook my head and cut off the link. Then I pressed the button for Randall.

He arrived quickly, but I couldn't talk anymore. I made him sit me up and get me a handheld. Everything in my body hurt. Nonetheless, I keyed in:

. . . Tell Sally she nearly ruined all alien contact for good. Make this very important. Very! Let her think everything hinges on her apology, let her make it, and get her a community service job on Earth with kids who really need her . . .

He snapped, "I'm not running a juvenile rehabilitation program, Celia!"

I glared at him and picked up the handheld again.

. . . Do it, or I quit as dance instructor . . .

Then I fell back on my pillows and closed my eyes, the exhausted dictator.

Would it work for Sally? I didn't know. We don't pick the things that define us—they pick us, which is a fucking random arrangement. But having an impact on *something* . . . yes. Even a negative impact was better than none. And a positive impact, however weird . . .

Yes.

When I had rested a bit, I'd call Randall again. I had to tell him he needed to reschedule my ballet students' recital of *Afternoon of a Faun.*

*   *   *

Nancy Kress is the author of twenty books: twelve novels of science fiction or fantasy, one YA novel, two thrillers, three story collections, and two books on writing. Her most recent book is **Probability Space**, *the conclusion of a trilogy that began with* **Probability Moon** *and* **Probability Sun**. *The trilogy concerns quantum physics, a space war, and the nature of reality. Kress' short fiction has won her three Nebulas and a*

Hugo. Her work has been translated into fourteen languages, including Croatian and Hebrew. She writes a monthly "Fiction" column for Writer's Digest *magazine, and lives in Maryland.*

THE SIREN STONE

by Derwin Mak

COLONEL Matthew Chang sat aboard the spaceship *Long Island* and stared at the sensor map, which showed asteroid 20 521 Odette de Proust flying steadily toward Space Station Reagan—and the two hundred and ninety people he'd had to leave there.

A video transmission from General Boyd on Olympus appeared on a monitor.

"Colonel," said Boyd, "all our fleet—what's left after the Mars disaster—is still carrying refugees away from Olympus.

The soonest any ship can get to Space Station Reagan is seven weeks."

"Odette will hit Reagan in six," said Chang plainly.

"Are you confident the demolition crew will blow up the asteroid well before that?" Boyd asked.

Chang shook his head. "They're still behind schedule. Two days now. Something's wrong." In the asteroid demolition business, rock blasters did not linger on an asteroid by choice. If they were late, they had run into trouble. A failed bomb, a premature explosion, a crashed ship, a collision with another asteroid, an injured crew . . . there were endless possibilities of how the mission could fail.

But these problems occurred on asteroids that wobbled erratically in orbits crowded with other rocks. They seldom occurred on asteroids like Odette, rocks that rotated smoothly in orbits with few neighbors.

"Rock Blasters, Inc., are the best in the business," said Boyd. "But if they've failed, you and the *Long Island* must be in position to blow up the asteroid."

"I should be evacuating the station. It's not worth risking anyone—" Chang protested. "We're not the experts—"

"I'll take full responsibility. I've put the order in writing," said Boyd. "Remember, the *Long Island* holds only ten people. Time isn't on your side—to save the personnel or the station itself. That's why I'm sending you to make sure that asteroid is destroyed. It's the only way to save all three hundred people."

After Boyd's transmission ended, Chang muttered, "We should've blown up Odette years ago. Those stupid civil servants don't take anything seriously until it becomes a crisis."

A lieutenant turned to Chang. "Sir," said the lieutenant, "we've reestablished contact with the *Rocky Road.*"

"Finally," said Chang. "What's going on now?"

"The crew is still acting crazy. They insist there are people living on the asteroid."

"Impossible," Chang growled. "How can anyone live on an airless rock?"

The lieutenant pointed at a monitor. "We're getting a transmission from the blasters now, sir."

On the monitor, the image of Andrew Lundman appeared, beamed from his ship the *Rocky Road*, now on Odette.

"Lundman, when are you going to blow up that rock?" said Chang.

"Not while there are people here," said Andrew.

For Andrew Lundman, owner of Rock Blasters, Inc., and captain of the *Rocky Road*, the project had seemed clear and simple: land on Odette, bore a hole into its core, plant a couple of nuclear bombs, leave, and detonate the bombs. Odette would break into pieces of varied trajectories instead of slamming into Space Station Reagan six weeks from now.

Scavengers would follow to pick up the chunks of iron ore and pay a commission of five million gold units to Rock Blasters, Inc. Along with the twenty million gold units for blowing up the asteroid, Rock Blasters, Inc., would make a good profit.

20 521 Odette de Proust, named after a character from the novel *Swann's Way* and the novelist who created her, should have been a routine assignment. Odette was small and deemed safe enough that the United Nations Committee on Asteroid and Meteor Collisions had simply outsourced the job to Rock Blasters, Inc.

On schedule, Andrew Lundman, George Hodding, and Ed Benton had landed on Odette without problems. Just another asteroid demolition. Or so they'd thought.

The first ghost had appeared when they were drilling into the asteroid. Andrew remembered the moment in every detail. They all did.

* * *

"Oh, God, look over there!" George shouted.

Ed gasped and pointed at the figure. "What's that?"

"Then you see her, too?" demanded George.

Andrew turned off the drill. "I see it, too," he said. "What is it? An alien?"

"No, it's Rachel," said George, both mystified and excited. "Rachel, my wife."

As he watched the figure walk closer, George muttered, "Rachel, Rachel. But Rachel is dead."

Andrew turned and stared straight at her so that his helmet camera would capture her image. "Reagan Mission Control, there's another person on the asteroid. I'm aiming my helmet camera at her. Do you see her?"

"Negative, Lundman," Mission Control replied warily from Space Station Reagan. "We don't see any person other than you and your crew."

George began walking toward Rachel. As he passed by, Andrew saw the dumbfounded look on George's face and the hesitant way he approached Rachel.

Mission Control addressed George: "Mr. Hodding, why are you moving away from the drill operation?"

"Investigating an anomaly," said George as he approached Rachel, who was now smiling.

Rachel put her arms around him. "Oh, George, it's been too long," she cooed. "Don't look so shocked. Look happy."

"Rachel, how—how on Earth did you get here?" George blurted.

"We're not on Earth," Rachel reminded him. "Just hold me for a little while."

Over his helmet radio, Andrew heard George and Rachel talk. "Mission Control, Hodding is talking to his wife. Do you hear them?" he asked.

"Negative on that. We hear Hodding talking to someone,

but we don't hear anyone talking back to him," said Mission Control. "What's going on over there?"

Even if she were alive, she should have been dead because she had no space suit and no air. Instead of any protection from the cold and vacuum of space, she wore a red jacket, a short black dress, and high heels. It was the outfit she had worn on their first date twenty years ago.

She also looked as young as she had been on their first date. Behind her, the stars shone like bright white pinpricks against the black fabric of space. The searchlight from the *Rocky Road* lit half her face, leaving the other half in shadow.

"George, it's so wonderful to see you again," she repeated.

George shook his head. How could she talk through the vacuum of space, and how could he hear her voice on his helmet radio? How could her wavy black hair blow in a wind that couldn't exist?

"Rachel, is it really you?"

Rachel smiled. "In the flesh."

George reached out and touched her again. She was solid.

"How can you stand there without a space suit, how can you talk to me?"

Rachel shrugged. "I don't know. I was suddenly here. I don't know how I got here or how I can live here."

She swung her arms around and danced. "But I feel so alive!"

Even though you died seven years ago, remembered George.

"George, how is Megan?" she asked.

"Megan's well. She turned fifteen a month ago. Listens to those Euro-rock groups. She got an A in English. Her teachers like her . . ." he rambled.

Rachel squealed. "Oh, how I wish I could see her grow up! And how about Crystal?"

George smiled. "She's well, too. Crystal's an athlete, pretty good for a twelve-year-old. Came in second at a school track and field meet. She got a blue ribbon."

Rachel pointed at the *Rocky Road*. "Can we go inside the ship? Did you bring photos of the girls? I want to see them!"

As they walked to the ship, George wondered how he would tell his wife's ghost that he had betrayed her.

Ed's father, who had died of lung cancer five years ago, appeared next. Ed had seen photos of his dad's last days, when he looked scrawny and wasted by disease inside an ill-fitting green hospital gown. But here on Odette, he looked healthy and fit, as he was in Ed's childhood, and wore his favorite red plaid shirt and blue jeans.

Ed walked slowly, cautiously, to his dad. Ed felt his throat go dry with fear and surprise, but he managed to talk.

"Dad, how did you get here?" Ed asked.

"I dunno. Suddenly appeared here. Glad I'm alive again, though."

"So you know—you know that you're—dead?" Ed asked.

His dad threw a pebble. It soared silently through the beam of light from Ed's flashlight and into the black depths of space.

Dad nodded. "Yeah, I know I'm supposed to be dead. I don't know how or why I'm here with you."

The final ghost to appear to the rock blasters was Sally, Andrew's sweetheart at the University of Oregon. She had died when terrorists bombed her train in their last year at university. Yet on Odette, Sally was alive and well, as young as she had been in her senior year, wearing the white, green, and yellow uniform of a University of Oregon cheerleader.

"Go, Ducks!" she yelled, referring to the University of Oregon's football team. After dropping her pom-poms to the ground, she jumped into a pike, kicking her legs up parallel to the ground and bending at the waist to touch her toes. When she landed in front of Andrew, a small cloud of rock dust rose from her feet.

With a gasp, Andrew stumbled and fell backward onto the ground. Up and down his spine, he felt both the heat of shock and the cold of fear. As he looked up at Sally, he saw and heard her laugh.

"Klutzy, just like at the spring dance! You haven't changed a bit!" she teased him. She bent and reached down to help him get up on his feet. He felt her solid hands grab his arm.

"Hey, Andy, let's go into the ship," she suggested. "You can take your space suit off in there. You'll be more comfortable. Yeah." She smiled. "Why don't you take some clothes off?"

Back aboard the *Rocky Road*, Andrew took off his space suit and led Sally to the control room. Used to a mere three-man crew, Andrew suddenly felt crowded in the control room, with George and Rachel holding hands in one corner, Ed and his dad huddled over a monitor at another area, and now he and Sally walking into the room.

Andrew had never seen George's green eyes so happy and bright as now, as Rachel ran her hands through his brown hair. Andrew also noticed that Ed's blond hair was thinning in the same spot, at the back of his head, where his dad had gone bald.

He turned around and saw Sally put her pom-poms down beside a computer console. As she sat down in a chair and stretched, he noticed how lifelike these ghosts were. Unlike the transparent spirits of horror movies and stories, these looked opaque and felt solid.

He saw his reflection in a shiny metal control console. Gray hair, induced by time and hard living. He'd aged so much since Sally died. What a contrast with her ghost's hair, still as blonde and shiny as it had been in college.

"How can you exist?" Andrew demanded. "Without air? Without food? Without, uh—"

"Without life?" said Sally. "Yes, I know I'm supposed to be dead. I don't know how I got here. Buy why does it matter? We can just pick up where we left off." She rose from the chair, put her arms around Andrew's shoulders, pulled his lips toward hers, and kissed him. It was a deep, wet kiss, full of love and longing and hunger.

Andrew gripped her and returned the kiss. Her skin felt warm and soft and smelled of the lilac perfume she had worn on their last date, two weeks before she died.

On Space Station Reagan, Mission Control still could not see Sally, Rachel, or Ed's dad through the *Rocky Road*'s cameras, nor could Mission Control hear the ghosts' voices. After Mission Control and Andrew had argued for hours, Colonel Chang, the station's commander was called in. Like his staff, the colonel could not see the ghosts either.

"All I see are you, Hodding, and Benton," said Chang. "I can't see anyone else."

"How can you not see them? They're right here beside us," said Andrew. He turned to Sally. "Sally, say something to the colonel."

"I can't explain this, sir, but I am here," said Sally.

Chang said nothing. *Hadn't he heard Sally?* Andrew wondered.

Finally, Chang spoke. "Lundman, who were you talking to a minute ago?"

"Sally," said Andrew. "Didn't you hear her?"

"Hear who?" Chang asked. "I heard nobody."

Over at another corner, Rachel sighed. "It's so stuffy in here, George. Can I go back outside? I feel more comfortable on the asteroid surface."

"Soon, Rachel, soon," said George as he rubbed Rachel's shoulder to soothe her.

On the monitor, Chang looked puzzled. "Hodding, what are you doing? Rubbing the air?"

"My wife," George said. "Her shoulders are a bit sore."

"Your wife? But Abby's in New York," Chang protested. "She called Mission Control last night."

"Not Abby. Rachel," explained George. "I was talking to Rachel."

"Rachel?" Chang said. "No, that's impossible."

Ed's dad waved dismissively at Chang's image on the monitor. "He doesn't believe we're here," he said. "He just wants you to blow up the asteroid."

"Don't worry, Dad. We won't blow it up," said Ed.

"Mr. Benton, did I hear you tell someone that you're not going to blow up the asteroid?" Chang erupted.

Ed nodded. "You heard correctly," he mumbled.

Andrew looked at Chang's image on the monitor. "Colonel, I know how incredible this all seems to you. We're very shocked and surprised, too. I think we shouldn't destroy the asteroid until we're had a chance to study it."

Chang looked alarmed. "You *must* blow up that rock."

"We can't blow up this rock. It's different."

"What do you think you've found?" Chang protested. "A Siren Stone? You know they're just a deep space myth."

As mermaids had been to ancient mariners, Siren Stones were to modern spacers. They were a way to explain the space crews who turned crazy and disappeared without a trace. In the vast deepness of space, what lonely spacer could resist the beautiful spirits who haunted the Siren Stones? Andrew hadn't taken the myth seriously—until now.

"Maybe there's some truth behind the myth," said Andrew. "That's more reason to preserve the rock until we learn more about it."

"What about the three hundred people on Space Station Reagan?" said Chang.

"We can still save them. Let's not blow up the asteroid. Let's move it instead," Andrew suggested eagerly. "We'll plant explosives on the rock's surface—the blast will nudge Odette into a new orbit, one that won't threaten Reagan or anything else."

Chang shook his head. "Attempts to move asteroids into safe orbits have a lousy success rate. The procedure is too complicated. That's why we blow up the damn things. I can't take the risk. I won't gamble with three hundred lives."

"We *can* move the asteroid into a safe orbit," Andrew insisted.

"You have your orders, Mr. Lundman. Blow up that rock."

Ed and his dad went outside the ship, back to the airless surface of Odette. Ed wore a space suit, but Dad did not.

"How is the family?" asked Dad.

"Mom's okay. She moved to California about two months ago," Ed replied. "Joan's not at Georgetown anymore. She chose a contract position at Stanford because she likes it there. And Trini and I had a son last year. His name is Norman."

"Wow, I'm a grandfather! Whoo-ee!" his dad yelled. "Too bad I couldn't be there for the boy, Norman's his name? It's bad enough that I missed a few years of your life, and now I'm not around for my grandson's."

A few years of your life: the words echoed in Ed's ears.

Ed's dad quit his job at the car factory when Ed was five years old and spent the next five years moving from one bad business deal to another. During that time, Dad never had money, and Mom never smiled. After five years of financial failures, he had simply walked out. To support Ed and Joan,

Mom worked two jobs, one cleaning an office building and another waiting tables at a restaurant.

Dad returned five years later, paler and thinner than ever before, but with a small amount he had earned in odd jobs in California. He was ready to lead his family again, he announced sheepishly. Mom wouldn't take him back, though. Without any argument, he gave her the money and moved into an apartment across town. He had exiled himself from his family when they had wanted him, and now they were exiling him when he wanted them.

He came to visit them from time to time, though. By the time Ed left to work on the Moon, Mom and Joan were just warming up to Dad again, starting to close the chasm in the family. Eventually, Mom and Joan forgave Dad for his disappearance. About seven years after his return, Dad and Mom renewed their vows, in essence, got married again, with Joan as bridesmaid. But Ed was away on the Moon and couldn't come back. He had said that his employer had no room for him on the next shuttle back to Earth. In fact, he had not even asked for a seat on the flight.

Ed visited his mom and dad only twice in the next five years. Unlike Mom and Joan, he could not forgive his dad for leaving him when he was ten years old.

And then his dad discovered he had cancer. When Ed got the space transmission from his mother, he realized that if he wanted his father again, he was running out of time. But Ed was on a rock blasting team heading for Mars. By the time the ship returned to Earth, his dad had already died.

Ed wanted to tell his dad that all was forgiven—but was this ghost really his dad?

"Before you arrived here, what was the last thing you remember?" Ed asked.

"Dying," said Dad.

Ed looked at the stars above them. *Is this what heaven*

looks like? he asked himself. *Is that where they were? In heaven?*

"INCOMING TRANSMISSION" flashed on the monitor. Andrew watched the words fade out and Colonel Chang's image fade in. The transmission was coming from the *Long Island;* Chang had left Space Station Reagan and was heading to Odette.

"You are now three days behind schedule on the demolition of Odette," Chang said. "Do you intend to blow it up?"

"I repeat, not while there are people here," said Andrew.

"There are no people there!" said Chang. He sounded agitated; Andrew had never seen him unnerved before.

Chang tried a more reasoning tone. "They're all in your imagination," he said.

Andrew looked at Sally. She straddled the floor, legs wide apart, and raised her arms over her shoulder to touch her feet. That was how cheerleaders stretched their hamstrings and calf muscles. He remembered seeing her do those stretches on a football field in Oregon many years ago.

She looked so warm, so lively. When they had kissed, he realized that he had never kissed as passionately as with her. Sally was a real woman again.

Andrew turned back to Chang. "No, sir, they are not our imagination. They are real."

"So are the two hundred and ninety people now on Space Station Reagan," Chang reminded him grimly. "That's two hundred and ninety dead if you don't blow up Odette."

"We're working on a way to move the asteroid into a safe orbit," Andrew said. "I'm confident we'll succeed."

"You know that's the riskier procedure." Chang scowled from the monitor. "You leave me no choice, Mr. Lundman. I will demolish Odette and arrest you and your crew."

"Arrest us?" questioned Andrew. "On what grounds?"

"*United States Space Stations Code,* section 52, 'Willful

Endangerment of a Space Station,'" Chang stated. "Minimum sentence, ten years. Don't make this mistake. Obey your orders."

George and Rachel strolled outside on the asteroid's surface, talking about the girls. Rachel laughed when she heard how her daughters had grown up.

"Oh, how I wish I could have seen all of it," she said finally. "Oh, if only I could have been there for them."

George nodded. "That has been the greatest sadness of my life, that you aren't there to see them grow up."

Rachel shook her head. "George, don't feel sad anymore. I'll always be with all three of you."

"Are you in heaven?" George asked.

She took his hand and placed it over his heart. "I'm right here, in your heart."

"You always have been," said George as they continued walking.

"I got to hand it to you, George," said Rachel. "It must have been hard to raise two girls by yourself for seven years."

George sighed. "There's something I have to tell you. I wasn't alone all that time."

"Oh?" said Rachel. "My mother has been helping out?"

"No. I remarried four years ago. Her name is Abby."

Rachel stopped walking and looked at George. "Abby. Is she a nice girl?"

"Yes."

"And how does she treat the girls?"

George said nothing.

"George, how does she treat the girls?" Rachel asked again, anxiously.

George took in a deep breath. "Extremely well. Abby loves them deeply, treats them as if they were her own daughters."

Rachel crossed her arms and shifted her gaze to a rock beside them, as if to avoid looking him in the eye.

"Oh, I see," she said softly.

For Andrew, Sally's death had ended all of their plans: getting married, getting jobs, and starting a family.

"So you never went to that job you had lined up after graduation, the one with the City of Eugene?" Sally asked.

"No, I went into the Navy instead," said Andrew. Without Sally, he had joined the U.S. Navy after graduation, hoping to fight the terrorists who had blown up her train.

He had felt a brief sense of joy when Navy missiles killed the last terrorist commander in Sudan, but it couldn't erase the sadness of losing Sally. Afterward, he volunteered for service on the farthest, loneliest space station, and later, went into rock blasting.

"No children?" asked Sally. "Why not?"

"Hard to do with my job," said Andrew. "I'm always traveling for months in space. No time to meet someone, much less raise a kid."

He paused. He knew he had been making excuses for years.

"But, remember, I *had* wanted children," he continued. "That's what we had planned. We would get married after graduation. We'd live in Eugene. We would get jobs there. I would be a road engineer. You would be an accountant for the bakery. We would have children."

Sally smiled. "We had our whole lives planned, didn't we?"

"We sure did, girl," said Andrew.

"Things didn't go according to plan, did they?"

"No, they didn't." Words came out of Andrew in a rush. "I was looking forward to life with you. It was the most important thing in my life. Instead, I wound up alone, no kids, living anywhere but in Eugene, blasting space rocks for a living. It wasn't what we had planned."

*   *   *

Ed and his dad passed by the drill, now motionless but still stuck into the asteroid. His dad pointed at the drill.

"Is it deep enough to plant those nuclear bombs?" his dad asked.

"We're not going to do it," Ed protested. "How can we? We would kill you."

"I'm already dead," said his dad. "But think of yourself. That military spacecraft will be here any day now. If you don't blow up Odette, they'll arrest you and blow it up anyway."

"We'll fight them," Ed declared. "I lost you once, I won't lose you again!"

"Ed, you can't have me forever. Stop clinging to me. Son, why do you keep clinging on to me?"

"Because, because," Ed started. He couldn't force the words out of his mouth. But it was time to tell him.

"Because I never got to tell you that I forgive you for leaving me and Joan and Mom," Ed said.

His dad put his hand on Ed's shoulder. "I know, son. I've known all this time."

A tear ran down Ed's cheek. "You mean, you died knowing I had forgiven you?"

"Sure did. Don't let that bother you anymore."

Ed heard a clicking sound over his helmet radio. He turned around and looked at the drill's sensor box. The sensor box's lights were lit up in red, blue, and green. He kneeled down to read the display.

"My, oh, my," said Ed. "Dad, you've got to see this."

He turned around to look at his dad, but his dad was not there.

Rachel uncrossed her arms. George remembered that she always crossed her arms when she was angry. Had she been angry? Was she still?

"Since Abby is the girls' mother now, " she said, "does she do everything that a mother should do?"

"Yes," said George.

"Do the girls love her?"

"Very much. You should see the three of them together."

"Ohhhh . . ."

"Oh, no, I shouldn't have said that," George said. "I'm sorry, so very sorry."

"No! Don't be sorry!" Rachel cried. "Oh, George, I'm so happy for you and Megan and Crystal! And Abby!"

She threw her arms around him and squeezed him. Even through his space suit, he could feel that it was the tightest hug she had ever given him.

"I'm thrilled that my family is happy," Rachel said. "Why wouldn't I want to hear that?"

George took a deep breath. "I felt I had betrayed you by marrying Abby. I'm sorry, I'm sorry."

"Stop apologizing." She kissed his helmet visor. "You haven't betrayed me. If anything, you've done exactly what I've wanted. You've raised our girls to be happy, confident young women. You've created a warm, caring family."

"Really?"

"If you're looking for my permission to love Abby and raise the girls with her, you have it. I wouldn't have it any other way."

They hugged, they kissed, and this time, George felt her lips press against his.

That's impossible, he thought. *I have my helmet on. Oh, God, I better still have my helmet on!*

He felt his helmet with one gloved hand; he was still wearing it. He looked around. He didn't see Rachel anywhere.

Inside the ship, Ed scrolled through the graphs and figures appearing on his computer monitor. A three-dimensional computer graphic of Odette appeared, showing how animated waves poured from the core of the asteroid.

"Incredible!" Ed exclaimed. "The drill's sensor detected electrochemical signals below the asteroid's surface. The asteroid is hollow, and it's emitting electrochemical signals."

"Like a battery?" asked Andrew.

"More like a brain. Look at this." Ed pointed at the animated image. "It's also absorbing electrochemical signals."

"From where? The only sources of electrochemical signals are us, from our brains," said Andrew.

"I can't prove it without further tests, but I think the asteroid is absorbing our brain waves and sending its own signals into our brains," Ed guessed.

"Holy smokes. Sally, Rachel, your dad. Could the ghosts be based on our memories and thoughts?"

Ed nodded. "That's possible. Dad's ghost knew how I've felt since he died."

They heard the sound of metal doors swinging open and boots pounding upon steel as George emerged from the air lock. After entering the control room, he began to take off his space suit.

"Funny thing happened out there," he said. "One minute, Rachel is standing there, hugging me, completely alive—"

"No," Andrew interrupted. "Rachel isn't alive. The *asteroid* is. This is a Siren Stone."

Aboard the *Long Island*, Colonel Chang returned to his usual calm, if humorless, mode after hearing Andrew's explanation of the ghosts. To Andrew, this was as close as Chang would get to showing happiness.

"Finally. Now that you've determined that there are no living human beings on Odette, proceed to destroy it," said Chang.

"Colonel, we still can't do that," said Andrew.

Chang glared at them through the thousands of miles of space. "Why not?"

"The asteroid is absorbing our brain waves and emitting its own brain waves. It's some kind of living being. We can't—we shouldn't—kill it."

"It's a rock!" Chang snapped. "Unlike Space Station Reagan. Reagan has two hundred and ninety permanent residents: scientists, tradespeople, artisans, farmers, settlers, and children born on the station. Don't forget that Reagan isn't just a space station; it's their home. You have to blow up the rock!"

"We've been working on the calculation for moving the asteroid. We'll know how many explosives to use, where to place them, and when to detonate them. We can do it," Andrew insisted.

"No, you won't. You're under arrest!" Chang yelled.

Andrew cut off the audio link to the *Long Island.* He could still see, if not hear, how Chang continued barking orders to restore the audio link.

"George, have you finished the prep for shifting the orbit?" Andrew asked.

"I've figured it out," said George, "but it's a complicated calculation. If I missed a variable, it might not work."

"It's a chance we'll have to take," said Andrew. "Ed, how's our flight plan coming?"

"Just finished it," said Ed, looking up from his computer monitor.

"Good, good," said Andrew. He moved toward the crew quarters. "Excuse me for a minute. There's one last thing I have to discuss with Sally."

"We should have died together," said Andrew.

"No, no," Sally said. "We should have *lived* together."

"But we didn't," he argued, "and that's what's haunted me for years. Life didn't go the way I wanted. No house in

Eugene, no job with the city, no cottage in the summer, no vacations to Disney World, no taking our kids to see their grandparents, no kids at all—"

"Hush," Sally ordered. "Listen to me. You've had a good life without me. You've beaten the enemies of our country. You've saved lives by blowing up asteroids before they hit people. You've been all over the world and beyond, from Oregon to Polynesia to the Moon to the asteroid belt. You've done things, seen things, helped and saved people. Don't ever think that your life was a waste of time."

"Even if I've lived it without you, Sally?" Andrew said.

"Even without me," she replied, smiling. "You've gotten on with your life, even if you don't know it. Stop mourning my loss and the loss of what could have been. What you made instead is great and wonderful."

"That's what I finally needed to hear," he said as his throat began to go dry, as the years of sadness ended with this moment of joy.

She kissed him, in the same deep, passionate way they had kissed in their college years.

Then suddenly, she was gone.

After they finished planting the bombs, Andrew, George, and Ed scrambled aboard the *Rocky Road*. An hour later, the *Rocky Road* soared away from the asteroid. They'd go beyond the range of the blast before detonating the bombs, but set them off soon enough to avoid danger to the oncoming *Long Island*.

A day later, the *Rocky Road* reached a safe distance from Odette. As planned, the *Long Island* was still out of range. Andrew smiled; they had outrun Chang.

Andrew typed the detonation code into the transmitter. He hit the "send" button.

"It's done," Andrew said. He began the countdown under his breath.

"We have a strong signal from the probe watching Odette," said Ed. He sent the asteroid's image to all the monitors.

They watched the bomb explode. Although fragments of rock flew in all directions, most of the asteroid stayed intact. Amidst a gray cloud of pulverized stone, slowly but surely, Odette shifted its path.

Aboard the *Long Island*, Colonel Chang and his crew silently watched Odette shift into its new orbit. Never before had they seen an asteroid move amidst a cloud of its own debris.

"This damn well better have worked," Chang said, breaking the silence.

"Colonel, your orders?" said Major Peters, the ship's first officer.

"Plot a course to intercept Odette," said Chang. "I want to be sure this trajectory is completely safe. We still might have to destroy it."

As the *Long Island* continued toward Odette, deep space probes monitored Odette and sent data to Space Station Reagan. With the data, asteroid trackers began mapping Odette's new orbit. Would Odette hit something sooner or later?

A day later, Mission Control sent the answer to Chang. "A one in a million chance, and they got it," he reported to General Boyd.

Back on Space Station Reagan, Mission Control sent the same relieved message to all ships and probes: Odette had changed its orbit and no longer threatened to strike Reagan or any other station.

The *Long Island* was preparing to head home, leaving Odette alone, when she received a distress signal from the *Rocky Road*. The rock blasters had returned to Odette for reasons unknown and now were in trouble. Calls to the

Rocky Road only returned a recorded mayday message. Chang had no choice but to respond. What could be going wrong aboard the *Rocky Road* now?

Andrew looked around. George was telling Rachel about her mother's vacation to Spain last year. At his station, Ed explained to his dad how probes and beacons sent images back to Earth and traveling ships. George and Ed were making up for lost time with their loved ones, talking about family and friends, hopes and plans.

Sally, still dressed as a Ducks cheerleader, came back into the control room. Andrew knew he could imagine her in other clothes, but he wanted to remember her this way. The college years had been the best time of their lives, when the present was full of life and happiness, when the future seemed eternally bright.

Sally sat down beside Andrew and took his hand. "Why did you return to us?" she asked.

"To bring Chang to the asteroid," said Andrew. "I've known Chang for several years, and he's always sad. I don't know why. Maybe it's someone in his past. If it is, he needs to come here."

Shortly after the *Long Island* landed on Odette, Colonel Chang and six commandos quietly boarded the *Rocky Road*. As the commandos took control of the engineering sections, Chang went to the control room.

Chang raised his helmet visor. "We received your distress signal," he said. "What's wrong, is anyone injured—oh, my God."

In addition to Andrew, George, and Ed, he saw other people on the ship: a woman in a red jacket; a man in blue jeans; and a girl in a cheerleader uniform.

"You're just figments of my imagination," Chan insisted.

"Captain Ross reporting for duty, sir!" someone announced from behind him.

Chang spun around. A soldier, dressed in green jungle combat camouflage, stood there. His name tag read "ROSS." He was unscratched and alive, the way he had been when Chang last saw him.

Chang put a hand on Ross' shoulder—his solid shoulder.

Chang tried fighting back the tears, but a single drop rolled down his cheek.

"Oh, dear God, why can't you be real?" he asked. "Why couldn't I take you home to your wife? Instead, I had only your dog tags to take to her. . . ."

One night in the U. S. camp in Haiti, Chang had heard strange sounds, like someone stumbling through the garbage dump just outside the camp. Change had ordered Captain Warren Ross to investigate the sounds. As he walked into the garbage dump, Ross had stepped on a land mine and been blown to pieces. Ross had been married only ten months.

If only he hadn't ordered Ross to investigate the sounds . . .

Chang had never fully recovered from meeting Ross' wife Karen and their newborn son Daniel. He had given her Ross' dog tags, and soon afterward, applied for space station service, away from Earth's fighting nations.

After Chang ordered the commandos to return to the *Long Island*, he talked to Ross in the control room, oblivious to the others, both living and dead. Finally, Chang heard the words he had needed to hear for nineteen years.

"Karen knew the risks, Major," Ross said, calling Chang by his rank during the Haitian War. "Her father and grandfather were both in the Army. She knew we could be killed in action anytime. I'm sure she never blamed the Army or you."

"Thank you, Captain," Chang said. "Let me say again that I was proud to have you under my command. I wish I had been able to tell you at the time."

Chang and Ross exchanged salutes. The colonel sighed and closed his eyes. When he opened his eyes, Ross was gone.

Sally, Rachel, and Dad left again, leaving the three rock blasters alone with their memories—and Colonel Chang.

"I'm gong to drop the charges of willful endangerment of a space station," said Chang, staring out the window at the stars above Odette.

Andrew joined Chang at the window. "Thank you, Colonel," said Andrew.

"It's the least I could do, considering you've lost five million gold units in scavengers' commissions," said Chang with a wry smile.

Andrew nodded. "That's a lot of money, but we can't put a value on this asteroid. It's priceless."

"And mysterious," said Chang. "We know nothing about it. Is it one of the legendary Siren Stones? Could there be more of them? Where did it come from? Did someone send it to us? Is it alive?"

"Do you think the asteroid is alive?" Andrew asked.

"I don't know," Chang answered, "but it doesn't matter. It does something wonderful, and that's what counts. You've done the human race a big favor."

"How's that?"

Chang gazed at the stars again. "You've saved something the human race desperately needs: a place where people can make peace with their pasts."

George and Ed joined them at the window. Up in the black sky, there seemed as many stars as there were lost souls in the human race, each wishing for a chance to say unsaid words.

"I have friends, family—we all do—who could be healed

by coming here," said Chang. "Too bad it's so far from Earth."

"You brought more explosives, didn't you?" asked Andrew. "I think we can give Odette another nudge. Drop her in behind Mars, for instance. Not so close to Earth as to endanger anything, but close enough so people can come here."

"I have the explosives," said Chang. He gave Andrew a serious, questioning look. "Are you sure you can do it again?"

"Yes, I'm sure," said Andrew without hesitating. "We've done it once already." Behind him, George and Ed nodded.

"Fine. You can have the explosives," Chang said. Then he became silent, deep in thought. "I have a problem, though," he said after his silence. "How will I explain this to General Boyd? He'll think I've gone crazy. I don't want to get discharged as a mental case."

"Don't worry about the general," Andrew said. "He'll understand after he comes here, just as you did."

"Of course," said Chang with a smile. "And he will come here. This is a Siren Stone, after all."

*   *   *

Derwin Mak lives in Toronto and writes quirky science fiction short stories. His stories are about ballerinas, tiny aliens, unlucky Titanic *survivors, and vile U-boat captains. He was an anime correspondent for the Canadian magazine* Parsec *and has written articles about royal families and nobility for* Monarchy Canada *magazine and the Napoleonic Society of America. He has university degrees in accounting, defense management, and military history.*

FEEF'S HOUSE

by Doranna Durgin

TEMPORARY HELP WANTED
Short-term contracts available for general laborers. Short-term and renew-for-kind available for those with experience in the service sector, skilled tradespeople, and certified technicians. Apply at any public interact screen by accessing the Toklaat Station's Temporary Job Placement System. Be aware that providing a false statement via a public system is a Category 4 offense and, if convicted, offenders face severe fines and imprisonment.

THE interact screen stared sternly at Shadia, showing her a form full of questions to which she had no answer. To which *no* duster would have an answer. *Local personal reference.* No chance of that. It's why she'd chosen the temp form.

Commonly known as the "duster form," but only if you said it with a sneer.

Local address. Wherever she landed on any given night.

Last posting. Three weeks Solward on Possita IV.

Shadia scanned the form with the contempt of a duster for the mag-footed perms and then, recalling that she sat in front of an interact screen connected to Toklaat Station's temp job placement system, she hastily schooled her expression to something more neutral. *Jobs no one wants, jobs with no guarantee of security.* The first she was used to; the second suited her. She didn't want still to be here in the first place and she certainly didn't want to tie herself to work or community.

There. There was an empty form-line she could fill. She manipulated the interface with absent ease.

Instantly, a woman's face filled the hitherto blank square in the upper left of the screen. "You had a terdog? A *real* terdog?"

A real terdog?
I didn't want to be here in the first place. Not filling out forms, not pretending it suited me, not remembering the sight of my friends boarding the hydropon repair ship, buying passage with three weeks of shoveling 'cycle products and glad to do it. Not hiding my reaction to such a question. A real *terdog? Was there any other kind?*

Politely, Shadia said, "A kennel of real terdogs, sir. Belvian Blues, which we used to find subterr rootings for export—"

"Yes, yes," the woman said, rude in her eagerness. "I have just the position for you. It pays well and suits your unique skills."

Her unique skills? She had a duster's skills. A little of this, a little of that, learn anything fast. Take what gets you off-planet or off-station when you feel like going.

Unless, of course, you fall on your ass in front of a zipscoot and rack up such a medical debt that you're stuck on-planet until you repay. Stuck. In one place.
Stuck.

Most wary, Shadia said, "What's the job?"

Her application screen rippled away, replaced by the familiar format of a job listing. Almost familiar . . . except for the header logo, which caught her eye before she had a chance to focus on anything else. *Permtemp.* "There's been a mistake, sir," Shadia said. Her recently healed thigh cramped with her sudden dread that it wasn't actually a mistake at all. She forced herself to relax. "I'm not a perm. Just a temp. I put it on my application."

"This is a priority position, young woman. In such cases we extend our search parameters."

"Apologies, sir, but temp is a preference, not a restriction."

The woman's eyes flicked aside to her own interact screen where Shadia's partially filled form would be displayed. Her demeanor cooled, enough to give Shadia that same prickly unease she got any time she stepped out of duster turf and into perm areas. "Shadia," the woman said, pronouncing it wrong, *shad-iya* instead of *shah-diya.*

Shadia didn't correct her.

"Shadia," the woman said, wrong again. "Why are you applying for work on Toklaat?"

I have the feeling you know. No doubt the woman had instantly called up all of the records Shadia had accumulated since disembarking here. "Med-debt, sir," said Shadia. *Damn perm.* They thought themselves so superior, with their airs about commitment and stability and dependability. Dusters thought them staid and boring and knew better than to expect permanence from any part of their lives.

"Then you won't be allowed to leave the station until the debt is paid?"

Shadia stopped herself from narrowing her eyes. Of course the woman knew the terms of duster med-debt. "Yes, sir."

"Filling this job is very important to us. Our permanent residents, by definition, have little chance for exposure to pets of any kind."

No, of course not. Only the affluent could afford a pet in

a station environment, even a station like Toklaat with copious gardens and play spaces and other luxuries. And the affluent wouldn't need to check station listings for jobs, temp *or* perm.

The woman smiled a grim little smile. "I can't say for sure, but I suspect that with the priority placed on filling this job, it would be very difficult to remove you as a candidate."

And as long as she was listed as a candidate for one job, she wouldn't be considered for others.

Oh, God. Stuck.

*   *   *

Until this moment she would have said all stations smelled the same. A whiff of artificial scent meant to cover the disinfectant that was ineffective in some places and astonishingly strong in others. But no disinfectant would handle this smell. No artificial scent stood a chance. Wildly exotic pet residue, abandoned and left to stew.

Blinking watering eyes, Shadia tried to evaluate her new home.

Home. How long had it been since—?

But no, this wasn't a home. This was enforced labor, and as soon as her med-debt was paid, she'd find some way out of this place. Off of this station. Back to the habits to which she'd become accustomed these past fifteen years, just over half her life. Her hip twinged, reminding her why she was still here; old memories twinged to remind her why she wanted to leave.

Shadia concentrated instead on her new environs. Two floors of space, an unimaginative floor plan that put living quarters above several rooms meant to simulate a home environment for pampered pets while offering a practical nod to the need for cleanup, food preparation, and isolation of cranky or antisocial animals. There was, of course, a tub.

Precious water, used on dirty pets.

There was even an old schedule tacked directly to the wall next to the tub. The hand-scrawled names were water-stained and worn, but Shadia got the gist of it. Once a week for most of them, twice for some of them. And not all of them were bathed with shampoo and water. There was one called Mokie; it seemed to be bathed with a special oil. And Tufru used a product she found in the storage bins over the tub . . . it reminded her of cat litter.

Cat litter. When was the last time I cleaned a litter box? Stinky old litter box, never could have the fancy self-cleaners because Ma and Dad said we needed to learn responsibility. As if working in the kennels wasn't enough. Worked in that damn kennel from six years old to—

Old enough.

Shadia left the tub area behind. Hastily. By the time she reached the spartan little office, she was full of anger. The way she liked it. Good cleansing anger, snarling that the very part of her *once-was* that had sent her on duster ways now had her trapped on Toklaat.

Nothing's permanent. See what you can see. Drift from station to planet to orbiter, grabbing catch-work rides and reveling in the newness of the next place until it got old, finding new friends when the old drifted away, your only true bond the very thing that would eventually drive you apart. Duster ways.

Still snarling, she found the paperwork that suggested she name the facility and directed her how to hire the assistants she was allowed—just enough help so she could sleep and acquire food and personal maintenance goods, for the pet care facility served all three shifts. There was a com-pin so she could be contacted by customers or assistants at any time, a cashchip for operating expenses, and an ID set. *Her* ID set.

Fast work.

Shadia picked it up, fumbling the slick bifold set. Employer information on one side, personal history on another, a large recent image of herself—source unknown to her— and a fourth side that sheened blankly but held all of the set's information and more in digital. She looked at the image. It showed her from the head up but somehow managed to capture her scrawniness beneath the patched duster's vest-over-coveralls she wore. Mementos covered the vest, from crew patches to a shiny bead made from a shell found only in a single place on a single planet. And they hung within her hair, an unimpressive dark blonde never given the opportunity to go sun-streaked, but long enough to hold beads and twists of woven goods. The tactile hair of a woman who encountered very few mirrors.

Her appearance clashed with the purple border around the image, the one that proclaimed her as a perm job worker. A purple border she'd never thought to see on her own ID set, not after being dragged into the duster's life while she was still young enough that her original ID lived in the back of her underwear drawer.

Dragged into it, maybe. But I embraced it. The very involuntary nature of my introduction to the life was a blessing, an event that taught me a duster's way is the only way. People think we're crazy, bouncing infinitely from station to station to planetside to station. Space dust. But in reality we're the wisest of them all. They count on their lives to continue as they know them. We admit up front that it'll never happen that way, and make the best of it.

The duster bar was easy to find from her new location; she'd been there often enough before she was hit by the zip-scoot. Like most stations, Toklaat was a glorified cylinder with travel tubes down the open axis, from north to south and back again, with east and west split according to function. East housed station maintenance and services; west housed the residences and personal services. Dusters worked the eastern station-side jobs, clung to station-side corners, slept in station-side nooks.

Now Shadia worked and lived in the west.

The duster bar, considered both a personal service and a duster accommodation, balanced on the border between east and west. With the com-pin tucked away in her vest pocket, a duster's ubiquitous utilities under the vest, and a small advance on her personal cashchip, Shadia stood at the edge of the bar nursing a featherdunk and considering her situation.

The pet-watching service came as a benefit to the elite on the station, so the station itself paid her salary, whether she had one pet on hand or twenty. Escalator clauses kicked in after ten of them, things like increased assistant hours, increased pay. . . .

Increased pay meant a quick debt reduction. A quick departure from this, a quick return to her own way of life.

"Out 'tending, are you?" said a growly alto voice in her ear. "Duster rig, all right—you take it off someone, 'tender? You someone's mag-bound little perm?"

Startled from her reverie, Shadia jerked around to discover herself flanked by two women whose musculature and vest pins marked them as cargo-loading dusters. Not a worry. Dusters left their own alone. "I'm no pretender."

Quick as that, one of them grabbed her arms, spilling her drink, while the other fished around inside Shadia's vest until a search of the many interior pockets offered success. The creditchip, the ID set. "Looks like your set to *me*," said the growly one. "Didn't anyone ever warn you that the only thing worse than a perm in a duster bar is a 'tender perm in a duster bar? Should've at least gotten a fake to proof your age."

Shadia kicked the woman who held her, a pointy-toed kick just below the knee. When the woman's grip fell away, Shadia snatched her ID set back, spitting a long string of blistering duster oaths. She didn't fight, she didn't get drunk, she didn't join the ranks of the dusters' practical jokers . . . but she had a vocabulary to make even a growly-voiced cargo loader blink. And while the one woman was blinking and the other was bent over her leg, Shadia snarled, "Med-debt. It's paid, I'm gone. Got it?" She turned her back on them and went back to her drink. They would have muttered apologies except that her turned back was a sign to be respected. Not a rudeness as the perms would have thought, but simply a gesture requesting privacy in a society where complete strangers made up a constantly shifting population. So they went away.

No one else bothered her.

But I didn't go back there. Because they were right. I might hate it, I might have been forced into it, but in the strictest sense, they were right. I was a perm in a duster bar . . . and elsewhere, a duster in perm ID. I just didn't intend to stay that way.

The smell was incredible.

"You're going to break down the 'fresher system again," Shadia told Feef the *akliat*, resigned to it. Each day, Feef arrived clinging to Claire Rowpin like a baby, deep blue eyes squinting fiercely against the morning sun. He might have been a cross between a three-toed sloth and a Chinese Crested Earth dog for all his appearance indicated—hairless with suedelike skin except for a poof of white powderpuff hair on the top of his head and a deep affinity for dark corners and high places. In spite of his slow and essentially sweet nature, he emitted the most astonishing odors under stress.

Feef. His owners, a couple named the Rowpins, had confessed to her upon first visit their intention to name the akliat *Fifi.* They hadn't—quite—gone through with it.

But despite their moment of weakness with the akliat's name, they clearly adored him. They gave her his favorite towel, hoping it would ease his stress, and they often called during the day to check on him. The other owners were much the same—loving their pets, checking on them, offering advice and expending worry.

As well they might. Of all the things that weren't permanent, pets topped the list. Shadia had known that even before she turned duster. But she didn't say anything, not to perms who would never understand anyway, people she would leave behind as soon as possible. She made the pets comfortable, read up on their various habits and habitats, and smiled at the owners who dropped them off each day. It brought her business; in some strange way the perms began to think of her as *their* duster.

Ugh.

Some of the animals gloried in their visits, with supervised playtime and more interaction than they'd get at home. Some were sullen and spent their time in hiding. They all had challenging habits that served them well enough in their own environments. Feef's odors were part of his communication system, although in the pet care facility they earned him a quiet and solitary room with high perches. The Jarlsens' *skitzcat* shed luxurious hair with mildly barbed tips intended to line its nest—Shadia made sure it had a private bedding area and invested in high-grade cleaning equipment. The roly-poly hamsterlike *rrhy* dripped scent-mucus wherever it went as a warning of its poisonous nature. And Gite the *tasglana*, who looked like nothing more than a flop-eared goat in extreme miniature, liked to sharpen its claws on everything and anything—or anyone—it could find. Shadia wore leather work chaps when Gite came to stay.

The work chaps belonged to the station-run business. But the plumy, feather-fronded houseplant in the entryway was hers. And along with her battered collapsible cup-bowl and pronged spoon, she also had a new plate and matte-finish steel mug.

As if I need those things. As if I need anything. How can I fit a plant into my duffel? Why did I even get it?

She'd liked it, that's why. She'd seen its pale soft fronds and she'd felt a tingle of pleasure and she'd smiled. She'd had the funds, and she'd seen it and liked it and bought it.

They can't make a perm of me. One set of coveralls on my back, one in the duffel, a toothcleaner and soap-pack and monthly supps. Whatever I can carry in the vest. That's all I'll ever need.

She wouldn't stay a single pay period longer than it took to pay off the med-debt. She'd take her experience—one more thing for her listings—and she'd take her inexpressible relief and she'd move on.

Too damn bad that zipscoot was going so fast when it hit me.

"Until they're *clean*," Shadia told the youthful first-jobber who had deluded himself into believing the pet room maintenance was completed. With a glare at the cleaner machine, he gave the handle a jerk and sullenly dragged it back into

Feef's unoccupied area. He'd been on the job a week and she was about to give him notice.

Toklaat's workers took so much for granted: that they could keep a job once they took it, no matter their performance; that they could find another. No matter their performance. Dusters knew to keep their records spotless for ease of transition from one situation to another. No one vouched for a careless worker, or digi-stamped their jobchips with the top rating that would draw that next good gig. Ever-imminent transitions kept them sharp.

Maybe she'd just start hiring dusters. If she could get the assistant's job listed as temp . . .

And why not, when she wasn't keeping most of the assistants beyond the time a duster would stay? Just one, a young woman named Amandajoy who loved the animals and applied herself to learning their routines with nearly Shadia's vigor. A more honest vigor, since Shadia used the work as a means to an end and Amandajoy did it for the work itself, although she was often too timid to act when she knew she should. Shadia could have loved the work, but didn't dare. She could have loved the memories it invoked, but didn't dare that either.

Those memories couldn't coexist with a duster's life, not and be cherished.

I don't have to think about that. Another few pay periods and I can turn this place over to Amandajoy, even if she doesn't know it yet. By then she'll have the confidence. She'll have to, even if she doesn't. That'll be a duster lesson for her. Never let the doubt show.

More airfreshener 'zymes in the rrhy-tub, that would probably help. Amandajoy must have had the same thought, for she emerged from the storage pantry with 'zyme packets in hand—

Shadia's world shifted. It looped in a strange manner her senses couldn't seem to perceive. She would have thought it was some unfathomable result of the zipscoot if her first jobber hadn't made a loud gurgle and dropped his cleaning equipment. As they all looked to one another for explanation, a series of hollow booming noises made the ground shake; the air fluttered in response. Shadia and Amandajoy clutched each other for the stability and ended up on the thickly carpeted floor anyway, gathering skitzcat hair.

For a moment there was silence. Then Gite bleated, leaping from the wire enclosure as the door slowly swung open on its own. He bounded out to land on them both, searching for a lap. Shadia winced as his claws dug in, automatically scooping his legs out from beneath him to place him on his back in his favored comfort position. Amandajoy looked like she wanted to climb right into Shadia's lap with him. "What was *that?*" she said, her eyes wide.

Shadia searched her duster experiences, years of different stations and different failures and accidents and emergencies, and then she searched her ten whole years on Belvia, all the time she'd had before she'd been snatched away.

I don't know. All those years, all those places . . . never anything like this. That's a duster's life, not knowing what's next, ready for anything. But I knew I wasn't ready for this.

Shadia shifted Gite from her arms to Amandajoy's. "Wait here," she said as the dwelling erupted into noisome protest—howls and chirps and screams and a few entirely new scents—though none as bad as the akliat's would have been. "Try to calm them." To the first jobber, she said, "Whatever Amandajoy says, you do."

"You're *leaving?*" Amandajoy's fear-widened eyes opened even further with surprise.

"You want an answer? Someone's got to go find it." Shadia climbed to her feet, not bothering to remove the Gite-defense chaps as she headed for the clearsteel door, her matter-of-fact brusqueness hiding her breathless fears.

She half expected to find the entrance lockdown engaged. Like all structures, this one had its own emergency air cleaner, its own independent—if finite—power supply. But the door slid smoothly aside for her, ejecting her out on the inner-ring walkway. Clearsteel lined that, too, separating her from the open station core.

But not blocking her view.

At first, all she saw was the movement. Down a few levels, center west; she had to push against the clearsteel, craning her neck against the arc of the inner ring and leaving smudges the autos would clean as soon as she moved away. Center west, location of the finest residences and normally the quietest slice of the station. Too far away to make out anything but the activity, and a wrongness so unexpected that she literally couldn't resolve what she was seeing into an image that made sense.

Nor did the alarms. The ones that had been going off for some time now. Not the screeching *you might die* breach alarms, but the swell-and-fade tones of the alarm that merely admitted something had happened, and if you paid attention the station techheads would eventually tell you what it was.

Except . . . in the distance, Shadia thought she heard shriller sounds. Harsher vicinity alarms, the ones that meant no breach, but if you were there to hear them, you might die anyway.

Or already be dead.

Duster reflexes kicked in, urging her to move off. The dusters knew all the safest nooks and crannies of a station— the structural strengths, the environmental neutral areas. She'd take the time to shout back into the shop and release Amandajoy and the first jobber from their duties here so they might secure the animals and follow if they wanted, but then she'd shed her shallowperm facade and take back the duster ways that had served her so well. Back to the east side.

At least until she understood what had happened. Until the skitter of fear along her spine eased and she trusted the disaster—whatever it was—wouldn't spread.

Wait a moment. Center west. The finest residences. The luxury residences. Half my clients live there. Gite's people. The Rowpins. They're perms . . . but they're nice *perms. Kind perms.*

Kind people.

Shadia's hand brushed over her vest, on which she'd recently sewn an exotic bit of weaving. Meant to be a small spot of wall decor, and acquired by Claire Rowpin on her latest off-station jaunt. She fingered the newest bead in her hair, something the rrhy's owner—a shy young man—had hesitantly offered, noticing her fondness for such things. Just something he'd had around the house, he'd said.

She'd doubted it.

She stuck her head back into the pet care facility, a building unidentifiable from the outside by anything other than a utilitarian number. "Something's happened in center west," she told Amandajoy, who'd succeeded in calming Gite enough to secure him in his den-cage. The starkly normal sounds of the cleaning machine emanated from Feef's room; Shadia nodded at it. "Let the 'jobber go home. You can go, too, if you want."

"Don't you want me to stay with the animals?" Amandajoy asked, torturing the corner of her work apron into a twisted knot.

Shadia couldn't answer right away; it wasn't the response she'd expected. After a moment she said, "Yes, I do. But it's up to you."

"I'll stay, then," Amandajoy said, not hesitating. "I don't want to leave them alone, and people might call in and get worried. But I want to turn on the gridnews. I know you think it bothers the animals sometimes, but—"

"Turn it on," Shadia said, and left. Heading for center west and not even sure why. All her instincts told her to run the other way, and all her habits warred with every step she took. Within moments—still true to duster ways in this, at least—she'd slipped down the maintenance poles few perms even knew existed and reentered the inner ring several levels below her own. New territory.

Chaos prevailed. Perms running away from the alarms, other perms running toward them. Perms crying and stark-faced and grim. Uniformed station personnel muttering into their inner wrist complants, one of whom she caught on the way by and said, "What's going on?"

"It's contained," she said, not even looking at Shadia, her eyes on some invisible goal . . . or maybe still seeing that from which she'd just come.

Shadia wouldn't be invisible. "*What?*"

Now the woman looked at her, swept her gaze up and down and took in Shadia's coveralls and vest. "Gravity generator surge," she said, clearly impatient. "The offending system is off-line—no more danger there. As if a duster would care. Just stay out of the way and you'll be fine."

As if—

Shadia jerked, stung, and then didn't know why she should be. By then the woman had moved on, pulling a flat PIM from her pocket to enter notations on the run. Shadia shouted after her, "Hey! I'm the one going in *this* direction."

Then again, why is that?

Shadia stopped short at the edge of the damaged area. She would have stopped short had the station uni not stood in front of his hastily erected low-tech barrier. She'd never imagined—

She *couldn't* have imagined—

Gravity generator surge.

Random lashings of unfathomable gravity, crumpling away the residences. Level after level, collapsed and twisted; she couldn't tell how deep it went, if it reached the next ring-hall or even went beyond. Narrow ribbons of damage spared some residences entirely, and destroyed others just as surely. Sullen, acrid smoke eased out of the wreckage, and Shadia pulled her loosely fitting coverall cuff past her hand and covered her mouth and nose.

There were other smells. Oils and coolants and hot metals, compressed beyond all tolerance. And a cacophony of sound—shouting and crying and orders and creaking, groaning structures. Someone jostled her; she barely noticed. She was too busy trying to orient herself, to find the residence ID numbers—but the chaos distracted her eyes, and she found nothing upon which to focus.

Until she glanced at the barrier, realized it was part of a residence. Her eyes widened at the number.

Not so very different from the Rowpins'.

The uni seemed to notice her then. The expression on her face, maybe. He swept his gaze over her much as the woman had done . . . and then it softened. "You know someone here?"

Behind him, there was a sudden flurry of alarm, shouted warnings; a chunk of a residence broke away and tipped off into the exposed core, falling in what seemed like slow motion. Shadia flinched at the hollow boom of its landing; they both did. And then she whispered, "I think so."

It wasn't loud enough to be heard over the noise, not even though the alarm cut off in the middle of her words. He seemed to understand anyway. "I can't let you through. Only unis."

Official hover scooters flashed through the core, strobing ident lights. Already starting to clear the debris. Towing things.

Stretchers, mainly.

Shadia puzzled in blank lack of understanding, knowing that any victims were more likely to come out in a bucket than on a stretcher. The long-coated uni saw that, too, and edged a little closer to her, like a confidant. "The edge zones," he said, gesturing. "The parts damaged by the *damage*, and not the gravity. You see?"

She saw. Unable to go forward, unable to leave, she waited and watched, an anomalous quiet spot in a brownian motion of perms and destruction. Trying to discern just where the Rowpins had lived, and to figure out if they'd had enough time after picking up Feef to make it back home. Listening to people around her recount the moments of the disaster—what they'd seen and what they'd heard and how they thought it might have been. Watching them pitch in as the rare survivor stumbled out of the edges of the damage, and as they pushed past the barriers, climbing into the wreckage and joining the unis as they tossed bits and pieces of what had been homes into the core net now strung below them for just that purpose.

Go back to the facility, Shadia Duster. You don't belong here. This is just one more story to take with you along the way. Walk away, finish out what little time you have left before the med-debt's gone, and then board the first ship you come to.

Except she didn't. She couldn't ease around the uni; her coveralls were far too conspicuous. But she couldn't go. She asked perm after perm if they knew where the Rowpins' address would have put their home, and she asked if anyone had seen them—or rather, she asked if they'd seen Feef, who would have made more of an impression than just another person in the bustle. She made herself useful on this side of the barrier, distracting the uni when another perm needed to slip by. When a handful of people came with warm drinks and what must have been their entire month's ration of treat bars, she knew who'd been working the longest and most needed the boost.

And when someone spotted the dangling pale tan arm amidst the edge wreckage, several levels up and with the inner ring destroyed between here and there, she knew how to get there. She glanced at the uni, who quite deliberately looked the other way, and then she slipped past the barrier to the half-height tech access door recessed invisibly into the slightly skewed wall, the seams not evident until released with the right touch in the right spot.

She led them into the tight darkness.

They murmured uneasily behind her, following at a slower pace so when she emerged into the maintenance shaft and flicked the control to release the stepholds folded into the pole for upward transit, she still had a moment to wait. They'd never been in such tunnels; their uneasy voices rang louder than they'd ever guess. They worried about the obvious warping in the walls, they murmured about the motionless arm they'd seen . . . and they wondered about her.

It's only fair. I'm wondering about them.

Who were these people, following her into the unknown for the sake of someone equally unknown? Who were any of them, defying unis to work among the wreckage of the neighborhood? Clustering around the dangers instead of running away as any duster would do? *Take nothing for granted and take what you can get,* one of the common duster phrases. One would say it, and all others within earshot would finish with the chorus of *And then move on!*

It's only fair. I'm wondering about me.

Shadia moved on, all right. She waited for the first tentative head to poke out of the half-height tunnel and she started climbing the pole. She took them up two levels and stepped off onto the platform . . . and then, remembering the layout of the wreckage they'd seen, took them farther into the structure, through an even smaller access hatch until they were just about to balk—and then she clambered out into the wreckage itself. So close to the edge, where it tumbled straight out into the core. The floor beneath her feet seemed to give a little quiver when the second person came out, and when the third appeared, there was no doubt.

The third was the uni. He gave her a guileless smile—and he bent down to instruct the others to wait. "It's not secure," he told them. "You shouldn't be here."

None of them should be here. And yet here they were.

"Found someone!" the second person, a woman in an expensive work suit from which she'd already ripped the frills so they wouldn't get in her way. Her voice held a vibration of excitement that made her next words seem lifeless. "No. Never mind. We're too late."

The uni joined her as Shadia inched around the wreckage; a fourth person eased out into the open and began to cast around, hunting the owner of the elusively dangling arm. What had seemed so obvious from below was hardly that from amidst the tangle of walls and upholstery and crushed electronics.

"Good Lord, what's that *smell?*" exclaimed the man who'd just joined them; his hand covered his nose and mouth, but from what remained of his expression, it had done no good. The woman caught a whiff of the odor as well, and was the first to spot the source.

"There!" she said, flinging up a hand to point. "*That.*"

That. Cowering into the smallest possible bundle in the only dark, intact corner left in the residence—the upper tier of a closet, it looked like—was a mostly hairless slothlike

creature. The crumpled remains of a den-cage, barely recog-
nizable, were not far away.

Aw, ties and chains. The Rowpins. And Feef, their
survivor.

She must have said some part of it out loud; the others
glanced at her. Then the uni said, "I found a second one,"
and the tone of his voice was clear enough. Too late. Both
dead.

"That's all there is," Shadia said, her voice very small as
it fought to get out of her throat. *Nothing's permanent.*

The uni looked at her, somber. "These are the people you
were asking about when you first came."

Shadia nodded.

He gave a little nod back at her, a small gesture that
shouldn't have made her feel as it did . . . as though she
were part of something. Something bigger than she was or
he was . . . bigger than all of them. She frowned, caught in
the moment.

"Go on back down," the uni told those people still waiting in the tunnel. Waiting to help . . . except no one here
needed it. "There'll be crews here to deal with . . . what
we've found." The flooring gave a decisive tremble beneath
them, and his voice grew crisp. "Go on, then. We'll get their
animal and be right after you."

They meant well.

They cooed and they called, unable to reach the akliat
through the rubble, wanting badly to preserve this creature
belonging to those people they *hadn't* been able to save. But
the flooring gave a wicked shudder and Feef's odor-signals
only grew more intensely offensive. A gridnews hovercam
floated past, stopped short, and wandered into the destruction, wavering slightly in midair as it soaked up the scene
for its operators. Shadia, retreated to familiar duster ways—
nothing's permanent—eased back toward her escape. It was
all too much, this *joining in,* this *caring* . . . she'd learned the

lesson once as a child and learned it well. She hadn't thought she'd be learning it again, that she'd been foolish enough to let herself care about these people who loved their akliat.

He was a disturbed old ex-duster. I didn't do any-thing besides bring him a few meals, sneak out some of the family's old clothing and once a pillow. An old ex-duster who wanted to return the kindness, to save me from the misleading perm ways of my family. I under-stood that later. And in a way I suppose he did. When he took me away from all I knew, it was the strongest lesson I ever could have learned. Nothing is forever. Things change, whenever and wherever. So embrace the change. No ties, no extended responsibilities to oth-ers, nothing to lose. Dive into the change and ride it like a wave.

The uni shouted a warning; a huge chunk of flooring broke away and tumbled down the levels, leaving the others scrambling for safety while Shadia clutched the edge of the maintenance shaft. Time to leave.

"That's it, people," the uni said. "He's not coming to us. I wish there were something we could do, but—"

"Give me your uni coat," Shadia said abruptly.

He gave her a baffled, resistant look, one arm raised to usher the other two back toward the shaft.

Shadia stepped away from it. "Your coat," she insisted. The man and woman hesitated by the exit, watching them. "You want to save the akliat? Hand it over!"

Still baffled, less resistant, he peeled it off and passed it to her, a long, dark tailored thing that smelled of sweat and stress and physical labor. Shadia tented the collar over her head, put her hands halfway up the sleeves that were way too long for her anyway, and turned the coat into a draping cloak, turned her upraised arms into cave-enclosed branches. She didn't have to warn the others to hush; they'd done so on their own, letting their hopes burst through to their faces.

Shadia raised her arms a little higher within her self-imposed cave and gave one of the casual little chirrups she'd often heard from Feef. A long trill with a few clucks at the end, a soft repetition . . .

He sprang from his corner, scuttled across the rubble, and climbed her like the nighttime tree she pretended to be. Fast enough to make them all gasp. And then she steeled herself for the stench of him . . . but the stench had transformed to perfume, a crisp pervading caress of a scent; his soft, suede-skin arms clung to her not with fierce intent, but gentle trust. Slowly, filled with a sweetness she could just barely remember, she let the coat slide down to her shoulders and closed it around the two of them.

They clapped for her. The man, the woman, the uni . . . the people several levels below on the first intact inner ring, watching it broadcast on their PIM gridviews. She met the grin of the uni with a surprised gaze, and he nodded at the maintenance shaft. "Go."

The others went. And Shadia turned to follow, awkward under the burden of coat and akliat, in wavering midstep when the uni shouted and the grid-watching crowd gave a collective gasp of horror. She saw it from the corner of her eye, the bulk of falling debris, its screech of metal against metal as it bounced once on the way down.

She'd never get out of the way. Not in time. Dusterlike, she was ready for that . . . except within her whispered a long-forgotten child's voice, something that treasured the newly rediscovered sweetness in life and didn't want to give it up again so soon. . . .

Something hit her hard. She twisted, trying to cushion the akliat even as she protected him, and all the while he exuded his scent of trust. A horrible crash buffeted her with sound and everything went dark, dark with a great heavy weight upon her.

She waited for the pain.

"Close one, eh?" said the uni's voice in her ear. "Come on, then. You're the one that knows the way, I think. Let's get you and your new friend out of here."

I don't understand. He could have been killed. He doesn't even know me, doesn't have any of a perm's affection for those they keep around them.

I don't understand.

She led him through the darkness and back to the dimly lit pole shaft. She did it in silence, moving carefully to protect Feef, moving slowly to accommodate the tremble in her limbs. When they reached the level they'd come from, he put a hand on his own coat and stopped her before she remembered that dusters didn't like to be touched by strangers, and *everyone* was a stranger.

"I work the duster turf, mainly," he said, and his voice held an understanding she'd never heard before. "Never yet met one who hadn't already lost too much to listen, but you . . ."

She looked at him, going wary. Feef snuggled against her and before she could stop herself, she stroked the absurd fluff of his topknot where it poked out at her neck.

The uni gave the smallest of smiles. "It's worth a try," he said. "This is it: we're not so dim as you dusters think, perms aren't. Most of us aren't fooled into thinking what we have is forever, whether what we have is a little or a lot. Things come and go . . . we just . . . we take 'em in as we can instead of skipping across the surface of life like so much space dust. Sure, we lose things, and then it hurts. It's just . . ." He shrugged, coming to the end of his little speech and apparently not quite sure what to do with it. "It's just that—it gives us—"

She thought of people rushing to help strangers and other strangers cheering her success with Feef and yet other strangers who mourned. Perm strangers, who somehow weren't really strangers at all, not as dusters defined them. Perms left themselves open and vulnerable to the hurt and disillusion that dusters scorned, but . . .

"You could have been killed," she said. Killed, tackling her to take them both flying into their only safety instead of diving there himself, a certain save.

"Yes," he admitted.

"A duster wouldn't have done it."

"No. A duster wouldn't."

"You leave yourself open to lose things," she said, and looked down at her hand a moment. Then, gently, more naturally than she'd have thought possible, she offered it to him. A perm gesture. "But it gives you this."

His uncertain expression made way for a smile. It cracked the dust on his face and crinkled the corners of his reddened, irritated eyes. He looked terrible, and he looked wonderful. "Yes," he said, taking her hand. Only for the briefest moment. Then he coughed and said rather brusquely, "Let's get you and your new friend home, then."

Feef's House. *Sounds like a good name for a pet care center.*

*　　*　　*

*After obtaining a degree in wildlife illustration and environmental education, Doranna Durgin spent a number of years deep in the Appalachian Mountains, riding the trails and writing SF and fantasy books (*__Dun Lady's Jess__*, __Wolverine's Daughter__, __Seer's Blood__, __A Feral Darkness__), ten of which have hit the shelves so far. She's moved on to the northern Arizona mountains, where she still writes and* *rides. There's a Lipizzan in her backyard, a mountain looming outside her office window, a pack of dogs romping in the house, and a laptop sitting on her desk—and that's just the way she likes it. You can find a complete list of her books at <http://www.doranna.net/>, along with scoops on new projects (and of course, tidbits about the four-legged kids).*

ATTACHED PLEASE FIND MY NOVEL

by Sean P. Fodera

ASSISTANT EDITOR SOUGHT

The well-known and respected publishing house K&T
Publishers has an immediate opening for an assistant editor. The successful applicant will not only have outstand-
ing academic and practical credentials, but will also be
thoroughly familiar with our current and past list of authors. A commitment to quality, a willingness to take on
disparate tasks, and the ability to work under tight dead-
lines are essential.

Send resumé and references via ColNet to K&T Publishers, 16 Elray Circle, Landfall, Christea

<dbra.ktp.chr.ColNet>
Mr. Del Bradden
Science Fiction Editor
K&T Publishers
16 Elray Circle
Landfall CHRISTEA

Dear Mr. Bradden:

Attached please find my novel *Beyond Here* for your consideration. It is a science fiction novel, 270 refrains long. I
have read the books published by K&T Publishers since arriving on Christea, and most enjoy the works of this kind
that you have published. I hope I have captured the format
properly.

Please listen to my novel, and be honest in your opinion.

Please do not reply to this message, as this account will no
longer be active after today. I will contact you in one week
with a private ColNet address for further communications.

Sincerely,
"Dr" Aly'wanshus
Christea Collegium
Office of Alien Studies

<File Attachment: BeyondHere.lyr>

THERE you have the letter that started it all. Simple. For-
mulaic, for the most part—"here's my book; I like the
books you publish; read mine and get back to me." Even if
it hadn't made me curious, I would have read it anyway.
That was my job.

I had to admit this was a new approach for a submission.
From an academic, obviously. Probably one about to lose
his job, or move to another collegium; hence his expiring
EdNet address. But 270 *refrains?* And an audio file? Unless
he was trying to recapture the days of the bards and min-
strels with an epic sf poem, I didn't know what to expect.

But this "Dr." Aly'wanshus' mysterious approach had
doubly caught my attention, as science fiction was my pet
project at K&T. Hardly anyone was writing science fiction
at the time; an understandable turn of events on a colony
world where nearly everyone's parent or grandparent had
been among the first humans to arrive. Even the people back
on Earth ("Homers" in colony slang) now perceived folks
from "outer space" as being no more distant than someone
half a globe away, though those of us who had made the trip
once or twice could tell them it was a bit farther. Still, there
was enough life left in my favorite genre to warrant the re-
discovery of works from the pre-colonial days, and the pub-

lication of novels by a handful of young colonial writers dreaming about faster-than-light fighters and space battles.

I'd read lots of junk during the year-and-change since I'd begun K&T Publishers' open-door policy on submissions. It was a simple enough policy, if unique on Christea and the other colony worlds. We would review any booktext sent to us, from anyone.

Actually, every 'text that came in was personally read by yours truly, Del Bradden, searching for a winner. I was only an assistant editor, working for Mr. Cyril Burke, our executive editor, but I had found a terrific one just a year before "Dr." Aly'wanshus sent me his message: Jeremy Raschon's *Starseeker*. The fifth best-selling novel on ColNet that year, and the best-selling novel in K&T's seventy-two-year history. If I hadn't found *Starseeker*, I doubt we would have retained the policy so long.

There were, at the time, only the original eight colony worlds: Christea (though we weren't the first), Almedia, Kuron, Wales, Jerral, New Rome, Beacon, and Hurst. Broadbent and Leeside had only just been discovered, and were not yet settled.

And among these worlds, there were seven colonial publishers: two on Christea; none on Wales or Beacon. Competition was fierce. A small number of Earth academics took notice of our literary output, but not in significant numbers. Colonial publications just didn't show good sales on SolNet. We were basically limited to ColNet.

We had a total potential audience of approximately seventeen million. Most of those were on the heavily populated worlds of Kuron, Christea, and Almedia ("heavily" is a relative term, as Kuron, the most crowded, had just under five million people). The rest were on the more recently settled worlds—"provincials" with little interest in general fiction (erotica and tech manuals were the top sellers on Beacon, Wales, and Jerral).

The other publishers required writers to send their 'texts through a licensed Mediator. Earth's government was smart when it started licensing mediators . . . "agents" as they used to be known. Since almost every human ever born probably fancies himself a writer at some time in his life, the population explosion on Earth in the late 2000s also caused an explosion in would-be authors. Agents already had a lock on the market, as any file submitted to a publisher that didn't come from a recognized agent would be automatically rejected by the comp system.

So agents started proliferating. And the government noticed. "Hey," someone in the Hague said, "these literary agents are becoming as powerful as the lawyers used to be. Time for them to be licensed." Vote-stamp-sign: Agents with licenses become government-sanctioned mediators. Unlicensed agents find other jobs. And the government starts getting a cut of the mediator's third of the author's earnings.

"A third?" you ask. Of course they're entitled to a third. They're licensed mediators, so they must be worth it. After all, they perform the mysterious task of popping the book-text into NetMail. It wasn't as if just anyone could do it for themselves—remember, only a recognized mediator could get a 'text through the system. Personally, I think if Shakespeare had an agent/mediator, that line about the lawyers would have read differently.

Despite the absurdity of such procedures, I am still glad to have discovered this profession, of which few colonists are even aware. I owe it all to my unique family and education. The colonies only have a handful of small collegia, which just don't rate with the big Earth universities. However, everyone in the colonies has a degree or two, since it's easy to advance one's education by completing coursework on EdNet. No need to even physically attend a collegium, though that gives a deeper experience to the education.

My father always hated that the colonies are so far from

Earth, making true interactive Net services almost impossible—time lag, you know. Despite the fact that we could get large transport ships jumped up faster-than-light, no one had managed to get the nets to clear that hurdle. Homers had the option of using EdNet in realtime, or actually attending one of their prestigious universities.

Thankfully, Dad is a brilliant man. One day, while teaching his physics class at the collegium, and using a NetPedia reference on screen, he had a *Eureka!* moment. Well . . . it actually took him a few more years to make Packet-Comm a reality. But, when he'd finished, it was possible to communicate with Earth, or other far-flung locations, instantly. Okay, so there's a three-second lag to Earth.

Suddenly EdNet, BuyNet, and the other NetServs were practical for the colonists. And Dad was (and still is) collecting licensing and royalty chits nonstop; a good portion of which go back into public works. On the colonies, the name Randall Bradden is always spoken in admiring tones.

When I came of age, he told me: "Del, you're going to Earth to attend university in person. Let all those EdNet grads pay for a real education for you."

So off I went. I studied Literature as my Primary, with a Secondary in Business and Finance, and a Tertiary in the Sciences (Dad needed to get his chits' worth.) But I have the best implants money can buy, so it wasn't too difficult.

While there, I took an internship at a venerable old publishing house. They actually maintained offices with staff. No telecommutes for them, except one executive editor.

During my time at Holburn House, I learned a lot. And really fell in love with the business. I knew I'd be applying to one of the colonial publishers when I went home. There was no question of my staying on Earth—my student permit would expire, and they'd be sending me back to the colonies. Besides, Christea was home.

So . . . how did that internship lead to K&T deciding to shrug at the system and become so writer-friendly?

Well, I take full credit for it. There is even an archive recording of the moment I got the idea, though I wasn't the center of the cams' attention that day.

During my internship, there was a retirement party for Mr. Malcolm Ramos. All 234 years' worth of him. One of the most distinguished editors in the business. He could easily have become a mediator at any time in his career, but he just loved editing.

At the party, he gave a talk about how the industry had changed during his career.

"When I came to this house in 2047," Mr. Ramos recounted, "we had an open-door policy on booktexts. The last year of it, mind you, but *anyone* could submit to us.

"The Web, as SolNet was called then, led to so many would-be authors finding us and submitting, we just couldn't keep on top of it." He chuckled. "Eight billion people on Earth in those days, and most of them submitted to us that year."

My instincts told me he was exaggerating, but I had little personal experience with bicentenarians. We colonials shy away from age-defying treatments—a normal 125 always seemed a sufficiently lengthy life to most of us. But I was intrigued.

As he sipped from his water glass, I called up to the dais, "Did you find anything worthwhile?"

"Oh, yes. We developed two eTimes Bestsellers out of that batch. One of them only made it to number fifty on the list, but that was high enough for bragging rights." Mr. Ramos raised his forefinger with a smile. "And we found a handful of midlist titles—the stuff you call 'fill' these days.

"You know," he continued, "there could have been more good stuff in there, but there were just too many submissions coming in. If only there had been fewer people in the pool, we could have read a lot more before we gave up."

He spoke quite a bit more—some interesting, some rambling, some downright incomprehensible—and you can view the archive recording for the rest, if you want. But that little bit had already hatched the idea in my head.

I returned to Christea with my degrees, and sent employment queries to several publishers. Only K&T was hiring for an actual in-office job, as I'd had at Holburn, and was satisfyingly Christean, so I took the position. Del Bradden became the newest assistant editor (in-person degrees and internships actually do mean something on a resumé—no starting as an editorial assistant for me).

I established myself and learned more about the company. Not wanting to seem too eager or eccentric, I waited through three personnel reviews (all stellar, I might add) before presenting my idea to Mr. Burke.

"An odd request, Del," Mr. Burke commented when I asked to be allowed to open things up to un-mediated 'texts. Thankfully, he was first-generation Christean, like my father, and still thought like a pioneer. To make the idea more appealing, I offered to do the reading on my own time (though I'd be compensated if I actually found anything publishable). It was agreed.

A subroutine was written into our sorting algorithm. Un-mediated 'texts would be sent to my comp for review, rather than rejected outright. And we quietly started letting people know they could submit to us this way, though I still received my usual share of mediated works for reading at the office.

The mediators weren't thrilled by our new policy, and threatened to stop submitting, but as we were a small Christean house, it was a useless threat. A few mediators made a point of telling us that certain top titles *would* have come to

K&T if not for our policy, but Mr. Burke knew better. He made a point of reading each one of those, and was convinced he wouldn't have published them anyway.

Luckily for me, Mr. Ramos had been correct about the pool size. Most Christeans are still pretty much your rugged pioneer types rather than would-be authors. So we weren't inundated with Christean 'texts.

Once we published Raschon's *Starseeker* and my project was better publicized, submissions from the other colonies increased. Nothing from Earth, but what Homer would want to be published by a colonial?

I opened the file attached to "Dr." Aly'wanshus' message, and settled back to listen to the good doc's novel.

The most amazing sound issued from my speakers. It wasn't amazing in that it was sweet and melodic like no music could ever be. Nor could I say I'd never heard its like before, because I certainly had. I'd heard it while taking a history course at university; a course that covered the discovery of each of the colony worlds and included audio/visual details of the few alien races we had encountered.

This was the sound of the speaking voice of an Aaul'inah.

The Aaul'inah are a secretive race. The exploration ship *Chicago* had discovered the planet Aaul'in, which lies not far from the mid-colonies. But they were turned away by the Aaul'inah when they tried to enter the atmosphere. No human has landed there since.

We did manage to finally communicate with them, after a small Aaul'inah ship crashed on Hurst while scouting the colony. The one survivor had a translation device with which they were monitoring our communications. We managed to reverse-engineer it, and could finally speak with them—not perfectly, but sufficiently.

Theirs is a flowing, tonal language, that sounds much like musical instruments. And it has a musical structure to it that goes beyond anything humans can produce. I'm told linguists believe that the language hides many layers of meaning in the subaudible bands that we cannot comprehend.

Whatever else, it is exceedingly beautiful to the human ear.

I stopped the playback, and looked back at the query. "Office of Alien Studies." I recalled my father telling me a few years before that the collegium had been thinking about offering a position to an Aaul'inah, but didn't recall him saying that it had happened.

I clicked over to the collegium's linguistics bank, and linked myself into the Aaul'inah translation matrix. Then, I opened the file again, experiencing a brief pause while the files connected.

When the story began, I was initially distracted by how the translation matrix took what was essentially a grand operatic performance and turned it into a piece of prose. Wonderful prose that would still need some small editing to be publishable in English.

That quickly became a secondary thought, because what I was hearing was the most fantastic story of interdimensional adventure I had ever come across in my short lifetime of reading and publishing science fiction.

The next nine days were agony.

I'd asked my father to check on "Dr." Aly'wanshus for me. All he reported was that Alien Studies had offered to sponsor an exchange program with Aaul'in. When the reply came, this "Doctor" said that his people would never agree to permit a human on their world. However, he would come to Christea in a personal research effort to see if his people could coexist and intermingle with humans. He had apparently arrived two years ago.

Finally, the second message arrived.

<dbra.ktp.chr.ColNet>
Mr. Del Bradden

Science Fiction Editor
K&T Publishers
16 Elray Circle
Landfall CHRISTEA

Dear Mr. Bradden:

I hope you have had time to listen to my novel. I look forward to hearing your response. Please contact me within the next three days at vjin.pse.chr.ColNet.

Sincerely,
"Dr." Aly'wanshus

I was hitting the reply key before I'd even finished reading the first sentence.

<vjin.pse.chr.ColNet>
"Dr." Aly'wanshus

Dear "Dr." Aly'wanshus:

I am very pleased that you have contacted me again. I have, in fact, listened to your novel. It is quite unique in my experience, and I would very much like to meet with you to discuss it. Would you be free to meet with me at my office tomorrow?

I greatly look forward to hearing from you.

Sincerely,
Del Bradden

The reply came back just as swiftly.

Dear Mr. Bradden:

It would not be prudent for us to meet where others might easily observe us. Can we please meet tomorrow in the rooms where

I am lodging? Perhaps about 1100 hours. The proprietor here is a discreet woman. Directions are attached.

Sincerely,
"Dr." Aly'wanshus

<File Attachment: Direct.scr>

Ever mysterious. But not a meeting I wanted to decline.

I arrived at the boarding house near the Landing Ground a few minutes early. It was the usual sort of place where travelers could settle in for a day or two before catching their ship. Quaint yet pleasant.

The door was open, but I knocked and entered when a voice told me to do so.

There was a small desk in the corner of the parlor just off the entry hall, and the woman there appeared to be shopping BuyNet for towels. She looked up at me.

"You must be here to meet the Doctor," she stated.

"How'd you know?" I asked with a smile.

"No bags. Not dressed for travel." She smiled, "And he left me a note that he was expecting a visitor about now. His room is the third on the left, top of the stairs." She turned back to her comp.

I started toward the stairs.

"May I ask you something?"

I stopped and turned. "Sure."

She looked uncertain. "Normally, I don't concern myself with the affairs of my guests—they don't stay long enough. I get all types, including some nonhumans. But . . . the Doctor's a singer. I'd always thought they don't like us much. But he's been perfectly pleasant, polite, and quiet. He seems different than I've been led to believe. Do you know why?"

She wouldn't have been satisfied with the simple "No"

that almost came from my lips. And being rather ignorant on the matter myself, all I could do was reassure her and hope I wasn't wrong. "I can't really say. This is our first meeting. I know he's an academic, and I don't think he's up to anything nefarious."

She smiled again. "Thank you. I've always gone by my own experience—not judging things based on other folks' say-so. If the other singers are like him, they'll be welcome in my house." And she turned back to the comp.

I went up the stairs, found the door, and knocked.

A voice called out, "Come in, please, Mr. Bradden."

I opened the door, and met my first Aaul'inah. I had learned somewhat about them at university and also done some refresher reading in the last week. So I wasn't too surprised to find that "Dr." Aly'wanshus was pretty much a textbook example of the Aaul'inah.

He stood about five and a half feet tall and was covered from top to bottom by a tan-colored pelt that wasn't quite fur or quite feathers. His eyes were set to the sides of a wide nasal passage, and appeared to operate independently of one another, much like Earth chameleons. His lips were fleshy, and the upper hung down over his mouth when he wasn't speaking. His arms and legs appeared to be slightly shorter than ours, but I knew the joints were far more supple than my own.

The Doctor held out a six-fingered hand and grasped my own in a hearty handshake. "Welcome to my rooms. I am so thrilled to have you here." His voice was fluid and clear, and seemed to have little trouble with the English words. There remained an undertone of music, even when not speaking his own language.

The handshake ended, long enough to express eagerness, short enough to prove he understood when to stop.

"A pleasure to finally meet you, 'Doctor' Aly'wanshus." I stated honestly.

He, for lack of a better word, smiled. "I'll not trouble you with the proper pronunciation, Mr. Bradden. Please have a seat."

Thanking him, I took the offered seat. I noticed as he took the one opposite that the motion seemed at once both graceful and awkward for him. No doubt the result of some time accustoming himself to human furniture.

"I notice you hesitate when you say my title. One can almost hear the quotation marks from my message around it. You wonder, perhaps, why they appear there?" He appeared quite relaxed and comfortable with me.

While I was nervous at meeting my first Aaul'inah, professional and personal curiosity overwhelmed that. I nodded. "I did wonder."

Again, that smile. "Quite understandable. Although I am not a medical doctor, nor do I have any advanced degrees from a human collegium, that is the nearest title your language has to express my position in my culture." The smile seemed to dim.

"The nearest, but not exact, yes?" I asked. "Should we be using some more prestigious title for you?"

The smile faded. "No, 'Doctor' is fine. As you will learn, I hold two positions in my society. Being an educator is my chosen life's work. But there is another more difficult task that I must undertake."

His voice and manner changed, becoming more forceful. "Mr. Bradden, I have read or listened to a great deal of human literature. Of all I have read, the science fiction stories you published attracted me the most. Explorers going out beyond their own known universe, seeking whatever is out there for good or ill. Those stories spoke to me—made me realize that I was doing something similar. I felt this story, *Beyond Here,* waiting to come out. As one of my kind who desires contact with humans, the title is somewhat meaningful to me. And so I dictated it. As my time at the collegium drew to a close, I decided to submit my work to you."

I was puzzled. "I'm not so familiar with your people. Is your book somehow related to this 'task' you mentioned?"

"No. And yes, I suppose," he responded, suddenly revealing four small budlike ears that erupted from the pelt at the sides of his head. "But I will get to that. Your language is quite simple, compared to our own, and I learned the spoken and written forms quickly. But, for me, it was only natural to dictate my book in my own language. And I am quite happy to have your attention. It is my situation that constantly reasserts itself in my mind, distracting me from our literary discussion."

"Your situation?"

He gave a quick birdlike nod. "I should like to explain. I assume you have the usual human familiarity with my people? Basic external physiology? General language sonotype?"

"Yes."

His ears settled back a bit as he began to tap his cheek with one finger. In a human, I could have taken it for thoughtfulness or nervousness; in him, I had no idea.

"Before we discuss my novel—and I am very interested to hear from you on that—I am going to tell you something about my people. I will hope that you are as trustworthy and discreet as Randall."

I couldn't help myself. I blurted out, "My father! You know my father?"

His smile returned. "Yes. And from your reaction, I know now that he *has* been trustworthy and discreet. We met at the collegium, but I will tell you more of that shortly. I only ask that you permit me to finish what I have to say before asking any questions."

If his novel wasn't enough to make me adhere to his request—and I assure you it was—Dr. Aly'wanshus of Aaul'in had a willingly captive audience now.

He began:

"My people have believed for many millennia that we were alone in the universe. In truth, we have never even contemplated the existence of other beings or systems beyond our own. Unlike humans, who have long had a tradition of literature that speculates about other life and worlds, we have no literature of the fantastic—no true literature at all. Writing is limited strictly to religious purposes for recording certain important events.

"Believing ourselves the only intelligent life in the universe, we have developed a philosophy of life, a religion, if you will. We have always believed that the universe *is* a deity—the *Unali'wahnah*. Everything in the universe, which we believed consisted of only the few planets of our solar system, our two moons and sun, make up the physical being of *Unali'wahnah*.

"We believe that we, the *Aaul'inah*, are the very mind of *Unali'wahnah*. As though each of us is one 'brain cell' of It. Thus, every action we take, every statement we make, every interaction we conduct, is a function of the thoughts of *Unali'wahnah*. This is why, were you to visit our world, you would see that most things are quite peaceful, orderly, and deliberate. After all, who would wish to disrupt the thoughts of a god?

"And so it was for countless millennia . . . until your ship came.

"We had developed technology, as innovation is seen as the maturing of *Unali'wahnah*. One of our advances was space travel. Some two hundred or so of your years ago, it was decided by our leadership council that we would reach out to the moons, for as part of *Unali'wahnah*'s mind, the Aaul'inah should have a presence there. And so it was that we had ships to turn the *Chicago* away.

"It was fear that made us do so. Genuine, all-encompassing fear. Suddenly, after so long alone, another part of *Unali'wahnah*—a part that should not exist—had come to us. And when we sent it away, it left and didn't come back. As the action of the mind of *Unali'wahnah*, our people should have automatically perceived this as a correct action. But, there was concern that we might have mistakenly denied *Unali'wahnah* another part of Its maturation.

"We had the capability of tracking this mysterious visitor, for we had long ago developed the technology to look out across *Unali'wahnah*, though we had apparently never looked in the proper direction to discover your kind. By tracking the *Chicago,* we discovered that there were other worlds, with living beings on them.

"Our leaders debated among themselves in closed council sessions for many years, and finally determined to officially ignore your existence. But, secretly, scouts were sent out, and we monitored your transmissions and nets. You may have discovered the scout on Hurst, but many others have monitored your colonies for a long time.

"Then, not only were our leaders and space teams aware of you, but our population became aware as well. For your people began to transmit messages to our planet, in a crude version of our language. Our leaders tried to deny your existence, saying that the transmissions were a garbled test of a new communications system for the moon bases. But it was too late.

"My colleagues and I are determined to discover the truth about your people. We knew the truth of your existence because we are the hereditary heirs to seats on the council. Our parents were obligated to keep us informed, should any of us need to succeed them on short notice. Obviously, we were forbidden from telling others about you.

"I am the senior member of the group. I will be the first of the 'new thinkers' to join the council, but we will not have a significant number of like-minded councillors for many years yet. In any event, it will be a difficult and lengthy process to get our people to recognize you in any substantial way. That is the daunting task that looms before me.

"Although we are expected to replace our parents at the appropriate time, we must also have an occupation until that time. I wished to be an educator, and was assigned to educate young adult Aaul'inah in space sciences. Such is my claim to the human title 'Doctor' or 'Professor.'

"When the transmission came from the collegium inviting us to exchange personnel, it was summarily dismissed by the council. But I knew of it and had the means to reply. So I secretly managed to leave our world and came to your collegium.

"Your father was among those with whom I worked. He is a brilliant physicist and he taught me much about the unseen universe, as well as how to improve communications between our planets.

"I sent you my novel both because your father spoke so highly of you, and because of my admiration for the books you have edited. I suppose I wanted to see if my effort was worthy of your attention. At the very least, it pleases me to have met both of the Bradden men—the man of science and the man of letters.

"My ship leaves in two days, and I will be essentially stranded on Aaul'in for many years. The time draws near for me to succeed my mother on the council. I must return home and discover whether my original excuse for this absence is still acceptable to my parents. If I am successful, I will take my seat on the council and begin to strive for open relations between our peoples.

"If I am unsuccessful, I will face the penalty for disobeying the orders of the council. I will spend the rest of my life in solitude; cut off from my people; unable to take my part in the mind of *Unali'wahnah*."

He didn't settle back into his chair, as a human who'd finished telling a story would, but the finger tapping stopped. It suddenly occurred to me that he'd been tapping to keep musical time while making such a lengthy speech in a foreign language—like a metronome with an odd timing I couldn't quite follow.

"This is certainly different from how I'd thought this meeting might go," I said.

He laughed a strong, hearty, musical laugh. "I don't suppose it is like anything I anticipated two years ago either. When I came here, I had no idea what to expect. And I have tried to repay the things I have learned with the many things I have taught my colleagues at the collegium, and the little I've shared with you today."

Now he sat forward, and it was obvious our species shared at least that outward expression of eagerness. "Please. I am so happy to have you here, but I've taken up more than enough of your valuable time. I must ask you about my novel."

I sat forward as well. "I'm in no hurry, Doctor. If what you say is true, I won't likely get the opportunity to share a conversation with an Aaul'inah for some time, if ever again. However, you've done me a great honor today. And I'm going to repay it now.

"In simple terms, *Beyond Here* is fabulous. Doctor, you have created the most riveting, original science fiction story I have ever come across. We humans are inured to space travel and alien races these days—the Aaul'inah excepted, I suppose. I can get decent re-creations of the classic sf story types from Terence Jool and Skye Perrin . . ."

"I did like Perrin's *Starship Waterloo,*" Aly'wanshus commented, "Though it wasn't as good as that Heinlein in your Twentieth-Century Classics collection last year."

I nodded. "That is my point. We're stuck on trite ideas of interstellar adventure and bipedal aliens—despite having relationships with four species that don't fit that bill. We just don't seem able to produce truly new ideas any more.

"You, however, have. I mean, we've done tales of interdimensional travel, alternate universes, and the like. But the one you've created is totally unique. And you've actually managed to capture the human element of your explorers, without our stereotypes.

"I want to publish *Beyond Here*. I *have* to publish *Beyond Here*."

His earbuds appeared again. "I am honored, Mr. Bradden."

"It's Del."

"Del." His earbuds slowed, settling back into place. "Del, I am not certain that would be possible. Publication would reveal my presence here. And everything my friends and I are working for would be compromised."

"Not necessarily." I quickly continued. "The work has to be translated into English, and slightly edited. It can be published under a human pseudonym. As much as I would love to broadcast all over NewsNet that K&T and Del Bradden are publishing the very first English-language novel by a nonhuman, I'm willing to forgo the recognition just so I can publish this book."

"You barely know me, Del. Why would you do that for me?"

I sighed, "I wish this could be the great uniting moment for our peoples, Doctor. But, at the very least, let me make you a published author. I'd hate to send you home with this novel still in your trunk."

He laughed again, "Two years ago, I wouldn't have understood what you meant by that. I wouldn't have known what an author or a trunk was, or why it might be important. Today . . . I want to give you your wish."

My jaw dropped. I'd thought the politics of his situation would outweigh all the rest.

He reached out to shake my hand. "Your father tells me it is customary to seal a business transaction like so."

I reached out as well. "In my business, we usually finalize it with a contract and payment."

"We will need to keep the contract itself secret, Del. Your father did arrange to use his corporation to quietly handle my affairs on Christea. I suppose the 'royalties'—is that the term?—can go into the spending account he set up for me when I arrived. Perhaps someday I will return to spend it. Or others of my kind will make use of it."

Our hands met.

So . . . why am I sitting here telling you all this? Is Del Bradden a man of his word or not? Is he so eager to publicize his grand publishing achievement that he'd betray an alien being too far away to do anything about it?

No. It's because circumstances change. Sometimes in ways we can't conceive.

Ordinarily, the acquisition stage of book publication is boring to the general public. And it may be so in this case. I'll give you the short version.

I returned to the office late in the afternoon and made a quick comm call to my father. He was smiling the instant he saw me on his screen. Apparently, Aly'wanshus had informed him of our meeting. Dad said he was thrilled that the cat was out of the bag with me. We agreed on how to set up the contract, and to have a *long* talk over (and after) dinner that night.

I printed out the basic translation for Mr. Burke's review. The author, I said, was an eccentric crewman from one of the original colony ships, who lived in Star Falls (the conveniently distant town where my father had set up the Doctor's account). I told Mr. Burke we could have the book for a song, and the author wanted any money from it to accrue to his account for any family members who might come to Christea at some later date.

Mr. Burke read it that night, and loved it. "Could use a bit of editorial polish, Del. But, I think you've got something special here. Give the old fellow ten percent above our usual first-timer advance. We all owe quite a bit to the ones who weren't born here."

About twenty minutes after the contract was signed, and

the advance transferred, Dr. Aly'wanshus' ship lifted off. And he left Christea for good.

Even in this age of the electronic distribution of books over ColNet and SolNet, book production is *not* instantaneous. Well . . . quality book production, anyway. And I'm a bit of a perfectionist when it comes to my work. It took me a few months to properly edit *Beyond Here*. Not because it needed a lot of work, but simply because any revisions I made had to be absolutely perfect. At the very least, I owed it to Aly'wanshus to be sure I delivered the closest thing to his original vision for the story. When I keyed it in as approved for distribution, I was sure I had delivered.

Mr. Burke agreed to do some publicity for the novel. We made no false claims about the author; just called him "a brilliant new talent in a classic mold."

Beyond Here was released to the general public under the pseudonym Steven Forrester. And sold like no novel had since the colonies were founded.

The reviews glowed like . . . well . . . like Aly'wanshus' fictitious transition coil drive. "Rich in detail and language." "A literary masterwork from a lost genre." "Should be required reading at all secondary school levels." And my favorite: "Here's hoping Forrester's follow-up is already on his editor's comp."

Ten months at #1 on every bestseller list, out here and on Earth.

In truth, the book lasted at #1 longer than that. But when it had been out for six months, things started to change.

I was promoted to full editor, with my science fiction releases coming out under our (my) new StarSong line.

Four months later, I arrived at the office one morning. My new assistant, Helene, also came in every day, and she greeted me cheerily. I was lucky to find someone who loved her job as much as I loved mine. I even made a promise to myself that if she stayed a year I'd let her choose a work-from-home day, if she wanted one.

I dropped into my chair, and read my internal messages. Meeting at midmorning. Lunch with Mr. Burke. Drinks with influential mediator in the evening.

Then, I opened my external messages.

And there it was.

<dbra.ktp.chr.ColNet>
Mr. Del Bradden
K&T Publishers
16 Elray Circle
Landfall CHRISTEA

Dear Mr. Bradden:

Attached please find my science fiction novel *The Terran Seven* for publication by your company.

I feel certain that you are the appropriate editor for this novel. While I do not know Steven Forrester personally, I believe he and I share a certain philosophy and upbringing. My reading indicates that *Beyond Here* carries far deeper levels of meaning than your regular readership can recognize. *The Terran Seven* is similarly composed.

Please listen to my novel. Messages to this address will reach me, subject to a slight delay in response.

Thank you for your time.

Sincerely,
Wilosh'yata

<File Attachment: TerranSeven.lyr>

It was the first of three such submissions that arrived on my comp that week. One more arrived the next week—two more the following. And it continues to this day. So far, I've published every one of them.

I often wonder if the Aaul'inah authors will ever reveal their very successful contact with humans to the rest of their kind. Dr. Aly'wanshus had hoped to change the ideas of his people. All I can do to assist him is to keep their secret as long as they wish.

<*end personal journal recording*>
<*file seal and encryption: activated*>

*   *   *

Sean P. Fodera spent his high school and college years attending SF cons and dreaming of working (and writing) in the science fiction and fantasy field. An unrevealed number of years later, he became the Director of Contracts, Subsidiary Rights and Electronic Publishing at a major New York science fiction/fantasy publishing house. "Attached Please Find My Novel" is Sean's first professionally published short story, and marks the fulfillment of the second of his genre dreams. He lives in Brooklyn, New York, with his lovely wife Amy and their two adorable children Christina and Austin.

FIELD TRIP

by S. M. and Janet Stirling

FREE SPACE TRAVEL!!
Interested in space? Always wanted to visit one of the
fabulous space stations, but couldn't afford the trip? Here's
your chance. Join our team of professional chaperons and
be paid to travel in space! Your duties will be to escort ac-
ademically advanced students from Earth via shuttle to
field trips on one of five orbital stations, overseeing their
scheduled tours while on-station, then returning home
again. Shuttle and station personnel will be on hand to ensure safety at all times. You can relax, enjoy the company
of these bright young people, and see space the way you
never thought you could!
Call today! Our operators are ready to interview you immediately. Open a vid link now to Professional Chaperon
Services, 0555-35GOTOSPACE. Get ready to soar!

LEREESA Norton watched the yellow-and-black shuttle
complete its docking maneuver and sighed, only partly at
the delicate beauty of the winged rocket-plane's movements
against the silver glitter of the stars and the blackness of
space, the stabbing flicker of the guidance rockets, and the
remnant red glow of its vents.

When I got this job . . . an actual chance to work in
space! *What's that old saying? Be careful what you wish for:*
you may get it.

What she'd wanted was to work for the station in a *real*

job, not as a glorified shepherd for groundlings. She felt like a fraud in her stone-gray close-fitting ship suit.

Here I am on the glorious high frontier ... bored now, she thought, running a hand over her close-cut, loosely-curled black hair—she was of North American-Columbian-Zulu-English descent, a wiry brown young woman with regular, high-cheeked features and green eyes. She'd never imagined then that she could be so bored.

God, I'd almost welcome a catastrophe!

Boredom had an actual physical sensation, something like a low-order tension headache combined with indigestion and sleepiness. It was like a cold—it made you feel stupid and lethargic without actually crippling you. Just *being* in space wasn't all that thrilling, once you'd been here for a while. The endless shiny whitish beige of the corridors and compartments, the recycled antiseptic cleanliness of the air and everything else, seeing the same people every day—unless you were doing something unusual, it was far too much like being imprisoned in a submarine. Granted the view was better, but a good holo could give you something so close you couldn't tell the difference.

The tourists she guided were carefully steered away from the station's real functions—where her interest lay—and were enthusiastically encouraged to visit and *stay* in the civilian entertainment and medical areas, which most preferred to do anyway. That was like New Disney World, only with low gravity.

A little more than half the station was devoted to civilian pursuits. That half paid for a lot of the rest of the station. There, travelers were offered the ultimate in luxury accommodations, food, and drink. Live entertainment by the best and most popular actors, singers, and comedians on Earth in every language and culture was available. Plus unique attractions like zero G ballet and "flying" with strapped-on wings.

There was also what Lereesa called, to herself and her friends, high-end sleaze. What some unkindly referred to as "hot and cold running whores." The station had its own laws about recreational chemicals, too—and they could be *enforced*, in this antiseptic environment. And good old-fashioned gambling was offered in elegant surroundings reminiscent of a time when the rich were safely separated from the hoi polloi by the simple expedient of being somewhere ordinary people couldn't afford to be.

"*I* couldn't afford to be here," she muttered. "When everyone can afford to go to Monte Carlo, Monte Carlo goes to space."

She couldn't afford a drink of water in those places. Even the charge for air was higher in the big clubs. Not that she had to worry about the air charge; that was the tourists' concern.

Sometimes all Lereesa could think about was escape. *Just a day away from here, where I could see blue sky, feel a breeze, a rainstorm, see a bug!* It wasn't until you'd left Earth that you realized how much everything there *changed* from day to day.

"I know I won't break down. The psych tests said so. Unfortunately!"

And the station was *safe*. Zero tolerance described a generous policy next to the station's attitude. This wasn't the Wild West; management controlled everything.

As she waited for her party, Lereesa switched the viewport beside her to an Earth view; there weren't any actual viewports in the long domed corridor of the passenger shuttle dock. She sighed again and activated the notebook computer that was part of her uniform sleeve to check the names of her new charges one more time. Ms. Lorraine Tosca, a high school science teacher and her four: Gina Mancuso, Russell Moore, Christine Wu, and Greg Baca. High school kids.

Lereesa had actually groaned when she pulled this assignment. These kids would be seeing parts of the station that most tourists weren't even remotely interested in, and would rarely be allowed to visit even if they were. They'd be wandering through the guts of the station and they'd even be allowed onto the original station, preserved in the center of the ring. The places she'd have liked to visit—on her own.

The kids were here on a special scholarship, so she supposed she could expect a certain degree of decorum. Meaning perhaps they wouldn't try to duck out of the tour to catch some of the action in the adult entertainment section. *I hope.* The only thing worse than being bored by the tourists was having them do something so reckless it would stop your heart. *And who better to do that,* Lereesa thought, *than teenagers?*

A couple of handlers came along and said hello as they stationed themselves on either side of the white-coated hatch. One of their jobs was to assist passengers from the zero G of the shuttle to the station's near-Earth-normal gravity. After so many months she knew them both well.

"I guess this has been one of those hell trips," Pete said with a grin.

Lereesa raised her brows.

"Some kid puked his guts out all the way up, I hear," he said. "Apparently, he sparked off an orgy of upchucking."

"The head stewardess said they'd have to fumigate the shuttle before it could be used again," said the other handler.

Oh, boy, she thought, her heart sinking. *Please let it be somebody else's kid.*

The hatch opened with a hydraulic hiss and passengers began to disembark, along with a faint sour odor, despite the best the airscrubbers could do.

First out was a black youth who was an interesting grayish-green shade. He staggered and almost fell, but the handlers kept a grip on him until they were sure he was steady. The kid lurched to the bulkhead opposite and leaned his forehead against it, swallowing and wiping at the clammy sweat on his face. Active misery made him look younger than he was, and Lereesa felt a stir of compassion.

This was Russell Moore, one of her guests. He was followed by an anxious-looking woman of about twenty-five; olive-skinned, with a curved nose and intelligent dark eyes. Lorraine Tosca, the chaperone. The other three members of Lereesa's group followed rapidly, looking both bored and shell-shocked, something she was sure only teenagers could manage.

"Hello," she said to the teacher. "I'm your guide, Lereesa Norton. We can take Russell down to the clinic if you like, to see if he needs to be rehydrated."

"Lorraine," the woman said. "Tosca. That might be a good idea. He's had rather a rough trip."

Other passengers filed by, casting resentful glances at the group.

"It wouldn't have been so bad," a pale Christine Wu muttered, "if he hadn't been so *loud*."

"It wouldn't have been so bad," Greg Baca returned, "if he hadn't started out by boasting how his astronaut uncle had never been sick once in space, and how he was looking forward to seeing *us* puke our guts out."

"Well, he sure got to see that," Gina Mancuso said with a grimace.

"How'm I gonna get home?" Russell asked with real horror. Ms. Tosca blinked.

"It might not happen again," Lereesa reassured him. "Or if you do get sick it might not be as severe. Try not to think about it," she suggested. "Why borrow trouble?"

"Yeah, maybe it was a fluke," Gina said.

Russell slid down the wall and rested his head on his knees. "I've got a headache," he complained quietly.

"Then he probably does need to be rehydrated," Lereesa said to Ms. Tosca.

The teacher rose from Russell's side and nodded. "Okay. Why don't you escort us down to the clinic, then you can take the kids to their rooms. We haven't got anything scheduled tonight but settling in and a quiet din . . ."

"I know," Lereesa said with a smile. "I've got your schedule."

"Of course. What about our bags?" Ms. Tosca asked distractedly.

"They'll be delivered to your quarters," Lereesa assured her. *After they're thoroughly inspected.*

There were more than a few fanatical groups who would love to blow up what they called the "Babylon of the sky." Since there was no easy way to determine who might be a member of said fanatical groups, everything that came aboard was checked and rechecked for possible weapons or explosives. And since most of their guests had to be handled delicately, the station simply pretended that delivering their bags to their quarters was for their convenience instead of for security. A pleasant fiction that everyone conspired to accept.

After they'd dropped off Ms. Tosca and Russell, Lereesa escorted the others to their quarters. The facade facing the corridor was grand with synthetic stone and lights, but within . . .

"My closet is bigger than this room!" Greg said in awe.

"So was mine when I lived in Seattle," Lereesa agreed. "These are just like the staff's quarters."

There were six of the tiny rooms opening into a small sitting room.

"Unbelievable," Gina said, shaking her head. "Good thing I'm not claustrophobic."

"Oh, you wouldn't have been allowed up here if you were," their guide explained. "The station is very careful about potential lawsuits."

"Hey." Christine came out of her cubby/room. "Can we, like, go out?"

"Yeah!" Gina said. "I don't need to rest. Can we explore a little?"

"I suppose so," Lereesa said understandingly. "Let's go down and check with your teacher."

Sick bay was slightly less cramped than the students' hostel, and it had a different odor—a slight trace of ozone and the chemicals which made sure that no mutant superbug lived long enough to divide.

Ms. Tosca left Russell's side. "He's going to be fine, I'm sure," Lereesa said with a smile.

"Yes, he is," Ms. Tosca said, with a trace of well-hidden anxiety. "But I'd like to stay with him for awhile."

"The kids want to stretch their legs," Lereesa explained. "I thought I'd take them to the arcade. It's an area cleared for adolescent entertainment, full of games and age-appropriate V.R." She caught Christine rolling her eyes and grinned. "This is good stuff; you won't be disappointed."

"I'll bet," Greg muttered.

"I'd appreciate it if you'd keep them entertained," Lorraine Tosca said. She made a torn-in-two gesture. "I wouldn't feel right leaving him, but . . ."

Lereesa reassured the teacher; it was something she had to be good at, in her line of work.

The arcade was one of the open areas of the station, a huge central area with balconies opening up to the twenty-fifth level of this module. At the farthest edges, the gravity was light enough to allow some spectacular bounds and the floor consisted of trampoline fabric, carefully calibrated to prevent head contact with the floor of the balcony above. The teens were instantly immersed; signs flickering and flashing in brilliant colors, air that pulsed with the latest music, subliminals catching at the corner of the eye. Game zones and restaurants and shops and booths to inspire the shopaholic hidden even in teenage males surrounded them.

Seeing her charges' eyes light up, Lereesa smiled. They might be very sophisticated and very smart, but there was still a lot of common-or-garden mallrat left in there.

She knew they'd be safe here—even better, they wouldn't go home bearing tales of nameless debauchery. At least they wouldn't if they didn't stray, so the guide laid down some ground rules and gave them a place to meet her in two hours—enough time for them to feel trusted and responsible, but not enough time to get into trouble or wander too far.

"And remember," Lereesa said sternly, "no wandering away from this area."

They assured her that of course they wouldn't think of such a thing and, after a moment, scattered like a handful of dropped beads, disappearing into the crowd too quickly for her to follow.

Half an hour ago I was bored, Lereesa thought, with a stab of anxiety—there should have been another adult helping her, and subtracting the sick kid didn't make up for losing the teacher. She keyed her computer to the surveillance cameras.

I prefer bored.

Greg stopped at a game terminal with an exclamation of awe; the visual portal projected images of a huge blond warrior flourishing a sword that dripped realistic gore, while two pneumatic beauties in highly unrealistic scraps of fur clung to his massive calves.

"Crom Thunder! This isn't even *out* yet, man!" In an instant he was plugged in and playing, his eyes dreamy as the machine fed him neural impulses that counterfeited reality.

Gina and Christine continued on their way with barely a glance at his discovery. There were times when it could be funny to watch someone plugged in, in a grotty sort of way, but they had a different agenda today.

"Boys," Gina said, throwing back her reddish-brown hair.

"Geek boys," Christine replied, wrinkling her snub nose.

"*Young* geek boys," Gina said, topping her.

"He's our age," Christine pointed out.

"That's pretty young, for a boy. He's not going to miss any good killing or bikini time, *that* one isn't."

"And we're not going to achieve program in this environment," Christine said. "Let's look for—"

In the crowd of sleek, well-dressed teens, he stood out like an Alsatian at a poodle convention. Soft black vat-leather, glittering with implanted spikes, and swirling motion from the tattoos on a slimly trim body nearly as hairless as theirs.

"Hey, those are great!" Gina said admiringly.

"Did you have them done here?" Catherine asked.

He looked them up and down for a long moment and asked, *"Parlez vous Français?"*

The girls looked at one another. "Uh, *petit pas,*" Gina said dubiously.

The boy laughed. "If that," he said in English with a distinctly North American accent.

"Sprechen zie deutsche?" Catherine muttered, and they all broke up.

"Sorry," he said, "just tryin' it on. Who knew you knew *petit pas.*" He held up his thumb and forefinger almost touching.

"Sooo," Gina said, her eyes roving over his colorful arms and shoulders. "Did you have any of this done here?"

"Check it out," he said, and flexed a bicep. A colorful band glowed into life around his upper arm. It glistened with some antiseptic barrier and stood out from the others—the little flock of geese seemed more alive, and the deep waves crashing on a rocky shore were so green and frothy you could feel the cool spray.

He pinched it slightly and the colors began to flow, giving the coiled design the illusion of movement, surge and retreat of the sea, the graceful flex of wings. . . .

"Oh!" cooed Gina. "It's a cybertat! That's just what I want!"

"It's gorgeous," Christine agreed. She reached out, one finger hovering above the glowing band. Then she realized what she was doing and, with a laugh, withdrew her hand.

He grinned. "No problem. My name's Joe."

"Well, that's prosaic," Gina said.

"I knew you two were geeks the minute I saw you," Joe said with a grin.

He had a very nice smile. That and his being a year or two older took some of the sting out of his words.

"C'mon," he coaxed. "Don't look so sour. Who else would use a word like prosaic?"

"Well," Christine said, looking down her nose, "you look like the kind of guy who has a name like Slash or something."

He clutched his heart and mimed a dying fall. "Nah, *Slash* is what groundsiders *think* a guy like me should be called," he said. "That is like, sooooo pressurized."

"So," Gina said. "Where can we get a tat like yours?"

"That could be a problem," Joe said thoughtfully. "You don't have an appointment and he's a busy guy. How long are you gonna be here?"

With a grimace, Gina said, "Just four days."

"Yeah," Christine nodded, "and this is the most free time we're likely to have."

Joe looked at them and raised one eyebrow; the row of spikes above it made a rippling, musical sound at the movement and he smiled to see Christine's mouth open in unconscious appreciation.

"Look," he said, "I've got an appointment for Lazro to

finish up some work on my back, but I'm gonna be here for
another week, so I can reschedule. If you have a couple of
hours right now, I'll let you have my appointment."

Cries of joy and delight met his suggestion and he rose
from his seat.

"C'mon then, we've got some traveling to do. You won't
find anybody like Laz here in cotton candy heaven."

Joe gestured contemptuously at the affluent crowd
around them. "Not a tat showing."

The shop was named *Torture Tattoo*, as a holo with a faint
sonic undertone of screaming proclaimed outside. Most of
the storefronts along this corridor were dark, and it was as
close to a run-down neighborhood as the station boasted,
with color-coded conduits thick on the low ceiling. Inside, it
was long and narrow, with a smell much like the hospital's,
but with a harder edge of disinfectant and old, old metal.

Laz was more of a pattern than a person. He was tall and
wide and bald, covered with swirling, flashing colors
worked into fanciful designs everywhere except the parts
covered by a twisted cotton loincloth—and, Gina thought
with a start, probably there, too.

He'd chosen bands of designs rather than building out
from a single image.

Christine whispered in Gina's ear. "An unkind person
would say he looks like the bargain bin in a ribbon shop."
Their giggles had a nervous edge, and Laz reacted not at all.

His face was hard to read with all that motion going on;
actually it was hard to even *see* his features, as wild horses
in galloping motion were superceded by abstract patterns.
But with a flick of a muscle his visage was suddenly naked.

And he was *still* hard to read, all massive bones and
coarse pores, but no trace of beard stubble. The gold rings in
his ears moved slightly as he raised his eyebrows.

"We . . . I want a tat," Gina said, fighting an impulse to turn half away and talk to him over her shoulder. "A cybertat."

"That's the reason people usually come here," Laz agreed, nodding. He looked at Joe. The boy in leather—and he suddenly looked much more like a *boy* to both of them—spread his hands.

"They're only here for four days, Laz," Joe explained. "I said they could have my appointment. I'll make another for . . . say the first week in June?"

"It's your money and time," Laz shrugged, with the slightest hint of a smile, before turning to the girls. "Bye."

He didn't say much and that was said curtly, and his prices were sky-high, but Gina immediately fell in love with a display of a three-color mandala that swirled clockwise and changed shades, simultaneously, never repeating itself.

"How does it do that?" she said.

Laz smiled again, with a quirking curve of his thick lips. "Chaotic pattern," he said. "The algorithm is simple, but the permutations are infinite. I call it *seminfinity*. It runs off your body heat, like the others. Lasts indefinitely."

"Oh, *yeah*," she replied dreamily.

He considered her with a technician's eye. "It would just about fit on your stomach," he said. "Use the navel as the pivot, and—"

"No!" Gina said. "What's the use of a tattoo you only show in the shower?"

"Or to your boyfriend," Christine said, chuckling even more at Gina's quelling look.

"I want it in the middle of my forehead."

He shrugged. "In order to center it right, it's gotta be smaller, so there'll be less detail."

Gina pouted. "I really like this design."

Laz shrugged. "It'll be seventy less for the smaller version—the detail's *there,* but you'd have to let your friends get real close and use a 'scope to see it all. We'll put the control here," he said, tapping her lightly on top of her head. "That way you won't turn it on and off by accident every time you change your expression."

"Sold!" Gina said instantly. She had a hundred and seventy-five in her account—half a year's scrimping, so she could afford to bring back something from this trip. His original price would have left her with nothing. Now, at least, she'd be able to afford an extra soda now and then.

Two hours later Gina was in the shop's tiny and not very sanitary bathroom wondering why she was feeling so drained. Worse. She felt logy and very faintly nauseous—the sort of sensation that made you hungry but the thought of eating repulsive.

Well, she reassured herself, *it's kind of like an operation. Not to mention all those hours on the vomit comet getting here.*

Gina sighed and laid her head against the cheap extruded synth of the partition behind her, a sensation neither hard nor soft, cold nor hot.

Then she heard voices coming through the wall. The nausea was forgotten as she pressed her ear to the synth. The material was very strong, but so thin it acted like a giant hearing membrane at close range.

"Okay, so what's the story? What's so important that you can't talk to me in a completely empty store?"

The voice was male and young, with an accent she didn't recognize until she thought of holo actors playing spacemen.

"Look at this," another male answered; his voice was gruff and deep but carried the same slight everywhere-and-nowhere twang.

There was silence, then, "Holy . . . you can't be serious!" the young voice said.

"As explosive decompression."

"Man." The young voice was filled with awe. "This will blow the whole station wide open—peel it like a banana!"

"Yeah," the gruff voice said. "And, sadly, they'll never see it coming."

"They should've hunh?" younger voice said.

"If they weren't idiots they would have. They deserve to be blindsided." The deep voice was bitter. "That'll teach 'em to make fun of me."

"This'll teach 'em all right," younger agreed.

"And too late to do 'em any good." There was a deep laugh that matched the voice. "They're gonna regret it, all those jokes, the lousy quarters. I'm gonna make them so sorry."

"Whaddaya mean?" the younger voice asked.

The answer was spoken so low that Gina couldn't make it out.

"You've got to be kidding!" younger said. "You can't do that!"

"Gina, are you all right?" Christine asked, banging on the door.

Gina jumped and gasped. She heard the sudden silence on the other side of the wall as threatening and fumbled with the lock. She rushed from the lavatory; snatching Christine's wrist to drag the other girl out of the shop and hustle her down the corridor.

"Whoa!" Christine said, digging her heels into the rubbery nonslip flooring; it was slightly worn here Gina suddenly noticed, which meant this part of the station was *ancient*.

So ancient it doesn't have surveillance? She thought, frightened—all the books and holos she'd read containing menacing conspirators and secret agents coming back with a rush.

"What are you *doing?*" Christine cried.

Gina turned to look back down the corridor. Laz had

closed his door—they'd paid by retina and voiceprint, as usual—and nothing else was moving.

"We've got to keep going!" she hissed. "I think I just heard someone plotting to blow up the station!"

A man's head popped out from between two shops, looking both ways.

"That's him!" Gina said.

"Hey!" the man shouted. "Wait!"

The two of them ran, bounding like long-legged gazelles in the low gravity and holding their hands over their heads to keep from hitting them on the conduits.

Ms. Tosca sat down at Lereesa's table with a heartfelt sigh. "First day and I'm exhausted," she said.

"I'm not surprised," Lereesa said sympathetically. "Have a cup of coffee. I take it Russell is okay."

Ms. Tosca nodded as she tapped in her order on the table's keypad; it was one of a dozen on a flying cantilevered platform overlooking the concourse. The view of the teeming, brightly-dressed crowd was excellent, but if you moved your head quickly, it blurred a little, the sign of a privacy screen. The palm-sized crimson-black-orange genengineered butterflies avoided the field as well.

"I got him bunked down in one of the cubbies at the hospital, with a sleepyfield on him. He looked like he might sleep until it's time for us to go home, even without it."

"Hah! He'll be up and raring to go by the time you get back," the guide said. "Kids are amazingly resilient."

"You said it." Ms. Tosca looked around. "And he'll be ready to use the suppressor net this time—no more Mr. Macho. Where are the others?"

"I saw Greg playing some game about twenty minutes ago. But I haven't seen the girls since we got here. Which, given the kind of clothing shops around here, doesn't surprise me."

Ms. Tosca checked her watch. "I'm just feeling anxious. Field trips are always insane, but we're not even on Earth. It adds a certain something. You know?" Her cup of coffee slid out of the table's surface and she drew it toward her, blowing on the hot frothy surface; it gave off a faint pleasantly bitter odor, slightly touched with cinnamon.

"I can imagine." Lereesa pointed. "Here they come now."

The two girls approached the table at a near run, looking sweaty and gasping for breath; to Lereesa's surprise they actually bumped into a few people on the way.

They were graceful enough before, she thought. Twenty-five wasn't so far from fifteen that she couldn't remember the horror of public embarrassment. Then she saw what swirled on the auburn-haired girl's face.

"Omighod!" Gina managed to say between huge gulps of air. "Omighod!"

Omighod is right, Lereesa thought faintly, hearing a slight choked sound from the teacher beside her. *Omighod!*

Christine frowned at her friend and cast a nervous glance at their teacher.

Ms. Tosca stared at the blazing mandala tattoo as though hypnotized. Meanwhile, Gina poured out her story as best she could being so out of breath. Then she demanded, "What are we gonna do?"

Christine took in the fascinated horror in the two women's expressions and slapped Gina on the top of the head; Laz had demonstrated how that would make it disappear.

"Ow!" Gina glared at her.

The tattoo was still visible, if no longer moving; Christine raised her hand again.

"I'll do it," Gina said and tapped her head lightly, dismissing the design.

The spell was broken; Ms. Tosca and the guide blinked and looked at one another.

"Explain," the teacher demanded.

"I just *did!*" Gina half-whined. "Weren't you paying attention? We've got to do something!"

"About the tattoo?" Ms. Tosca asked, frowning.

Christine rolled her eyes. "Gina thinks she heard someone planning to blow up the station."

Lereesa sat up straighter. "That isn't something to joke about," she warned, her voice stern. It wasn't. That sort of joke was a criminal offense. "A false alarm could get you heavily fined, possibly jailed, and banned from the station for life."

"I'm not making this up!" Gina insisted. "One guy said this will blow the station wide open and the other guy was talking about how they'd all regret making fun of him!"

"Maybe we'd better report this," Lereesa said. She activated her telephone implant with a twitch of her ear-cocking muscle.

"*Security*," she said. Machines read her voiceprint and routed the call. "*Possible 7-4. Repeat, possible 7-4.*"

7-4 was *breach of hull integrity*, and it was about the dirtiest word on a station. Only *fire* on one of the ancient wooden ships of Earth had quite the same ring of horror.

"Do you think she heard?" Ray Cowper asked his friend Bob Masud, wiping sweat from his face with a palm.

"Ye-ah," Bob said with doleful certainty, his voice oddly young. "That wall is paper-thin. The only way she couldn't have heard is if she's deaf."

Ray could see that Bob didn't understand. "She'll *tell!*"

With a sigh Bob pushed himself away from the counter of his shop, a big-shouldered troll-like bronze figure that seemed to go with the racked machine parts in their cubbyholes.

"Okay, let's go next door and find out who she was from Laz. Then, when you find her, you can ask her not to spread the word." He smiled, showing thick yellow teeth he'd never bothered to have cosmeticized. "If you ask the right way, she'll be real quiet. How's that?"

Ray brushed his sleek black hair back and took a couple of anxious steps back and forth, a thin man who moved like a whippet. That showed the degree of his agitation; usually he had the distinctive stillness of a spaceman used to single-handing utility craft, the habit of those who spent much time in confined spaces crammed with delicate controls.

"Yeah," he said after a moment. "Good idea. Let's go."

"Coupla high school kids on a field trip," Laz said. "Why do ya wanna know?"

"Ray was telling me something confidential and he wants to ask the kid to keep it quiet, if she heard."

"Yeah?" Laz's face turned toward Ray. "What was it?"

"He finally got a positive reading," Bob said.

Ray punched him in the arm. "What are you doing?"

"Look," Bob said, rubbing his arm, "with Laz you've got to give to get. Okay?"

Ray scowled at Laz. The thickset man's eyes had opened wide enough that they could easily be seen among the myriad flashing, rolling patterns, a trace of cold blue that did not waver.

"Are you serious?" Laz asked.

"As explosive decompression," Bob said airily.

Ray cast him a nasty look.

Laz said, "So what exactly did you get?"

Looking trapped, Ray demanded, "You gotta swear not to tell anyone."

Laz shrugged. "Sure, whatever."

It wasn't the firm commitment that Ray had been hoping for. *But I figure it's the best I'm going to get.* He reached inside his coverall and withdrew a file; he bit his lips, then handed it over.

"Hard copy?" Laz said.

"You can't take a disk in or out of that section," Ray explained. "Nobody pays much attention to printout—you'd need a dolly and a lifter to get out hard copy of any really valuable data."

"Hunh." Then there was silence as the tattoo artist read the file. "My God," he said when he was finished. He shook his head. "*Bozhemoi.*"

"Proof positive of intelligent alien life," Bob said proudly. "I had pretty much the same reaction."

"You can't tell anybody," Ray insisted.

"Why not? This is the biggest news since . . . ever!" Laz said.

"Yeah, and everybody is gonna know. But there's somebody I've gotta tell first."

"Lloyd Witham," Bob said.

"That guy who goes the VR porn?" Laz asked, a slight edge of scorn in his voice. "What's he got to do with this?"

"He offered a prize—ten million after taxes—to the person who could prove the existence of other intelligent life in the universe," Ray explained. "On the condition that the proof was given to him first."

"Is this ethical?" Laz asked.

"That depends on what I intend to do with the money," Ray said. "You know I was about to lose my funding. I was going to have to leave the station in less than a month."

"Yeah, but with this," Laz said, spreading his hands, "they wouldn't just stop the funding. Why would they?"

"Because once this comes out, the world governments will step in and they'll kick me aside like a junkyard dog."

"Melodramatically phrased," Bob nodded, "but probably true."

"But if I've got ten million credits I get to stay here and keep tabs on what the governments are doing. This is definitely something that needs a watchdog."

Laz and Bob looked at one another. "Well, Ray, here's a

miracle," Laz said. "I actually *agree* with you about something besides the fact that Schiller isn't really beer. So these kids overheard you telling Ray about it and now you're afraid they'll tell station security or maybe the media about it and you'll lose your chance."

"Yeah."

"And all you want to do is ask them to not tell anyone, right?"

"Yeah."

Laz tapped a few keys on his computer. "She's Gina Mancuso, lodged on deck five, section thirty-eight, suite twelve thirty-eight. High school student, NE Megplex, on a tour. Don't make me regret giving you this, Ray. If I do, so will you."

"I won't," Ray promised. "I just want to keep my edge."

"So you didn't actually hear anyone say, 'I'm going to blow up the station'?" security officer Loh asked.

He was a slight, slender, amber-hued man with lines in his face and white in his close-cropped cap of black hair; somehow he took less than his share of the narrow space at the hostel, despite the holstered stunner on the belt of his plain gray coverall.

"What he said was, '*this will blow the whole station wide open,*'" Gina insisted. "Which sounded close enough to me."

She heard the edge of a whine in her voice and corrected it. The officer didn't seem to be taking her very seriously, but that was no reason to sound like a brat. "And he chased us."

Christine nodded. "Chased us for, oh, a couple of corridors. We really had to *run,* but then he got into a place with lots of people and stopped."

"I'll check it out, ladies," Loh said, rising. "It may be a misunderstanding. At least I hope it is. Thank you for filing a report; all threats are taken seriously here." He turned to look at them from the doorway. "But this had better not be a prank. We take *that* seriously, too."

"It's not a prank!" Gina said, almost shouting in frustration. "If it was a prank, I'd have made an anonymous call. What am I, an idiot?"

Loh smiled. "No, miss," he said. "If you were an idiot, you wouldn't have earned this trip. But smart people make the worst sort of fools."

He thanked the teacher and the guide and left. At least he *hoped* she wasn't an idiot. He called in a report and headed for the *Torture Tattoo* parlor.

"This space is illegally divided," Loh told the tattoo parlor's proprietor. "I'm going to have to write you a ticket."

"The place was like this when I subleased it," Laz said. "I can show you my contract."

In fact, Loh could have scanned it from the Station files, and they both knew it. There would be no point in lying.

"How was I supposed to know?" the thickset artist went on, scratching idly at a design that slowly transformed itself from *Nude Descending A Staircase* into Holman Hunt's *The Awakening Conscience.*

"This is just a ticket," Loh replied reasonably. *Something to make you sit up and pay attention,* the security officer thought, *like a shovel in the face in the old days on Earth. With some people you have to use visual aids.* "The original leaseholder is going to find himself in *big* trouble."

He finished writing and the imager at his belt purred as it printed out a hard copy, registering the ticket with security's ROM data bank at the same instant. "Now, about this underage girl you tattooed without her parents' permission."

Sweat didn't hide the designs on the artist's skin, but it did give them a rippling sheen in the harsh bright light of the parlor's cubicle-office.

"She had a notarized recording of her mother giving permission," Laz said. "I took a copy." He tapped a few keys and a holo image of a thirtysomething blonde woman hovered above the table.

"I authorize Gina to have any nonpermanent body modifications of Level III and below she wishes," the woman said, smiling indulgently. "Subject to immediate payment from account #—"

Loh looked at the artist and raised his eyebrows. "Nonpermanent?" he said. "Level III?"

"Hey, give me a break," Laz said, shrugging and making a symphony of color run from his bald head to his toes. "Do you think I was giving the tourist girl *this?*"

"Could be a fake," Loh said, nodding toward the holograph that repeated its message.

"It's *notarized*," Laz pointed out. "Our beloved Station Security comp can check the encryption. Query groundside if you want."

Loh nodded. "Could you make me a copy for our files?" he asked. "Notarization and all?"

"Sure," Laz said wearily. "I never would have done it if it hadn't been notarized. What am I, an idiot?"

Loh smiled politely. "I seem to be hearing that phrase a lot lately. Of course you aren't—but if nobody was an idiot, what would we need Security for?"

On the other side of the illegally divided space, Loh confronted Bob. The place sold small machine parts and consisted of a front counter and, visible through a doorway, rows of storage shelves.

"There's been a report of a very alarming conversation taking place here today," the security officer said.

"Oh, yeah?" Bob said. "Alarming, huh? What was it about?"

"Something about blowing the station wide open."

Bob widened his eyes and gave a choked little laugh.

"Hey, somebody has big ears. A buddy of mine came over to share some hot gossip, and I used the expression, *this will blow the station wide open*. Nothing to do with actually blowing anything up."

"What was this piece of gossip?" Loh asked, in his best Dubious Official Tone.

Bob looked uncomfortable and shifted his feet. "I'd really rather not say. It's kind of personal and I don't feel comfortable talking about it."

"I see. Well, perhaps your friend will feel more comfortable talking about it to me."

Loh was writing out a ticket as he spoke and Bob kept shifting nervous glances between the officer's face and his pad. After a moment, the pad spit out a ticket and Loh held it out to the storekeeper.

Bob backed away. "What's that for?"

"It's a ticket for the illegal division of a commercial space."

"Just because I don't want to repeat gossip? You can't do that."

"No," Loh said, allowing himself to look surprised. "The ticket is for having an illegally divided commercial space. For not telling me how to find your friend, you might be charged with . . . oh, obstruction . . . assault on a constable—"

"What assault?"

"The assault you'll commit when I'm through thinking up things to charge you with."

"I didn't say that I wouldn't tell you about Ray! I just said I didn't want to repeat something he told me in confidence." Bob brushed his hair back. "He's Ray Cowper."

"The nut?" Loh said, straightening.

"He isn't a nut," Bob said. "I don't know where he is right now."

"I'll find him," Loh said, laying the ticket on the counter. "The Station thanks you for your cooperation."

*   *   *

Ray Cowper, Loh thought, as he walked out into the deserted corridor. *This is as good a place as any.*

He called up the man's file on the screen built into his sleeve; the problem with having information always accessible was finding a quiet moment to absorb it without distraction or someone looking over your shoulder.

Cowper was an independent scientist searching for deep space signals that might indicate intelligent life outside the solar system. Due to poor financing, he had access to a very, very narrow band of space. Records indicated that his financing was about to run out—and his space on the station was eagerly sought after by a number of Earth's governments and businesses. It was unlikely the station would renew Cowper's lease even if he could come up with the money.

"This looking for aliens crap really doesn't fit the staid image the station likes to project for its science section," Loh muttered to himself.

Cowper had lodged numerous, increasingly angry complaints about the situation. He seemed to be exactly the kind of person who did things like blowing up space stations. He was certainly intelligent enough, having degrees in electronic engineering, computers, and chemistry.

All of which suggest unpleasant possibilities, Loh thought.

I shall have to talk to the man.

Loh didn't like possibilities. Most of the random possibilities possible on a station couldn't possibly be good.

He allowed himself a quiet chuckle at the thought as he began the search for Mr. Cowper.

"I don't see why I have to stay in," Greg said, looking around the bare confines of the hostel. "I didn't do anything wrong."

"And I wasn't even awake," Russell protested. "I missed out this afternoon. I want to see the station."

"We didn't do anything wrong!" Christine added her voice.

"What about that thing on Gina's forehead?" Ms. Tosca demanded.

"What thing?" Gina reasoned. "It's turned off, you can't see anything."

"What about the fact that you sure didn't acquire it at the arcade," Lereesa snapped. "You promised me you wouldn't wander."

"And I didn't," Greg said. "That's my point."

Ms. Tosca slapped her knees and rose. "You know what, Greg? You're right. You and Russell deserve more time in the arcade if you want it. But you two," she pointed a finger at the girls, "are going to stay here."

There were the expected cries of dismay, growing increasingly shrill until Lereesa put a stop to it by saying: "If Security wants you again, they'll want to speak to you in confidence. You're staying here."

The girls looked at one another, pouting.

"Okay," Gina said.

"You can order dinner sent up," Ms. Tosca told her. "Just keep it under budget, okay?"

They left the suite to resentful mutterings of "Yes, Ms. Tosca."

Outside the suite, Lereesa tapped a code into the key panel. "That will keep them inside unless there's a station emergency," she explained.

Ms. Tosca raised her eyebrows. "Don't be too sure about that. Those two are good with that sort of thing."

"Maybe so," Lereesa said, "but they'd have to access this panel. I'm betting their cutting-through-walls skills aren't up to their computer abilities."

Ms. Tosca laughed, and Lereesa chuckled herself.

Behind her, the two boys looked at each other and smiled slightly.

Ray watched the small group walk down the corridor and hop onto the people mover, dodging past a group of biotechs. He licked his lips nervously, tasting the acrid salt of nervous sweat.

The two girls aren't with them.

Which might mean that they had stayed behind, the voice of hope struggled to convince him. But it might also mean they were at Security headquarters telling anyone who would listen about his secret.

When the group was out of sight, he snuck over to the door of their quarters and, after a swift, nervous glance around, pressed the call button.

An Oriental girl's image appeared on the screen. "Did you forget something?" The question was followed almost immediately by screaming as his image appeared on the inner screen. "I'm calling security!" the girl said.

"NO! Wait!" Ray said desperately. "Just give me a chance to talk to you. It's very important. Please."

"I heard what you said!" Another girl's face appeared beside the first's. "You want to blow up the station!"

"What!" Ray had trouble getting his mouth to close for a moment. "I do not!" he insisted. "Where did you get that idea?"

"Your friend said so!" the one who must be Gina told him. "This will blow the station wide open. I heard him!"

"Nooo," Ray said, his eyes bulging. "He only said that as a metaphor."

That stopped them cold. Neither girl could believe that a mad bomber would use a word like metaphor.

"Please, wait, let me explain," Ray begged. "Just give me a minute. But you've got to let me come in—I can't talk about this in the corridor."

The girls looked at one another. "There *are* two of us," Christine said.

"I don't like it," Gina said. "You didn't hear him."

"I don't want to hurt anybody," Ray said, his voice falling in despair. "Believe me, I don't think that the station canceling my lease is reason to kill a lot of innocent people. I may be a little, umm, peculiar, but I'm not a murderer."

"What do you think?" Christine asked Gina.

"I think you're going to let him in whether I like it or not," Gina snapped.

"It's the only way to get to the bottom of this."

Gina threw her hands up. "All right, do what you want. If anything happens, it's your fault."

"Like, it's ever not my fault?" Christine asked. "Was it not my fault when you jacked the game screen at the football match to show—"

"*I* jacked the screen? Soooo *not!* I *helped* when *you*—"

Christine's thumb hit the open key with unnecessary violence; she muttered a word under her breath and shook it. Apart from that, nothing happened except that Ray's face in the screen grew more desperate.

"It won't work!" Christine said.

Gina came back to her side and tapped it a few times. "Unless you broke it," she said. "But I don't think one thumb could do that."

"They locked us in!" Christine said in astonishment. "I can't *believe* they locked us in."

"I can take care of that," Ray offered.

"Well, so could we, if we could get at the keypad," Gina said. "It can't be too hard."

Ray gave them a haggard grin. "I'm sure you could. You probably hacked your way out of your playpens."

"No," Gina said. "But I got this set of cydolls when I was six, and I hacked their controller so I could make them run all through the house and hide things."

Ray stopped in the middle of unclipping an instrument from his belt. "You didn't!"

"She did," Christine affirmed. "I was there. The cat climbed on top of the porcelain cabinet and wouldn't come down for days."

"Well," Gina pointed out, "it was *your* idea to make them carry matches like a torch relay race."

Ray tore his attention away and shuddered. "And to think I've regretted not having children," he muttered, and set the square featureless box over the keypad. "With my luck and genes, they'd probably be brilliant and depraved, like this bunch."

The little box beeped contentedly as it achieved electronic communion with the hostel's system. In a few seconds, he was tapping in a code and the door swished open.

The girls glanced at one another and relaxed. He was smaller than they'd thought, and skinnier. They both thought they could take him with one hand tied behind their backs.

"I've got something I guess I should show you," he said.

"Like . . . a gun, maybe?" Christine asked. "Or a knife?"

Ray rolled his eyes and began unzipping his coverall. "Of course not," he said impatiently.

"I guess it's the *other* thing that strange guys always say they've got to show you," Gina muttered. "Now I'm definitely calling security."

"Wait," Ray said and reached for her wrist.

Before he knew what was happening, Christine gripped his wrist, half-turning it with a thumb pressed down on the sensitive spot above his thumb.

"Wait—"

Gina grabbed the other hand in an identical grip. "We tied for second place in self-defense class," she said. "Hey, this really works!" she went on, as he sank to his knees and made a choked sound.

The girls quickly stuffed a roll of spare socks into Ray's

mouth. "Does this count as an Adventure in Outer Space?"
To Ray: "No, don't try to get up. You could hurt yourself
pushing against the joint like that."

"Urruruk!" Ray agreed.

"I don't know," Christine said seriously. "I mean, it could
have happened on a trip to, oh, Marseilles, just as easily.
Have you got something we could tie him up with?"

"Tights?" Gina suggested with a shrug. "I've got plenty
of extras. I really don't like that pair with the spangles now,
anyway."

"I guess if we pull them tight enough," Christine said
skeptically. "We can't leave enough stretch for him to work
loose."

In less than a minute, Ray was trussed at ankles and
wrists. The two girls each held an extra pair of tights and
discussed whether they should tie his wrists to his ankles.

"Arrgh! Pfffthtt!" The roll of socks, somewhat damp, spat
across the room. "Wait a minute," Ray said in a hoarse exas-
peration. "This has gone far enough. I am not dangerous!"

"Well, you aren't now," Gina said. "Ms. Kourosoppolu
always said to immobilize a potential danger first. Then figure out what else to do."

"I do not have any kind of a weapon on me. I have no intention of threatening or hurting you or anybody else!
Where did you get these crazy ideas?"

"From you," Gina said offhandedly.

"All I want to *show* you is a file I have tucked into the top
of my coverall." He rolled onto his side and the girls could
just see the tip of the paper folder leaning out from his open
zipper.

"What the heck is it?" Gina asked.

Christine reached down and very cautiously slid it out
and opened it.

"It looks just like that plaque they put on the *Voyager*
spacecraft," she said, looking at what was inside.

"Yeah," Gina agreed, "but . . ."

"Different," Ray finished for her. "Very different, if you check it against the original from Earth."

The girls looked at one another and then at him. Christine whistled. "You know, Gina, I think maybe this does qualify as an Adventure in Outer Space. Cool!"

"Yeah, if it's not a fake. Where did it come from?" Gina demanded.

"The data stream came from the direction of Epsilon—"

"That's over seven light-years away."

"I seriously doubt *Voyager* could have gotten that far," Christine sneered.

"Exactly," Ray said smugly. "But without a doubt, that's how far away the closest star in that direction lies, and the figures prove that the signal came from a vast distance. It's not one of my fellow scientists jerking me around. That was the first thing I checked." He looked up at them. "Do you realize what this means?"

Gina's face began to turn pink. "It means I misunderstood what I heard," she muttered. "I'm very sorry."

"Sorry enough to untie me?" he asked, somewhat sharply.

Just as the girls bent to untie him, the door opened. Ms. Tosca entered, saying, "I've changed my mind, girls . . ."

She stopped cold and stared. Behind her, Lereesa and the boys took in the very peculiar scene.

"This is the guy I overheard this afternoon," Gina said quickly. "But he's explained everything. I was totally mistaken."

"Mistaken to the point of tying him up?" Ms. Tosca asked weakly.

"Yes," Ray said cheerfully. "But it's all cleared up now."

"Not exactly," Lereesa frowned. "How did you get in here?"

Ray grinned sheepishly. "I figured out the lock code."

"Oh, you did, did you?" Lereesa said grimly. "I think we'd better call security," she told Ms. Tosca.

"NO!" the two girls and the scientist shouted.

Ms. Tosca pressed her hand to her forehead. "Maybe we should allow them to explain," she suggested.

"Could I be untied first?" Ray asked plaintively. "I can't feel my hands anymore. They got *all* of the stretch out of these tights. Ms. Kourosoppolu would be very proud."

"Isn't this a bit unethical?" Ms. Tosca asked when the explanations were done. "I mean, shouldn't you tell your support group first?"

"I and my colleagues have spent everything we have on this project," Ray said. "If I tell them first, we'll lose a chance at ten million credits, and we need those credits to keep going. I think it would be more unethical to blow this chance, and I'm convinced my colleagues would agree."

"Um, but you've already blown it," Russell said. "You've told us, and your friend earlier today."

Ray's shoulders drooped. "You're right," he said. He buried his face in his hands. "You're right."

"Not to mention station security is probably looking for you," Lereesa said. "If you attempt to make a call to Earth, they'd probably block it and find you in seconds."

Ray lowered his hands, there were actual tears in his eyes. "For all I know, it was a scam anyway," he said, his voice choked.

"That's right," Gina said, patting his shoulder consolingly. "Lloyd Witham is a pornographer, after all."

"Wait a minute," Greg said. "There's no reason he has to know that we've been told. I mean, I won't tell anybody; what about you guys?"

They looked at one another. "Sure," Russell said, "I don't mind. Ray did some major work on this. He *deserves* to get some of the credit. Not to mention the ten million. Hey, man, what you going to spend it on?"

"A Foundation," Ray said. "We need an independent agency to communicate with—"

"There's still the problem of getting a message past station security," Lereesa pointed out, shifting slightly in her seat, visibly uncomfortable at the rising enthusiasm.

"And we still don't know if this guy would pony up once you do show him proof," Christine said. "I mean, Gina's right. He *is* a sleazebag."

Ms. Tosca cleared her throat. "Actually," she said, "in my opinion, Lloyd is a stand-up guy."

They all looked at her.

"I used to go with him in high school. Until my parents found out about these soft porn movies he was putting on the internet." She bit her lip. "Lloyd said he understood. My father was a minister, after all. But I always felt like a coward."

Lereesa put a sympathetic hand on her shoulder.

"Cool," said Gina brightly. "Then you can call Witham for Ray and say he didn't think he'd be able to get through on his own." She looked around at their solemn faces. "What?"

"Just that the lies are getting pretty thick on the ground here," Lereesa said. *Was it just this morning she was so bored?*

"But this is our chance to do something important—"

"I . . . I . . ." Lereesa stammered.

"Hey, you're qualified," Ray pointed out.

The hushed tinkle of cutlery came from other parts of the restaurant. It was one the guide had never been able to afford; some of the paneling was actual *wood*, shipped all the way up the gravity well from Earth. The ambience was lost on her right now, and even the savory smells of a meal worth every exorbitant penny.

"I'm a tour guide!" she blurted.

"The Outsider Foundation's going to need PR work," Ray said. "The Lost Gods of the Galaxy know *I'm* not fit to do it. I mean, imagine me dealing with the media, VIPs who want tours—"

Lereesa blanched slightly. "Okay," she said. "I *do* have a degree in Communications."

"And you earned it," Ray said earnestly. "If you hadn't helped convince Ms. Tosca, there wouldn't *be* an Outsider Foundation to handle establishing communications with the Outsiders. It'd all be official—and me and my friends would be reading about it on the newswebs." He paused and smiled brightly. "And pretty soon, you'll be working with some other old friends!"

"Oh?" Lereesa said cautiously.

"Yeah! Gina, Christine, Greg, and Russell are taking the prelim courses. They're all bright as tacks—they want to work for the Outsider Foundation. I mean, so do all the other bright kids in the Solar System now, but we owe—"

The thought of working with those four made Lereesa hesitate, but not for long. Her thumb came down on the signature patch with an audible *thump*. Boredom in space wasn't going to be her problem much longer.

Terror, embarrassment, sheer funk, yes, she thought happily. *Boredom, no.*

*   *   *

Stephen Michael Stirling has been writing science fiction and fantasy for more than fifteen years, producing such excellent novels as **Marching Through Georgia**, **Snowbrother**, **Against the Tide of Years**, *and most recently* The **Peshawar Lancers**. *He has also collaborated with many of the best authors in the business, including Judith Tarr, David Drake, and Harry Turtledove. He was born in Metz,*

Alsace, France, and educated at the Carleton University in Canada. He lives with his wife Janet in New Mexico.

Born Janet Moore in Milford, Massachusetts, Janet Stirling has been a science fiction buff since her teens. She sold her first story to **Chicks in Chainmail***, an anthology of amazonian fantasy edited by Esther Friesner. She married S. M. Stirling in 1988, after a courtship conducted largely at World Fantasy conventions, and now lives with him and their two cats in Santa Fe, New Mexico.*

COME ALL YE FAITHFUL

by Robert J. Sawyer

NEW YORK DIOCESE, INTERNAL MEMO
. . . yes, Bishop, I was frankly surprised by the number of
applicants. Such interest bodes well for our newest parish.
I do believe we have selected the best candidate under the
circumstances. After all, his qualifications combine several
key elements. Still, his will be a lonely job. . . .

"DAMNED social engineers," said Boothby, a frown distorting his freckled face. He looked at me, as if expecting an objection to the profanity, and seemed disappointed that I didn't rise to the bait.

"As you said earlier," I replied calmly, "it doesn't make any practical difference."

He tried to get me again: "Damn straight. Whether Jody and I just live together or are legally married shouldn't matter one whit to anyone but us."

I wasn't going to give him the pleasure of telling him it mattered to God; I just let him go on. "Anyway," he said, spreading hands that were also freckled, "since we have to be married before the Company will give us a license to have a baby, Jody's decided she wants the whole shebang: the cake, the fancy reception, the big service."

I nodded. "And that's where I come in."

"That's right, Padre." It seemed to tickle him to call me

that. "Only you and Judge Hiromi can perform ceremonies here, and, well . . ."

"Her honor's office doesn't have room for a real ceremony, with a lot of attendees," I offered.

"That's it!" crowed Boothby, as if I'd put my finger on a heinous conspiracy. "That's exactly it. So, you see my predicament, Padre."

I nodded. "You're an atheist. You don't hold with any religious mumbo jumbo. But, to please your bride-to-be, you're willing to have the ceremony here at Saint Teresa's."

"Right. But don't get the wrong idea about Jody. She's not . . ."

He trailed off. Anywhere else on Mars, declaring someone wasn't religious, wasn't a practicing Christian or Muslim or Jew, would be perfectly acceptable—indeed, would be the expected thing. Scientists, after all, looked askance at anyone who professed religion; it was as socially unacceptable as farting in an air lock.

But now Boothby was unsure about giving voice to what in all other circumstances would have been an easy disclaimer. He'd stopped in here at Saint Teresa's over his lunch hour to see if I would perform the service, but was afraid now that I'd turn him down if he revealed that I was being asked to unite two nonbelievers in the most holy of institutions.

He didn't understand why I was here—why the Archdiocese of New York had put up the money to bring a priest to Mars. The Roman Catholic Church would always rather see two people married by clergy than living in sin—and so, since touching down at Utopia Planitia, I'd united putative Protestants, secular Jews, and more. And I'd gladly marry Boothby and his fiancée. "Not to worry," I said. "I'd be honored if you had your ceremony here."

Boothby looked relieved. "Thank you," he replied. "Just, you know, not too many prayers."

I forced a smile. "Only the bare minimum."

* * *

Boothby wasn't alone. Almost everyone here thought having me on Mars was a waste of oxygen. But the New York Diocese was rich, and they knew that if the church didn't have a presence early on in Bradbury Colony, room would never be made for it.

There had been several priests who had wanted this job, many with much better theological credentials than I had. But two things were in my favor. First, I had low food requirements, doing fine on just 1200 calories a day. And second, I have a PhD in astronomy, and had spent four years with the Vatican observatory.

The stars had been my first love; it was only later that I'd wondered who put them there. Ironically, taking the priest job here on Mars had meant giving up my celestial research, although being an astronomer meant that I could double for one of the "more important" colonists, if he or she happened to get sick. That fact appeased some of those who had tried to prevent my traveling here.

It had been a no-brainer for me: studying space from the ground, or actually going into space. Still, it seemed as though I was the only person on all of Mars who was really happy that I was here.

Hatch 'em, match 'em, and dispatch 'em—that was the usual lot for clergy. Well, we hadn't had any births yet, although we would soon. And no one had died since I'd arrived. That left marriages.

Of course, I did perform Mass every Sunday, and people did come out. But it wasn't like a Mass on Earth. Oh, we had a choir—but the people who had joined it all made a point of letting each other know that they weren't religious; they simply liked to sing. And, yes, there were some bodies warming the pews, but they seemed just to be looking for something to do; leisure-time activities were mighty scarce on Mars.

Perhaps that's why there were so few troubled consciences: there was nothing to get into mischief with. Certainly, no one had yet come for confession. And when we had communion, people always took the wine—of which there wasn't much available elsewhere—but I usually had a bunch of wafers left at the end.

Ah, well. I would do a bang-up job for Boothby and Jody on the wedding—so good that maybe they'd let me perform a baptism later.

"Father Bailey?" said a voice.

I turned around. Someone else needing me for something, and on a Thursday? Well, well, well . . .

"Yes?" I said, looking at the young woman.

"I'm Loni Sinclair," she said. "From the Communications Center."

"What can I do for you, my child?"

"Nothing," she said. "But a message came in from Earth for you—scrambled." She held out her hand, proffering a thin white wafer. I took it, thanked her, and waited for her to depart. Then I slipped it into my computer, typed my access code, and watched in astonishment as the message played.

"Greetings, Father Bailey," said the voice that had identified itself as Cardinal Pirandello of the Vatican's Congregation for the Causes of Saints. "I hope all is well with you. The Holy Father sends his special apostolic blessing." Pirandello paused, as if perhaps reluctant to go on, then: "I know that Earth news gets little play at Bradbury Colony, so perhaps you haven't seen the reports of the supposed miracle at Cydonia."

My heart jumped. Pirandello was right about us mostly ignoring the mother planet: it was supposed to make living permanently on another world easier. But Cydonia—why, that was here, on Mars. . . .

The cardinal went on: "A televangelist based in New Zealand has claimed to have seen the Virgin Mary while viewing Cydonia through a telescope. These new ground-

based scopes with their adaptive optics have astonishing re-
solving power, I'm told—but I guess I don't have to tell you
that, after all your time at Castel Gandolfo. Anyway, ordinarily, of course, we'd give no credence to such a claim—
putative miracles have a way of working themselves out,
after all. But the televangelist in question is Jurgen Emat,
who was at seminary fifty years ago with the Holy Father,
and is watched by hundreds of millions of Roman Catholics.
Emat claims that his vision has relevance to the Third Secret
of Fatima. As you know, Fatima is much on the Holy Father's mind these days, since he intends to canonize Lucia
dos Santos next month. Both the postulator and the *advoca-
tus diaboli* feel this needs to be clarified before Leo XIV visits Portugal for this ceremony."

I shifted in my chair, trying to absorb it all.

"It would, of course," continued the recorded voice,
"take a minimum of two years for a properly trained cardinal to travel from the Vatican to Mars. We know you have
no special expertise in the area of miracles, but, as the
highest-ranking Catholic official on Mars, His Holiness
requests that you visit Cydonia, and prepare a report. Full
details of the putative miracle follow. . . ."

Rome didn't commit itself easily to miracles, I knew.
After all, there were charlatans who faked such things, and
there was always the possibility of us getting egg on our collective faces. Also, the dogma was that all revelations required for faith were in the scriptures; there was no need for
further miracles.

I looked out the shuttle's windows. The sun—tiny and
dim compared with how it appeared from Earth—was
touching the western horizon. I watched it set.

The shuttle sped on, into the darkness.

*　　*　　*

"We speak today of the Third Secret of Fatima," said Jurgen Emat, robust and red of face at almost eighty, as he looked out at his flock. I was watching a playback of his broadcast on my datapad. "The Third Secret, and the miracle I myself have observed.

"As all of those who are pure of heart know, on May 13, 1917, and again every month of that year until October, three little peasant children saw visions of our Blessed Lady. The children were Lucia dos Santos, then aged ten, and her cousins Francisco and Jacinta Marto, ages eight and seven.

"Three prophecies were revealed to the children. The third was known only to a succession of Popes until 2000, when, while beatifying the two younger visionaries, who had died in childhood, John Paul II ordered the Congregation for the Doctrine of Faith to make that secret public, accompanied by what he called 'an appropriate commentary.'

"Well, the secret *is* indeed public, and has been for almost seventy years, but that commentary was anything but appropriate, twisting the events in the prophecy to relate to the 1981 attempt on John Paul II's life by Mehmet Ali Agca. No, that interpretation is incorrect—for I myself have had a vision of the true meaning of Fatima."

Puh-leeze, I thought. But I continued to watch.

"Why did I, alone, see this?" asked Emat. "Because unlike modern astronomers, who don't bother with eyepieces anymore, I looked upon Mars directly through a telescope, rather than on a computer monitor. Holy Visions are revealed only to those who gaze directly upon them."

An odd thing for a televangelist to say, I thought, as the recording played on.

"You have to remember, brethren," said Jurgen, "that the 1917 visions at Fatima were witnessed by children, and that the only one who survived childhood spent her life a cloistered nun—the same woman Pope Leo XIV intends to beatify in a few weeks' time. Although she didn't write down the Third Secret until 1944, she'd seen little of the world in the intervening years. So everything she says has to be reinterpreted in light of that. As Vatican Secretary of State Cardinal Angelo Sodano said upon on the occasion of the Third Secret's release, 'The text must be interpreted as a symbolic key.'"

Jurgen turned around briefly, and holographic words floated behind him: *We saw an Angel with a flaming sword in his left hand; flashing, it gave out flames that looked as though they would set the world on fire . . .*

"Clearly," said Jurgen, indicating the words with his hand, "this is a rocket launch."

I shook my head in wonder. The words changed: *And we saw in an immense light that is God—something similar to how people appear in a mirror when they pass in front of it—a Bishop dressed in white . . .*

Jurgen spread his arms now, appealing for common sense. "Well, how do you recognize a bishop? By his miter—his liturgical headdress. And what sort of headdress do we associate with odd reflections? The visors on space helmets! And what color are space suits? White—always white, to reflect the heat of the sun! Here, the children doubtless saw an astronaut. But where? Where?"

New words, replacing old: *. . . passed through a big city . . . half in ruins . . .*

"And that," said Jurgen, "is our first clue that the vision was specifically of Mars, of the Cydonia region, where, since the days of *Viking,* mystics have thought they could detect the ruins of a city, just west of the so-called Face on Mars."

Gracious Christ, I thought. Surely the Vatican can't have sent me off to investigate that? The so-called "Face" had, when photographed later, turned out to be nothing but a series of buttes with chasms running through them.

Again, the words floating behind Jurgen changed: *Beneath the two arms of the Cross there were two Angels . . .*

"Ah!" said Jurgen, as if he himself were surprised by the revealed text, although doubtless he'd studied it minutely, working up this ridiculous story.

"The famed Northern Cross," continued Jurgen, "part of the constellation of Cygnus, is as clearly visible from Mars' surface as it is from Earth's. And Mars' two moons, Phobos and Deimos, depending on their phases, might appear as two angels beneath the cross . . ."

Might, I thought. *And monkeys might fly out of my butt.*

But Jurgen's audience was taking it all in. He was an old-fashioned preacher—flamboyant, mesmerizing, long on rhetoric and short on logic, the kind that, regrettably, had become all too common in Catholicism since Vatican III.

The floating words morphed yet again: . . . *two Angels each with a crystal aspersorium in his hand . . .*

"An aspersorium," said Jurgen, his tone begging indulgence from all those who must already know, "is a vessel for holding holy water. And where, brethren, is water more holy than on desiccated Mars?" He beamed at his flock. I shook my head.

"And what," said Jurgen, "did the angels Phobos and Deimos do with their aspersoria?" More words from the Third Secret appeared behind him in answer: *They gathered up the blood of the Martyrs.*

"Blood?" said Jurgen, raising his bushy white eyebrows in mock surprise. "Ah, but again, we have only blessed Sister Lucia's interpretation. Surely what she saw was simply red liquid—or liquid that *appeared* to be red. And, on Mars, with its oxide soil and butterscotch sky, *everything* appears to be red, even water!"

Well, he had a point there. The people of Mars dressed in fashions those of Earth would find gaudy in the extreme, just to inject some color other than red into their lives.

"And, when I gazed upon Cydonia, my brethren, on the one hundred and fiftieth anniversary of the first appearance of Our Lady of the Rosary at Fatima, I saw her in all her glory: the Blessed Virgin.

"How did I know to look at Cydonia, you might ask? Because the words of Our Lady had come to me, telling me to turn my telescope on to Mars. I heard the words in my head late one night, and I knew at once they were from blessed Mary. I went to my telescope and looked where she had told me to. And nine minutes later, I saw her, pure and white, a dot of perfection moving about Cydonia. Hear me, my children! Nine minutes later! Our Lady's thoughts had come to me instantaneously, but even her most holy radiance had to travel at the speed of light, and Mars that evening was 160 million kilometers from Earth—nine light-minutes!"

I must have dozed off. Elizabeth Chen was standing over me, speaking softly. "Father Bailey? Father Bailey? Time to get up . . ."

I opened my eyes. Liz Chen was plenty fine to look at—hey, I'm celibate, not dead!—but I was unnerved to see her standing here, in the passenger cabin, instead of sitting up front at the controls. It was obvious from the panorama flashing by outside my window that we were still speeding along a few meters above the Martian surface. I'll gladly put my faith in God, but autopilots give me the willies.

"Hmm?" I said.

"We're approaching Cydonia. Rise and shine."

And give God the glory, glory . . . "All right," I said. I always slept well on Mars—better than I ever did on Earth. Something to do with the 37 percent gravity, I suppose.

She went back into the cabin. I looked out the window. There, off in the distance, was a side view of the famous Face. From this angle, I never would have given it a second glance if I hadn't known its history among crackpots.

Well, if we were passing the Face, that meant the so-called cityscape was just twenty kilometers southwest of here. We'd already discussed our travel plans: she'd take us in between the "pyramid" and the "fortress," setting down just outside the "city square."

I started suiting up.

The original names had stuck: the pyramid, the fortress, the city square. Of course, up close, they seemed not in the least artificial. I was bent over now, looking out a window.

"Kind of sad, isn't it?" said Liz, standing behind me, still in her coveralls. "People are willing to believe the most outlandish things on the scantest of evidence."

There was just a hint of condescension in her tone. Like almost everyone else on Mars, she thought me a fool—and not just for coming out here to Cydonia, but for the things I'd built my whole life around.

I straightened up, faced her. "You're not coming out?"

She shook her head. "You had your nap on the way here. Now it's my turn. Holler if you need anything." She touched a control, and the inner door of the cylindrical air lock chamber rolled aside, like the stone covering Jesus' sepulchre.

What, I wondered, would the Mother of our Lord be doing here, on this ancient, desolate world? Of course, apparitions of her were famous for occurring in out-of-the-way places: Lourdes, France; La'Vang, Vietnam; Fatima, Portugal; Guadalupe, Mexico. All of them were off the beaten track.

And yet, people did come to these obscure places in their millions after the fact. It had been a century and a half since the apparitions at Fatima, and that village still attracted five million pilgrims annually.

Annually. I mean *Earth* annually, of course. Only the

anal retentive worry about the piddling difference between a terrestrial day and a Martian sol, but the Martian year was twice as long as Earth's. So, Fatima, I guess gets *ten* million visitors per Martian year. . . .

I felt cold as I looked at the landscape of rusty sand and towering rock faces. It was psychosomatic, I knew: my surface suit—indeed white, as Jurgen Emat had noted—provided perfect temperature control.

The city square was really just an open area, defined by wind-sculpted sandstone mounds. Although in the earliest photos it had perhaps resembled a piazza, it didn't look special from within. I walked a few dozen meters, then turned around, the lamp from my helmet piercing the darkness.

My footprints stretched out behind me. There were no others. I was hardly the first to visit Cydonia, but, unlike on the Moon, dust storms on Mars made such marks transitory.

I then looked up at the night sky. Earth was easy enough to spot—it was always on the ecliptic, of course, and right now was in . . . my goodness, isn't that a coincidence!

It was in Virgo, the constellation of the Virgin, a dazzling blue point, a sapphire outshining even mighty Spica.

Of course, Virgo doesn't depict the Mother of Our Lord; the constellation dates back to ancient times. Most likely, it represents the Assyrian fertility goddess, Ishtar, or the Greek harvest maiden, Persephone.

I found myself smiling. Actually, it doesn't depict anything at all. It's just a random smattering of stars. To see a virgin in it was as much a folly as seeing the ruins of an ancient Martian city in the rocks rising up around me. But I knew the . . . well, not the *heavens,* but the night sky . . . like the back of my hand. Once you'd learned to see the patterns, it was almost impossible *not* to see them.

And, say, there was Cygnus, and—whaddaya know!— Phobos, and, yes, if I squinted, Deimos, too, just beneath it.

But no. Surely the Holy Virgin had not revealed herself

to Jurgen Emat. Peasant children, yes; the poor and sick, yes. But a televangelist? A rich broadcast preacher? No, that was ridiculous.

It wasn't explicitly in Cardinal Pirandello's message, but I knew enough of Vatican politics to understand what was going on. As he'd said, Jurgen Emat had been at seminary with Viktorio Lazzari—the man who was now known as Leo XIV. Although both were Catholics, they'd ended up going down widely different paths—and they were anything but friends.

I'd only met the Pontiff once, and then late in his life. It was almost impossible to imagine the poised, wise Bishop of Rome as a young man. But Jurgen had known him as such, and—my thoughts were my own; as long as I never gave them voice, I was entitled to think whatever I wished—and to know a person in his youth is to know him before he has developed the mask of guile. Jurgen Emat perhaps felt that Viktorio Lazzari had not deserved to ascend to the Holy See. And now, with this silly announcement of a Martian Marian vision, he was stealing Leo's thunder as the Pope prepared to visit Fatima.

Martian. Marian. Funny I'd never noticed how similar those words were before. The only difference . . .

My God.

The only difference is the lowercase t—the *cross*—in the middle of the word pertaining to Mars.

No. No. I shook my head inside the suit's helmet. Ridiculous. A crazy notion. What had I been thinking about? Oh, yes: Emat trying to undermine the Pope. By the time I got back to Utopia Planitia, it would be late Saturday evening. I hadn't thought of a sermon yet, but perhaps that could be the topic. In matters of faith, by definition, the Holy Father was infallible, and those who called themselves Catholics—even celebrities like Jurgen Emat—had to accept that, or leave the faith.

It wouldn't mean much to the . . . yes, I thought of them as my *congregation*, even sometimes my flock . . . but of course the group that only half-filled the pews at Saint Teresa's each Sunday morn were hardly that. Just the bored, the lonely, those with nothing better to do. Ah, well. At least I wouldn't be preaching to the converted. . . .

I looked around at the barren landscape, and took a drink of pure water through the tube in my helmet. The wind howled, plaintive, attenuated, barely audible inside the suit.

Of course, I knew I was being unfairly cynical. I *did* believe with all my heart in Our Lady of the Rosary. I knew—knew, as I know my own soul!—that she had in the past shown herself to the faithful, and . . .

And *I* was one of the faithful. Yes, pride goeth before destruction, and a haughty spirit before a fall—but I was more faithful than Jurgen Emat. It was true that Buzz Aldrin had taken Holy Communion upon landing on the Moon, but I was bringing Jesus' teachings farther than anyone else had, here, in humanity's first baby step out toward the stars. . . .

So, Mary, where are you? If you're here—if you're with us here on Mars, then show yourself! My heart is pure, and I'd love to see you.

Show yourself, Mother of Jesus! Show yourself, Blessed Virgin! Show yourself!

Elizabeth Chen's tone had the same mocking undercurrent as before. "Have a nice walk, Father?"

I nodded.

"See anything?"

I handed her my helmet. "Mars is an interesting place," I said. "There are always things to see."

She smiled, a self-satisfied smirk. "Don't worry, Father," she said, as she put the helmet away in the suit locker. "We'll have you back to Bradbury in plenty of time for Sunday morning."

* * *

I sat in my office, behind my desk, dressed in cassock and clerical collar, facing the camera eye. I took a deep breath, crossed myself, and told the camera to start recording.

"Cardinal Pirandello," I said, trying to keep my voice from quavering, "as requested, I visited Cydonia. The sands of Mars drifted about me, the invisible hand of the thin wind moving them. I looked and looked and looked. And then, blessed Cardinal, it happened."

I took another deep breath. "I saw *her*, Eminence. I saw the Holy Virgin. She appeared to float in front of me, a meter or more off the ground. And she was surrounded by spectral light, as if a rainbow had been bent to the contours of her venerable form. And she spoke to me, and I heard her voice three times over, and yet with each layer nonetheless clear and easily discernible: one in Aramaic, the language Our Lady spoke in life; a second in Latin, the tongue of our Church; and again in beautiful, cultured English. Her voice was like song, like liquid gold, like pure love, and she said unto me . . ."

Simply sending a message to Cardinal Pirandello wouldn't be enough. It might conveniently get lost. Even with the reforms of Vatican III, the Church of Rome was still a bureaucracy, and still protected itself.

I took the recording wafer to the Communications Center myself, handing it to Loni Sinclair, the woman who had brought Pirandello's original message to me.

"How would you like this sent, Father?"

"It is of some import," I said. "What are my options?"

"Well, I can send it now, although I'll have to bill the . . . um, the . . ."

"The parish, my child."

She nodded, then looked at the wafer. "And you want it to go to both of these addresses? The Vatican and CNN?"

"Yes."

She pointed to an illuminated globe of the Earth, half embedded in the wall. "CNN headquarters is in Atlanta. I can send it to the Vatican right now, but the United States is currently on the far side of Earth. It'll be hours before I can transmit it there."

Of course. "No," I said. "No, then wait. There are times when both Italy and the U.S. simultaneously face Mars, right?"

"Not all of the U.S.—but Georgia, yes. A brief period."

"Wait till then, and send the message to both places at the same time."

"Whatever you say, Father."

"God bless you, child."

Loni Sinclair couldn't quite mask her amusement at my words. "You're welcome," she replied.

Four years have passed. Leo XIV has passed on, and Benedict XVI is now pontiff. I have no idea if Jurgen Emat approves of him or not—nor do I care. Dwelling on Earthly matters is frowned upon here, after all.

Five million people a year still come to Fatima. Millions visit Lourdes and Guadalupe and La'Vang.

And then they go home—some feeling they've been touched by the Holy Spirit, some saying they've been healed.

Millions of faithful haven't made it to Mars. Not yet; that will take time. But tens of thousands have come, and, unlike those who visited the other shrines, most of them stay. After traveling for years, the last thing they want to do is turn around and go home, especially since, by the time they'd arrived here, the propitious alignment of Earth and Mars that made their journey out take only two years has changed; it would take much longer to get home if they left shortly after arriving.

And so, they stay, and make their home here, and contribute to our community.

And come to my Masses. Not out of boredom. Not out of loneliness. But out of belief. Belief that miracles do still occur, and can happen as easily off Earth as on it.

I am fulfilled, and Mars, I honestly believe, is now a better place. This *is* a congregation, a flock. I beam out at its members from the pulpit, feeling their warmth, their love.

Now I only have one problem left. To lie to Cardinal Pirandello had been a violation of my oath, of the teachings of my faith. But given that I'm the only priest on all of Mars, to whom will I confess my sin?

*   *   *

Dubbed "the dean of Canadian science fiction" by The Ottawa Citizen, *Toronto's Robert J. Sawyer is the author of the Hugo Award finalists* **Starplex, Frameshift, Factoring Humanity,** *and* **Calculating God,** *and the Nebula Award winner* **The Terminal Experiment.** *His story from the DAW anthology* **Sherlock Holmes in Orbit** *won France's top SF award, Le Grand Prix de l'Imaginaire, and his story from the DAW anthology* **Dinosaur Fantastic** *won Canada's top SF award, the Aurora. Rob's latest novel is* **Hominids,** *the first volume in his "Neanderthal Parallax" trilogy. His Web site at www.sfwriter.com has been called "the largest genre writer's home page in existence" by* Interzone.

RIGGERS

by Michael E. Picray

SOLAR SAIL RIGGERS, APPRENTICES SOUGHT
The factory ship *Inner Space* is offering apprenticeships
to qualified candidates interested in working toward their
certification as Master Riggers. The first portion of the program will take place on Earth, followed by extensive,
hands-on training aboard ship. Transport to and from
Earth will be provided.
A commitment to four years working as a rigger for the
Company is required. We pay top wages, offer a complete
benefits and bonus package, and provide the highest
standards in safety. Apply at your local employment office
or contact Human Resources, ExtraTerra Corp.

THE Solar Sail Factory Ship *Inner Space* cruised ten million miles above the plane of the ecliptic. If a rocket
were launched nearly straight up from the North geographic
pole of the Earth, it would have hit the *Inner Space* right in
the center of its wheel spokes, where the main zero G factory works were located. Radiating outward from this center
body was the structure that supported the solar sails. The
ship's wheeled shape seemed to be rolling through space as
it spun to maintain the stability of the structure, and to keep
tension on the fabric of the sails.

On the far side of the sun from the *Inner Space,* a sunspot
formed. The opposing magnetic fields formed a loop be-

tween them that ran across the neutral line, thus achieving stability. As the sunspot rotated toward the Earth, the magnetic environment changed and the loop twisted, creating a shear that pointed along the neutral dividing line. The change in the magnetic field caused a filament suspended above the surface of the sun to collapse. Seconds later a solar flare, formed by a tremendous explosion of gases and solar material, and heated to one million degrees Celsius, leaped into the lower heliosphere at nearly 1800 kilometers per second, toward the area commonly known as inner space. At this temperature, electrons were stripped from component atoms and sent spaceward as ionized particles, accompanied by gamma rays and X-rays. A shock wave from this explosion raced across the intervening space.

On Earth, the solar weather forecasters sent out a general warning that a Coronal Mass Ejection, a CME, had occurred and applied their formulas to project the exact path of the Solar Particle Storm. The Solar Sail Factory Ship *Inner Space* was centered in that path in four dimensions. A specific warning was sent.

But aboard the *Inner Space* a small resistor in the electronic tracking system of the Main Radio Antenna Array, after working faithfully for nearly fifteen years, failed. Since the highly directional array still functioned within defined parameters, the redundant systems did not kick on-line and take over tracking. At a distance of ten million miles it doesn't take much variance to miss a target. The highly-directional antenna array still functioned, but it was no longer pointed at the Earth.

Master Rigger John "Cap" Hardesty, senior rigger aboard the *Inner Space,* released the stay-brake. Centrifugal force began to act on the bright silver two-seat creeper's boxy shape, and slowly began pushing it out Radial Arm Three's guide wire toward the rim of the sail. At the same time, an automated weight began its journey out Radial Arm Eleven, providing the balance so necessary to the stability of the structure. The grabber-gears attached to the undercarriage of the creeper were crawling along the radial with agonizing slowness, metering its speed, keeping it from flying out to the rim and being flung into space. The seat next to Cap's held Apprentice Rigger Bob "Ace" Harley.

"I've been aboard for two months," Harley was saying, "and this is the first time I get to go out on the sails."

Cap responded, "When I first came aboard, I lived to come out here." He reached a hand forward and tweaked the tension adjustment on the Alpha set of clamps. They had a tendency to expand and drag as the friction heated them. Then he leaned back in the driver's seat. "I got over it."

Cap's adjustment of the clamps required Harley to lean into his own control panel and loosen the forward set of grabbers so that they operated smoothly and didn't bind on the cable. Cap watched him fuss and fidget with them, first turning the knob the wrong way and tightening, then nearly losing the wire as he loosened them too much. Although Cap saw everything, he said nothing. The kid had to learn, and hands-on experience was still the best teacher.

"Why don't you like going out anymore?" Harley asked.

Cap continued to look out the port, listening to the muted ticking sound as the grabber-gears meshed with the radial track. Eventually he spoke. "What do they tell you kids these days when you come up here? What do they tell you about the dangers?"

"Well, they tell us that radiation can kill us, but everybody knows that." Harley thought back to his orientation training. "They tell us that working here is safer than being a farmer on Earth, that we'll get less radiation than the farmer will. Oh, and they tell us to listen to you when you tell us how to do things so we don't get hurt."

Cap nodded his head. "That's about what I figured."

Harley looked startled. "Did they lie to us?"

Cap's face acquired a grim smirk. "No. They didn't lie. They just left out a few things. Like they probably used the words 'on average' when they told you that bit about the farmers and the radiation, didn't they? What they told you is absolute truth, as far as it goes. Those radiation risk estimates they told you about are based on increased rates of cancer. But if you get zapped out here and die quickly, you'll never have a chance to get cancer. You won't even be a statistic.

"How do you think you got your job? Did you think we were building an addition to the factory and needed extra riggers?" Cap's voice sneered, and then became hard and flat. "You are here because the guy you replaced isn't, and I'm here to tell you that he didn't get old and retire. I've been up here on rotation with Beta-partners for five years and I'm the senior rigger. What does that tell you? It should tell you that up here we live until we die, and that's all we expect." He paused. "They told you about Beta-partners, didn't they?"

Harley looked confident. "Yes, sir. A Beta-partner is your opposite number so that you can rotate back to the Earth to rebuild muscle tone and bone mass, and therefore not become debilitated by working for extended periods in space. The Company can employ you longer that way and it spends less in training costs, allowing them to pay us more. I haven't met my Beta-partner yet."

Cap nodded his head. "You probably never will. You're up, he's down, with no overlap. You're a smart kid. You know about redundancy in space systems? Your Beta is also your spare, your replacement if something happens to you. There is one advantage to the system for you, though. It allows you to get out of the radiation up here for a while."

Harley nodded in understanding. Then he got a concerned look on his face. "Cap? What do we do if the gears slip?"

Cap could see all of Harley's gauges from his own seat and had noticed the progress indicator showing zero progress some time ago. He had been wondering how long it would take the kid to notice. The kid was quicker than some, slower than others. Cap leaned over and looked at the indicator, then straightened up and looked out his porthole. "Sometimes not much," he said and pointed out Harley's port.

Harley looked outside and saw that their progress continued. Then he looked back at the indicator, which still said that the creeper wasn't moving, and got a puzzled look on his face.

Cap reached under the control panel's bottom lip and took a large screwdriver from a homemade rack. He gave the progress indicator gauge a hard whack with the handle. The gauge immediately jumped from zero to their earlier indicated speed. "Sometimes ya gotta do a field calibration with a technical tool," he explained. "I used to keep a little tack hammer under there, but the brass figured out what I did with it and took it away from me. When they still didn't replace the indicator, I 'found' that screwdriver in one of the shops and nobody's the wiser." Harley smiled, nodding. Cap went on to explain, "I think the indicator locking up like that has something to do with the centrifugal force out here near the rim. At C 20, we will weigh an apparent 1.5 times our Earth normal. Then, too," he grinned as he put the screwdriver back, "some things just act differently out here."

After he straightened up, he gave Harley a speculative look. "So, Ace. What made you want to come into space? The pay? Running away from an ugly girlfriend?"

Harley flushed. "You'll laugh at me if I tell you."

"No. I won't. Trust me," Cap encouraged and grinned benignly.

Harley chuckled. "Okay. I came into space because I wanted to be a part of it. I mean here we are, human beings expanding out into the universe, going out to explore the galaxy! This has got to be the grandest time in history." He paused, and his face fell. "But most of the people down there don't even pay attention to it anymore. We're just part of the little lights in the sky. They don't care." He looked directly at Cap. "I want to be part of it. I want my kids and their kids to be able to say that their dad was up here doing something to help us get to the stars!"

Further small talk was suspended when the creeper lurched as it hit the end-of-radial stop block, which automatically shut down the grabber-gears and engaged the safety clamps.

Cap reached down and reengaged the stay-brake. "Well, here we are, Ace; the end of the line. Concentric Stiffener Ring #20, home of random effects, edge monsters, and the place voted most likely to need repair. You now know what it's like to be on the edge of one of those toy disks the kids throw around." He double-checked the safety equipment's indicators, and his voice grew serious. "On this trip your primary function will be just to watch me. Next time, if you're really polite and beg a lot, I might let you handle the waldos."

The Master Rigger stood in order to reach a contraption that was all wires and joints with two gloves on the end. Then he leaned his body back and pulled until the contraption started to move toward him. He quickly put his forearms on the gloves and bore down with his full weight. The machine rode smoothly to just above his chair and then he sat down, putting the gloves on while Harley watched. Cap reached with the gloves to take hold of a helmet that was also wired and put it on. A display screen automatically folded down in front of Harley so he could see what Cap saw in the helmet, and Cap began giving voice commands.

"Butthead. Access C3. Repair arm to gross position nine zero degrees left, SS plus max extension."

Then he started teaching Harley. "As you may be aware,

waldos are remote manipulation units that allow us to work with things that are in hostile environments. To use them you need several things. First you need the computer's name, which in this case is Butthead." Harley grinned as Cap went on in a dry tone. "The next time we come out you'll be sitting here. There will be an initialization sequence and, if it suits you, you can name the computer whatever you want. If you rename it, you'd better remember the name. It won't work for you unless you do, and you can't rename it.

"Second you'll need an access code. When I tell them to, the central office will issue you one. No need to worry about someone else using it. It's keyed to your voice."

Harley looked puzzled. "Then why have a code? If it's keyed to my voice, why can't I just tell it what I want it to do?"

Cap sighed at the familiar question. "Because when they designed these systems, they didn't think being ten million miles from Earth and moving at over 1.5 million miles a day just to keep up with the ball of dirt was sufficient security. The waldo is top secret equipment that has only been around since Adam and Eve got caught with their fig leaves down. How should I know why they did it? Sometimes I think they do things like this just to give us something to bitch about. So, of course, we oblige them.

"Third, you need to learn the abbreviations we use with the computer. For example . . ."

"I know them," Harley interrupted. "They've had us memorizing them for the past two months and practicing with waldo simulators. You just told the computer to swing the arm out ninety degrees and as high as it would go over the sail surface."

Cap turned so Harley could see his face through the helmet and winked. "You got the basics. There are some commands we taught the computers that the boss doesn't know about. You'll learn those in time." As soon as he had the waldos in position, he nodded his head toward the screen. "Now watch this real close. The sail is thin enough to slip between one second and the next, and as fragile as anything ever made. That's why we have to be out here fixing it all the time. If God so much as farts, we get a hole in it.

"Butthead, Access C3. Hold access code to terminate. View equals three meters squared." The view on the screen widened until it showed the requested area. The reason the sensors were reporting slackness in the sail became readily apparent. They could both see that it had torn loose at the corner and was slowly flapping in the solar wind.

"Crap!" Cap said to himself. "The bugger is loose. There'll be no safe, secure job today." He put the waldos away and then called the ship. "Bridge, C3."

The bridge answered, "C3."

"Bridge, we have a corner tear at R3/C20."

"Roger C3. I hear a corner tear at R3/C20. What do you recommend?"

Cap responded, "Recommend forty percent reduction of spin and five percent reduction of area, then EVA to reattach."

"Roger. I hear a request for four zero percent reduction of ship spin and take in the sails to reduce total area by point zero fiver, then EVA to reattach. Stand by, C3."

Cap turned to Harley. "They will, of course, deny the request because to reduce sail area means to slow down. To slow down means to fall behind the Earth. To fall behind means that they'll have to fire the ion engines to catch up . . . which means they'll have to spend a lot of money. The question our Captain and CEO is now asking himself is why he should spend a lot of money and risk his performance bonus just to make a sail rigger's job easier. The answer will be that he shouldn't, that's what we get paid for, and he'll say no. Which should take him about . . . five . . . four . . . three . . . two . . . one . . . zero seconds to do."

Exactly when Cap said zero, the radio scratched to life. "C3, Bridge."

"C3."

"C3, it has been determined that the repair as described can be effected without reducing area or spin. You have permission to go EVA and proceed with repair while observing all safety regulations and procedures. Space weather is in a no-warning condition."

"Roger, Bridge." Cap turned the radio off.

Harley brightened. "Actually, this is something I've always wanted to do. To be outside with nothing between me and the stars but a sheet of plastic over my face!"

Cap smiled grimly and nodded his head. "Well, a sheet of plastic and a couple of million miles of vacuum. Helmet on, Ace! It's time you and Daddy went for a little walk, and we have to hustle. If we don't get that beast fixed in short order, it could shred the whole sail. In the time it takes to mount a replacement sail, the whole ship would be unbalanced. To prevent that, they'd have to roll all sails, which would get really expensive! Then, since it will no doubt be our fault, you and Daddy will be out of a job. No brave new galaxy for you. No comfy retirement for me."

"Ace? Take hold of this sail clamp." Cap handed Harley a device that looked like a spring clip that was six inches wide with padded strips where the clamp faces would come together on each side of the sail, squeezing it between them. "Clamp it there. Yeah, good. Now, pull! *Harder!*" Waving a hand at Harley to ease off, Cap stopped pulling. "Crap. It's not going to work. Whatever tore through here must have taken a piece of the sail with it. Take your clamp and tie it off with a snap line so it will hold that piece of sail about where it belongs."

"Does this mean they'll have to let tension off the sail so we can fix it?" Harley asked.

"Not in this life," Cap laughed cynically. "No. What that means is that instead of taking us half an hour to fix, it will take two hours. See, we have to get another piece of sail from the patch box on the back of our sailcreeper, then fuse it to this one and seal it down with the sealing kit. The glue stuff takes a long time to set, and we have to hold the sail in place until it does. One screwup and we start all over."

Cap heard the sigh in Harley's suit-to-suit microphone. Then Harley said, "Well, it'll give me more time to look around, I guess."

Cap laughed. "Yeah. That's about all you'll be able to do while it sets." Then he called the bridge. "Bridge, C3."

"Bridge."

"Bridge, there is a piece of sail missing here. We plan to effect a patch. Estimated repair time is two hours. Submitting modified recommendation."

"C3, stand by."

On his suit-to-suit radio Cap said, "Why don't we go ahead and get the patch gear out while they're dithering. It'll save us some time."

Harley answered, "But don't they have to authorize us to use that stuff?"

Cap shook his helmeted head. "So what else are they going to do? Tell us to forget it; the ship is beyond repair and to call a tow truck? Come on. This thin stuff is really hard to corral if it gets away from you. And grab a couple more snap lines. We'll use them to tie the stuff down until we're ready for it. You set something down out here on the rim without attaching it to something and ka-zing! Off it goes into the dark, and your pay gets docked for the replacement. Ever price a wrench that has to come ten million miles?"

Once all the equipment and supplies were gathered, they settled back to take it easy until the official go-ahead. They were lying on the inner surface of the concentric ring looking "up" toward the rest of the ship. The inner rings and sail supports blocked the ship itself from view, and the glare of the reflected sun on the sails blotted out the stars on the sunward side, but they could see the stars streaking overhead on the shadowed side of it as they wheeled through space.

Bored, Cap decided to tease the kid. "If someone was on the top of this thing up there and fell, could we catch them before they dropped past us into space?"

Harley responded, "Nope."

"Why not?" Cap asked.

"Well, I could give you the long-winded answer that they would go the other way because of centrifugal force, but that wouldn't be as much fun. I think that if someone fell this way instead of that way, it would have to be Fat Jim. Fat Jim is so fat I doubt that even centrifugal force could budge him if he didn't want to go. So, if he fell this way, it would be on purpose, and I don't know about you, but I'm not getting under him!"

"Fat Jim?" Cap asked, thinking perhaps the teasing had been turned around.

"Yeah. He's a guy I met on Earth who really wanted to come up here. He got perfect scores on all his tests, but he just couldn't make weight. I heard a Company guy say that no matter how good Jim's scores were they could spend the same money and boost three riggers up here instead of just one. Last I heard, Jim was still down there trying, but they might have changed their minds. Let's face it. There are only just so many crazy people around."

The radio call intruded on their stargazing. "C3, Bridge."

"C3."

"You are authorized to proceed with the repair plan as modified. Bridge out."

"C3, out," Cap said. Then in the suit radio he said to Harley, "Okay. Time to get to work." He grabbed a sail clamp and held it up for Harley. "Now this is a sail clamp. If it looks familiar and the name sounds familiar, that's be-

cause I just showed you one of these and told you about it a
little bit ago. You even used one. It is not a doohickey. It is
not a thingamajig. It is not a dweedle-bob. Learning proper
nomenclature is important." He handed the sail clamp to
Harley.

"Now, you take that sail clamp and clamp it onto the sail,
but not just anywhere. You must first locate an imaginary
line-segment that runs from one edge of the sail to the other
edge of the sail with no tears intersecting that line." He took
a marker from a pocket in his suit and eyeballed the sail material. After several false starts, he put the soft marker point
on the sail and made a decisive line across the corner. "So.
Then you apply your sail clamp anywhere on the tear side of
the sail material." He watched as Harley did so.

"Good. Next, you take another sail clamp and do it again
only at a different spot. When the entire line is 'edged' with
sail clamps, we take the snap cords and snap them to the little snaps on the sail clamps, so, and then pull them until our
guts pop out, then hook the little hook on the other end of
the line to a cleat. Then we tighten the cord with the little
ratchet provided for that purpose, thereby stretching the material until it is as firm as a board."

They hooked the snap cords to the sail clamps, then
hooked the other ends to the cleats and tightened them
down. "Next, we measure the size of the hole, add a factor
of fifty percent, and cut the material." Cap took a small cutter from another pocket and expertly slashed the sail material before returning the cutter to the pocket and reclamping
the unused material to the ring.

"Then we just lightly stretch the material over the sail to
make sure it will fit; smooth that little corner over there."
Cap pointed to the errant material. Harley ran his gauntlet
over the spot. Cap nodded the upper half of his suit. "Yeah.
That's good. Now we glue it down." The "glue" was a tube
of sealer. He rolled the material back, smeared the glue over

the joint area, then replaced the patch material and pressed it down into the glue. The operation was completed when he took out a small electronic tool and slowly passed it over the joint, fusing the materials together much like a welder fuses metal. Then he stood up on the ring. "Now we put the material and tools away except for the cords and clamps that are in use, and wait. It takes approximately an hour for the sealant to achieve maximum strength." Cap looked at his wrist chrono. "Tie yourself down if you're going to take a nap," he warned. "Keep in mind that although your safety tether will stop you from flying off into space, it won't make you lighter. If you fall off, when you reach the end of your tether centrifugal force will make you weigh an apparent 1.5 to 1.75 times your Earth normal weight. Then a shuttle will have to go after you, as you won't be able to climb the rope—especially in a suit that weighs as much as you do. All the tether really does is make you easy to find and hard to catch. Any questions?"

Harley was looking closely at the shiny sail material. "How do you see the edge of this stuff? It just kind of disappears into nothing."

"With a microscope. We don't worry about the actual edge too much. We just grab it where we can see it and go with it."

Harley looked out over the sails. "So the sunlight hits the sails and pushes us along. Pretty simple, huh?"

Cap agreed. "Yeah. When a photon hits the sail, it bounces off and gives us a teensy push. The part I don't get is they tell me that when it does that it gives up twice the momentum it had coming in. It's like getting something for free. At least that's what the physicists claim."

Harley went on. "I don't know how it does it either, but I know about the bouncing thing. When I was a kid, I had one of those solar cookers. You know, the ones where you stab a hot dog on a spike and the little curved dish focuses the sunlight on the dog and burns a hole in one spot while leaving the rest of it raw?"

Cap laughed, "I had one of those, too!"

They sat down on the ring to wait for the patch to set and watched the stars for a while without speaking. Then Harley broke the silence. "Are we there yet?"

They both laughed again and Cap looked at the kid. "Ace, you know? You're all right. I think we're going to get along."

Harley looked out at the stars again and said, "I don't know. I was looking for a rich wife. I don't think you qualify."

They both laughed as the stars wheeled overhead and they waited.

The radio instruments aboard the *Inner Space* first detected the CME as a slowly drifting type II radio emission, which was indicative of a CME heading their way. The onboard weather staff was rousted and sent to their computers and instruments to determine the severity and probable threat level and duration to the ship and its crew. Within fifteen minutes of the radio detection, the first highly-energized particles arrived. The weather section supervisor called the bridge on the intercom and suggested protective measures be taken just in case it turned out to be a bad storm. The watch officer called the Captain, who verbally approved the standard potential CME measures. The watch officer, after logging the series of orders, stuck his finger on the button for the external radiation storm warning light and then activated the GEMS unit, the Generated Magnetic Shield that mimicked the Earth's own geomagnetic field and captured the ionized particles to keep them form getting to the main body of the ship.

Cap was thinking about his family dirtside when the radio intruded.

"C3, *scratch skurtchh*."

Cap was puzzled. He keyed his radio. "Bridge, C3. You need something?"

The only answer he received was more noise. "Something wrong?" Harley asked.

"Don't know. I think the bridge just tried to call me, but they were eaten by static. Maybe if I stand up I'll get a better signal."

The second Cap's head cleared the thickness of the inner rings he knew they had trouble. A red strobe light was blinking on the top of the factory. "Ace, I want you to do just exactly as I say, no response, no argument, no bullshit. Got it? Now stand up and follow your tether to me."

Harley did as he was told. As he was moving toward Cap, Cap raised his arm and pointed to the blinking red light. "Do you know what that is?"

Harley knew. They'd talked a lot about it in the classes. It was the radiation storm warning light.

Cap said, "That is a bucket full of shit and we are squarely in it." Cap was afraid. He had never been outside when the red light was on. He could already see the auroral glow as the ship's GEMS unit intercepted charged particles and protected the main ship. Out here on the sails, though, there was no GEMS.

As he began to lead Harley toward the creeper, he started to feel lighter on his feet. "They're slowing the spin rate. That means they are going to take in the sails." As he said it, he felt the direction that was "down" begin to change. "They're precessing the wheel, too, turning it sideways so the peak of the radiation storm will hit the ship's edge."

Cap looked around as he moved, figuring angles. Then to Harley over the radio static he said, "We're heading for the creeper. We gotta get behind it. That's where we'll have the most passive shielding." Halfway to the creeper, they heard the high-pitched squeal of their active dosimeters. When they got to the shadowed side of the creeper, Cap squatted up against it and told Harley, "Hunker down. Smaller cross section gets you less total whole-body exposure.

"Bridge, C3 at D20. Mayday. Mayday." Cap glanced toward the ship and saw the high-speed shuttle already on its way. Someone had remembered they were out here. He'd have to thank the officer of the watch.

The whole situation was unreal to Harley. He hadn't enough experience or knowledge to be properly scared. So far it seemed like an adventure that he could write home about! "Funny," Harley said. "I *believe* the fact that there is a ton of radiation zipping by me, but I don't see a thing. A person should be able to see what might kill him."

Cap nodded his helmet in agreement and pointed to the main ship. "You can, and that's the worst view of it you'll ever have . . . from outside the GEMS field." They waited until the shuttle matched trajectories down light from the creeper. When the hatch opened, they scrambled inside and floated to the far side of the cargo area. The shuttle pilot in a full radiation protection suit looked at them to make sure they were clear of the hatch, then closed it and spun his craft around to streak for the ship's hangar bay, bouncing them off of the aft bulkhead.

The fully suited hazard control crew met them in the hangar bay. They were escorted to a nearby decontamination area before their EVA suits were stripped off of them, then their Anti-Cs. The material was all put in a large foil bag with radiation symbols and the words "Danger! Radioactive Material" on it in case they had picked up charged particles. The radiation hazard evaluation team collected their dosimeter sets, the active dosimeters' alarms screaming their electronic heads off at the indignity of being exposed to so much radiation. Then the riggers were scanned for discrete particles, issued new dosimeters, and escorted to sick bay. The medical team was waiting for them.

*   *   *

The doctor looked up from the records on his desk as Cap entered his office. "Master Rigger Hardesty? I thought you'd like to know that your lab results are in. How do you feel?"

Cap answered calmly. "Well, pretty much okay now that I quit barfing. I mean I think I might have a little temperature, and feel a bit tired, but I've felt worse. I'll get over it."

The doctor was nodding his head. "Well, that is consistent with your lymphocyte count and about what I expected." The doctor made a note on the record before him, the silence in the room stretching as his stylus tapped data into the chart. Finally he sighed and looked into Cap's expectant eyes. He quietly said, "I'm afraid I have some bad news for you. Your lymphocyte count was really low. It was just above fifty percent. Do you know what that means?"

Cap's mind went blank, then seeing the doctor was waiting for a response said, "Yeah, I know what it means. It means I've got anywhere from a couple of hours to a week of feeling normal, then my body parts start falling off. How much radiation did we get?"

The doctor looked at the chart. "Not enough to make body parts fall off, at least. There's actually no way to tell for sure exactly how much. It was significant. Apprentice Rigger Harley got the most, I believe."

Cap stiffened in surprise. "How could he get the most? We were standing side by side! Besides, I have four-plus years of accumulated dose."

The doctor shuffled the records and read for a second. "As of right now he's almost caught up. We wondered the same thing, so we checked it out. A careful analysis of the sensors indicated that a heavy dose covered your location from the shadowed side. The preliminary incident report suggests that as we took in the sails, something—a gust, a surge of photons and charged particulate matter, maybe even a filament plug in the solar wind—caused a sail to dimple. In short, it acted like a dish and focused on your area. Rigger Harley must have been on the side the beam came in from. It's the only explanation that works."

Cap's face became wary as he asked, "Are we treatable?"

The doctor nodded, "I believe so."

"Believe so? Can't you do better than that?" Cap demanded.

The doctor responded quickly. "I'm sorry, no. In a week, as soon as the storm is over and it's safe to do so without getting you additional exposure, we'll ship you both to one of the orbital treatment centers and get things rolling. While you're up here, we'll want to see you at least once a day at a consistent time. Meanwhile, you just take it easy and rest. I'm taking you off the duty roster. If your symptoms change, call us. We'll do all we can for you, but we are not set up to do the major work in these cases. We can, however, make it somewhat easier for you, you know." The doctor's eyes had drifted down to the desk as he spoke. Now he made direct eye contact. "I'm terribly sorry. I do wish there was something more I could do."

Cap nodded in understanding and resolved to put a good face on the situation. "That's okay, Doc. It's not your fault." He rose slowly to his feet. "See you tomorrow, then. Thanks," Cap said as he stuck out his hand and shook the doctor's. Then he turned and left the office.

Harley was in the tiny waiting room, waiting for his turn. In a small voice he asked, "Well, Cap. We gonna live?"

Cap smiled grimly and said, "At least until we die, Ace." Cap could see that the situation was finally becoming real to the kid. He sat down and watched Harley go into the office and close the door. A few minutes later he came out with a numb expression on his face and they both left the office and headed for the inner spaces where their rooms were and where there was less spin-gravity.

Feeling that something needed to be said, Cap finally spoke. "Well, Ace, looks like we're going to be grounded."

Harley cleared his throat before he said, "Yeah. Short career, huh? They said we were probably treatable." Harley looked searchingly at Cap. "What do you think? I mean you've seen this sort of thing before. What are our chances?"

Cap turned and looked full at him and lifted an eyebrow. "Of what?"

"Of living. Of surviving this?" Harley's eyes drilled into Cap's.

Cap answered as he made the transition from light on his feet to weightless and began pulling himself along the passageway by grabbing the rings on the bulkheads. "Like I said before, Ace. We'll live until we die. A man can't ask for more than that, now, can he?"

As Harley less gracefully followed Cap along the grab-rings, he thought about what Cap said and finally understood what Cap had been telling him since their first conversation. It was an attitude, a necessary attitude for those who worked under dangerous conditions. Soldiers, high steel walkers, deep-sea construction workers, space workers were all subject to it because they worked in unforgiving environments. "You live until you die." He liked it. It struck him as funny that he had no sooner learned it than he wouldn't need it any more.

*   *   *

Michael E. Picray was born in Des Moines, Iowa, and left the state at the first reasonable opportunity. A graduate of Northwest Missouri State University ('91) with a major in accounting, he now resides in Missouri with his wife and such children who have not yet lost all patience with him and moved out. In "Riggers," he combines firsthand knowledge of the blue-collar world with his experience as a U.S.

Navy veteran to provide a view of working in space from near the bottom of the human food chain. "If we could send humanity into space without sending people, it would be perfect." Mike hopes you enjoy the story and thanks Julie E. Czerneda, the editor, for putting up with him along the way.

SUSPENDED LIVES

by Alison Sinclair

GENERAL SURGEON

The IMS series of Medical Space Stations provides medical services to all orbital facilities and traffic, including government-run, privately-run, and nonprofit freehabs. Currently, each station serves over 15,000 personnel. To provide this level of service, the IMS stations are fully-functioning hospitals, with telesurgery and other specialists available at all times.

Immediate openings exist for three full-time telesurgeons. These positions have a mixed cycle of shifts, including the required three-month time Earthside.

Qualifications: As per IMS regulations, including a specialization in space-related trauma.

Personal: Must pass all physical and psychological tests required for prolonged work in space, including tolerance to zero G and a genome screen for susceptibility to radiation-induced cancer.

Responsibilities: As per IMS policies, procedures, and directives.

Compensation: Based on the existing IMS grid, which includes substantial incentives and benefits as well as insurance coverage.

Please apply in confidence to: IMS Hospital Services, Attention: Human Resources: File #5672298A-06

Only candidates to be interviewed will receive a reply.

FIVE facets of the icosahedral doctor's lounge look up, or down, if you will, on Earth. The dayshift surgeon, Ygevney Barishenkov, slouches beneath the window, rumpled and bleached in the Earth light. I'd think he'd had a bad shift, but that Y' always looks as though he hasn't grown to fit his skin, never mind his scrubs.

I attach my coffee-sac to my belt and monkey along the perimeter struts in the approved manner. No microgravity aerobatics in the doctor's lounge.

"I accepted two transfers from Franklin, Artemis construction crew," Y' says, by way of evening greeting. "Both stable."

"Tell me about them; I'm awake." I suck on coffee, to ensure I can live up to the promise. I could ask the genie for the hand-over, since all the information is databased, but nobody comes up here to be a hermit.

"The first one's Maria José Elliott, twenty-seven, closed-suit crush injury to right leg. Vascular repair was successful with recovery of good perfusion; some ischemic damage and rhabdomyolysis. No genetic risk factors for muscle breakdown, however, slightly increased risk of thrombosis. The gene-genii flagged two separate polymorphisms associated with mild thrombophilia.

"Second one is Li Shu Quen, thirty-four, decompression injury to left arm, sustained when she went to assist the first casualty. Transferred primarily for pain management; she's a known hypo-responder to synthetic opioids and Franklin didn't have the drugs to cover her." I agree with his scowl; if they have a known hypo-responder, they should have the drugs to cover her.

"I thought Artemis' argument for all-female work crews was that they had a better record in hazardous work environments?"

Out of the corner of my eye I see the nearest genie's eye brighten. "Genii, cancel review request," I get in, before the

knowledge system starts to pontificate on the world literature on gender differences in safety practices. "When are
they going to give us an upgrade that can recognize a rhetorical question?"

Y' can recognize a rhetorical question. "Stephe Te
Kawana has a hot gallbladder over at Sharman. The auditor-
genii says she doesn't have acceptable live experience, and
so she wants to know whether she should transfer or
whether you'll operate from here."

"How'd someone get up here with a hot gallbladder?
They should have been screened out and treated Earthside."
Y' produces another from his repertoire of shrugs. "What
should I know about him?"

"Forty-eight-year-old male, Ellis Keene. Engineer with
Faber. No known health problems."

"I'll review him, see whether we should transfer him
here. What's the lag between Sharman and here?"

"Seventy-one milliseconds," supplies the genie, on cue.

Telesurgery is limited by, among other things, the signal
round trip. Humans can only accommodate two, two fifty
milliseconds delay between their movement within the operating station and the visual feedback from the OR suite.
Much more than that, and the rhythm is broken, instruments
get out of position, incisions are too shallow or too deep, su-
tures are ill-placed.

Then Y' adds the joker to the pack. "We heard an
hour ago that there is an IBDD shuttle due in at 2307 for
Semmelweis."

Another platter of dainties left over from the bioterrors.
HIV-'flu, for instance, or Jerusalem hemorrhagic fever.

Although the last proven biowarfare release was seventeen years ago, and decommissioning of the former biowarfare labs is slowly proceeding worldwide, nobody quite
wants to let go. Hence Semmelweis, another example of a
small, not so bad idea that grew into a monster. We can see

it from here, off to the right, a clutch of polyhedral pods, tube-linked, with solar collector deployed.

Unlike any other department of the IMS, there are no tubes linking it to the rest of the platform, only support struts. Semmelweis is entirely self-contained, shuttle and bubble-car being the only way to reach it. Initially, it was intended to be a temporary research and storage facility; now, because the IMS is the organization that all bodies and states distrust least, it has become the repository for all the ostensibly decommissioned pathogens . . . just in case.

"Genii, please confirm that all departments have been officially notified that ambulances are *exempt* from the standard security lockdown?" Two years ago a critical transfer was delayed by security, such that we nearly lost the patient. I might forgive and forget; space doesn't.

Roll on the happy day when Semmelweis gets floated off on its own. Roll on the happier day when Semmelweis gets dropped into the sun.

"What else?"

What else is our current cadre of trauma inpatients, tucked away in the flare-shielded infirmary pods toward the center of the platform. Given the screening our crews undergo, they're as near to perfect specimens as the human race produces: young or middle-aged adults selected for excellent health, low cancer risk, mental stability, intelligence, adaptability, and a variety of other assets.

Not that we are underemployed, since the five IMS platforms are effectively the tertiary care centers for the orbital population, the fifteen thousand or so inhabitants of everything from the great solar taps to long-term experiments in closed-environment living, with various materials manufacturing, materials research, and pharmaceutical research and manufacturing platforms in between. Trauma accounts for most of the surgical caseload. Platform construction crews are disproportionately represented, because of the number

of new and short-term workers, then platform maintenance,
particularly the outdoor monkeys, those whose work in-
volves EVA. Inboard and teleconstruction crews are less
likely to wind up in here, though we currently have two survivors from an explosive depressurization that killed one
over on McAuliffe. One might be discharged back to McAuliffe today, assuming traffic control can clear the backlog
created by the IBDD shuttle in time. The other is likely to be
transferred Earthside if the anti-PTSD pharmacotherapy
doesn't take effect soon.

"G'night," I said to Ygevney, who waves an idle hand at
me and monkeys toward the nearest hatch. I tuck myself
into one of the lounge's blebs—recessed communications
alcoves—to look in the genii's eye. I'm considered eccentric
for my appetite for Earth news, but my family, like myself,
incline toward dangerous places. My plant geneticist parents
are currently working in the Christian States of America,
whose attitude to gene-engineering is nothing if not am-
bivalent, even though climate change has so altered the
Prairie and Southern landscape that no unengineered crop
plants can survive. My marine-biologist sister, the radical
conservationist, is campaigning against the expansion of the
fish plantations in former New Zealand waters. Since a third
of the world's population is now dependent on the sea for
food, the campaign has been, and will continue to be, violent.
My peacekeeper brother is guarding a forensics team investigating accusations of bioagent release somewhere in Mid-
Europe. And my ex-marital partners, a mobile group practice, have just been granted license to practice in a region of
United Africa formerly closed to, and still very suspicious of,
Western medicine.

I don't want to be taken by surprise by the official message that begins with the words "We regret to inform
you . . ." though I know I probably will be.

None of my spiders snag anything of interest, except for

an item on the case before the World Court determining plat-
formers' rights to rear children in microgravity. A verdict is
pending.

Pregnancy is both achievable and sustainable in a platform habitat, though there are challenges involving oxy-
genation and circulation. Study of mammals in microgravity
suggests that the postnatal maturation of skeleton, muscle,
and circulation under gravity is likely to be abnormal. Perhaps abnormal enough that any child raised purely or mostly
in space would have serious difficulty readapting to Earth.

As far as those on the international and commercial platforms are concerned, the issue is academic. Our contracts
stipulate contraceptive implants, and our benefits include
gene-banking and IVF. But several platforms established by
smaller governments, private foundations, and organizations
explicitly promote procreation in space. Four infants have
been born in the freehabs over the past three years, and the
Earthside relatives of two have taken the argument over
their well-being to court. The freehabber parents are refus-
ing to take the children Earthside at all until their rights are
upheld.

Personally, I regard our tenancy in space as entirely too
precarious to think of colonization. But if the World Court
rules the children have to be transferred Earthside, someone's going to have to enforce the order. I can see the whole
mess being recast as a child-health issue and dumped hot
and quivering in the IMS' jurisdiction. And *that* is something I want to see coming.

No verdict so far, and so to work.

I see no reason to transfer the patient from Sharman; indeed, knowing about the IBDD shuttle, I prefer to keep what
grace we had for accidents and true emergencies. Hence at
2030, I've done rounds and am configuring the operating
station Y' and I both favor to my own preferences, fitting the

headset, loading the VR interface, and adjusting the surgical gloves. For a small man, Ygeveny has big hands.

I study Keene's anatomical reconstructions and lab results. He has a hot gallbladder, all right, taut and inflamed, with an impacted stone in the bladder neck. With the surgical expert system in simulation mode, I run through the procedure, a remote laparoscopy. In microgravity things flip and bounce far more than you'd expect, particularly a slippery bag of fluid on a stalk. But since the operating field is entirely reconstructed from 3D imaging data, when I nick the biliary artery, the gory cloud filling the abdominal cavity does not obscure the surgical field, as it might under camera Earthside. I spend about thirty minutes refining my approach so that *won't* happen *in vivo,* all the time with a little clock ticking in my head. As though the arrival of medical emergencies is guided by any natural law—unless it's the one that says the pager never goes off just *before* you go to sleep.

I've spoken to Ellis Keene before I start my setup, and I bundle up the result of the simulations with the expert system commentary and squirt them over to him, adding the information to the statistics on my record. If he's unhappy with my experience and performance, we can prepare him for drop, but I gather from our talk that, like most people up here, he'd rather not drop out of turn. For someone who has been working on short-term contracts, he has accumulated a lot of hours.

While I'm waiting for a final conversation or a registered consent, I take a quick virtual trot around the ward and the parts and activities in the platform that experience has taught me are most accident-prone. The security lockdown helps, because nobody in the area is outside who does not absolutely need to be because something needs to be fixed now, and not in four hours. Who knows: it might be a quiet night. There's a suspected atmosphere leak over in one of the seven bioreactor pods where these days we grow most of our pharmacopeia. The suit and implanted biosensors of the team outside are normal, not even one raised heartbeat. If they've got a problem, they don't know it yet, and in any case, the duty internist will have them on his screen.

Lastly, I watch the IBDD shuttle emerging from Earth's shadow, its trefoil symbol orange on shining white. Precious little information available on what it's carrying—I, after all, will only have a need-to-know if something goes very wrong. Several IBDD teams have been visiting Serbiastan over the past months, so odds-on it's fungi. While the Americans liked viruses, the Europeans were partial to fungi.

Ellis Keene calls me, with a question as to how serious my nicking the biliary artery would have been. He could get the answers from the genie, of course, and let the decision-assist software assist his interpretation, but I already sense he prides himself in making up his own mind. He'll let me do this surgery if he decides to trust me. Which, in the end, he does, because, he informs me, I personally sent him my screwups and didn't make him look them up.

The surgery itself is straightforward—hardly a drop of blood spilled. What is less so is the results of some of the blood work. PCR shows one of the more common leukemic chromosomal translocations. There's a higher incidence of various cancers among space workers, and often a more rapid progression. I dislike the medical exemptions given for short-term contract workers, and the way companies like Faber take advantage of them. Those of us with long-term contracts have been screened for a low-risk genotype, as well as being fully dosed with the latest tumor suppressants. Ellis Keene's predicted cancer risk was lower than average, but still below the standards of the IMS, and I don't regard his tumor suppressant regimen as optimal. He'll be medically discharged Earthside for a full workup and treatment. The leukemia is eminently curable, particularly at this early stage, but he won't be back, not with a history of malignancy; no one would insure him.

Stephe Te Kawana seems as depressed as I am. We regard each other glumly across the virtual link, having agreed that she will be the one to tell our patient.

Like myself, Stephe is Unified Pacifican, though her ethnic blend is Asian Pacific, while mine is American Coast. Olive skin, light hazel eyes, black hair that she wears compressed under an elastic cap on duty and in baroque sculptures when not. She always looks slightly puffy-eyed, shifting fluids and the never-settling dust and dander even in our filtered air. Or that's how she has always explained it. I brace myself when I ask, "How was your time Earthside? With your family."

She smiles radiantly. "Hikaru's moving them to Canberra was the best decision we ever made. The kids were being exposed to so much propaganda against space development," the smile turns wry in acknowledgment that the big Space Centers are papered with their own propaganda, "never mind the relatives constantly dripping 'poor little things' into their ears and preaching about material goods being less important than family happiness. They're not the ones with nearly half a million in pro-school debt."

"To be honest, I wondered if you'd be back."

"Yes," she said. "You would. It's hard, isn't it? When it looks like it has to be a choice."

I don't talk about the divorce much: respect for my ex-partners and my own pride. I loved them, I honor their commitment to the ideals we once shared—still do, I believe, though we express them differently now. But their rejection still hurts, even after five years. "Not the same," I tell Stephe. "No kids, for one thing. And there were five of us. The dynamics are different."

"Where are your exes now?"

"They've moved the clinic down to the southern part of United Africa."

"Isn't that dangerous?"

"Less than it was; Africa is more stable and prosperous than it has been for a century." United Africa has been an unexpected beneficiary of global climate change, with the transformation of large areas once-desert by rainfall; for the last decade, they have been exporting wheat and corn.

Stephe has just drawn breath when our entire surround breaks up in red bars. A beat later, the alarm sounds, a sequence I've never heard before.

Behind the pulsing red bars, Stephe's lips move soundlessly. I'm seeing red myself. I never knew *any* platform system or alert could interrupt the visuals on a surgical link, even if we're not engaged in surgery. "Genii! This is a surgical circuit. A closed circuit. What's the hell's happening?"

Then I'm hanging over blue space, over the Earth. Looking down at the IBDD shuttle, pearl white on blue, gliding by an installation that twinkles coyly in the sunlight. I recognize it, one of our nearest neighbors, a quirky little bauble we all call the Desert Rose. It looks too decorative to be what it is, one of the most state-of-the-art experimental habitats.

I almost expect to hear music, Vaughn Williams, perhaps, or Elgar. But what I do hear, or rather, feel, is an irregular vibration through the pod, and then there's a cascade of text down the side of the image, including the symbol we can all recognize in our sleep, the warning to get to the shielded areas, *now*. I never knew the thumping of bodies in the tunnels transmitted through the walls.

Shielded areas—including the infirmary and telesurgery stations—are reinforced against meteorites and solar flares. But this is neither. Now I can hear the pilot's voice through my audio, speaking very fast, reciting what she's seeing, what she's doing, as though her instruments, her actions, were not being recorded and transmitted. And then she says, "Initiating cargo sterilization. Ejecting," and the cabin-pod cracks away on a cleft of fire, cast into the shallowness of space.

Text screeds down both sides of my screen. At such moments I go word-blind, even as my visual perception expands and my time sense explodes. The pilot is still reciting what she's doing as she rides the shuttle through the telelink, trying to turn it away from the platforms. She's still talking when the whole side of the shuttle peels apart from an eruption that is for the briefest of moments brighter than the clouds of Earth. And then there's a silence and murmured prayer.

Against the Earth light, the fragments are invisible, except for those large enough to contain their own shadow; they flicker, tumbling, Earthward, or obliquely past IMS-1. But we know the unseen ones by their passing: thin through the walls of the pod, the decompression alarms begin to squeal, and in the periphery of the display, as I have programmed it to do, the decompression warning icon blinks.

Faces bloom across my display, all the duty-docs, Julian Sutherland, space medicine; Tonia Sundralingham, radiation medicine; Nuria al-Hassam, psychiatry; and Y', who must just have gotten to sleep. Medical emergency coordinator comes around in rotation, rather like the one shell in Russian roulette. Guess who is gazing into the little black eye of fate tonight?

"Load medical emergency coordinator expert system," I . . . squeak. No, it's not the atmosphere. Deep breathing.

Earth, clouds, the absent shuttle, are all replaced by a schematic of nodes, my preferred representation. Each node indicates a particular function or aspect of the disaster, color-coded according to priority for my attention. The colors dance as everyone except Y' starts routing data toward it and me. The bioreads of scared and injured people. A map of the immediate vicinity, charting impacts, decompression reports. A report from Desert Rose's duty-doc: They've been struck by debris, have lost solar panels, have four—five— perfed pods, one torn open to the point of explosive decompression, and can anyone kindly tell them *what just came through their walls?*

Luther Igorin, the IBDD specialist on Semmelweis, is trying to answer that question. No question about the need-to-know now, and he spreads out the shuttle's manifest for us. It's fungi. In the later years of the bioterrors, fungi in particular were bioengineered to withstand heat, desiccation, radiation, taking tips from *Deinococcus radiodurans* and other extremophiles. He's highlighted two entries on the cargo manifest as radiation-resistants. The question is whether the radiation dose was adjusted to take account of that, whether the shuttle's cargo got the full sterilization before the shuttle came apart. I've never seen Luther sweat the way he's sweating now.

The shuttle crew announces their survival with a restrained, "I realize this may not be a good time, but we could use a pickup here." Someone in the background is retching.

Luther withdraws from the team room temporarily to get more information from the shuttle pilot. He's replaced by Jay McPhearson Leaphorn, responsible for rescue and retrieval. Jay traces descent from chiefs of clan and tribe, and his square, terra-cotta face reflects the stoicism of both traditions; nobody has ever sees *him* sweat.

Jay says, with his usual politeness, "My team have almost completed their hazard assessment. Do you have a casualty assessment, please?"

The expert system is crunching the biosensor readings, emergency calls, environmental readout, and other data, generating a list of urgent-attention cases in all the affected platforms. "I'm still waiting on a provisional list—"

"I'll be back for your review. Excuse me," and he blinks out.

The lit-up nodes now include: decompression, environmental compromise, radiation exposure, potential infectious agent exposure, psychological trauma.

Luther dumps the fingerprints of the shuttle's manifest to the pathogen-sensors of all platforms above our horizon. I have a bad feeling that this means he is not satisfied that the cargo was sterilized. We should all be grateful for a man who appreciates priorities; some of his IBDD colleagues would still be trying to limit "exposure" of sensitive information. This doesn't address the problem that, although there's a minimum standard for platform atmospheric monitoring, not everyone has the grade of biosensors that we do, affinity sensors with a wide range of receptors associated with pathogenicity rather than specific to individual pathogens. But . . . I subclone the display again, in time to see one, two, three, four, five . . . potential positives.

I've gone cold, seeing the signal imposed on the familiar blueprint.

Now, the fingerprints Luther sent over have a strong bias for sensitivity over specificity: no surprise, since the consequences of failing to detect these spores are far worse than the consequences of getting excited over some innocuous mold.

Only my parents and I were in Montana in June 2034. Global warming coming atop sustained overuse and over-irrigation had cost the Prairies their place as the continent's breadbasket; most of the Americas were dependent upon the sea, or imports from outside. I was on a student elective at a rural clinic and my parents were working on one of multiple drought-resistant engineering projects, efforts violently opposed by the Earth Redeemers. Since the Redeemers opposed genetic engineering of any organism, no one anticipated the anthrax bombing. My family had been vaccinated against all known strains ourselves, because of other areas my parents had worked; so we only got to watch other people die.

Transport of medicines and vaccines was delayed; the delay, it emerged, was because of concerns in Washington that further attacks might come, that the vaccines might be needed and better used elsewhere . . . in the important, economically valuable regions of the country, rather than in the depopulated, dust bowl Prairies.

Out of the outrage unslaked by the impeachment of the president, John Rand Brierly established his own Senate in Atlanta and built the New Secessionist movement. Four years after that, after an el Ninõ decimated the sea's relied-upon harvest, Brierly's forces launched the first attack in what became the pan-American War. By then, I was in Africa, completing my training, falling in love with Luis and Michel, planning a future that had nothing to do with a continent half a world away splintering under environmental stress and political, religious, and racial extremities—Africa's renaissance, after all, had come after decades of it.

"Helen," says Nuria.

Almost unseen in all the clutter of texts and symbols is the warning signal of excessive stress on the surgical gloves. I unlock my hands and pull them out of the gloves. This is not the time to break equipment.

The other faces in the team room freeze. Only Nuria's is animate. "I've locked them out for a moment," she said. "I wanted to talk to you privately. Would you prefer to—"

"*No*." And, more temperately, "The expert system will backstop my judgment. So will my colleagues and friends. We all lived through these times."

She has a still, well-schooled face; even after five years in such proximity I cannot say I know her. Yet some shift of expression makes me wonder what she herself lived through, during the years the Islamic nations were isolated behind the "Iron Veil."

Another flashing icon: the triage-list is complete, and Jay is waiting. We review the triage-list, *stat,* so Jay can start directing retrieval efforts. His job is not one I envy: besides IMS-1, four other platforms have been damaged by debris. All of those have lost one or more pods to total or severe decompression and have known casualties. Our size works for us: none of the holes were large enough to evacuate a standard IMS pod before they could be sealed. We now have four suspected sites of contamination. It was up to nine, but Luther has established by reanalysis of the sensor's past recordings that, in five, the suspect signal actually preceded the shuttle's destruction: false positive. Ours, unfortunately, is not one of those; the signal is new, persistent, and adjacent to one of the two pods that were penetrated. By quarantine protocols established thirty years ago, the signal, false or not, means that until we obtain IBDD clearance, we can neither send out rescue craft nor receive survivors, and until we obtain IBDD clearance, none of the staff from Semmelweis— enclosed in its own, inviolate, environment—can come aboard to do their own monitoring.

"I recommend," says Nuria, "that someone else relieves Helen as coordinator of emergency medical response—" My mouth opens, though I'm not sure what would have emerged. "I recommend it," Nuria leans on me, "because she's the most experienced telesurgeon we have in the medical staff and we are likely to need that expertise, given that we cannot accept transfers for the foreseeable future."

A private note flashes up, in green. "And that's my only reason."

Reassuringly, she does not say "believe me" or "trust me," assertions anyone over thirteen knows to receive with skepticism.

Julian, as my successor by acclamation, squints at his suddenly cluttered work field. "Who'd have thought the old man had that many *bits* in him."

That, no doubt is a literary allusion, but this is not the time to ask genie for enlightenment.

I slip my hands back into the gloves, and open synchs to the suites at the four priority platforms. All, fortunately, are within the lag-limit. Two have OR facilities; two have emergency medical stations. I squirt a message to Luther asking that priority consideration be given to lifting restrictions on transfers between one quarantined platform and the next. There's a limit to what I can do with an EMS, which is designed primarily for stabilization prior to transfer.

I've no sooner done that than the first casualty arrives in an EMS, a woman with blown-out lungs—pulmonary over-inflation syndrome—a newcomer who has never been through even a mild decompression and so never put into practice the prohibition against breath holding. Not a surgical case, but it quickly emerges that this platform's paramedics were partners. She, sleeping in her cabin, is one of the two dead, and shock has him fumbling in microgravity as though he was only launched yesterday. So I find myself assisting with her intubation, assisting with placing lines, getting the expert support system up and running to backstop him. Her oxygen sats are lousy, her blood's fizzy, she needs to go on bypass circulation both to get the oxygen in and to get the fizz out . . . And I've got another urgent from one of the OR stations, and Y' is already involved with the most serious casualty from Desert Rose, decompression and chest trauma from the impact of a sizable chunk of shuttle that crushed the pod. A candidate for transfer if there ever was one. But the IBDD on the ground hasn't changed its prohibitions: no transfers.

Julian drops in to my link, synching in Stephe from Sharman to take over. Guiltily, I wonder if Nuria *wasn't* right to get me to pass this off to Julian: He's the better manager. Doubt lasts all of three seconds, then I boot up the software which will aid me in coupling expertise in the form of the telesurgeons within lag limit to need in the form of the cases pending, reserving myself for those cases that need my experience. The urgent request gets passed to the duty surgeon on IMS-2, and I get a chance to think *I shouldn't have had that cup of coffee,* before Y' pages me.

Y's patient on Desert Rose is unstable with a thoracic cavity full of blood, Y's going to have to open the chest, and he's having technical problems. His visuals are degrading, his imaging input is losing resolution, and even worse, beginning to stutter. Since he's going to be working on breathing lungs and a beating heart, he needs the system to track the motion, stabilizing the images and synchronizing his instruments with the natural movement. I route his synch through my station temporarily and call on genie for a diagnostic. It turns out that Y's OR suite contact-priorities haven't been set high enough, and with the current state of emergency other links are poaching some of his bandwidth. Since only sysadmin, the genie-minders, get to meddle with those settings, I call them with a *"fix,* please, *stat."*

I've no sooner reclaimed my bandwidth when Stephe pages me, wanting help with the bypass setup in her patient with the badly damaged lungs; with a nervous glance at the waiting casualty list—three of whom could get into trouble very quickly—I synch with her to assist as she establishes the jugular lines and watch until the woman's oxygen saturation and her blood pressure finally begin to come up. Then the genie pages me over to the other EMS, aboard a material research platform, where the duty-doc and paramedic are running a code on a patient who has just arrested with an arterial blood embolism. There is nothing else I can do for them: they know what they're doing, they have the expert system support, they've given the recommended drugs, and they have the hyperbaric chamber ready.

I freeze all links, giving myself a chance to breathe. When I pull my hands out of the gloves, sweat glitters in the

creases of my palms. I check the other departments: The
shuttle capsule has been retrieved and towed to Semmelweis, its original destination. Luther has issued another set
of recommendations, this time for prophylactic treatments
to begin immediately for all staff in all platforms with
known penetration. That means turning over three of our
bioreactors to the synthesis of his recommended myco-
statins, and he has recommended that they be given by intra-
muscular bead implants, as well as aerosolized through the
ventilation system; he's going to be a popular man.

His prediction is that prophylaxis should be ninety percent effective in preventing infection; and immediate identi-
fication and aggressive treatment of the actual diseases
should produce around an eighty-five percent cure rate, even
for the bad actors. He adds, comfortingly, that additional information from Earthside suggests a better-than-even probability that the abbreviated sterilization will have been
effective even on the radiation-resistants, in the presently in-
calculable event that one of the impact fragments was carrying infectious material. I don't bother asking genie to try
the arithmetic to tell me the probability that one of us will
die of fungal sepsis within the month.

I review the operations in progress, the patients waiting,
and unhook myself from the surgical station for a quick visit
to the head. It's a small triumph over circumstances that I
actually make it there and back before Y' pages me. His
link's stable, but the damage to his patient's pulmonary
veins is more extensive than the diagnostic imaging suggested; now he's in there moving things around. I confer
quickly with Julian, who accepts coordination of the surgical roster from me without even a literary quip, and drop
into synch with Y' and Desert Rose. Y' has the Rose's second paramedic suited and scrubbed to do fluid control and
monitor the sterility of the field, while the duty anesthetist
from ISM-2 is working anesthesia and life support, and an

on-site technician is managing the mounting of transfusions
and drugs onto the operating assembly. It's a brute of an operation. IMS-1's communications system manager over-
loads and crashes, and the backup system comes up with the
old settings, so Y's bandwidth steal recurs and I have to take
over clipping and gluing oozing vessels while he gets that
corrected. Then Desert Rose starts having power problems,
and while the engineers there are rejigging circuits to keep
power going to the OR suite, we run out of SynthaHeme-M
and have to go to an alternative blood substitute, and the patient's blood pressure promptly bottoms out with an adverse
reaction. But Y' and I work as though our thoughts have
synched as well, the anesthetist is sharp and solid, the patient is young, fit, and tough, and God, or whoever decides
these things, toys with us all and then decides he doesn't
need another angel right now.

One for our side.

I check our status: Three ORs still going, two at quarantined platforms, one something that has nothing to do with
the emergency—an incarcerated hernia. Julian looks like he
has been squeezed through a fist-sized hole in the outer wall,
very slowly. He gives me a precis: Final casualties, seven
dead, including the patient with the arterial gas embolism,
twelve injured, mostly decompression. The IBDD confirms
the original estimates of radiation-resistance, so Luther's
numbers stand. Further analysis of the shuttle's disintegra-
tion suggest that it really was a malfunction, enough by the
sound of things to lead to heads rolling but not, we trust, to
wars starting. The same analysis gives us some hope that the
trajectory of the cargo carried it away from the platforms,
toward Earth atmosphere—although there's an understandable reluctance to disclose that reassuring tidbit Earthside,
even though reentry would have charred it.

Julian and I review the rota. Y' has already worked nearly
two full shifts; I have worked one, and none of the people

who would ordinarily cover have overdosed on sleep. So we decide I'll continue through this next shift, Y' will pick up the two after that, and then we'll be righted; I'll just owe Y'. We'd switch, only Y' has a partner among the environmental engineers; their shifts are coordinated.

Julian orders me to find something to eat. I order him to do likewise. Besides, we've both been notified we're due our first dose of antifungal prophylaxis. We make an appointment for the doctor's lounge in ten.

I'm almost out of the chair before the page comes in, so I throw it up on the flat-screen. Stephe, hair unraveling in long plaits, like a handsome Polynesian medusa. No preamble: "The World Court just announced their decision. The freehabbers get to keep their kids."

This is surely the last outcome I could have predicted, given the recent demonstration of the extraordinary dangers of our suspended lives.

Stephe is saying, "There's a strong recommendation that the kids be taken down on the normal three-month rotation, and they're requiring medical monitoring—but the research that we're doing on bone and muscle protection and the development of rotating platforms decided the judges. And we knew that three of them were pro-space, but it was a five-four decision."

"Some of that bone-protection research doesn't stand up to critical review." That's not what I would have said; it is only the most accessible objection.

"But there are quality trials in there as well, two random controlled trials in the last year. We're finally getting the numbers to up here to get grade 1 evidence. We've been accepting being tied to Earth all those years, with that three-month down rotation, and families staying downside—" She blinks at me, eyes suddenly a lighter green, and starry. "Wow!" she says. "That's going to change things."

"Stephe," I say slowly, "your partner's a physician. Did he pass the genotype tests?"

"Yeah," she breathes. "We knew that before we married. But we decided that one of us should stay down with the kids. The kids should pass, too. I wonder if the freehabs need a couple of doctors. I expect it'll be a while before the commercial stations come to terms with kids in space."

"You need sleep," I tell her, quellingly.

She laughs, hair flying. "I need to call Hikaru, before somebody wants me. Don't say anything about this to anyone, will you?"

"Cross my heart," I say, more than a little bemused. And she leaves me to think of the twelve hours we have just lived through, the hours we are going to live through, waiting for any contamination to declare itself.

If there's news coming in, there must be bandwidth to spare. I settle back into the chair, fit the virtual array over my head again and request a channel to Earth.

It's the middle of the night, but Luis is not asleep. Nor is he alone: I can hear movement around him, in the common area of the clinic's living caravan.

Luis looks good, and that's not only because I've been celibate too long. He has one of those faces that time only improves, since age reveals character. Though he was almost as light-skinned as Stephe when we met, Africa has darkened him, set squint-lines around his eyes, made him thoughtful in motion, careful of his energies. Like many of us, he's a mongrel, born in a country that no longer exists, but unlike many of us, he has found his heart's home. He was always the one I was closest to, my friend, my preferred lover; our intimacy at times made the others jealous. I'm not surprised at his greeting, "Helen, thank God. I've been trying to get through from this end. We heard the news—what's been getting through the UA government filters. Are you all right?"

Terence, unseen behind him, says, "Ask her if it *was* sabotage, like the EEN said."

A woman—Charmaine, probably—shushes him. Luis looks pained. This is certainly being monitored from my end, and probably from his, and Luis has always been cautious. Terence, on the other hand, thinks his radical credentials are imperiled if he's not on some official shit list—and if the African governments are filtering the news, then quoting the Earth Ekumenical Network is a fine way to get there.

"How should I know what anyone on Earth is saying?" I parry. "I've had my head in the hood for the past nine hours. I'm all right, Luis. We weren't one of the platforms with decompression emergencies. Needless to say, I've been busy assisting the ones that did." That I judge safe to say. I will leave off mention of the contamination, lest that is not to be public knowledge where they are. "How is it with you?"

"We wanted to thank you for that last cash transfer."

I flutter my hands. They look puffy and dry, with red pressure marks from hours in the gloves. His will be long, thin, weathered—I corral my vagrant thoughts. "You know I believe in the work, Luis, and it's no hardship for me."

After the pan-American War, support to the African restoration was cut, including support to our mobile clinic. With the cynicism of young, bruised idealists, we decided that those of us who could would find the highest salaried jobs until we had banked enough for five years' self-sufficiency. I was the only one who qualified for space.

For my first three-month downtime, I joined Luis and Charmaine on the edge of the Sahara. After nine months in the confined, regulated, precarious environment of the space habs, I was utterly disoriented, starting at any shift of light, any change in the wind. I fainted when I stood up; I developed sunstroke; I had constant diarrhea, infectious and nonfectious. Luis was alarmed; Charmaine, contemptuous.

By the end of my third year, the others had reunited in the

field, working in the Ganges delta. I was better at managing my readaptation, but Terence and I argued constantly. I saw how to expand our practice beyond the mobile clinic, using one or more telesurgery stations, but that would have required negotiation with local and regional governments, obtaining access to bandwidth and infrastructure—trusting and buying in; to Terrence, a deal with the devil.

One more year, I told us all. One more year, to give us more of a cash reserve, and then we'll work it all out. Three months into that year there was an opening for a surgeon on IMS-1; I was invited to apply. And we all confronted how much I wanted that post, how much more satisfying I found the mastery of skills and technology required of this work, than the enervating struggle with Earth's chronic afflictions.

Charmaine demanded a divorce; Terence called me a traitor; Michel withdrew. Luis alone gave me his blessing, and for him, alone, I would have stayed.

Luis is saying, "We were able to license some recombinants producing the proprietary antiparasitics, the ones effective against the super *Plasmodium*. Maybe now things have settled down politically, the WHO will get permission to release their new mosquito sterilization vector."

I smile, despite myself. I'm sitting in a space platform under IBDD quarantine, after a decomissioning shuttle disintegrated in orbit. Half the world's media is yelling screwup and the other half conspiracy; the IBDD has canceled all its inspections until further notice and three countries have issued statements declaring they've decided to review IBDD participation in their own decommissioning operations. But things are quiet in Africa.

After that long, slow moment of lag—well beyond operating distance—he returns my smile. "Any chance I could talk you into coming out into the field again, next time you're down? We should still be here; we've got some excellent colleagues, including some I'm sure you'll have heard about, in telesurgery."

"Luis . . . let me think. That's not an evasion, I do need to think."

He nods. "You should go. I don't want you spending all your salary on expensive calls—"

"When you've expensive drugs to spend it on. I'll send you a vmail. Look after yourselves. All of you. Stay safe."

His smile is sweetly ironic, and fades just as one hand begins to reach out to me, as I, deceived by the virtual image of him, reach out in turn, into the unseen space beyond the virtual image. The surgery interface re-forms around me, a series of windows on the two ORs still running, the biosensor outputs from recovering patients, a reminder from Julian about our appointment in the doctor's lounge, from Luther about the need to start antifungal prophylaxis, from the research coordinator about the necessity of registering our optouts if we object to the medical information gained from our exposure (putative exposure) and prophylaxis being distributed to the scientific community. . . .

Five facets of the icosahedral doctor's lounge look up, or down, if you will, on Earth. It's dark now, though if we turned off all our lighting, we could see the civilizations of Earth sprinkled across the landmasses. Only the seas of Earth are dark. And the space above.

Y' slouches beneath the window, rumpled and squinting. Even without the contrast, Nuria would look graceful, even in the knees-up astronaut tuck. Julian hangs beside her, tethered by one arm to a strut, sucking on a coffee-sac. The dayshift duty-docs orbit them gently, as though they are convalescents and their recovery, precarious.

Julian lifts an eyebrow to me. "And how was your night?"

*   *   *

Alison Sinclair is the author of **Legacies, Blueheart, Cav-
alcade** *(nominated for the Arthur C. Clarke Award) and*
Throne Price *(with Lynda Jane Williams). She has lived in
Colchester (England), Edinburgh, Victoria (BC), Hamilton,
Boston, Leeds (England), Calgary, and Ottawa. She has
done basic and medical research. In 1999 she graduated
from the University of Calgary with an MD and now works
in Victoria as a medical writer. When not working or writing she sings, swims, dabbles in computers, and fantasizes
about being perfectly organized. Her Web site is at
http://www.sff.net/people/asinclair/.*

I KNEW A GUY ONCE

by *Tanya Huff*

WANTED: SERVERS, CLEANUP CREWS
Temporary and permanent staffers needed for station recreation facilities. Apply in person to the Quartermaster's Office. On-the-job training provided. Minimum wage. Shift negotiable, but failure to appear for scheduled work will result in immediate dismissal.
Applicants must show proof of station residence or have a valid employee number.

ALTHOUGH there were only two people in the passenger compartment of the supply shuttle, the cramped quarters had them practically in each other's laps. The company had no intention of wasting shipping space on privacy; nearly every square millimeter of the four-by-eight-meter compartment they weren't actually occupying had been filled with labeled containers.

As the shuttle left Io, they were a study in contrasts.

The young man, his environmental suit still so new it crinkled softly when he moved, gripped his helmet tightly in both gloved hands. He wore his dark hair at the Company's regulation length, but it looked to have been styled rather than cut. His face was tanned with high spots of color on both cheeks, and he was trying too hard to appear unafraid.

The older woman's short gray hair seemed to have been hacked off during a power shortage, when lights, as unessential, were the first thing to be shut down. Her skin had the almost translucent paleness of someone who'd spent her entire life protecting it from high UV, and her environmental suit was so old it had digital readouts in the cuff. As soon as the main engines cut off, she closed her eyes and went to sleep.

Tried to go to sleep.

"They say that this last bit from Io to the station isn't as dangerous as it used to be."

She opened her eyes and turned her head enough to see him smiling at her, his teeth very white, his lips pulled back just a little too far. "They're right," she said at last.

His smile relaxed a little although the rest of him remained visibly tense. "I'm Simon Porter. Dr. Simon Porter. I'm the new station psychologist."

"What happened to the old one?"

"What? Oh. Well, actually, there wasn't one. The Company only brings a psychologist out to the mining stations when there's a problem they can't solve through the usual channels."

"Wouldn't it make more sense to keep you on staff?"

"Too expensive." He seemed proud of it.

"So, what's the problem?"

"I'm afraid that's privileged information." He seemed proud of that, too. "But I can tell you that things seem very shaky on the station right now. Stress levels rising. You know . . ."

"Yeah." And something in that single syllable suggested she did. Probably better than he did.

"I specialize in isolation psychosis. This is sort of a dream job for me."

The following pause lengthened into expectation.

"Able Harris. I'm the new bartender for downside."

"So we're in the same line of work. You listen, I listen."

"You pour drinks?"

"No, but . . ."

"Well, there's your difference. I'm a bartender."

"Okay." His tone touched patronizing. "I've never been in a downside bar."

Able turned just enough to look him full in the face.

"I've never actually been *downside,*" he admitted. "Or on a mining station at all." He cleared his throat, as though confused by his confession. "So what happened to the old bartender?"

"He died."

Dr. Porter nodded sympathetically. Everyone knew death and downside were intimately acquainted. "Of what?"

"Well, they said it was the sucking chest wound, but I suspect it was actually the wrench to the back of the head."

"He was *killed?*"

Able shrugged philosophically. "Might've been an accident."

"He was accidentally hit on the back of the head with a wrench?"

"It happens."

He studied her face, dark brows knit together so tightly they met over the bridge of his nose. After a long moment, he nodded and relaxed. "I may be fresh out of the gravity well, but I'm not totally gullible. You're making fun of the new guy. I'm onto you, Able . . . may I call you Able?"

"Everybody does," she told him, unaffected by his accusation.

"It's an unusual name. I assume it's not the one you were born with?"

"Why?"

"Well, it's just . . . unusual."

She stretched as far as the straps allowed. "I knew a guy once named Strawberry Cho."

"He had a birthmark?"

"No, he had a mother who was so homesick she didn't consider the consequences."

"Consequences?"

"You name your boy Strawberry and there's going to *be* consequences."

Dr. Potter opened his mouth, closed it, and shook his head. "You're doing it again, aren't you, Able? You're pulling my . . ."

The klaxon's sudden bellow clamped his hands to the arms of his seat, his helmet floating out to the end of its tether.

Able glanced down at her cuff, then reached out, hooked a gloved finger around the cable, and tugged it back. "They're warning us they're about to hit the brakes, start decelerating."

His ears scarlet, Dr. Porter clutched the helmet so tightly his gloves squeaked against the plastic.

"Pilot knows it's your first time out. Knows people have been feeding you bullshit stories since you blew off Earth. Probably hit the klaxon trying to get you to piss yourself."

Embarrassment rose off the psychologist in nearly visible waves.

"Don't worry, the suit'll take care of it. I knew a guy once, had the shits all the way from L5 Alpha to Darkside. Suit took care of it." Able closed her eyes and didn't open them again until the shuttle kissed its assigned nipple on the docking ring and the "all clear" sounded.

By the time Dr. Porter had fumbled free of his straps, the hatch was open and the dockers were barely controlling their anger as they waited to start unloading. Able snagged her carryall from behind her seat and followed him to the bottom of the ramp, arriving just in time to keep him from being flattened by a wagon piled high with containers from the aft compartment.

"They're on tracks," she yelled, leaning closer to make

herself heard over the noise. "You get in front of them, they'll squash you flat. I knew a guy once, lost a foot under one. Crushed too bad to be reattached."

The doctor's cheeks paled, his embarrassment forgotten. "What happened to him?"

"Got himself a whole bunch of prosthetics. Got one with a full entertainment unit in it."

"In his foot?"

Able shrugged. "Takes all kinds."

She slipped between two wagons and headed for a set of metal stairs against the starboard wall. The doctor trailed behind.

"There should be someone here to meet me," he shouted as they climbed.

"There is, back behind that glass."

At the top of the stairs was a wire-enclosed catwalk. At the end of the catwalk, a platform. In the wall overlooking the platform, two hatches. Between the hatches was a mirrored window.

"There's no way you can know who's back there, Able." Safely above the wagons, he regained his professional voice.

"Presence of suits kept the dockers from hauling your ass out of the shuttle. Only place the suits could be is behind that glass. They're not going to be out here in the nipple risking a seal rupture. I knew a guy once, got sucked through a seal rupture and ended up in a low Mars orbit." When no question prodded her to continue, she grinned. "Bounce satellite signals off him now. This is your exit." She nodded toward the right as they clanged out onto the platform.

Dr. Porter stared at the hatches. Aside from the varying wear and tear, they were identical. "How can you tell?"

"Company policy; suits are always right. We're what's left."

He stared at her for a long moment, he glanced toward

the mirrored glass, then he held out his hand. "I appreciate you making the effort to distract me, Able. Perhaps we'll meet again."

"Could happen. It's a small station in a big universe."

His grip was a little too emphatic. A young man with something to prove.

Don't need to prove it to me. Her grip matched his exactly.

EVS in a temporary locker, Able took a moment to watch the Company news on the small vid in lock. Possible lay-offs. Cutbacks. Accidents. Price freezes. One hundred per-cent bad. She sighed, scanned her chip into the station's database, stepped through the inner hatch, and went looking for the Quartermaster's Office. QMO was never far from the docks so she expected to have no trouble finding it. And the yelling was pretty much a dead giveaway.

"I don't freakin' care what the invoice says, my people unloaded sixteen crates of seven dash seven three two *not* seventeen." Hands planted firmly on the desk, the quarter-master leaned closer to the pickup and went for volume. "You short-shipped us, you bastard! For the second god-damned time!" Then she straightened, flipped pale blonde hair back from her face, and smiled across the room at Able. "Jesus, Able, what'd you do? Hijack a military transport?"

Able stepped over the threshold and shrugged. "Just made all the right connections."

"Just? You broke the freakin' Phoebus to GaMO speed record. And who told you lot to god-damned stop working?" she snapped, as the four clerks along one side of the room turned to look. "I can't say I'm not glad to see you, though, situation's been going to freakin' hell in a handcart since Rich Webster died. Asshole. I close the place down, the rig-gers riot. I open the place up, the riggers get drunk and riot. The fitters are talking freakin' union again and that's got the suits on my ass. Whole god-damned place is falling a . . ." The desk receiver chimed. "Hang on a nano, Able. I need to get this."

"I'm sorry, Quartermaster Nasjonal, but our packing orders clearly show that all seventeen crates were loaded. I suggest that you take the matter up with the transfer supervisor on Io."

"PJ's got more freakin' brains than to screw with me! Now get your thumb out of your ass, get Yuen on this thing, and stop wasting my god-damned time!" Shaking her head, she dropped down into the desk chair. "Freakin' distance delays make it impossible to hold a conversation. You've got standard quarters behind the bar. You got six servers, burnouts for the most part—I think Webster was paying at least one of them in booze."

"I won't."

"I know. I'm the one who asked you to drag your ass out to the armpit of the universe, remember? Usual drill. Company expects you to turn a profit and keep the workers happy. You should be fully stocked, I've kept supplies coming in during this whole freakin' mess. And . . . Jonathon!"

One of the clerks jerked and peered over the top of his monitor.

"Where's my freakin' ass-Quart?"

"He's at 07, Quartermaster. Supervising the loading . . ."

"Right. Okay, you take Able to the Hole."

"But . . ."

"Quartermaster Nasjonal, Supervisor Yuen is not currently available. Would you be able to call back after 1700 hours?"

"Tell Yuen I'm about to start talking about what happened last December. And if that doesn't haul his skinny ass to a pickup, nothing will," she added, sitting back in the chair. "I'll be down to see you as soon as I get this freakin' short ship straightened out. Jonathon!"

He jerked again, the movement propelling him out from behind his terminal.

"Go!"

Able paused on the threshold, allowing Jonathon to proceed her into the corridor. "Always a pleasure talking to you, Quartermaster Nasjonal."

The quartermaster grinned. "Suck up."

Jonathon was waiting an arm's length away, nervously clutching his hands together in front of his belt.

"Do you know where the Hole is?" Able's tone made it clear she very much doubted it.

He flushed. "Yes, theoretically, but I've never . . . I mean . . ."

"It's downside. You drink amid." She slung her carryall over one shoulder, and started to walk.

"Not that I . . ." His protest trailed off as he hurried to catch up. "It's just, it's . . ."

"Downside?" When he nodded, Able snorted. "Tell you what, take me to lower amid and the nearest shaft, give me decent directions, and I'll cover downside myself. We won't mention it to the quartermaster."

"She'll find out."

"Then tell her I didn't have the time to waste escorting you back and there was no way I was letting you walk through downside alone. She'll let it go if you tell her it was my idea."

"You've known her for a long time?"

"Pretty much since she was born."

Jonathon flattened against the bulkhead as Able and the approaching docker merely shifted their shoulders sideways and slid past each other. "She's actually really good to work for," he declared scrambling back to Able's side. "Her bark is worse than her bite."

"Most days." Able paused at the hatch that would take

them from dockside into the station proper. "I knew a guy once that she bit."

Sucking chest wound or wrench to the back of the head, after a cursory inspection of the only bar in downside, Able was sure of one thing: that Richard Webster had gotten what he deserved. The place was everything people like Jonathon expected a downside bar to be. Dark and filthy and stinking of despair and rage about equally mixed—as well as a distinct miasma of odors less metaphorical.

She ripped a yellowing list of rules off the outside of the hatch—splash marks making the vector for the yellowing plain—and stepped over the threshold. The panel just inside the door responded to her chip and once she'd pried the cover off, she hit the overhead lights. The amount of grime that had sealed the cover shut suggested it had been a while since the overheads had been turned on.

A pile of rags in the far corner coughed, cursed, and turned into a skinny person of indeterminate gender.

"I didn't do nothing," it whined, squinting across the room.

"That's obvious." Able pushed a dented chair out of the way and moved close enough to see that the rags had covered a balding man who could have been anywhere from forty to seventy, his mottled scalp a clear indication that hair loss had been caused by other than genetic factors. Toxic spills were endemic to downside. "Who are you?"

"Bob."

She'd be willing to bet that Bob was the guy Webster had been paying in booze. One way or another, and there were a number of ways, he'd gotten so far in debt to the Company that they'd written him off. He'd lost his access to the ship's database, his quarters, and his food allotment, leaving him with two choices, the kindness of strangers—only people who'd burned off their friends fell quite so far—or the tubes.

Clearing the tubes of blockages was usually a mecho's job but the little robots were expensive and they didn't last long. People like Bob didn't last long in the tubes either, but they were cheap.

Arms curled around his chest, he rubbed his hands up and down filthy sleeves. "I need a drink."

"I don't doubt it."

"'s cheaper than paying me. Keeps your profits up."

"Who told you that?"

"Webster. Lets me sleep here, too."

"Webster's dead."

"I didn't do it."

"I don't care."

If Bob was sleeping in the bar during the eight in twenty-four it was closed, he was using the bathroom sinks to keep clean. And not very often.

"I knew a guy once who smelled like you. Somebody kicked his skinny ass out of an air lock and nobody missed him."

Without waiting for a response, she ducked behind the bar. The door on the right led to the storeroom, to the left, her quarters. Both smelled strongly of disinfectant. The QMO. If they'd been attempting to run the Hole, the only thing they'd care about was the stock. Wiping Webster out of her quarters had probably been a personal courtesy from Nasjonal. Able'd thank her later.

"I *need* a drink."

The whine came from directly behind her left shoulder. Up close the smell was nearly overpowering.

Fortunately, disinfectant was cheap.

Grabbing the back of Bob's overalls, she frog-marched him through her quarters, ignoring his struggles and incoherent protests, carefully touching him to as few surfaces as possible. The showers on downside all had the same two settings. Hard clean. Soft clean. Hard clean for when the riggers and the fitters came off shift. Soft clean for the rest of the time. The Company saved money by keeping the pressure and temperature consistent.

Bob went in, as he was, on Hard.

When the cycle finished, Able checked to see he hadn't drowned, efficiently stripped him of overalls and ragged cloth slippers, and hit the button again.

By the time the second cycle finished, his clothes were dry, the industrial solvents in the Hard clean having taken care of most of the grime.

She dressed him, ran a depilatory pad over his head, and marched him back to the bar.

The whole thing had taken just under twenty minutes.

"I assume you sold your shoes?"

Bob stared at her, wide-eyed and trembling.

"Then the slippers will do for now. Here's the deal . . . you work for me, I pay you like everybody else. You can decide what you do with it. You can start paying down your debt to the Company, or you can drink it away—after you pay me what you owe me for the two showers. Until you're clear and can get quarters again, you can keep sleeping in the bar but not on that crap. I'll pull a couple of shipping pads out of stores. You don't do your job—well, a smart man will keep in mind that I'm the only thing between him and the tubes. Oh, and you will shower every two days. You can use a communal cleanup off the hives."

He was panting now. "I *need* a drink."

"You *need* to haul the big steam cleaner out of the storeroom. Or you need to let the Company know they've got a new tube man. I knew a guy once, survived four trips down the tubes. His record still stands."

By the time Bob had dragged the cleaner out into the bar, the five other servers were standing, blinking in the light. None of them looked too pleased about being summoned.

"I didn't even know this place had overheads," one muttered.

"Then how did you see to get it clean?" Able asked, coming out from behind the bar, wiping her hands on a dark green apron.

"Fuck that, how clean do you need to get a place like this?" one of the others snorted. "Nobody who drinks here gives a crap."

"What difference does that make? My name's Able Harris and I'm the new bartender. You're Helen, Tasha, Toby, Nick . . ." With each name, she nodded toward an incredulous server. ". . . and Spike." She studied the last woman curiously. "Spike?"

Spike folded heavy arms over an ample chest. "Able?"

"Good point. So . . ." Her attention switched back to the group. "Is that what you wear to work?"

The four women and two men looked down at their overalls and exchanged amused glances.

Able waited.

Toby finally shrugged and muttered, "Yeah."

"It'll do for now, but when the first shift's back for opening, I want the overalls to be clean. There's a dozen or so aprons like this one in stores. You're in them while you're working." When the protests died down, Able nodded. "Okay. You don't have to wear them if you don't want to. You don't have to do anything you don't want to do. If you work for me, you wear the aprons, but you don't have to work for me."

"And if we could get other jobs on this fucking station, we'd be fucking working at them."

Toby moved up behind Spike's shoulder. "Webster didn't care what we wore."

"Webster's dead."

Bob jerked up from behind the steam cleaner. "I didn't do it."

After the snickering died down, Spike growled, "He wasn't killed because he wasn't wearing a fucking apron, was he?"

Able shrugged. "I knew a guy once, got killed by an apron. He lost his job and got so hungry he tried to eat it. Managed fine until he got to the ties and then he got one wrapped around that dangly thing at the back of his mouth and choked to death."

"Was that a threat?" Toby wondered as their new boss walked over to Bob and hauled a length of hose off him then hauled Bob back to his feet.

"I have no fucking idea," Spike admitted.

Even with the pressurized steam, it took the seven of them three hours to get the bar clean.

"Who the fuck washes the bottom of tables?"

"I'd guess nobody in living memory." Tasha swiped on more solvent and grimaced at the dissolving grime. "This is disgusting."

Helen nodded and sat back on her heels. "Well, at least we won't have to do it again . . ."

"We'll do it after every shift."

The two women glanced over at Able, working the steam against the upper wall.

"Why?" Helen demanded. "Hell, with only the drinking lights on, nobody can even see the dirt."

"Doesn't mean it's not there."

"Are you fucking obsessive or something?"

"Keeping the bar clean's part of the job."

"But nobody cares!"

"That doesn't change the definition of clean. I knew a guy once, tried to change the definition of Tuesday. Ended up with a fish up his nose."

"That makes no fucking sense . . ."

"And that's what I said to him at the time. How long has the big vid not worked?"

Discussion narrowed it down to a couple of months.

"Bar's not making enough of a profit for the Company to send maintenance in."

Everyone turned to stare at Bob, who dropped his sponge, hugged himself, and announced that he needed a drink.

"Downside maintenance never drinks here?" Able asked after a moment.

"Well, yeah," Toby snorted. "But they can't shit without a Company work order."

"Okay, bar opens in half an hour. First shift go home, get cleaned up. Second shift, your time's your own." Standing by the light panel, Able looked around and nodded. "Good work, people."

Spike poked Toby hard in the side. "Why the fuck are you looking so pleased?"

He shook his head. "I dunno. It just sounded like she meant it."

"Meant what?"

"When she said, good work. When was the last time you heard somebody say that, and mean it? Webster never said it."

"And when was the last time you did good work for Webster?" Tasha snorted as they left.

With only the drinking lights on, Able went back behind the bar, put a new sponge in a shallow bowl, filled the bowl with beer, and kept filling it until the sponge was soaked through. She looked up to see Bob leaning on the end of the bar, his eyes wide.

Able pried the cover off the main air vent, set the bowl inside, and put the cover back on. "No one wants to drink in a bar that smells like disinfectant. It's annoying. They start out annoyed, they end up as nasty drunks. On the flip side, no one wants to drink in a bar that smells like old piss and stale sweat. They start out disgusted, they end up as nasty drunks. You don't want nasty drunks, you start your drinkers out in a good mood."

Bob opened his mouth and closed it again.

Carrying a box of textured protein patties in from the storeroom, she dropped a stack out on the counter and began cutting them into strips. "I knew a guy once lived on these things for twelve years. What he didn't know about making them edible you could write on the ass end of a flea. Lots of chili, a little oil, bake 'em until they're crisp and they're almost food. Works with garlic and onion, too."

"They won't pay for it," Bob muttered, staring longingly at the taps.

"I'm not expecting them to."

"Company won't like it."

"Company expects me to turn a profit. You give the drinkers something to eat, they can drink more and it affects them less." She slid the first tray into the tiny oven on the back wall. The bar had a kitchen unit, so her quarters didn't. "You make this stuff right and it's got a bite. The more they drink, the less they feel it, the more they can eat. Since the patties are enriched, the serious drinkers are getting fed. Which makes them less shaky, which means fewer accidents on the pipes. Fewer accidents puts everyone in a better mood. With everyone in a better mood, fewer nasty drunks. Fewer nasty drunks, fewer fights, fewer things get broken and need to be replaced, less drinking gets interrupted, the bar turns a profit. The Company's happy." The oven chimed and she slid the tray out, juggling a strip from hand to hand, finally passing it to Bob.

He took a cautious bite and sneezed. "It's good."

"I know what I'm doing." She drew a 500 of beer and handed it to him.

After emptying it, he blinked at her a few times, his eyes
the clearest they'd been. "Who the fuck *are* you?"

"I'm the new bartender."

When she opened the hatch, half a dozen riggers and fitters stood in the corridor; weight shifting back and forth
from foot to foot, hands curled into fists, a fight waiting to
happen. They knew who she was. The only thing that got
processed faster than the gas pumped up off Jupiter was
gossip.

"What happened to Webster's rules?" one of them
growled.

"You guys do the most dangerous work on the station,
you don't need someone to tell you how to act like adults."

"So there ain't no rules?"

Able stepped back out of the way. "I didn't say that."

The big rigger leaned across the bar, grabbed a bottle in
one scarred hand, and grinned at Able as he settled back on
his stool. "Webster let us serve ourselves."

"Webster's dead. Put it back."

He cracked the seal and took a long messy swallow.
"Make me, old woman."

A heartbeat later, he was lying on the floor and everyone
in the immediate vicinity stood openmouthed, blinking
away the afterimages of an electrical discharge.

"I knew a guy once took a second hit from one of these
things." Able bounced the rod against the palm of her other
hand. "He's still striking sparks when he takes a shit. I'm
charging the bottle against your chip. Oh, and by the way,"
she raised her voice so that it filled all the listening spaces
in the Hole, "it's coded to my DNA. Anyone else touches it,
and . . ." A nod toward the rigger blinking stupidly up at her
from the floor. "I knew a guy once who designed weapons
systems for the military."

"Fuck," someone sneered, "you knew a lot of guys."

Able grinned. "Would you believe I used to be a raven-haired beauty?"

"Not without a few more drinks!"

"You're lucky his friends didn't rush you," Nick muttered under the laughter.

"First guy who tries something never has friends." Able drew a beer and set it on his tray. "That's why he's trying something. Second guy who tries something's always a little trickier."

She drew some beer, poured some shots, and scanned the crowd for maintenance overalls. They weren't hard to spot. Two women sitting alone in a booth; one of them had a bandage wrapped around her right hand, both of them were drinking boilermakers. Two beers, two shots, basket of chili strips on a tray and Able slid out from behind the bar.

They watched her approach and when she paused at their booth, the uninjured woman snarled, "We didn't order those."

"On the house." Able set the drinks down and picked up the empties. "My big vid's busted."

"So?"

"I'd like one of you to fix it."

"No." The injured woman downed the whiskey and took a long pull on the beer. "Crew boss'd stuff us naked out an air lock if we did shit without a work order. And the Company won't approve a work order until this place turns a profit."

"Your crew boss says anything to you, you tell him I knew a guy once, used to work maintenance on L5Beta. He knew a seal was fucked but waited for a Company work order before he'd fix it. Six people died."

"You knew a guy?"

Able shrugged. "Haven't you heard? I know a lot of guys."

"Yeah, but . . ."

The uninjured woman raised her hand. "What's in it for us?"

"Repairs go on your tab. You drink free until it's cleared."

"You do know that the Company expects you to make a profit here, right?"

"Vid's fixed, people are happy and stay longer, they drink more, the bar profits. Excuse me." She slid the empties back on the table, took a long step to the right, pivoted on one heel and slammed the edge of the tray down on a fitter's wrist. He howled and dropped back into his seat.

"I was way over there and I distinctly heard her tell you to keep your hands to yourself. You want to grope my servers, you make damned sure they're into it first or you find someplace else to drink."

"There is no place else to fuckin' drink!"

"So if you're going to keep drinking here, what are you going to do?" She met his glare with a steady gaze and waited.

And kept waiting.

Slowly, the room fell silent.

Able kept waiting.

He rubbed his wrist and sighed. "I'm gonna keep my hands to myself."

"Unless?"

"Unless the person I'm gropin's okay with it?"

Able smiled. "Spike, give him his drink."

The large vid was showing zero G lacrosse from one of the L5s, the small vid behind the bar ran the station's news channel.

"Why the fuck is that on?" The rigger slid forward on his barstool and squinted at the screen. "News is all bad."

"Eighty percent bad."

"Bad enough."

"I like to know when it's getting better."

"Yeah? Well, what I'd like to know is where you get off tellin' us how to fuckin' behave."

Able wiped up a spill and pushed the basket of garlic-seasoned protein strips down the bar, closer to the rigger's reaching hand. "I don't. I tell you what I won't put up with. You choose how to behave."

"No choices on a Company station, you should know that."

"There's choices in here."

He chewed, swallowed, and finished his beer. "What; you not gonna tell me that you knew a guy once who had no choices?"

"I knew lots of guys like that."

"Yeah." He tapped for a refill. "What happened to them?"

"That depended on the choices they made."

"Who the fuck *are* you?"

She threw her rag in the sink and held out a hand. "Able Harris. I'm the bartender."

"Took you three freakin' weeks to make a profit, Able."

"Took you three weeks to fix that short ship, Quartermaster."

"I got busy. Freakin' sue me." She slid onto a barstool. "Jesus, you got coffee running. Let me have a mug. Too damned early for booze. You know, I don't think Webster even knew what that pot was for."

"Webster's dead."

The quartermaster started as half a dozen voices chorused, "Bob didn't do it!"

"What the hell was that?" she demanded as Able snickered.

"Private joke." The mug hit the bar along with two packets of creamer and three of sugar. "So, I make the news at about sixty-forty."

"Yeah, things are looking up. What happened over there?"

Over there was a stack of chairs waiting repair and a table that had moved significantly past *broken* and into *scrap*.

"Oh, one of the riggers told the 'two fitters in a suction pipe joke.' "

"Shit. What did you do?"

"Cleaned up afterward. I like to make stupidity its own reward."

"Able, you better get out here."

She rubbed a hand through her hair so that it stuck straight up in pale gray spikes. "Shift just started, what's wrong?"

"There's a table of supervisors out there."

"I knew a guy once, insisted on hanging out with the guys he supervised."

"What happened to him?"

Able finished entering the top shelf and handed Toby her data pad. "Let's just say *hanging out* became the definitive phrase."

There were five of them at one of the big round tables; two women, three men. The tables around them were empty. In the booths and at the bar, the regulars sat scowling over their drinks.

Able walked over, drying her hands on her apron. "Evening. Don't you lot usually drink in lower amid?"

"We've been hearing good things about this place." He folded his arms and managed to simultaneously look up at her and stare down his nose. "Thought we'd check it out."

One of the women smiled, showing recently repaired teeth. "Downside drudge like you ought to be happy we're here. Might get the Company to put you someplace a little . . . better."

"Better?"

"Than this . . . hole."

Able reached out and touched her chip to the table's scanner, then transferred the screen to the big vid. "I'm an independent contractor. I'm here because I want to be. You want to be here, that's fine. You're trying to make a point—make it somewhere else."

"The Company . . ."

"Doesn't care how I do it as long as this bar makes a profit. Now, what can I get you?"

"How about a little respect?" His lip curled.

"I knew a guy once, wanted respect he hadn't earned."

The regulars sat up a little straighter.

"What happened to him, Able?" a senior fitter called.

Able's eyes narrowed. "I didn't know him long."

They didn't stay long.

Beckoning Bob forward to clean off the table, she started back for the stockroom.

He caught at her arm as she passed. "Able?"

When she turned, every eye in the house was on her.

"You chose to be here?"

"I did."

"Are you out of your fuckin' mind?"

"Hole's a downside bar, isn't it?"

"Yeah, but . . ."

"I'm a bartender." She swept an exasperated gaze around the room. "Not a hard concept, people. Bar. Bartender. Sorge, I just got that god-damned pool table. Get your beer off the felt or it'll be the last beer you have that Bob hasn't pissed in."

"More good news than bad these days."

"You want bad news, I'll give you bad news." The rigger downed his shot, and slapped the bar for another one. "Fuckin' storms on Jupiter's flinging the lines around. We lock it down, we risk losing the gas pocket. We let it run, we got no control and we risk losing the whole fuckin' line."

"Does sound bad."

"Yeah. I don't suppose you knew a guy once who solved the problem?"

"Nope." Able polished another length of the bar, cloth moving in long, smooth sweeps. "But I expect to."

"You expect . . . Oh." Frowning thoughtfully he tossed back his shot. He was still looking thoughtful nearly half an hour later as he headed out the hatch.

Able polished her way down the bar—not so much because it needed it but because it was one of the things a good bartender did—and when she came back she smiled at the man sitting in the rigger's place. "Dr. Porter."

"It's a small station in a big universe, Able. How've you been?"

"Good. What can I get you?"

"Coffee's fine."

She set the mug down, studied him for a moment, then slid over two sugars. No creamer.

"Nice trick." He stirred them in, his spoon chiming against the heavy porcelain sides of the mug. "You know that problem the Company brought me on board for? Seems to be solved."

"Congratulations."

"I didn't say I solved it, Able. Company thinks I did, though. Upside, they're saying things started to change the moment I came on board. Except I wasn't the only one who came on board that day." He took a long drink and looked around. "So this is the Hole. It's not so bad; why the Hole?"

"Because this is downside, Dr. Porter. And they call this the asshole of the station."

"Do they, Able?"

"They do, Dr. Porter. I knew a guy once, his asshole seized up on him. Eventually, his head exploded." A sudden loud burst of music cut off the psychologist's reply. "Strawberry! Tell Logan to turn his damned foot down!"

The music dimmed.

Dr. Porter smiled into his coffee. "You knew a guy once?"

"I knew a lot of guys, Doc."

"And you say you're just a bartender."

"No, I don't."

"But . . ."

Able drew a beer and set it on Spike's tray. "I don't believe I ever used the word *just*."

* * *

Tanya Huff lives and writes in rural Ontario with her partner, four cats, and an unintentional chihuahua. After sixteen fantasies, she has written two space operas, **Valor's Choice** *and* **The Better Part of Valor**, *now out from DAW. Just published by DAW is* **Long Hot Summoning**, *the third novel in her* Keeper *series, which began with* **Summon the Keeper** *and* **The Second Summoning**. *In her spare time she gardens and complains about the weather.*

EDITOR'S BIO

Julie E. Czerneda comes by her interest in space and work naturally. A former biologist turned educational writer, she has been writing and editing science and career books for almost two decades, contributing to more than 125 texts. She is also an internationally best-selling science fiction author, with six novels published by DAW Books Inc. (including two series: the Trade Pact Universe *and the* Webshifters*), with more to come. Her short fiction and novels have been nominated for several awards, including the John W. Campbell Award for Best New Writer, the Philip K. Dick Award for Distinguished Science Fiction, and the Prix Aurora Award, as well as being on the preliminary ballot for the Nebula. A strong proponent of using science fiction in classrooms, Julie is series editor for* Tales from the Wonder Zone *and author of the acclaimed* **No Limits: Developing Scientific Literacy Using Science Fiction***. And, given any chance at all, she looks up into space and imagines how busy we'll be there.*